# CHILLING EFFECT

# CHILLING EFFECT

A novel by Marianne Wesson

UNIVERSITY PRESS OF COLORADO

Published by the University Press of Colorado
5589 Arapahoe Avenue, Suite 206C
Boulder, Colorado 80303

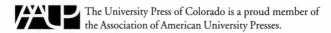 The University Press of Colorado is a proud member of
the Association of American University Presses.

The University Press of Colorado is a cooperative publishing enterprise supported, in part, by Adams
State College, Colorado State University, Fort Lewis College, Mesa State College, Metropolitan State
College of Denver, University of Colorado, University of Northern Colorado, and Western State
College of Colorado.

Library of Congress Cataloging-in-Publication Data

Wesson, Marianne.
  Chilling effect : a novel / by Marianne Wesson.
    p. cm.
  ISBN 0-87081-787-6 (hardcover : alk. paper)
  1. Women lawyers—Fiction. 2. Children—Crimes against—Fiction. 3. Boulder (Colo.)—Fiction.
4. Erotic films—Fiction. I. Title.
  PS3573.E81498C48 2004
  813'.54—dc22

2004011323

13  12  11  10  09  08  07  06  05  04        10  9  8  7  6  5  4  3  2  1

This book is lovingly dedicated to Judy and Larry Wesson

# ACKNOWLEDGMENTS

I am grateful to my writing friends in Boulder for suggestions (even if disregarded), thoughtful criticism, and inspiration. Thanks to Karen Palmer, Clay Bonnyman Evans, Janis Hallowell, Jeff Long, Ellen Gault, Jeanne Winer, Daniela Kuper, Tom Lamarr, Tim Hillmer, and Baine Kerr. For friendship and courage, thanks to Mary Hey, Maria Krenz, Dagny Scott Barrios, Stephanie and John Kane, and Manuel Ramos. For his generosity and also his invaluable advice about psychopathology and its diagnosis, I thank Stephen White. I appreciate Tom Kelly and Gene Nichol for their willingness to entertain my heretical ideas about the first amendment, and Mel Lockhart for a useful early critique of this manuscript. Thanks to Cynthia Carter, again, for superior manuscript preparation and excellent proofreading, and to Diana Stahl and Jenifer Martin for their help with all things technical. I must mention the unmatched support I've enjoyed from my brilliant and patient colleagues at the University of Colorado Law School, especially Sarah Krakoff, Phil Weiser, Scott Peppet, Lakshman Guruswamy, Art Travers, Emily Calhoun, Paul Campos, Barbara Bintliff, and Charles Wilkinson, from our Dean David Getches, a true Renaissance man, and from my irreplaceable former colleagues Hiroshi Motomura and Glenn George.

It has a been a deep pleasure to work with the University Press of Colorado and Darrin Pratt, Sandy Crooms, Laura Furney, Dan Pratt, Michelle McIrvin, and Ann Wendland.

Although I do not know them, I want to acknowledge how much I have learned from the writings of Catharine MacKinnon and Susan Faludi. I do know Robin West, and her insights into law and literature never fail to astonish me and disrupt my careless conclusions; I hope that some of what I have learned from her is at work in this book.

Ben Cantrick has taught me that children humble our illusioned pride in what we imagine we've created, and fill us with something better and truer.

Ben Herr's love and faith have made everything possible.

Once we narrow the ambit of the First Amendment, creative writing is imperiled and the chilling effect on free expression . . . is almost sure to take place.

—Mr. Justice William O. Douglas,
concurring in *Time, Inc., v. Hill*

Unlike the Court, I obtain no assistance . . . from the ubiquitous and slippery "chilling effect" doctrine.

—Mr. Justice John M. Harlan,
concurring in *Zwickler v. Koota*

Chances that a movie released in the U.S. last year was pornographic: 9 in 10

—Harper's Index/March 2002
(*Sources:* Adult Video News [Chatsworth, California]/
ACNeilsen [Hollywood, California]/Adams Media
Research [Carmel Valley, California])

He was the ghastliest hitchhiker who ever thumbed me.
—Ross Macdonald, *Find a Victim*

# PART ONE

✧✧✧

It was the ghastliest fax I ever received.

I was alone in the office, sitting at our secretary's desk, when it arrived. I'd been looking through the jumble of supplies in Beverly's bottom drawer, hoping to find a new cartridge for my printer, and just as I gave up the search I heard the rattle of the fax machine. It's an old one, and it groans when summoned into service like an arthritic doorman whose stiff joints protest when he has to get up to admit a visitor.

I watched idly as the first sheet emerged, expecting to see the letterhead of some other law firm, or perhaps a meeting announcement from the Boulder County Bar Association. But as it rolled out I saw that the page was blank, except for the unreadably small source information at the top— and the neat even handwriting, a single line about a third of the way down:

Is this the kind of case you handle? I'll be calling.

All these months later I can still summon up those tidy letters if I close my eyes and try, but it's the sheet that followed this one that sometimes still unrolls in the eye of my memory unbidden, and unwelcome. I watched the second page of the fax slide from the machine, so dark in spots that it glistened and curled with the weight of the ink. I pulled it out straight and as the image resolved in my perception I hunched my shoulders, as though by folding up my own body I could protect it from the knowledge of that one, so small, so violated, and even in black and white so obviously dead.

I looked away, but not before noting that the eyes were wide open, watching things that nobody should ever have to see.

I wanted nothing to do with it. You'd have to be crazy in some particularly ugly way to send something like that, I figured—to fax it, for God's sake, to someone you didn't know. I'd had enough crazy in my law practice the past few years; it wasn't romantic or interesting any longer. So when the phone rang ten minutes later I pretended to be a secretary, and told the woman she'd have to call back when one of the lawyers was in. I didn't really think she would, but I was wrong. She called back that evening, late, while I was preparing to leave for the day. My partner Tory took the call, and that was where all the trouble started, our first step along the crusade route.

At first it seemed the crusader would be Tory, and she's a far more plausible knight than I am—fearless, even reckless sometimes. But the mission became mine almost without my noticing. My friend Andy Kahrlsrud has recommended that I make an effort to understand why it happened that way.

I'm Lucinda Hayes, attorney, practicing in Boulder, Colorado. I wasn't born in Colorado. I came here to go to law school, and stayed. Boulder is a garden of transplants; almost everyone here is from somewhere else, so that's not unusual. But sometimes I think the particular place of my birth and upbringing, and my chosen exile from it, have shaped my path more than any other influence.

Try it yourself. Ask an American born before about 1957: What's the first thing you think of when you hear *Dallas*?

*Where Kennedy was shot.* Or maybe *John Kennedy,* or *President Kennedy.* That's the response you'll get, almost every time.

Nearly anyone old enough to remember it will give you that answer. Except for people who lived there at the time—you'd expect them to say something else, perhaps *my hometown,* or *where I was born,* and most Dallasites will. But not me: I answer like an outsider. It's my hometown all right, but for me it will always be first the place where the president was shot and killed.

Perhaps it's because that day I experienced for the first time a feeling that's haunted me, on and off, ever since: the impression that nearly everyone else understands something that I don't, has signed on to some agreement without inviting me to join it. I was a bit older when I started to think that those of us who were somehow excluded from this arrangement needed to look out for each other. And older still before I realized how many of us believe we're in that category, including some I wouldn't necessarily commit myself to looking out for. Leonard Fitzgerald, for example. No doubt there's more to this strange fragment of identity that I still haven't understood. But I know it started that day, or perhaps the day before.

## NOVEMBER 1963

I was nine, in the third grade, Miss Brewer's class. President Kennedy was going to be in Dallas. That's what he was called in my house, at least by my father: President Kennedy. Others, I knew, just called him Kennedy.

The day before he was to come, Miss Brewer told us we'd be making flag pictures during Art. Because of the President's visit, she said.

Kennedy is a traitor, said one of the boys.

Do you know what that means? asked Miss Brewer.

It means he's a faggot, said another boy, and some of them laughed. I didn't know what faggot meant, and I was unsure about traitor, but I raised my hand and said my father said he was a good president.

That day, after school, the boy who'd said President Kennedy was a faggot informed me that my father was a nigger-lover.

I know, I said, although I hadn't. From the way he said it, it was like being a faggot. But I was loyal to my father and said I know, without flinching. The boy looked at me hard and spat on the ground at my feet. But what he said then was not as mean as I had expected: *I hate this school. Nothing ever happens here.*

Maybe he would have been meaner if I hadn't been a girl, and hardly worth bothering about. I can't remember any of the boys' names, and not that many of the girls'. But I remember Celia, of course. She was my best friend.

Tory's my best friend now, I suppose, although I think her best friend is her lover Linda, so where does that leave me? We've been law partners for nearly nine years, Tory and I. Hayes and Meadows, P.C. Sometimes she's granite, and I lean against her when I start to wobble. Other times I worry that the burden of the bad times a few years ago will drag her back to the dark place in her mind, where she's already done enough time. I try to keep an eye on Tory's moods, and around the time we met Peggy Grayling I thought she was getting edgy. Her sarcasm was less playful, more stinging, and she'd taken to correcting my grammar, not just on paper when she proofread my legal work, but while we were talking. When I'd mention this to her, she'd disclaim any worries other than the usual one about how we were going to survive as lawyers in a town where there were too many of them, but I thought I knew better.

That evening—the evening of the day the fax arrived—she stood framed in my office door, one hip cocked. "Do you know anything about a Margaret Grayling calling this morning? She's on the phone now, says our secretary told her to call back later. Has Beverly stopped taking messages?"

"It was me," I admitted. "I got the call, but I thought she was a nut case, so I put her off. I didn't think she'd call back."

"Well she did. She's on the line now. What's so nutty about her?"

I was reluctant to mention the fax, and knew I didn't want Tory to see it. She needs crazy even less than I do, and she's more drawn to it. But I realized I needed some evidence to back up my impression of the woman's instability. "It looks like some little girl was murdered horribly. I don't know who this woman is or what she wants, but I guess she actually had a crime scene photograph, and faxed it here before she called. It was awful. Worst I've ever seen. We don't need those kinds of clients, Tory. Can't you refer her to Billy?" Bill Woodruff officed across the hall from us, a nice young lawyer with so much enthusiasm and so little judgment that he would take any client that moved.

Tory inclined her close-shorn copper head. "Depends. What does she want with a lawyer?"

I shrugged. "I think she knew the little girl, maybe she was related to her. So she faxes over the photo and asks me if that's the kind of case we might be interested in. I don't know why she picked on us. Maybe our ad." After some debate, we'd recently placed an ad in the Yellow Pages.

"Where's this fax?" asked Tory.

"I don't know, Tory. Jesus, I threw it away. Why would you want to see it? Didn't you get enough of that at the DA's office? It was horrible."

"What's this, then?" Some uncanny impulse had turned her gaze toward the chair next to me. My battered leather briefcase rested there, a sheet of paper protruding unevenly from the top. She walked over and pulled out the spotty-looking page.

I peered at it. "I guess that's it. I must have stuffed it in there."

But she wasn't listening. She was looking at the photograph.

"Tory? Don't look at it. It's pointless. Throw it away, okay? No, give it to me, I'll toss it. Here." I held out my hand.

She shook her head abstractedly and turned to walk back toward her office, gripping the fax with both hands. As she passed under the old chandelier in the reception area her face caught the light and I could see her expression—one that I knew and didn't like. The child's photograph had drawn her in, forged some connection to her tangle of loyalties and yearnings in the instant it struck her eyes. I heard her sit down in her creaky desk chair, could barely discern her murmur into the phone. I tried to shrug and get back to the billing records I was working on, but ten minutes later I could see that one of the lights on the telephone was still lit and I knew that Tory had not told the woman that we were the wrong firm to help her.

I rose and walked to her office, dread rising in my body like a fever. The only light in there was the greenish glow from the banker's lamp on her desk.

"I think I know how you must feel," she was saying. She swiveled around in her chair, seeing me at the door. *What?* I mouthed at her, but she just shook her head and turned back to the phone. The gruesome fax was lying on her desk next to the phone, its creases softening slightly as though she had smoothed it out.

"Sure we can. Sure," she said. "In person would be much better, I agree. I think tomorrow would be okay. Let me look. Hold on for a moment, please. Please. I'll be right back." She punched the mute button on her phone, and laid the receiver down tenderly next to the photo.

"She's the mom," she said.

"What?"

"Hers." She gestured toward the fax. "Her mom."

"Well, is she okay?"

"She's not okay, Cinda. Her little girl was tortured and murdered. She's never going to be okay. She wants to come talk with us."

"What about?"

"A lawsuit. For her daughter's death. We're the ones she wants to represent her. She says she's met you. Do you remember her?"

I shook my head and looked down at the carpet, which I noticed was stained pretty badly in spots. "I don't know her. I don't think we can do anything for her, Tory. You know we can't bring her daughter back."

She looked at me with scorn, then picked up the receiver again and punched the mute button. "Mrs. Grayling? Why don't you come over here about ten tomorrow, and we'll talk with you then? We don't charge for an initial consultation. One thousand seven Pearl Street, right over Pasta Jay's. Are you all right now? Is your husband there? Oh. Well can you call a friend? Good, why don't you do that? Right. Take care, and we'll see you at ten."

She hung up and sat down in her wooden swivel chair, then swung it round to face me. *"Can't bring her daughter back,"* she mimicked. "When was the last time we represented someone who actually hoped to get back what she'd lost? The one whose husband ruptured her spleen and messed her head up so bad she'll be in therapy until she dies? The one who got raped at knifepoint and then the guy slashed her face up because she didn't fake an orgasm?"

I made a gesture of surrender.

"That lady knows we can't bring her daughter back," said Tory. "Or I think she does. And if she doesn't we can certainly make that clear. She just wants the same thing our other clients want."

"I've been wondering about that lately," I said, sinking into the chair across from her desk. "What is that?"

"What is what?" She was pacing now, the room too small to contain her energy.

"What our clients want."

"I think they want a person on a tall bench in a black robe to tell them and the world that it's not right what happened to them. It's not *acceptable*. They want to know that someone is responsible for what they lost, and is going to have to pay for it."

"Well, someone killed her daughter. Does she know who it was?"

"Yeah, she knows. A guy confessed."

"So she wants us to sue him?"

"He was prosecuted for it last year," said Tory. "In Chicago. Acquitted, NGI."

Not guilty by reason of insanity. "I suppose we could sue him anyway," I said skeptically. "Insanity's not quite as good a defense to a tort as it is to a crime."

Tory shook her head. "She says she doesn't want to sue him. He's locked up in the psych ward, he's never gonna get out, and he's got no money."

"Then who?" I asked. "Who does she want us to sue?"

Tory turned back to her desk, scrabbling through piles of paper, looking for something. "I believe the word is *whom*. And I don't know whom she wants to sue. Something about an accomplice, I couldn't quite get it; she got very quiet toward the end of the conversation. She's coming in tomorrow, ten o'clock. We'll find out then. Now you better go home." She found a half-gone yellow legal pad, and started to make a bulleted list.

"What about you?"

"I'll be right behind you," she replied without looking up, and added another bullet to her list. I could almost smell the mania rising in her veins, and I thought, *God help you, whoever you are.*

I woke up the next morning in time for a run, but it was snowing lightly, a drippy puky nuisance snow that extinguished my interest in outdoor exercise. Even after an exceptionally thorough pass through the *Boulder Daily Camera,* I was dressed and ready for work by 7:45. When I got there the place felt chilly and awfully quiet under the fluorescent lights. Margaret Grayling wasn't expected until ten, and I knew that Beverly wouldn't be in until eleven because Tuesday is the day she and her chronically unemployed husband Charley have couples therapy. I didn't want to sit down in the bleak emptiness of my office, so I left my briefcase on my desk, stuffed a printout of the brief I was working on into my backpack, and decamped for the Trident across the street. Half coffee shop, half used bookstore, the Trident is an old Boulder tradition that Starbuck's will never replace. It's Buddhist-owned and operated and they make great coffee there, but I like it mostly for the curious stillness that permeates the air and underlies the buzz of steam and reggae music and conversation.

I kept my eye on the time as I marked up the brief, and dashed back across the street to the office at five minutes to ten, but Grayling must have arrived early. I could hear talking as I entered the reception area, two voices drifting out of Tory's office.

"Journalism," the not-Tory voice was saying. "University of Illinois at Chicago."

"And Alison's father?" Tory's voice had none of its usual edge.

"We're separated," she said. "Divorce underway. He's an academic too. Geology, Northwestern University. Glaciers, mostly. He's still there."

I stepped into the room. "Hi, sorry. I guess I'm a little late. I'm Cinda Hayes." I offered my hand to the slender gray-haired woman sitting in

Tory's guest chair. She turned her face up as she took my hand in hers; the face and the hand were both worn, both beautiful. About fifty, I guessed; no makeup, no hair dye. Her hair fell in careless streaky ripples to her shoulders, and the only jewelry in sight was a thin gold chain around her tanned neck. She certainly didn't look crazy.

"Cinda," she said softly, in the voice I had heard on the telephone. "I'm so glad to see you again."

"Me too," I said inadequately and probably ungrammatically, but her greeting had made me uncomfortable. I had no memory of ever having met this woman before. "Let me unload this thing"—I hefted the backpack off my shoulder—"and get a notepad, and I'll be right back." The red light on my desk phone blinked, suggesting that a caller had left a message on my voicemail, but I ignored it and rummaged for a legal pad, then rejoined Tory and Margaret Grayling.

"Yes, it was," she was saying in response to some question of Tory's I had not heard. "He thought the only thing was to go on, with our lives, you know. I don't mean right away, of course. But after the funeral, and then the investigation, and then this man who called himself Wolf was arrested, and then the trial, everything." Her voice trailed off. "After that he said to me, you can't be mired in grief forever. You have to go on. Life is good. I know he meant well, and I didn't want to force my grieving onto him. So we went our own ways." She fell silent, nibbling thoughtfully on her thumbnail.

I looked at Tory, and her look back said *Your turn.*

"I'm sorry, I know I came in late," I began. "Who is Wolf? What trial was this?"

"Wolf is the one who killed my daughter Alison," she said. "He was a young man, from a dreadful family, apparently. He was charged with sexual assault, sexual assault on a child, felony murder, murder with premeditation, various crimes. Quite serious crimes. There was something terribly wrong with him, of course."

"So the picture you faxed me yesterday—that was Alison?"

She nodded. "I thought you needed to see the photograph to understand why I want to pursue this. There was no doubt this man was the one who . . . did those things. He confessed almost as soon as the police came to his door. He lived across the street from Alison's school. Apparently he had watched her for weeks from the upstairs window when she and the other kids were on the playground. She was, I don't know. Noticeable. She was a shining star. I know every parent thinks that, but it was true of Alison. She was very blonde and had long, long legs for a nine-year-old, and she just ran rings around the other kids, in every possible way." Her voice dropped to a whisper. "Then—then he saw her and I believe he wanted to make her a part of his own world, which was very dark and ugly."

My pen completely still, I watched her face then; not a single tear glazed the surface of her eyes, and her voice was steady but extremely soft. Her words were eloquent enough to have been rehearsed, but I didn't think they had been. Despite the violence and loss in her story a curious peace clung to her, rather like the silence beneath the clatter of coffee cups in the Trident. She sighed and looked down at her ringless hands, spreading the fingers as if to dispel some tension there.

"Mrs. Grayling," I began.

"Please, Cinda, call me Peggy. You don't remember me, do you?"

I could feel a flush of embarrassment crawling around my hairline. "I'm sorry. I meet so many people and I'm not good at—"

"No, of course. No reason you should. My sister Celia was a friend of yours when we were all growing up. Back in Dallas."

"Celia," I said, blank for a moment until light broke through. "Celia Quinn? Oh my God, you're Peggy Quinn? Of course I remember you."

She smiled again, that Madonna-like blessing. "It's been a lot of years, hasn't it? A couple of years ago Celia ran into your sister—Dana, is it?—in Neiman-Marcus, and asked her about you. When she heard I was moving to Boulder she told me that you were living here, that you were a lawyer. So—" She spread the slender hands again.

Peggy Quinn had been eight years older than we were, an aloof princess whose boyfriends, dates, and clubs I heard about from Celia. My clearest memory of her didn't feature her presence at all—one Friday night when I slept over at Celia's and Peggy was out on a date, the two of us had raided her closet and tried on her clothes, her wool suits and high-heeled shoes as desirable and distant as the outfits we saw in magazines. Her parents were proud of both of them, but it was Peggy's photographs, in strapless gowns and cheerleader uniforms, that dominated their living room.

Then something went wrong, I never knew what. Only that Peggy had left home abruptly, before graduation, and gone to live with an aunt in

Chicago. When I went to stay at Celia's after that, most of the photographs were gone, and Peggy's closet was empty.

"Oh my God," I said again, mindlessly. "How is Celia?"

"She's fine. Her husband is a dermatologist, they live in Fort Worth. They have"—here she paused for the merest of moments—"two little girls."

There was more I could have asked about why she had left home and what she had done, but I thought I could sense Tory growing restive. "So," I said, "what brought you to Boulder, after you decided to leave Chicago?"

"Oh," she said. "The *sangha,* my community. Dorje Dzong." I knew I had heard the words but had to think for a moment where, then remembered. It was the name of the local Buddhist congregation.

"I see," I said. Perhaps this explained something, at the very least her air of calm and control. "So, this man Wolf lived near your daughter's school. And this was where?"

"Oak Park," she replied. "The public schools there are very good."

Another silence. "And so," said Tory eventually. "The trial?"

She shook her head; at first I thought she was trying to shake off the memory, but her words described a different negation. "I wasn't allowed to attend," she said.

*"What?"* Tory said it, but I had the same reaction.

"The prosecutor," said Peggy Grayling. "He was a very nice young man, John. He explained that witnesses couldn't be in the courtroom, except during their own testimony."

"Oh, yes," I said. "The Rule."

Full name: The Rule on Sequestration of Witnesses. Rule 615 of the Colorado Rules of Evidence. Like most lawyers, I had learned about it in law school. Any party to a trial can invoke The Rule to keep witnesses out of the courtroom until after they've testified. It prevents them from consciously or unconsciously conforming their testimony to that of the preceding witnesses. My Evidence professor had taught it to us, but he had neglected to mention that judges often refer to it simply as The Rule, or perhaps he didn't know—he was many years past his last courtroom appearance. At the beginning of my first trial as a young prosecutor, when I was as nervous as coffee, Judge Harold Ramos had summoned me and defense counsel to the bench and asked formally if either party wished to invoke The Rule. My opponent said "We do not, Your Honor," and then Ramos looked sternly at me. I had no idea what he was asking, and neither his expression nor anything else in the situation made it look like a good idea to inquire. Finally I said, in desperation: "Your Honor, we would like to invoke *all* the rules." Ramos, who had the best poker face of any judge I have ever encountered, burst into a massive belly laugh, joined by the defense lawyer and the stenographer who had heard the exchange. I wished only that the floor would open up and swallow me, but somehow I got through the morning. At the noon recess, the defense lawyer took me aside and sympathetically explained which rule The Rule was. His name was Sam Holt, and his unstudied kindness made me wonder why I'd never tried harder to know him when we had been law school classmates.

A few years after he taught me about The Rule, Sam and I became lovers. I sometimes felt as though he'd taught me half of everything I knew about law, and as much about love. But he didn't live in Boulder any longer; he had moved to New York to practice law in a place where an accomplished black man was not an object of curiosity or admiration simply for being that. I had spent a few days there with him about a month before Margaret Grayling sent her fax to our office. We had enjoyed our time together, but I didn't know when I would see him again.

I realized I had let my attention lapse, and I forced it back to Margaret Grayling and her story.

"But *were* you a witness?" Tory was asking. "I mean, did you have some evidence to give?"

"No, I wasn't, not in the end, because the verdict was not guilty. By reason of insanity. But if he had been convicted, I would have testified at the sentencing, is what this young man John told me. On—I think he called it the victim impact. So, just in case it happened that way, I couldn't be allowed into the trial."

It was Tory's turn to shake her head. "Doesn't sound right to me. If it had been me prosecuting, I would have argued that a witness who's just going to testify at sentencing isn't subject to The Rule."

Mrs. Grayling shrugged lightly. *What do I know?* said her expression. "But I've been told that in a civil trial, I'd be allowed to attend every day of the trial, even if I were going to be a witness."

"That's right," said Tory quickly. "Because you'd be a party to the case. The Rule doesn't apply to parties."

"So this man, Wolf—he was acquitted?" I prompted her. "By reason of insanity?"

She nodded. "I wasn't there to hear the testimony, of course, but apparently he was a very, very disturbed man. His name was Leonard Fitzgerald, but he had decided to call himself Wolf. Or sometimes Dire Wolf, I'm told. He had a whole fantasy life, and this basement apartment where he pursued it. The psychiatrists didn't agree altogether, John told me later, but every one of them thought he was severely . . . I don't know what. Impaired. Damaged. But there are so many people like that, aren't there?" She opened her hands outward like a book, a gesture of resignation, or benediction.

"Mrs. Grayling," Tory began.

"Peggy, please," she said. Her calm amazed me; I wondered if it was chemically maintained.

"Peggy," Tory agreed. "Peggy, when you called last night, you asked me about what happens when one person suggests that another commit a crime. Do you have some reason to think that someone else suggested your daughter's murder to Leonard Fitzgerald?"

"That's the thing, exactly, that I wanted to ask you about. Yes, I have some reason, but I need to know for sure. I really need to know," she repeated, with the first hint of urgency I had heard.

"What is your reason for thinking someone else was involved?" I asked. Tory's notepad, I noticed, was nearly as blank as mine. Nothing appeared on it after Peggy Grayling's name, address, and telephone number.

"John, the prosecutor, told me that part of what convinced the jury that Wolf was not guilty by reason of insanity was the videotape." This was the first I'd heard about a videotape. A small shard of memory turned and stirred in my mind.

"Apparently it was a pornographic tape," she continued. "A snuff film, John called it. They found it in Wolf's VCR, and the lab said he probably had copied it off of one he rented from a shop somewhere. They never found the place he rented it from. Chicago is a big place," she added unnecessarily.

Then I remembered. The Chicago Snuff Film Trial, the papers had called it. I had read about it the previous spring. It had featured many elements that made it a show trial: the lucid but very crazy defendant, the battle of the psychiatric experts, the film that some of them opined had finally pushed him over the edge, the NGI verdict.

"This was all about a year ago, right?" I asked her.

She nodded and then crossed her arms and leaned forward, the hem of her pale linen shirt sliding down over the knees of her corduroy jeans.

"I want to see that tape," she said.

*No,* was my first reaction. *No, you don't. No, you can't. Not if I can help it.* I was already harboring a passionate wish to protect this woman from any further sorrow. But Tory's reaction was more professional, and more constructive.

"Did you say the jury watched the tape?" she asked.

Peggy nodded.

"Then it must have been an exhibit. It will be an official part of the trial record. That's a public document," she concluded confidently. "I'm sure we can arrange for you to see it. If you really want to," she added more soberly, having caught my look, perhaps.

"Well, yes," said Peggy Grayling. "I did think of that. I'm a trained journalist, you know. Here's what I discovered. The trial record, including the exhibits, including the videotape, is in the clerk's office of the court. It cannot be removed, although copies may be made if they are made within the confines of the clerk's office. There is a copying machine there for that purpose. Only, of course, a copying machine is not useful for making a copy of a videotape. For that you need a videocassette machine. And there is none there."

"Shit, they really get you coming and going, don't they?" offered Tory.

"I did try bringing in a dual-deck videocassette machine, to make a copy," Peggy went on. "That request got me an audience with the clerk, himself. The first time I met with him, he listened to my request and then asked me to come back the next day. When I did, he informed me that he had reviewed the exhibit and that in his opinion it was copyrighted material, and consequently could not be copied without the permission of the copyright holder. I asked him who that was, and he said he did not know. By now I was thinking this conversation could have been a case study for my students in interviewing a reluctant public official. I'm afraid I rather gave up, then. I was getting ready to move here, and my husband was encouraging me to let it go. But I can't, you know," she said, the urgency in her voice again. "I can't."

"This accomplice you mentioned," I asked her. "You meant by that the videotape?"

"Whoever made it," she replied. "I haven't seen it, of course. But if the jury thought it made the Wolf do what he did, it must have more or less recommended the assault and mutilation and murder of little girls. Like mine." Her voice grew soft again, and on her face I saw for an instant the anguish that had hidden behind her professional rendition.

I looked at Tory, but she was staring rigorously out the window, although there was nothing to see but a pair of finches flitting around our bird feeder. "So," I ventured, turning back to Peggy Grayling, "you think you want to sue whoever it was made this videotape, if it seems that the tape encouraged Leonard, Wolf, to do what he did?"

"Precisely. Can you do that?"

"I don't know," I said doubtfully. "There's a big First Amendment question here, isn't there?"

I had meant the comment for Tory, but Peggy spoke first. "I'm a journalist. Nobody understands the importance of freedom of speech better than I do. But—"

Tory rose from her desk chair. "Peggy," she said firmly, "Cinda and I need to talk about this, do some research. This is an extremely interesting question you've brought us, and a hasty answer would be ill-advised. Can we call you in a day or two?"

"Of course," she said at once, rising to her own feet. She was even smaller than she had looked in the chair, much shorter than either me or Tory, and quite slender. "Thank you so much," she said, holding out her hand to me.

"Good to see you again," I said as I pressed it. "Did we get your phone number?"

She nodded. "Tory has it. Thank you, too, Tory."

"No problem," said Tory. I could almost feel a cold front sweeping through the small room; I nearly heard the windows rattle.

"I can let myself out," said Peggy, and she turned and vanished with a dancer's light grace. We watched her departure in silence.

*"No problem?"* I repeated after I heard the main office door close behind her. "What is that supposed to signify, Sister Frostbite? Last night

you were falling all over yourself to get the woman in here. Suddenly you can't wait to hustle her out the door."

"What hustle? I didn't *hustle* anything."

"Well, I sure think you would've, if you'd had to. You just didn't have to because she has such lovely manners that she hustled herself out to save you the trouble. What's going on?"

Tory paced over to the window and back, then sat down again and played a tattoo on the desktop with her pencil before finally speaking. "Cinda, I hate this idea of blame the book, blame the movie. We can't do what she's asking. It's censorship. Trying to stop someone's speech because some wacko acted out his fantasies then blamed his crime on pornography. Ted Bundy all over again. It's bullshit."

"What censorship? I didn't hear her say she wanted to stop anyone's speech."

"It's the same thing. Like making a filmmaker pay a huge fine if you don't like what he shows in his movies. You said yourself it's a First Amendment issue."

"I said *question*. I don't know the answer. Anyway, it's not a matter of whether we like it, Tory. It's whether it encourages someone to murder a little girl."

She muttered something then, but I didn't catch it.

"Say that again?"

"I *said* Brianna Fucking Bainbridge. Is who you sound like. Maybe you and she ought to get together on this, really step all over the First Amendment. I'm going over to the gym. See you later."

See, she *has* been getting edgy, I told myself. It wasn't until much later that it occurred to me how completely we had traded positions on Margaret Grayling and her lawsuit.

Going through the heavy old doors into the university's Fleming Hall building never failed to induce a mild case of the jumps, a souvenir of the terrors of the first year of law school. Even after I finished that year third in my class, I never entirely lost the dread of failure, of exposure as an impostor. Later, judges replaced professors as the source of my mental torments, and I learned to live with the anxiety, coming to understand that I needed a jolt of fear to work at the top of my form. But the vestigial quiver that seized me as I pushed open the doors and walked out of the blazing sunshine into the dim quiet of the hall was nothing but an annoyance; I had nothing to worry about here, not any more.

The directory by the elevator said that Brianna Bainbridge's office was on the fourth floor, and I decided to walk. In the dank old stairwell, between the second and third floors, I passed a couple of thirty-something men leaning against the railing, arguing desultorily. They were dressed alike in Dockers and Banana Republic shirts, and they were both pale, but the resemblance ended there. One was very tall and thin, with a thatchy mop of brown hair; the other was short and plump and nearly bald, and carried a wadded-up handkerchief, apparently for brow-mopping purposes.

"—*clueless,*" Handkerchief was saying. "He actually asked me, 'Well, how would you have voted if you had been on the Court at the time *Roe v. Wade* was decided?' I mean, he totally fails to understand that it's simply *not an interesting question.*"

Thatch nodded sadly. "Such a farce. He just doesn't get it that it's all a *metaphor.* I mean, how does a guy like that even get *tenure,* much less a *chaired professorship* . . . ." He brightened. "Hey, what about that game?"

"Shaq was great, wasn't he? I told my wife . . ." I turned the corner of the staircase and could hear no more.

Must be new faculty, I thought, hired since I graduated back in the pre-postmodern era, before law and everything else were demoted to metaphors (except, it seemed, possibly professional sports). I shuddered briefly, glad beyond belief that I was no longer a law student. As I left the stairs I saw that some things had not changed: the corridor of faculty offices on the fourth floor was as dark and claustrophobic as I remembered. Many of the fluorescent overhead lights were unlit, whether from neglect or a misguided desire for energy conservation I had never known. Most of the office doors along the corridor were closed, but I could see light shining out of one onto the dingy hall carpet; as I drew nearer I could hear music, too, something baroque.

Brianna Bainbridge had joined the law school faculty after my graduation, so I had never met her, but I read about her often in the alumni magazine. The school never tired of boasting about its success in hiring the "founder of feminist jurisprudence," as they often referred to her. Her books, in which she argued that pornography was both the perfect expression of discrimination against women and the cause of many crimes, had made nationwide bestseller lists and been translated into several languages. She had been a leader in the movement to pass laws making the distribution of pornography a crime, and her efforts had succeeded in four states. In the end, however, the laws had all been struck down by the courts, as violations of the First Amendment.

I thought her writings were unnecessarily abstruse—I had finally given up on her last book after one too many encounters with the word "epistemology." Even those who agreed with her legal theories had warned me that she was difficult. But at least Brianna Bainbridge still seemed to think the law mattered—that it was something more than a shopworn figure of speech.

"Hello?" I peered around the door into her office.

The woman who looked up from the desk had the face of a seraphim, complete with a cloud of pre-Raphaelite red hair. Yellow light shone from an art deco brass lamp onto her desk, which held a breathtaking bouquet of fresh flowers. The office appeared to have been decorated by a trendy eclectic designer—Japanese prints, off-white bookcases, an Iranian *gabbeh* underfoot—and the effect was disconcerting. The small room looked as though it belonged in an entirely different building from this aging utilitarian box.

"Cinda Hayes?" She rose from behind the desk and came forward with an outstretched hand. I smiled as I shook it, but my flutters had returned. Brianna Bainbridge had to be six feet tall in her spike heels, yet there was nothing even slightly wobbly about her—I imagined her dribbling down a basketball court in those shoes, like in some television commercial, going in for the layup and making a perfect four-point landing. God, she was intimidating. Vivaldi or something flowed out of a wonderfully miniature silver case on a bookshelf, the sound reproduction flawless. "Come in, please. Have a seat." She pointed toward a spindly sculpture with a small shelf built into it, evidently a chair. "Tell me again what brings you here?"

"You were very kind to make time to talk to me," I began as I sat down gingerly. She waved a hand regally, as though shooing a mosquito.

"The school encourages us to interact with alums," she said, smiling. "Do you have a local practice here in Boulder?" She pronounced the words *local practice* daintily, as though they might leave a slightly unpleasant taste in her mouth if given an opportunity to linger there.

"Like I mentioned on the phone, I went to law school here, but before you joined the faculty. Actually, I don't think there were any women professors then—well, one, but she left after a year. After law school, I worked in the DA's office for nearly ten years, the last four as chief of the Sex Crimes Prosecution Unit. Then I worked for two and a half years as director of the Boulder County Rape Crisis Center. I worked for a while, court-appointed, on a death penalty case, and then I went into private practice with a friend, Tory Meadows."

"Yes, I heard about your work on the Jason Smiley case," she said. "Some of my friends criticized you for it, but I admire it. As much as I detest crime against women, I don't support the death penalty. And I've met your partner Tory. At a conference about legal protection for gays and lesbians," she said. "Quite a wit, Tory."

"Yeah, she's rarely at a loss for attitude. She said you were a brilliant speaker." I had practiced this part, knowing I ought to have some alternative to *She thinks you're a threat to the Constitution and a bitch to boot.* And it was true that Tory, who agreed with nothing Bainbridge had said, had expressed surly admiration for her eloquence.

Brianna Bainbridge shrugged dismissively. "It was nothing special."

"Tory was the one who suggested you might be able to help with a legal problem I'm researching, Professor Bainbridge." *Suggested by telling me I sounded like Brianna Fucking Bainbridge,* I didn't add. "We're working on a case now that presents some First Amendment questions of the kind you've written about. Our client's daughter was murdered by a man who apparently watched a snuff film over and over before the killing, and tried to imitate it. She wants to find out who made the film, and who distributed it, and then sue them for damages. Have you ever heard of a case like that?"

Bainbridge sighed hugely. "Such a case would be very unlikely to succeed, because of the myths and simulacra that seem to addict the judiciary in this country."

"What do you mean?"

"Exactly that," she said rather snappishly. "Judges have invested in a tremendous amount of faulty meta-categorical analysis when it comes to the First Amendment, to the point that the written or spoken word, or the drawn or painted or photographed or filmed image, or the live performance, is deemed untouchable by the law. Except, of course, when it isn't.

Do you remember the famous pronouncement of Justice Potter Stewart about obscenity: 'I know it when I see it'?"

I nodded. *"Jacobellis v. Ohio.* We read it in my Con Law class. God, I haven't thought of that in years."

"Tell me," said Bainbridge, "what was your general impression of Justice Stewart's remark? I mean, what did it make you think about the man who said it?"

"I don't know." I frowned, a student trying to come up with the right answer again. I wasn't entirely enjoying the flashback. "Humorous, I guess. Sort of self-deprecating. Honest."

She nodded with satisfaction. "Exactly the way it's usually presented to law students. Go on."

It was just like being back in class. Tory would have frosted her in her tracks with the observation that she hadn't come for another dose of the Socratic method, of which she'd had a more than sufficient snootful in law school, but I wasn't Tory and so I played along. "Um, I think I remember that he was admitting that he couldn't actually give a good definition of pornography in theory, but that he could recognize it in practice. And it was kind of, you know, endearing that he actually admitted it."

"Exactly," Brianna Bainbridge jabbed a forefinger at me for emphasis. "Arrogance masquerading as modesty. You see it over and over again. *I* know it when I see it. Not *you* know it, or *anyone* knows it. *I* know it."

"So you mean this is an example of—"

"Male dominance, of course," she finished the sentence, evidently forgetting The Method for now. "Can you imagine a woman judge, Sandra Day O'Connor perhaps, saying that? Of course not," she answered her own question. "Only men reserve the right to rule without rules, to pronounce without justifying. *I know it when I see it.* It's a metaphor for two centuries of American constitutional law. And so when the Dayton antipornography ordinance came before the Court, of course they *knew,* as soon as they *saw,* that it was a violation of the First Amendment. They can't say *why,* of course, that's why they decided the case in that pitiful *per curiam* opinion, not even two hundred words to decide the most important constitutional case the Court had before it in the last twenty-five years, possibly in the last century."

"Wow, I see what you mean," I said humbly. The passion behind her argument made any objections seem shabby and pettifogging. "So their

explanation—they said the ordinance violated the First Amendment because it discriminated against certain viewpoints, right? You don't buy
that, I take it."

A look of withering scorn. "*Of course* it's viewpoint discrimination. It
discriminates against the viewpoint that women are objects who deserve to
be degraded and objectified and hurt, and that sex is most satisfying when
it consists of doing those things to women. And children. I don't deny it's
viewpoint discrimination—but what are they trying to tell us? That libel,
which they say is not protected by the First Amendment, has no viewpoint? That a sign that says "Whites Only," which they agree is not protected by the First Amendment, has no viewpoint? That a newspaper ad in
which I solicit the commission of a murder has no viewpoint? All of those
things have viewpoints, and the law discriminates against those viewpoints
without violating the First Amendment, because they're *wrong*. It's only
when the viewpoint is that it's okay to hurt women and children that
suddenly freedom of speech becomes so important. You see, Cinda? See
the shell game? It's ontology by decree, the utterly arbitrary invention of a
categorical jurisprudence designed finally to reify and make permanent
the subordination of women."

She lost me some there at the end, but I did see at that moment.
Suddenly everything seemed brilliantly clear.

"Professor Bainbridge . . ." I began.

"Brianna," she smiled. "Call me Brianna," with the air of one bestow-
ing a gift.

"Thank you," I replied automatically. "May I tell you about our case?"

She sat back, folding her red-tipped fingers. "Of course. Tell me all
about it."

When I was done, she looked over my shoulder, into the distance. The
direction was roughly east-northeast, so perhaps she was looking toward
Washington and the Supreme Court, considering whether they ought to
be given another chance to do the right thing. "How committed are you to
this litigation?" she said finally, turning her burning eyes toward mine.

"I don't know yet."

"Do you have any idea what you would be putting yourself up against?"

"That doesn't worry me," I said quickly, hoping that it would prove to
be true if necessary.

"It won't matter if the person who made that videotape was a three-strikes felon, or a documented child molester, or a cannibal. Your case has some emotional appeal, but if you pursue it, your opponent won't be an easy out. You're going to find yourself fighting the entire American entertainment industry, do you understand? You'll be up against the best-financed, most talented, and least scrupulous lawyers in the world."

I took a deep breath, trying to fill up my belly like a yoga teacher had once taught me would calm my mind. It didn't work all that well this time. "What else?" I said.

"If you're serious, start thinking about these obstacles to success. First, you have to have a client who will not waver, won't want to quit when it gets ugly."

"I think we've got that."

She moved her head impatiently. "Everyone always thinks they have that, but you'd be surprised how often they're wrong. Second, how are you going to find out who made the videotape? These snuff videos don't have credits at the end, you know. Or, if they do, they just give the fake names of the actors."

"I don't know," I admitted. "I haven't even seen it yet. Our first step is just to try to get a copy from the clerk's office. I'm going to Chicago next week for that purpose."

"You need to count on a long and uncertain investigative process to find the maker, and there's a good chance you may not succeed."

I nodded. "What else?"

She sighed, widened her eyes, and set her jaw. A memory tugged at me: waiting for a table once at a noisy family-style restaurant, I had passed the time by watching a pair of brothers, both under ten, standing at the cockpit of a video game. The older was warning the younger about the various monsters and other dangers that stood between him and the treasure. The younger did not seem to be very attentive to this instruction, and was charging hell-bent through dungeons and rivers, often enough getting his little electronic character killed in the process. The older brother had finally given vent to his frustration and cried out, "*Jeremy,* you gotta take the Sword of Fire *much more seriously!*"

The expression on Brianna Bainbridge's face had reminded me of that thwarted boy's, but when I looked at her again I saw she had decided to move on. "Then there's causation," she said briskly. "You might think it self-evident that watching a film in which certain acts give an actor an orgasm might encourage the watcher to try those acts himself, hoping for a similar result. But I am sorry to tell you that many judges and lawyers profess to find this proposition doubtful, even unbelievable. You're going to need expert testimony on this point. Someone is going to need to interview your perpetrator, do an in-depth psychological study, write a report, no doubt sit for a deposition. Testify at trial."

"I understand," I said, making a note on my pad.

"It will be very expensive," she said, moving her fingers to pick up an inlaid fountain pen lying on her desk. She twirled it in slow rotation as though enjoying its smooth texture.

I nodded, putting off any thoughts about how I was going to persuade Tory that the firm ought to finance this case. Unless Peggy Grayling had more money than most of our clients.

"There will be many other difficulties, of course," she said. "Jurisdiction, for example. Your account suggests no connection between Colorado and this matter except that your client lives here now. By itself, that is not sufficient. On the other hand, it does appear this tape was distributed in Illinois, which would confer jurisdiction on the courts there. Are you admitted to practice in Illinois?"

"No," I confessed. "I was hoping to find some jurisdictional theory that would allow litigation here, in Colorado. So was my client."

"That may be very challenging. And I haven't even gotten to the First Amendment arguments you are sure to encounter. Should you manage, against the odds, to surmount the difficulties of locating and identifying the defendant, acquiring jurisdiction over him or it in a court where you are admitted to practice, providing proof of a causal relationship between the defendant's creation and your client's loss, and financing all of this while maintaining your client's motivation to proceed, then you have merely arrived at the scene of your greatest battle."

"Persuading the court that the First Amendment doesn't rule out this kind of a lawsuit," I suggested.

"Precisely. Do you still want to take on this case?"

"Of course," I said. "More than ever."

Brianna Bainbridge smiled, almost beatifically, and suddenly I was swept by the barely remembered rush I would occasionally feel as a law student, when after a long and discouraging classroom grilling I finally came up with the right answer.

"But may I ask you something?" I said.

She inclined her head in assent.

"The tape, as it was described to my client, appears to have featured a child in a pornographic performance, ending in the child's death. Would such an item really qualify for the protection of the First Amendment? I thought the Supreme Court had said that child pornography was excluded from the protection given to other speech."

"It has," she agreed. "But it's not as simple as that because there's no agreement about what constitutes child pornography. There's a federal criminal statute that defines it as a sexually explicit depiction of a minor under eighteen, but prosecution is hard because unless the child performer—if that's what you call her, which I don't—can be located, then proving her age is impossible. She may look like she's eight, but these pornographers have experts who will testify that there's a possibility that she's really a small eighteen-year-old made up and enhanced with digitized special effects to *look* eight. And the courts have bought the argument of the pornography lawyers that a film using an adult performer made up or altered electronically to look like a child is protected by the First Amendment. So federal prosecutors won't pursue a case unless they can prove the age of the child."

"Which is often—"

"Impossible," she finished for me. "So you shouldn't count on arguing that the First Amendment doesn't apply because the film is child pornography. Unless you can find the child who was shown in it. Which, I can almost guarantee, you won't. Whether they killed her for the cameras or later, she's almost certainly dead. Now, any other questions?"

I shook my head, still taking in what she had told me.

"In that case," she said, "I think I'll suggest some homework."

"Anything," I said gratefully, completely forgetting for the moment how recently I had been thankful that I would never again need to be a law student.

She reached into a filing drawer built into her elegant desk and leafed through a sheaf of papers, finally extracting a stack about an inch thick. "Read this," she said. "It's the most recent word on the kind of thing you're attempting. Pay particular attention to the stuff by Detweiler on the relationship between violent pornography and violent behavior. And here." She wrote three lines on a small pad with the inlaid pen. "Call her and say you're a friend of mine."

I read the name as she pushed the paper across the desk. "Mindy Cookson?"

"A former client. She knows as much as anyone about the industry you're about to take on, and she lives right here in Boulder."

I don't know what I was expecting—no, that's not true. I *do* know what I was expecting, and it wasn't this meticulously tended condo development with the trimmed hedge and flower borders. I was looking to find a trailer park at the address Mindy Cookson had given me over the telephone: 1408 Greenwood Parkway, Unit 9. I suppose I had also expected big hair, fake fingernails, the entire litany of low-rent bad-girl features invented by William Jefferson Clinton's spin doctors when they were trying to make us despise and disbelieve Paula Jones and Gennifer Flowers. I could only laugh at myself for falling for the stereotype, and I tried to put my other expectations aside as I walked up the sidewalk to the door bearing a heavy brass numeral and a brass knocker shaped like a hummingbird.

She opened it before I knocked. "Hi. Are you Cinda?"

"That's me," I said. "Thanks for seeing me." She gestured me into the condo. Mindy Cookson, rather short in her bare feet, with chopped-up brown hair, looked like any of the thousands of lithe young women you see drinking (or serving) margaritas and seltzer in Boulder's sidewalk cafés. She could have been a waitress, aerobics instructor, rock-climbing instructor, personal trainer—or nanny, graduate student, emergency room nurse, lawyer. Nothing about her suggested what Brianna Bainbridge had told me: that she had made more than a hundred pornographic films, that her stage name was Venus Valentine, or that she had recently retired at twenty-six after Bainbridge settled a lawsuit in her favor against a well-known pornographic film director. I had been thinking this settlement sounded kind of cushy when Bainbridge told me about it, until she added that the lawsuit was based on a gang rape that took place on the set of *Chain My Body, Unchain My Dreams*—a wrap-day present to the crew from the director.

Brianna had admitted to me that she was disappointed by Mindy's decision to take the money. ("I can't tell you how much," she had said, "but it was a lot.") Even more upsetting to her, a term of the settlement had been a three-year confidentiality agreement. But apparently the two women were still friendly: the merest mention of Bainbridge's name had been enough to get me this appointment with Mindy Cookson, no questions asked. And judging from the furnishings I could see behind her, Mindy seemed to have made good use of her settlement check.

"Come on in," she invited me again. "Let's sit out on the deck. Would you like some iced tea?"

"Sure," I agreed, wandering into a soft interior of dove-gray carpet and mauve walls hung with artfully lit paintings. "What a lovely place."

"Thanks," she called out as she strode into the next room. "Come on in—the deck is through this way."

I walked through the kitchen, a wonder of copper pots hanging like Calder mobiles and more dramatic lighting. A sliding glass door gave out onto a small wooden deck surrounded by planters full of pink and red geraniums; beyond, the swiftly sloping ground led up to the Mesa Trail and, above that, the Second Flatiron. A hummingbird fluttered around a feeder hanging from the branches of a nearby aspen tree. I followed her out to the deck.

She was setting down a pitcher of amber liquid and two tall glasses onto a lacquered tray between two cushioned wrought-iron chairs. "Do you like lemon or sugar?"

"I love lemon, thanks. Even though my dentist says it's bad for me."

She shook her head while swiftly cutting wedges out of a fat yellow lemon on a cutting board. "Don't you hate that? The way everything that's good is bad for you?" She turned and flashed a smile of daunting whiteness but not quite perfection: there was a small gap between her two front teeth.

She poured the iced tea with the offhand confidence of a duchess, or a waitress, and we settled into the chairs under the shade of the overhanging roof. "Fresh mint?"

"Oh my God, yes," I said. "Did you grow that?"

"Sure." She tossed her curly head as she handed me the glass. "It's like a weed, you know. It's not hard to grow. It might be hard to *stop* it from growing, if you should want to do that." I had not expected this mastery of the subjunctive from a porn film actress—nor her bitten, unpainted nails, nor her baggy jeans and plain white t-shirt. She curled a bare foot up onto the opposite thigh, semi-lotus fashion, and said, "I'm glad to talk to any friend of Brianna's—she's one of my heroines. But she told you I can't talk about my lawsuit? Not for another, oh, seven months I think it is."

"I understand about that. I'm more interested in trying to learn about the pornographic film industry in general. Brianna said you know a great deal. That is, if you don't mind talking about it," I added, suddenly reluctant to interrogate this girl.

"I don't mind. I want a lot of people to know what it's really like, especially young men and women who imagine it's a way to break into the entertainment business. I know that's what they believe—it's what I believed. You know: Hollywood!" Here she fashioned each of her tanned hands into a right angle and raised them with a twist that framed her face, while producing the dazzling smile again. The sun bounced off her satin cheeks like the caress of a proud father, and I saw what I had not before: despite the ordinariness of her appearance, this young woman was made to be photographed.

"Can you tell me how you got started in the business, then?" I asked.

"Sure," she said, wiggling a bit to sink further into her chair. "When I was a sophomore in high school, in a little town in Iowa, I went into Des Moines to have my picture taken for the yearbook, just like a lot of my girlfriends did. After he took the regular shots, the photographer asked me if I would be interested in doing some professional modeling. I mean, can you imagine a high school girl saying no to that?"

"No," I confessed, remembering how much I wanted to look like Cheryl Tiegs when I was fifteen, even though I knew that no amount of Cover Girl makeup was going to make that happen.

"Yeah, well, I didn't either. Say no, I mean. He told me to come back the next Sunday; said I would get paid ten dollars an hour. I was thrilled, and you know what? So was my mom. She boasted about it all over town, to her bridge club, everything. My friends were all totally jealous, and I was on cloud nine."

I nodded encouragement, even though I could see where the story was going and it made my heart shrink in my chest to think of it. Fifteen. She probably still had a bed covered with stuffed animals, and dotted her i's with little circles when she wrote notes to her friends.

"So, when I went back, the first day it was fine. There was nobody in the studio but him and me, and that was a little creepy, but my mom was waiting for me out in the parking lot reading a paperback, and he acted okay. I had come in wearing jeans and a sweatshirt, and he just tossed me a black long-sleeved pullover made out of some slinky material, and showed me a dressing room where I could put it on instead of the sweatshirt. It fit a little tight and didn't smell all that good, but it wasn't revealing or anything. The opposite, in fact. He took a lot of pictures of me in poses that seemed sort of artificial—stuff like 'Tilt your head up, now look down, no don't move your head, just move your eyes.' He'd laugh and click away and move all over the studio from one side to the other like he was dancing, sort of like that guy in *Dirty Dancing*, and he'd say things like 'Amazing! You're just amazingly beautiful!' and of course I was just having a great time. He was a very foxy guy, wore these slinky jeans and a t-shirt with a picture of Andy Warhol on it, and after a while he said he was really hot under all the lights, and did I mind if he took his shirt off, and of course I said no. I mean at that very moment all my friends were at the swimming pool and all of the guys had their shirts off, so what was the big deal, you know?"

I nodded, liking this story less and less. "So—what happened then?"

"So, nothing really," she said. "He gave me twenty-dollars—these crisp, brand-new bills—and said he'd call me again, then I went home. I went back to school the next day and everyone asked me all about it, and I was like Queen for a Day at Woodrow Wilson Regional High School. My mom was the one who asked me who was the client, and I didn't know what she meant, and she said, like, 'Who is the *client*, Melinda, who is going to use all the pictures?' I guessed she wanted to tell her friends like whether to look for me on TV or in a magazine or what. And I told her I didn't know. So she told me to find out, and I said okay." This time Mindy's voice drifted off and I thought she looked reluctant to continue.

"Do you want to talk about something else for a few minutes?"

She shook her head and took a long drink from her glass. "You know, the part I don't like to admit, but it's true, is that I was really turned on by this guy, Ray, and by the whole scene in there—him with his shirt off, and he had all these muscles like not many guys at Woodrow Wilson had, and hair on his chest, and the paper on the walls and the lights. Me in this tight velveteen top that smelled like someone's body plus some perfume, tossing my head around and getting told I was beautiful. All week long I couldn't think about anything else, and my friends and our little parties and boyfriends somehow seemed so juvenile. I had this boyfriend, Terry, but after I'd been posing for Ray for a while, Terry seemed like such an infant, and so did all of them. I was going to see Ray every Sunday in Des

Moines by that time, driving myself with my new driver's license in my mom's car. Whew," she said, putting down her glass. "I guess I got a little carried away by that part, huh? Probably you're not too interested in my high school stories."

"I am interested, it's very interesting. But I don't want to make you—"

"You're not making me. Just give me a minute." She closed her green eyes and tilted her head back. The hummingbird was back, or maybe it had been there all along, chittering around the feeder. The breeze disturbed a wind chime and it intoned melodiously, innocent as an Iowa high-schooler with a sweet face.

"It's such a *stupid* story," she said suddenly, leaning forward again with her eyes open. "You could probably guess every bit of it, almost."

"Not at all. You're a good storyteller."

"Brianna says that maybe someday, after I'm allowed to talk about my lawsuit, I could write a book about all this. But writing's different, isn't it?"

"I'm not sure, really. All I ever write are legal things, briefs and stuff. They're all in legalese, which is a language designed for arguing. It's not a very good language for telling stories."

"Oh, yeah? Like, say something in legalese," she said, her eyes mischievous now.

"Like, *assuming arguendo.* That's a really good phrase in legalese."

She wrinkled her nose. "What does it mean?"

"It's a way of saying that your opponent, well, that even if he's right he's wrong."

"I still don't get it."

"Well, like this." I stood up and straightened my spine, made my face serious and mean as though I were delivering an argument on a motion for summary judgment to the sternest judge I had ever appeared before. "And so, Your Honor, assuming arguendo that Mr. Bogus is correct in his interpretation of *Irresistible Force versus Immovable Object,* he is still in error when he urges that the precedent controls here, inasmuch as the portions he cites are mere dictum, and moreover even the ruling has been questioned or distinguished in seven of the eleven circuits. Thank you, Your Honor." Here I took a little bow, then sat back down.

Mindy Cookson covered her nose with her hand and snickered. "That's a terrible language, Cinda. Do lawyers really talk like that? No wonder people don't like them much."

I laughed too. "I may have exaggerated a little. Not much, actually. It is terrible. The language of the law—usually it's ugly, but powerful, like a Sherman tank. Some lawyers can make it sound like poetry, but I admit that's a rare gift."

"What's *dictum?*"

"Do you really want to know? I mean, legalese? Wouldn't you rather learn, say, Sanskrit?"

"No, don't tease me, Cinda. I think the law is interesting, even if you do talk funny when you do it."

So we spent the rest of the afternoon talking; I taught her *dictum,* and then *precedent* (because you couldn't understand *dictum* without it), and then *tortfeasor* and *subrogation, nunc pro tunc* and *sua sponte,* and I think even *condition precedent* and *condition subsequent.*

Then, as the daylight dwindled and grew soft, she took up her narrative again. Brianna had told me most of the story but I wanted to hear Mindy's own version of the camera's requited love affair with her, with her face and body, and where it had led. It was nearly dark by the time she fell silent, leaving me with a final image I wished I could banish to Hell, as for all her composure she surely must have wished as well. It's another one of the pictures that sometimes appears in my private Gallery of Horrors, where my imagination occasionally wanders without asking permission. When it does, there she is: Mindy, naked and choking and helpless on a filthy mattress in a porn film studio in the San Fernando Valley, a sound tech's penis in her mouth, her hands bound with chains.

The chains were only props, she told me, but they did the job. We fell silent then. She had nothing more to say, and I couldn't find the right words to console her, or even be sure that consolation was what she needed. I asked her if I could come back to talk with her again some time, and she said of course. I touched her shoulder as we said goodbye at her front door, and she put her hand on mine for a moment. "Take care," she said, and then, "Beware the deadly nunc pro tunc." And, surprising me altogether, she giggled.

I met Peggy at the trailhead of the Mesa Trail; she'd suggested it when I told her I needed to talk with her.

"I hope you don't mind meeting here," she said as we walked along. She was a fast hiker, effortlessly skirting the rocks and roots that made that section of the trail a hazard to the unfit or unwary. "It's such a lovely day I didn't like the idea of sitting indoors, and I dislike the telephone."

"I'm glad to get the workout," I said. "Ought to do it more often."

She nodded, almost dancing up a series of steps formed from railroad ties. "I was thirty before I learned to like exercise. It was pretty different when I was a kid—none of these girls' soccer teams or basketball teams like they had for Alison and her friends. The biggest challenge in gym class was making up an excuse not to suit up. 'I have my period' was always good, I remember. They didn't dare contradict you."

"It was the same when I got to high school," I said, panting harder than she had as I ascended the same steps. "That reminds me of something I wanted to ask you."

"Sure, what?"

"I remember that you left Dallas sort of suddenly, in high school. Do I have that right?"

"Um-hmm. My parents sent me to live with my aunt because they found out I was having sex with my boyfriend."

"You're kidding! Were you pregnant or something?"

"No. He was a football player, and his father was president of the bank that financed *my* father's business. In retrospect I think it was his parents, really, that put pressure on mine. There was a big meeting in his parents' living room, and we refused to promise that we'd never touch each other again until we were married, and they agreed there was no way they could watch us like a hawk every minute, and next thing I knew I was packed up and sent to live with Rose."

"But what about him? Why were you the one who had to be sent away?"

She paused and turned around to look at me. The sun behind her fired her springy hair to a white heat and I couldn't see her expression. "He was a football player," she said again. "You remember what that was like, don't you? The team needed him to finish the season. I think they won State that year, but by then I was gone. And he had a new girlfriend, at least that's what I heard."

"That must have been terrible for you." I thought of myself at that age, competent at nothing but schoolwork and getting around to the local hangouts with my friends. For all my changeling fantasies, I would have been feckless and miserable if I'd had to navigate through an unfamiliar environment.

"At first, maybe. I can't remember it that well any more, frankly. And it turned out to be the best thing that ever happened to me. Rose was great, she was the black sheep of her generation just like I was of mine, and she took good care of me. I finished high school in Chicago and ended up going to the University of Chicago and then graduate school. I think I was the lucky one, really, getting away. I never belonged in Dallas."

I hurried to catch up with her; I wanted to see her face, see what she meant. "You're kidding, I always thought you were the perfect Texas princess, all the right clothes, the photographs, everything."

She stopped then, and sat down on a large boulder, plucked a sheaf of fountain grass from a patch of the stuff growing by her foot. "I guess you could say I was a gifted impersonator, but that's not the way it seemed at the time. I didn't realize until I was gone, in Chicago with Rose, how exiled I'd felt in Dallas. I think I didn't really draw a deep breath until I was seventeen."

"This is amazing," I said, hunkering down across the trail on a slight rise in the ground. "This is exactly how I feel about the place. Like I can't breathe when I'm there. Even now."

"I believe there are a lot of us, actually. Sort of a Dallas diaspora. I think I started to get some glimmering of things when Kennedy was killed, not so much from what happened as from the way people reacted to it. My parents hated Kennedy—it seemed like everyone we knew did. They actually seemed to think he had it coming, somehow. You probably don't remember much about it," she said. "You're that much younger."

"Oh, I remember it," I said.

1963

On Friday it wasn't too cold on the playground so Celia and I were out there at recess, sitting in a sunny corner of the sidewalk where the surface was smooth, playing jacks. A group of boys was huddled near the fence. I don't know what they were doing, or playing. Not jacks, anyway, which was a girls' game.

The bell rang much too early—we were just getting started with Around the World. Instead of one long peal it rang three quick times, like a fire drill, but then Miss Brewer was standing at the door calling us all to come in and she wouldn't have done that in a fire drill. In a fire drill you were supposed to get out of the building—quickly, but you had to be quiet and orderly.

Oh, man, said one of the boys, but they broke their huddle and started trudging toward the door. Celia and I rose reluctantly, scrabbling dirt under our fingernails as we scooped up the glittery red jacks. I carried most of them but Celia had a few of them and the ball. I hoped we would be allowed to come back outside and finish the game after whatever it was, but the three bells had worried me and I tried to be quiet and orderly, the pointed ends of the jacks poking into my palms as I swung my hands.

Miss Brewer told us to sit down and be silent, and for once we did. Maybe her red eyes made us understand it was an unusual occasion. There was an invisible stirring in my chest and I think it was in everyone's. Our flag pictures from the day before made a repeating border over the blackboard, and I could hear the bubbling of the tank where the classroom guppies lived.

Something terrible has happened, said Miss Brewer. I must ask you not to become too upset. I thought of the guppies again and the time my goldfish had died, and turned to look at the tank, but the little gray fish were darting around just like always.

The president has been shot, said Miss Brewer.

Did he die? said someone quickly.

They are saying, she said. Then she cried, in her throat sort of, just a very little but it frightened me. I didn't think teachers cried, or anyway I didn't think they were allowed to in school. I saw her swallow, saw the bubble in her throat move up and down.

They are saying that yes. He has died. Please remain calm, children.

It was very quiet. For a second the pump in the fish tank made the only noise, a foamy sound rolling over the rows of desks, but only for a second. My desk was on the second row, so I don't know how it started. There was a popping sound behind me, loud. Another pop, then more, then lots of popping all at once. Celia, sitting beside me, put the jacks and ball down on her desk and slowly started popping her hands together too. Clapping. The ball rolled off the desk and bounced once on the floor before rolling away, but she didn't stop. The clapping roared around the room like a train.

Yay, she said, looking at me sideways tentatively, moving her hands slowly at first, then faster and harder. Yay. They got him.

"Sorry," I said.

"I thought I'd lost you there for a moment," said Peggy.

I looked up to the empty sky, thinking it might clear my crowded head. "It just came back over me, as though it happened last week." A related memory struck me. "And then, two days later, Jack Ruby killing Oswald? Remember?"

Peggy nodded. "I was watching on television. I'd stayed home when the rest of my family went to church that morning. I'll never forget that, seeing the fat man step forward and put a bullet right into the skinny one." Her eyes narrowed. "I never put much stock in all those conspiracy theories, but how could they let that happen?"

"That was incredible, wasn't it?" I said. "Killing someone right in a courthouse."

"Unbelievable," she agreed, but her thoughts seemed to be elsewhere. She turned her face toward me, her air of reverie replaced by briskness, and rose in one graceful motion without even putting a hand down. "What did we need to talk about anyway?" she asked, brushing off the seat of her shorts.

My struggle to get up from the ground was unimpressive by comparison. I've got to get back into those yoga lessons, I thought. "I'm ready to start pursuing the investigation of your lawsuit, if you're sure it's what you want. I want to start by going to Chicago to see whether I can pry a copy of the videotape out of the clerk's office at the court there."

"The videotape that killed my daughter."

"The one that Fitzgerald was watching when he killed her, yes."

"Go," she said briefly, and stepped back onto the trail, leaving me once again to follow along behind. I hastened after her, trying to remember what she had looked like when she was Celia Quinn's big sister, but all I could remember was the photographs in the Quinn family living room. I couldn't say there was any striking resemblance, but that had been a very long time ago.

✧✧✧

Chicago was sunny and cool; even inside the airport a holiday air prevailed, the locals walking about in shorts and t-shirts as though they couldn't believe their luck. Sam wouldn't be arriving for another couple of hours, and he had reserved the car in his name. As much as I wanted to see him, I didn't want to linger in the hermetic atmosphere of the airport, and I had to make a phone call that I didn't want to place from the cramped quarter circle of a telephone booth. So I left a message for Sam at the Avis desk saying I had gone on into the city and would meet him at our hotel. After claiming my bag I followed the signs to the El, where I caught a train headed for the Loop and applied myself to figuring out where I should get off.

In the end I only had to walk a few blocks to the Raphael, a small old-world hotel with a wooden chandelier in the lobby and various other Gothic features. After checking in and being escorted to a spacious room, I sat down on the puffy duvet that covered the bed and paged through the telephone book, looking for the local government section. The number wasn't hard to find.

The first person who answered in the clerk's office explained three times, with increasing degrees of elaboration, that case number CR96-132 was closed. I responded each time, with decreasing graciousness, that I knew that, and needed to know how one might get access to the case file anyway. She disappeared eventually, leaving me on Hold to listen for eight minutes to a syrupy version of "Layla" that I could not believe Eric Clapton would ever approve of. The next person who came on was a deep-voiced and very calm Mr. Montgomery, who was more authoritative but no more helpful; I had the impression he was the Designated Nutcase Handler of the office. I finally convinced him I was not one of his charges, and managed to get an appointment to see the clerk herself at four o'clock.

I looked at the clock: forty minutes to get there. I changed hastily out of my travel jeans into borderline professional clothes and dashed down and out through the lobby, finding a taxi from which a well-dressed couple was just emerging. I walked around to the driver's window while the doorman was unloading the couple's matched luggage from the trunk.

"Do you know where the courthouse is?" I asked the driver.

He produced a broken-toothed grin and said, "State or federal?"

"State."

"Criminal or civil?"

"Criminal."

"You don't want to be going there, lady."

"Yes I do," I said firmly, opening the door behind him and climbing in. "As fast as possible."

"Okay then," said Dragoljub Ristic, whose cab license photo, now inches from my face, showed the man with a fine head of flowing hair. In the front seat, he adjusted the Cubs cap that concealed it, and said "Hold on," before pulling out into the traffic.

I took out my small tape recorder and fiddled with its controls to ascertain whether its batteries were alive. They seemed fine. As I looked up I saw Mr. Ristic's eyes looking at mine in the rearview mirror. I smiled at him. "I was hoping you'd know where the courthouse was," I said. "I've never been there."

"Yes, I understand this already," he said cheerfully. "You aren't asking Drago to take you there if you do. What are you, journalist?"

"Not exactly," I said.

"I drive many journalist in Sarajevo," he said. "Always in a hurry." We rode for a while in silence, Ristic being quite properly preoccupied with some challenging traffic situations. We headed away from the lake, and after seven or eight minutes he turned onto a narrow street where bicyclists competed with cars for a piece of the insufficient pavement, and the storefronts were mostly food shops with window signs in Spanish and at least a couple of central European languages. I wasn't sure, but it didn't seem to me we were headed toward the Loop.

"Excuse me," I said, "but are you sure we're going to the courthouse? We don't seem to be headed downtown."

He startled me by pulling all the way to the curb, prompting the car behind him to swerve and honk furiously, and turning around to face me. "You want to go to creeminal courts?" he said fiercely. "Say yes-no right now, or get out my taxi."

"Yes," I said meekly, and without another word he turned back around and pulled the cab back into the street. "Focking journalists," he snorted.

Fifteen more minutes through crowded streets brought us to a shattered neighborhood, where blackened empty buildings were partially concealed by immense billboards advertising prepaid telephone cards, money orders, check-cashing services, and immigration counseling. Ristic pulled over to the curb, more carefully this time, and pointed to a looming stone building across the street. I regarded it with dismay; Lubyanka Prison could not have been grimmer, or in greater disrepair.

"Hah!" he said, pointing. "Creeminal courts. Not downtown. Did I tell you? You want to go back to hotel now?" A concrete walkway bridged the sidewalk to the building's entrance, its sides flanked by a utilitarian metal railing apparently intended to prevent those crossing it from falling into the muddy moatlike area below. A small boy, his shorts bunched over to one side of his crotch, was urinating over the side of the walkway under the supervision of a teenager. Metal lettering on the side of the structure dripped rust and advised that this was the Chicago Criminal Courts Building.

"I am sorry, Mr. Ristic," I said humbly. "It was my mistake."

"No problem, then," he said, and moved to restart the engine.

"No," I said. "This is where I wanted to come. How much do I owe you?"

"Twelve dollar ninety," he said. "How you think you going to get back to hotel?"

I looked around. No taxis cruising; it wasn't that kind of neighborhood. "Can't I call a cab from inside the building?" I said.

"Yah, of course," said Ristic. "Anybody can. But will it come?" He smiled, pleased with his wit. "Better I come back for you. What time?"

"That's very kind of you."

"What time?"

"About an hour?" I suggested, handing him a ten and a five. He nodded as I stepped out onto the sidewalk, then he turned the taxi in a skillful U-turn and headed back toward the Loop. I looked at my watch: six minutes to find the clerk's office for my four o'clock appointment.


It was late in the day for a courthouse, but there was still a sizable crowd milling about on the sidewalk and along the concrete walkway. Very few were wearing what I would have called suitable courthouse attire. One heavy African American girl, her hair in numerous springy braids, carried the sentiment Fuck The Pigs appliquéd to the back of her shiny black and gold shirt. As she walked through the heavy door ahead of me I thought I caught a whiff of deja vu, but then placed it as a different memory: a case we had read in Con Law about a guy who wore a jacket embroidered Fuck the Draft into a courthouse during the Vietnam era. I thought hard and remembered that the Supreme Court had said he had a right to wear the jacket, a form of free speech. Not a very useful exercise, I know, that laborious act of recall. What was I going to do, tap this girl on the shoulder and give her some free legal advice? *Just in case you were wondering, you have a perfect right to wear that shirt in here, unless some Reagan-era appointees to the Supreme Court might vote the other way if the question were to arise today.* She didn't look as though she was very worried about it, and anyway if I were giving advice I think I might have struck a less legalistic and more prudential note. Something like *You have a perfect right to wear that shirt, but if you happen to be on your way to be sentenced by a judge for a felony or even a serious misdemeanor, I don't think it's a good idea.*

The girl stopped ahead of me, just inside the doors, and called out to another who stood on the far side of a fence-like barrier in the vast entry hall.

"Where she at?" she shouted.

The other girl, in miniscule tank top and denim cargo pants so wide at the ankles that they billowed as she turned, shrugged and shook her head. The girl ahead of me made an exasperated noise and headed for a break in the mazelike fencing.

"Hey!" called out a uniformed security guard. "Over there!" He pointed her to a line of about a half-dozen people who were waiting to go through a metal detector. She didn't protest, but shuffled over to the end of the line. I watched for a moment. Everyone in the line was dark, and dressed in clothing suggesting some admixture of poverty and defiance. In addition to submitting to the metal screening, they were opening their bags to be searched; in some cases they were being patted down by male and female officers who stood just inside the barrier. I started walking over to join the line myself.

"Hey!" It was the same officer who had directed the girl to the line. He beckoned me to a different break in the barrier, at which nobody was waiting, and whisked my briefcase swiftly through the metal detector there.

"That's all?" I asked.

He nodded, and I turned to look at the other line, where my imaginary client in the shirt was still four people away from the front. When I turned back to the officer he gestured toward me impatiently as if to ask whether I wished to look this gift in the mouth, and I realized that my dark skirt and black pumps, very likely in conjunction with my white skin, had saved me from a patdown.

"Where is the clerk's office?" I asked him.

"Fifth floor."

"The elevator?" He pointed impassively to the far corner of the entry hall of this grimy palace of justice.

"And, is there a ladies' room?"

"One up there," he said. "But you shoulda went before you came here."

"Thanks," I said.

"You'll see what I mean." And he turned from me to wave a plump pale man in a blue suit over to his express entrance.

The elevator was hot and crowded, reeking of unthinkable stale secretions, and it stalled for six minutes between the third and fourth floors. My companions in the abominable little car included cops, civilian workers with identification badges, and at least one other lawyer—I saw *U.S. Law Week* sticking out of her briefcase—as well as obvious clients of the system like those I had seen in the entry hall. But nobody except me appeared surprised by the elevator's inexplicable refusal to move; the lawyer even pulled out *Law Week* and started reading. Nobody even looked especially relieved when it started up again with a clank, from which I concluded that this was not unusual behavior for this elevator. The door finally slid open on the fifth floor and I stepped out gratefully with most of the remaining others, leaving in the emptied compartment only an apparent derelict in a black felt hat, mumbling to himself and scratching his bare navel back in the corner.

"Did you want to get out here, sir?" I asked, but he paid me no attention as the door closed.

The clerk's office was just ahead, but I walked about a bit looking for a bathroom, and after passing a couple of doors marked Authorized Personnel Only I was rewarded by the sight of a smeared-looking portal bearing the universal symbol for female comfort. The door stuck as I pushed it before giving way suddenly. I stumbled a little as I entered, then stopped short. At first I thought the room had been vandalized, that I ought to report it to someone, perhaps in the clerk's office. The doors to the two stalls had been ripped off the hinges and tilted against the wall. One toilet seat was missing altogether, the bowl below the bare rim containing matter from which I quickly averted my eyes. The other toilet's seat was broken in two, one jagged piece lying on the floor; a splintery compound fracture at about one o'clock on the piece that remained suggested the unwisdom of sitting down. The sink had been pulled away from the wall until the pipes had broken. But the pipes had been sealed off, the sink and floor were dry, and I realized that this damage was not recent. I decided to contain my discomfort, and try to accomplish my business with the clerk as efficiently as possible.

Fortunately, Ruth Suarez was all business. She received me in her small office behind the larger clerk's office. It was the neatest place I had seen in the whole building and she matched it for tidiness and propriety, the knot in her white jabot blouse a perfect square. After shaking my hand and examining my business card, she sat behind a desk stacked with meticulous piles of paper and motioned me to sit as well.

"Yes, of course, it is possible for the case file to be retrieved," she said when I had explained my mission. "Including the exhibits, if any."

"Then could you—" I started to write the case number Peggy Grayling had given on the pad of paper I held, but she put up her hand.

"I can't order the file back on your say-so, Miss Hayes," she said. "And even if I did, I couldn't give you an original exhibit. And if it's a film like you say, I don't see how you could make a copy here in the office."

I thought of the neat memo I was carrying in my briefcase, product of several nights at the law library back in Boulder. "My client told me she was prevented from making a copy here on the premises by someone who told her the copyright laws would be violated. I've done a little research and don't believe—"

She stopped me again, this time with an expression of weariness, and I thought I had worn out my slender goodwill. But she rolled her dark eyes slightly and said, "My predecessor. He was—shall we say, a bit authoritarian. Miss Hayes, we are not here to enforce the copyright laws. That is someone else's business. The document you describe is a public record if it was made an exhibit at a trial. If you can get a court order that instructs me to release the exhibit to you, I will get it for you. Then you can make a copy yourself before you return it."

"Thank you," I said gratefully. "May I ask which judge I ought to apply to for such an order?"

Ruth Suarez turned to a computer behind here and tapped in a few entries. "What was the case number again?" I read it to her and she tapped for a few more minutes before reaching for a slip of paper and writing a few words.

"Judge Vincent Ricci?" I said, reading it upside down.

She nodded, handing it to me. "Courtroom 14, in the East Wing."

"And could you tell me where the district attorney's office is?"

"I could tell you, of course. *States attorney* we call him here. Are you looking for someone in particular?"

"John," I said, trying to remember the name Peggy had told me. "John— Scarpelli."

Ruth Suarez nodded. "Same place. Courtroom 14. He's the prosecutor assigned to Judge Ricci's courtroom."

"You've been so kind," I said, rising and holding out my hand. "I wonder if I could ask for one more favor."

"If I can," she said.

"Is there any place I could use the restroom other than the one down the hall?"

"Of course," she said. "Never use the public bathrooms in this building. They're not safe. Hilda," she said to a woman who had just entered with an armful of file folders, "will you show Miss Hayes the staff facilities?"

Hilda showed me to a usable bathroom, apparently accessible only through the clerk's office. As I washed my hands in the clean sink and dried them with an absorbent white paper towel from a dispenser, I reflected with renewed sympathy on the boy I had seen on the entrance walkway, urging his little brother to pee over the side.

My search for Judge Vincent Ricci's courtroom took me back through the cavernous entrance hall, where there were fewer people than before. I looked at my watch, thinking worriedly of Mr. Ristic, who had said he would be back a little before 5:00 and might represent my only hope of getting back to the Raphael before Sam started to worry. I looked around the lobby for pay telephones, but didn't see any, and it occurred to me that even if I found one its condition might resemble that of the fifth floor bathroom. So I followed the perplexing signs up to the third floor of the courtroom wing, and wandered through dark corridors with sticky floors until I finally found a door that said COURTROOM FOURTEEN, HON. VINCENT S. RICCI.

I pulled the door toward me, puzzled that the inside seemed no lighter than the gloomy hall. Maybe court was over for the day and the lights in the courtroom had been turned off? But I heard voices, although tinny and distant, and when I stepped inside I found myself in a small enclosed area, with seats for at most ten people. A barrier separated this darkened gallery from the courtroom proper, which I could see, although not very well, through the smoked glass of the partition. The glass's dark glare made the figures moving beyond it look like characters in a badly lit and indifferently directed television program. A loudspeaker was mounted insecurely where the glass met the roof of our viewing area—I say *ours,* for there was one other occupant, a thin dark-haired woman. She ignored me as she leaned forward to catch the words being spoken on the other side of the glass. They came through the speaker at varying volume, sometimes resounding, often faint, apparently as the person speaking moved toward or away from a microphone.

"—further conditions of probation?" the judge was saying. His voice was thick but loud. "Because I want your counsel to make clear to you—*capisce,* Ms. Lawson?—that your future choices are becoming very limited very fast here as a result of your past choices."

A thin young man in a wrinkled white shirt and black pants stood at a podium facing the judge; even his back, which was all I could see, radiated dejection. He turned his head to the side, toward a suited woman standing there, and seemed to whisper something.

"He understands, Your Honor," said the woman, her voice high but firm, "and he is prepared to sign the Consent to Additional Conditions." She nudged her client, a gesture obvious from our rear view, but he still stood silent.

*"Madre de Dios,"* said the woman sitting next to me. "Say something, Diego, or *el juezo* is going to send you back to jail."

But the judge, ignoring Diego's silence, turned his head toward the other podium and a muscular man who stood there. The man's neat gray suit seemed slightly too snug through the back, or perhaps it was just the way his shoulders flexed as though they wished they could escape from it.

"Mr. Scarpelli?" said the judge. "Are the People really willing to agree to give Mr. Fuentes here another chance?"

"We are, Your Honor," said Scarpelli, "taking into account his willingness to agree to daily urine testing and participation in the program at

*Casa de Esperanza.* But I agree with Your Honor this should be the last chance." Scarpelli didn't even look up as he said the words, but shook his arms slightly and rose up onto the balls of his feet as though anticipating a game of hoops or racquetball before too long.

"It's more than—" the judge's confident baritone broke off with a scratch, even though it looked as though he was still speaking. The woman cursed softly at my side and looked up at the speaker.

"Is it broken?" I said to her, looking up at the flimsy-looking box.

*"No es roto,"* she hissed. "This judge, he turns it off."

I looked through the glass at the judge, and it was true his left hand was out of sight behind the bench. He continued to speak, and then it seemed that Scarpelli was saying something. The judge broke into a grin, then his lips parted and his head tilted back in laughter. Scarpelli laughed too, and even Diego's lawyer nodded in apparent appreciation.

Abruptly the speaker started to work again with a crackle. "—you know I love when you speak Italian to me," the judge was saying, apparently to Scarpelli. "So, are we done here?" His hands were both visible again.

"I believe so, Your Honor," said Scarpelli, paging through some papers on his podium while spreading his shoulders again against the confines of the suit jacket.

"Yes, sir," said the woman lawyer. Diego turned back as though to look at us, and the dark-haired woman raised her hand to him in a gesture both longing and resigned. He nodded a brief salute; then Judge Vincent Ricci pounded his gavel, an event that sent a shuddering boom through the loudspeaker, and court was adjourned.

The woman was gathering her belongings—a paper bag, a shawl—as if to leave, and I spoke hastily.

"Do you know where the lawyers will come out?" I asked her.

Her eyes narrowed, taking in my shoes and briefcase. "No," she said, and left the little room. The door to the corridor banged behind her.

I turned for one last look at the chamber where the laws of the sovereign state of Illinois were interpreted and enforced—an activity that must surely have been venerated at one time. I noticed for the first time that the smoky glass window rose only from waist height to the ceiling; below, the barrier was made of metal. Sturdier, I suppose. Someone—more than one someone, judging from the various handwriting styles—had scratched graffiti into the dull red paint. SOUTH SIDE DISCIPLES RULE! boasted one. THE COURT IS A CUNT, opined another.

As I left the court viewing room—I could not think of it as a courtroom—I saw the woman who had represented Diego Fuentes coming out of a door marked Authorized Personnel Only. She looked hot and in a hurry, the throat buttons of her crisp white blouse already unbuttoned. "Excuse me," I said quickly, earning an irritated glance. "Can you tell me whether Mr. Scarpelli will be coming out this way?"

"I have no idea," she said shortly. "He doesn't advise me of his plans." Then she looked at me a little more closely, hesitated, and sighed. "Just a minute," she said, and reopened the door just long enough to stick her head back in. "Johnny!" she shouted, "someone here for you!" before walking off rapidly toward the stairwell.

He was out the door before she had finished disappearing around the corner. "Don't forget to call me about that douchebag Rashid!" he yelled after her, before turning to me. "John Scarpelli," he said. "What can I do for you?" Without waiting for an answer he removed his jacket and raised and lowered his shoulders gratefully. "Whew!"

I handed him my business card. "Boulder, hey?" he said, looking at me again, more closely this time. "I went skiing there once, close to there. So what brings you here from Boulder? Wait, wait—you're not representing that *pezznovante* child molester Seth Meyer? He was talking about Barry Scheck, Johnny Cochran, I donno who else. You some famous criminal lawyer?" He didn't seem concerned about this possibility, however. He was rapidly unbuttoning the top buttons of his shirt and rolling up his sleeves to the elbows.

I assured him I had no relationship with Mr. Meyer, and explained about Peggy Grayling, her daughter, and her interest in seeing the videotape that had been used at Leonard Fitzgerald's trial. "And," I added, "I'd just like to talk to you about that trial in general. If you have time."

He stepped back for a second, jacket slung over his shoulder on a crooked finger, and smiled. "Sure," he said. "I think about that trial a lot. I was going to go get some exercise, but sure. You want to grab a drink somewhere?"

I looked at my watch: 5:10. "I would," I said. "I'll even buy. But I have to take a taxi to wherever your favorite drinking hole is."

"What for? We'll go in my car. Then I can drop you where you're staying, no problem. Where are you staying?"

"I don't have time to explain right now," I said. "But I just have to take a taxi. I'm staying at the Raphael, but I'll be glad to meet you anywhere you say."

He shook his head ruefully and massaged his forearm. "I never met a guy who had less luck understanding women than I do. Okay, how about the Old Town Ale House? Here." He pulled out a pen and scribbled on the back of the business card I had given him. "It's not too far from where you're staying. Since you're providing your own transportation, I might swing home for a quick shower, meet you there in about an hour?"

I thought of mentioning Sam, but decided against it. "Sure," I agreed. "See you there at 6:15."

"Later, then," said John Scarpelli, and disappeared again through the authorized persons door. Walking down the dusty stairs, it occurred to me I might have asked him to come outside with me to see whether Mr. Ristic had kept our appointment, but I needn't have worried: as soon as I emerged from the entrance I heard a horn honking. It was Ristic, sitting across the street in his taxi smoking a cheroot. "Come on, lady journalist," he called, waving the cigar at me. "Just in time for National Public Radio news!"

I was so grateful for his loyalty that I didn't complain about the cigar, even when its cinders blew back into my hair. As we drove past a movie theater whose marquee displayed *Shakespeare in Love* he said, over the drone of the radio, "You see this movie, hah?" When I said that I had, he informed me that it was not really Shakespeare.

"Well, no," I agreed.

"I go to classes at De Paul University, study Shakespeare," he told me. "To better my English."

"Your English is excellent," I said politely. After a block or two I remembered something. "When you were leaving me at the courthouse earlier," I said, "and I asked about whether I could call a taxi from there, you were saying something from Shakespeare, weren't you?"

I could see his grin in the mirror. "I was thinking maybe you don't know it," he said proudly. "Henry the Fourth. Part One, I am thinking, but about this I am not so sure."

"What was it again?"

"I don't know it perfect. Hotspur is talking to some other man, another soldier, you know? This man likes to boast. 'I can call spirits from the vasty deep,' he says. And Hotspur tells him 'So can I, so can anybody. But will they come when you call?' "

I laughed. "That's what you said about the taxi."

He nodded, looking at me again in the mirror. I looked back into his gray eyes; he was younger than I had first thought. "My son speaks English perfect," he said. "He will not drive a taxi when he is grown."

I nodded and said, "That's good. But still, it's an honorable profession."

"Oh sure," said Ristic. "But he has no foot on one side. From a mine. He plays the piano perfect anyway."

"You must be very proud of him," I stammered, and he nodded brusquely. After that neither of us had much to say; I sat back against the seat and listened with humble attention while one of NPR's velvet voices summarized the news from the former Yugoslavia.

Ristic got me to the Old Town Ale House in under half an hour, despite the rush-hour traffic. He stuck out his hand to shake mine as I handed him the fare through the window. It was slender, with long fingers that stank faintly of cigar. He held the cheroot between his teeth, narrowing his eyes against the smoke, as he bade me farewell.

The tavern was cheerful and noisy. I phoned the Raphael and asked for our room, but the phone rang several times before the desk operator came on again. When I asked about messages for me he found one. "From a Mr. Holt," he said. "His plane has been delayed, but he hopes he'll be here at the hotel by about ten."

I sipped a Black and Tan for about half an hour and looked from time to time at the television above the bar. The Cubs were not getting the bat on very many balls, but at the tables around me a number of yuppies were hitting on each other with more success. After about half an hour John Scarpelli appeared, looking damp but far more comfortable than before in jeans and a polo shirt. "Come on into the next room," he urged me, his hand touching my elbow momentarily, and I followed him to a booth, where he ordered another Black and Tan for me and a Guinness for himself. He was a good talker and a good listener, the alcohol relaxed me, and before long John Scarpelli had elicited most of my recent life story from me with the assurance of an experienced trial lawyer.

"So then what happened?" he asked at several junctures, a phrase I had employed in countless direct examinations. When I got to the part about leaving rape crisis work to represent Jason Smiley, and Jason's eventual execution, he leaned across the table to close the space and make it possible for me to speak more softly. "I'm sorry," he said. "But let me ask you something. You weren't a defense lawyer. You were a rape counselor, you'd been a prosecutor. Why did you agree to represent him?"

"I'm still not sure. But I've always been against the death penalty. That was part of it."

He nodded, his eyes looking at something over my shoulder—perhaps many miles over my shoulder. "Yeah. I did a capital case a couple years ago. After that I told my supervisor I didn't want to do any more. She gave me a lot of shit about it, but she hasn't assigned me any more of them. Instead she gives me the nutrolls. I think she intends it as some form of harassment; she doesn't know I like them. Crimes by mentally ill defendants have some of that same dark thrill as capital cases, but—well, they bother me less."

"The capital case you tried," I said. "Did you win it?"

He started to say something, stopped, and finally spoke. "I don't know," he said, turning in his seat to order another beer from a passing waitress. When he turned back to me he said, "Tell me about Mrs. Grayling. I admired her a lot—I think she's a very brave lady."

I pretended not to notice that he had changed the subject. "I think so too. She's very calm but very determined. Her first goal is just to see the videotape your guys found in Fitzgerald's VCR. During our first meeting she explained to me that she was not permitted to be in the courtroom when it was played there."

John nodded in assent. "At that point she was still a possible witness at sentencing, if Fitzgerald had been convicted."

"And The Rule had been invoked?"

He nodded again. "I had invoked it myself, before opening statements. I always do. Didn't you, when you were a prosecutor?"

"Yeah, but I think I might have argued that a witness who would be called only for victim impact testimony at sentencing shouldn't fall under The Rule."

Scarpelli had begun to slump a little over his glass, but here he looked up, his face rigid.

"I'm not trying to be critical," I said. "I know things might be very different here."

"I've made that exact argument to Ricci a couple of times. He doesn't buy it. You know how judges are: when in doubt during trial, rule for the defense. You'll never get reversed that way, because if there's an acquittal the government can't appeal."

"I do know how that works. I didn't mean to suggest you'd been less than zealous. Peggy thinks you're wonderful."

"Yeah?" A halfhearted grin. "Glad to hear there's one woman in the world that thinks so."

"Are you having woman trouble, John?"

He waved his hand in dismissal. "Not worth talking about. Listen, it's true Ricci would never have exempted her from The Rule, so I had to keep her out of the courtroom. But you know what? I was glad. That film was vile. Garbage. I'm not sure the sack of shit who made it didn't kill some other little girl just to film it. And Mrs. Grayling's little girl died just like the one on the tape. No way I wanted her to see it. You can make that present tense. I think you ought to talk her out of it."

"I may do that. After I've seen it. I thought maybe you could help me get an order from Judge Ricci releasing it to me long enough to make a copy."

His eyes looked steadily into mine as he shook his head slightly. "No. I don't see that any good can come from it, just a lot of pain. Go back to Boulder and tell your client she needs to bury the child in her mind just like she did the real one." And then he said something that really pissed me off. "In my opinion she ought to have another child."

An angry surge blew through my blood and I started to stand up, but the booth was small and sliding out would have been a production. Instead I drained my glass and said, "Do you have children, John?"

"Got nothing to do with it."

"Yeah, well fuck you, you don't know what you're talking about. For one thing she's fifty years old and recently divorced. She's not going to have another child. And even if she were, what kind of thinking is that? Just replace the dead one with another one? That doesn't even work with dogs."

"Yeah well fuck you twice, lady, you don't know what you're talking about either. And yeah, I do have a daughter, when her mother lets me see her." His eyes were red when he looked up, whether from drink or sorrow I could not tell, and my anger receded some.

"I'm sorry," I said.

"Yeah." He looked embarrassed. "I'll be right back." He slid clumsily across the seat, angled his way out of the booth, and walked toward the restrooms at the back of the bar. I looked toward the bar, where a brass-faced clock mounted on the mirror showed 7:45.

When Scarpelli came back he had another pair of beers in his hand. I accepted one with a nod. "Look," he said. "I was out of line there, sorry. It's just—I've known a few other lawyers like you. You're all filled up with a passion for something that's not available. Looking for truth, justice, and the American Way in all the wrong places. Don't get me wrong, I think it's great to believe in something, but true believers have been known to blunder from time to time. I just don't want you blundering into something."

"Into what?"

"Cinda, you don't want Peggy Grayling to see that tape. You don't want to see it, yourself. I don't want to ever see it again, and I'd give a lot to go back and arrange that I never had seen it. Do you know what I'm saying?"

"I think so."

"I don't think you do. Do you ever have bad dreams, Cinda?"

"Sure," I confessed, thinking of the one where I'm looking and looking for something: sometimes the room where a law school exam I'm supposed to be taking is going on, sometimes the barn where a judge is being stoned to death, sometimes a stained dress that will save my client from the needle that conveys potassium chloride into the big vein of his arm. I looked up and saw Scarpelli's eyes, dark stones.

"They could be worse," he said.

"You dream about this tape?"

"For a while. Not any more, I guess, or at least if I do, I don't remember it after I wake up. Thanks to many months of psychotherapy and the nightly use of a powerful sedative. And then there's losing joint custody of my daughter. After I worked on this case, it got so when she was with me I couldn't let her out of my sight. I wouldn't let her go to a friend's house, or play in the park, or go to a movie without me. She got tired of it, complained to her mother, and next thing you know I'm talking to some social worker about my inappropriate behavior."

"I'm sorry, John." At some point during the last couple of minutes I had concluded that John Scarpelli was not going to help me dislodge a copy of the videotape. I felt bad for him but I had a job to do, and one more idea. "What about a transcript of the trial, then? At least with that she could understand the psychiatric evidence about what motivated Fitzgerald."

Short emphatic headshake. "No conviction, no appeal. No appeal, nobody orders a transcript. I'm sure the trial record has never been transcribed."

Of course. I should have figured that out myself. "How about psych reports on Fitzgerald? You must have kept a copy of those."

He nodded reluctantly. "I probably can dig those up for you."

"Thanks," I said, checking the clock again. "And listen, thanks for talking with me about this case. Now I'd better go. My boyfriend's flying in, and I ought to try to get back to the hotel before he gets there."

"Boyfriend, huh? I didn't realize." His eyes narrowed for a moment and then his face changed again, into that of the cheerful *paisan* I had seen in the courtroom. He leaned forward confidingly. "Anyway, the bad dreams and the stuff with my daughter, that's not even the worst part about that tape."

Ah, I thought, still have that tape on your mind, do you? Maybe I had given up too soon. "What's the worst, then?" I asked.

He took another swallow of the beer and wiped the back of his hand across his mouth. "Nah. Maybe it wouldn't be that way for you. Women are different, right?"

"What are you talking about?"

"The hell. Why shouldn't you make your own decision? Big girl, am I right?"

I nodded unsurely. "So you'll ask Ricci for the order?"

"Sure, why not? You'll watch it before you show it to Grayling, right? I mean, you'll decide after you see it yourself whether you want to let her see it?"

"Sure," I agreed, although the minute I said it I realized I'd have no right to withhold it from my client after I'd obtained it by invoking her name.

"Good. Here's my office number." He scribbled on a napkin. "Call tomorrow, toward the end of the day. Ask for Olivia, my assistant. I'll have her prepare the order first thing in the morning, and I'll hit Ricci up to sign it if it seems like he's in a good mood. Then we talk about it later, you and me."

"You mean after you get the order?"

"Don't worry, I'll get it. I mean we'll talk after you've seen the tape. Come on, I'll walk you over to the Raphael. Safer that way."

The mask of affability had descended again over his handsome features, and it was pleasant walking along the sidewalk with him in the redolent night air of the city. "So, John, can I ask you something?"

"Yeah." But he said it cautiously.

"You seemed so Italian when you were in court. Even when I talked to you in the courthouse. But not since you met me at the bar."

He shrugged a little, and coughed. "Look, Cinda, I was born in this country. My mother was born in Chicago—her mother was Italian, but her father was Polish. My father was born in Pisa, but he came to this country when he was like, two, okay? I don't even speak Italian, except for lately I've learned a few phrases."

"You don't?"

"Ricci likes it, that's all," he muttered. "You get assigned to a judge, you have to appear before him every day, you figure out what he likes and doesn't like, you do the one and stay away from the other. Didn't you, when you were a prosecutor?"

I thought about it. "We weren't assigned to the same judge all the time."

"So you had to figure out how to get along with ten *pezzonavantes* instead of one. Still, didn't you play the same game I'm taking about?"

"I guess so, sure. But if Ricci really does speak Italian, aren't you afraid he'll find you out?"

"Sure, that's why I'm taking classes now. Thursday nights. The nights I used to see my daughter." I smiled to myself, wondering what Dragoljub Ristic would think of John Scarpelli's efforts to recover the language of his ancestors in order to gain an advantage in the American criminal justice system.

"Here we are," I said, glad of it. The hotel seemed to lean over the sidewalk, floodlights emphasizing the shadowy recesses of its Gothic facade. The doorman, blonde and very slight, stood at the curb in a maroon uniform.

Looking at him, John grinned suddenly. "Quasimodo must be off tonight." I laughed and took his hand in farewell.

"Thanks for everything," I said. "I'll call Olivia tomorrow about four."

"Call me after you've seen it," he said, withdrawing his hand. "That's the deal. You have to tell me what you think of it."

The desk clerk told me that Mr. Holt had arrived about a half hour before. On the way up to the room I realized that I was buzzed from the Black and Tans. My head kept rising even after the elevator stopped, and the thought of seeing Sam after so long provoked a frothy sensation in my chest region.

He was waiting in the room watching basketball, probably his beloved Knicks, and drinking from one of the minibar's half bottles of cheap wine. He looked up as I entered, then rose without a word, the television's sound vanishing as his hand pressed and then discarded the remote control. The inside of his mouth tasted like red wine, and below that his own delicious and indescribable essence.

"I believe I feel some weather approaching," was all that he said. One of our old expressions. And I was just intoxicated enough that it did seem an atmospheric disturbance was rolling in. As he slid his hands under my skirt I closed my eyes against the dizzying sudden fall in pressure. The friction of his hands against my stockings sparked jagged little bolts of electricity and the sky opened, like it does during the tender violent thunderstorms that roll over the Rockies in the summer. Heat and cool collided, moisture and drought met to consume one another. The storm lasted for quite a while, then finally died down to be succeeded by a deep peace of some duration, interrupted only by the flickering of the silenced television's light on the ceiling like lightning retreating to the east. I closed my eyes again.

But all that was just me, abetted by the alcohol. Sam would never have described it that way; he isn't that extravagant, or that sentimental, and he has not much use for metaphors. When he finally spoke, the first thing he said was, "Which room was it you were looking for, Miss?"

Later he called room service: an omelet for me, pie for him. He'd eaten on the plane, he said, if you call it that.

We spent the next morning like tourists, riding a boat on the river and ordering lunch from one of the famously rude waiters at the Berghof. Then

Sam retrieved the rental car from the hotel garage and we drove out to Oak Park, where we walked around admiring the clean quiet lines of the Frank Lloyd Wright houses. We found Peggy Grayling's former house a few blocks from Wright's studio. It wasn't one of his, but it was a pleasant prairie-style framed two-story, with vines sprouting leaves on the trellis that framed the spacious front porch and a hopscotch board drawn on the sidewalk in colored chalk. As we stood on the sidewalk the front door of the house banged and three girls ran out, pushing against each other to be first to jump the board.

There was some delicate girlish shoving, and then the tallest one said firmly, "Stoppit! It's Nellie's turn, I remember."

"Must be nice," said Sam, as the shortest one, plump in her red leggings, started to hop expertly from square to square.

"What?"

"Live some place where it's safe to let your kids play outside."

"Yeah," I said. "You ready to look for Leonard Fitzgerald's rooming house?"

Sam squinted into the sun as he turned toward me. "That was stupid, wasn't it? What I just said."

I shrugged. "I'm sure this place is safe. Mostly. Come on." I tugged gently at his hand.

It was yellow brick, three stories, and while it didn't have a distinguished architectural pedigree or even a shaded front porch, it did have a concrete stoop that faced the elementary school across the street. The school's playground was immense, perhaps four or five acres. I surveyed shady plots screened by the dozens of leafy trees that stippled the flat terrain, and imagined a blonde girl with long legs jumping rope in the sun, then seeking the shade. And Leonard Fitzgerald standing on the stoop, watching.

As we strolled by the building, a young man wearing a severe buzz cut and a sleeveless t-shirt that showcased a bad case of acne on his upper arms lounged on the steps, smoking a cigarette in the fire-in-the-palm style.

"Hi," I said, squinting up into the sun to look at him. He nodded wordlessly. "You mind if I ask you a few questions?"

He flicked the cigarette away and studied his biceps as he flexed them. "I didn't know him," he said. "Same as I told that other guy. I just moved in here five months ago."

"You know who I was going to ask about?"

"That Wolfman or whatever. I heard about him same as everyone else but I never seen him. Some girl lives in his old apartment now, I never seen it either."

I nodded at him, "Thanks anyway, then." As he turned back toward the doorway I said, "Someone else was asking?"

He shrugged. "Some other reporter, probably. I told him the same as I told you. I could make up something and ask for money, but that wouldn't be right, would it?"

"No," I said, and he retreated back into the yellow building.

At 4:30 I called the number John Scarpelli had given me, and his sweet-voiced assistant told me she had the tape I wanted, and that it was mine until nine o'clock on Thursday. "Not tomorrow, but the next day," she said helpfully. "So you'll have time to get a copy. The order says you can duplicate it once and once only, and that there are to be no public showings or admission charged."

"Of course," I said with relief. "I'll pick it up from you first thing tomorrow, all right?" She gave me the address, and I stepped out of the phone booth to tell Sam.

"Good. Then we're free until tomorrow. You ready to listen to some serious music after dinner tonight?" Sam said.

"Sure." I wasn't really paying attention.

"I mean serious, girl. The kind that makes you hurt. I don't think you're mean enough to listen to dirty old Chicago blues up from the delta."

"What do you *mean* not mean enough, playah?" I scrunched my face up as mean as I could manage.

"Okay," he said hastily. "I take it back."

We got to Bucket o' Blues about nine o'clock, having left the rental car at the hotel in favor of a taxi. The sign at the door said the headline act was Magic Slim.

"We're going to listen to a diet plan?" I said as Sam paid the cover charge.

"Wait'll you see," he said. "Wait'll you *hear*. Meantime, keep your ignorant white girl trash talk to you'self, hear?" We had fallen into the roles we sometimes occupied: airhead hippie white girl, tough black street dude. It was dumb, but got us through some moments. I looked around the smoky room, hoping for a comfortable racial mix, aware with some sense of shame that for me that meant fifty-fifty or more white people. It was close, but the room was still half empty. All the booths along the sides were occupied, but there were plenty of vacant tables.

"Where do you want to sit?" said Sam, looking around.

"Right up front."

"Want to catch old Slim's eye? Sometimes he likes to get something going with the ladies."

"That's right," I said. *This white airhead hippie chick isn't afraid of anything, see?* We squeezed into the nearest table to the stage, and Sam went to get margaritas from the bar. I didn't see a jukebox, but the sound system was playing good stuff, Aretha and Little Richard. It was too loud to talk unless you wanted to shout, so we sipped margaritas and listened to the music and to the guys at the next table who didn't seem to mind shouting. Bankers or stockbrokers, complaining about Alan Greenspan and the Fed and then, one of them, about the asshole who keyed his Lexus and the shithead insurance adjuster. And these were guys I had counted on *my* side of the mix. The place was filling up now, the shouting becoming hollow and thick as smoke, and sweat started to press in.

A worn-looking black guy who had been propped against a barstool talking to a waitress stood up and walked toward the stage, and the room's buzz grew softer and more attentive.

"Is that him?" I asked Sam, unimpressed. He wasn't very slim at all, for one thing. But Sam didn't answer, just watched intently as the man walked over to the center mike and blew into it gently. It huffed in a satisfying way, and he took a guitar from a stand behind the mike and straightened up to look at us.

"Somebody ask me once," he said, passing the strap of the guitar behind his head, "why none of my songs is wrote down. What he meant was, is it because I can't write? I can write, but blues is not about writing. See, you cannot find no blues on no paper, because you can't write on paper from your heart. You have to play it. You play the blues the way you feel, that's all. Come on now."

And he started to play, and he was right. You cannot find no blues on no paper, and I don't propose to try to put them down on this one. After the first song, Slim was joined by his band, the Teardrops. The driven bass and insistent drums flowed out and through the room, and the blues got louder then, and maybe a little more aggressive. But not any more complicated. *Woke up this morning. Woman done gone. Time pass so slow.* More along those lines.

After an hour I felt wrung out by the jagged energy and accumulated sorrows of the music, but the Teardrops were just getting warmed up. So were many others in the room; several couples were dancing in the inadequate spaces between the tables. One of the bankers, a man with a graying goatee, kept calling out the names of songs. *"Spider in My Stew!"* he yelled once, but Slim ignored him. When he shouted *"Wake Me Up Early!"* Slim finally looked at him, with quiet contempt. The room hushed some, so the loudest sound was the clatter behind the bar.

"Your voice is too heavy, man," Slim said finally. "I don't take no request from no heavy-voice guy. You get you a lady to ax me, and maybe I do it." And he turned aside to drink from his paper cup.

I needed to visit the bathroom. "I'll be right back," I whispered to Sam. He nodded, his eyes on Slim, who was talking and laughing softly with his little brother Nick, one of the Teardrops. There were three women waiting so I had to stand in line for a while but it was kind of nice, hearing Slim's guitar and Nick's bass driving through the wall, a little fuzzy. *Muffled Blues,* the new album by Magic Slim and the Teardrops. This thought was so stupid I realized I was drunk again. That's two nights in a row, I thought, sighing. Then the bathroom door opened and it was my turn.

The bathroom was small and close, and I felt sweaty and breathless when I came out of it. As I started back toward the bar I could feel cool air drifting in from somewhere behind me, and looked back. Beyond the bathroom, a dark door below an red-lit EXIT sign was propped open with a chair. Thinking to take in a few gulps of fresh air I walked back to the door and opened it far enough to slip out, carefully resting it against the chair back as it closed.

The alley was not very dark, and I saw immediately that I wasn't alone in it. Two of the bankers were there, one of them bent over at the waist, his face in his cupped hands. The other, the bearded one who had called out his requests to Magic Slim with so little success, was rubbing his hands up and down his arms below the sleeves of his polo shirt. At first I thought the bent-over banker was ill, but when he straightened up he snuffled his nose and rubbed the back of one hand across it.

"Hey," said the goatee. "What are you looking at?" I didn't answer, but I didn't turn away either. Fuck if I was going to get chased away by these creeps.

"Chill," the snuffly one instructed his companion, and then he walked toward me, his hand extended. I could see a small cylinder in it, like a film container. "Like a taste?" he asked.

"No," I said shortly.

"Come on," he said. "It's free. Only maybe you could ask old Slim to play 'Spider in My Stew' when we go back in. It's my friend's favorite. That's all we ask, see?" He thrust his hand toward me, more insistently.

"Fuck," I advised him, "off."

"Hey, Princess," he said, tucking the cylinder into his pocket. "You don't have to get snooty. We saw who you were with in there." He looked at the other one and they smirked.

That was it; I was going back inside. What happened next was my fault, partly. If I hadn't been cotton-mouthed and half-dizzy from tequila I would have found my way back through the door without any trouble, but instead I stumbled against a ragged pile of bricks stacked by the side of the building as I turned, and nearly fell to one knee. "Shit," I muttered. By the time I regained my footing, one of them had whisked the chair out into the alley, and the door had banged shut. I tugged at it, but it was locked, so I faced the two men, drawing a deep breath. They were standing side by side calmly, hands in pockets; then one of them looked at the other and raised his eyebrows.

"Worried about leaving your boyfriend alone, Princess?" one of them said. "It's cool. Let him spank the monkey while you hang out with us." He stepped forward and put his hand on my arm. I looked toward the other, the one with the goatee; he grinned and rubbed his crotch, deliberately.

"Don't even think about it," I said to the nearest one, but he tightened his grip above my elbow and said, "Too late Princess. I've been thinking about it for some time now."

I don't know how to fight; I never took karate or a Model Mugger course. Studying yoga had been good but I didn't think deep breaths were going to help much right then. I took one anyway, then made a round-house leg motion and clipped the guy just at the knee. He went down, cursing, which was very satisfying, but I lost my balance and fell myself; my elbow hit the gravelly ground hard.

The goatee started to haul me up but the other one said, "Fuck. Let her go. Fucking bitch. Let's book." He staggered to his feet, then spat onto the ground beside me. Then the door screeched open and Sam appeared,

as if pushed into the alley by the thunderous guitar chords pulsating behind him. He took in the scene in an instant.

"You white motherfucking cowards," he began through clenched teeth,
but I scrambled up and shook my head.

"Don't, Sam," I said. "They're just leaving." The man I had kicked
started to back away, but the one with the goatee and polo shirt must have
decided it would be a good idea to start a shoving match. Something to
justify all those hours at the gym, maybe, or to make up for the way Slim
had snubbed him. I couldn't hear what he said, but I was close enough to
see, in the harsh glare of the floodlight, the sneer that contorted his face as
he put the heels of his hands against Sam's chest. And I saw the sudden
stillness in Sam's body, and knew what it meant.

It was over very fast, in less than a minute. I was no use, but Sam didn't
need any help. Then a tall black man with a glistening bald head emerged
from the door, followed by two bouncer-looking characters. When the tall
man saw the bankers, one of them sprawled in the alley, the other yelping
with both hands pressed against his nose, he gave a snort of exasperated
recognition.

"You assholes again! Didn't I tell you before I didn't want to see you
around here?"

"You better call the police," said Sam.

"Are you hurt?" asked the bald man, addressing himself to Sam.

"Not me," said Sam quietly, rubbing his hand.

"Did you want me to call the police, sir?" the man said mock-politely
to the one who was leaning over, blood dripping onto his shoes. He didn't
respond, but the other held up his hands in mock surrender.

"No need for Smokey," he said.

The man turned to the pair who had come out with him and jerked a
thumb toward the bankers. "Get them to their car. If they left anything
inside, go get it for them. Don't let them back in." Then he turned to us.
"Sorry. You two want to come back in, or would you like me to call a cab
for you?"

It left me angry and frightened, of course. But, and this was the part
that worried me later, somehow aroused. I leaned against Sam in the taxi
all the way back to the hotel, enjoying the feel of his shirtsleeve against my
cheek. He didn't seem to want to talk any more than I did, but once inside
the hotel he pulled me to him in the mirrored elevator and put his hand

under my sweater, pushing aside the bra to brush my nipple back and forth with his thumb. I opened my mouth under his and grasped his belt buckle to keep from losing my balance, but the car slid to a stop too soon. A lit-up-looking foursome stood outside the elevator, looking in crookedly.

"Down? Are you going down?" said one of the women.

"Up," said Sam, as he pushed the Close Door button. "Definitely up," as he guided my hand to the zipper of his jeans. I pressed there while the car carried us up two more floors and spilled us out, gasping, into the corridor.

Once in the dim room, I lay under the sheets listening to the sounds of Sam running water in the bathroom, wondering why the image that kept returning to my head was of Sam's fist hitting the face of the goateed man; I was pretty sure I could remember the sound of bone breaking. The memory was exciting, and for the same reason shaming. When Sam pulled back the sheet and sat down beside me, I touched him quietly for a few moments, then slid the condom on tenderly. "Be sweet," I whispered as I pulled him toward me and wrapped my legs around his narrow buttocks.

Then he was just Sam again and it was all right. Much better than all right. I didn't think again about that terrible frisson, its blended elements of someone else's pain and my desire, until the next night.

The phone rang early the next morning. Sam can sleep through anything, so I rolled over to grab it.

"Wassup, Cinda?" It was Sam's law partner, Johnny. "Lemme speak to the man."

"Hold on, Johnny. Nice to hear your voice, too." I nudged the backs of Sam's knees with the fronts of mine, and put the receiver against his ear. "Johnny," I said.

"Is there no end to tribulation?" Sam said in his best Martin Luther King voice. I rose and went into the bathroom. When I came back Sam was sitting on the side of the bed, the phone back in its cradle.

"Tomorrow," he said, "we're gonna sleep late."

"I'm not," I said sadly. "I have to return that tape, then catch a 10:35 flight from O'Hare."

"When are you going to get that tape?"

"This morning. Then maybe we can find a place that will duplicate it, or rent us a machine so we can do it ourselves."

"What you mean we, white girl? According to my esteemed partner, I have to go down to the desk for a fax he's sending me, then spend the morning in a law library drafting a response to some bullshit motion a judge gave us forty-eight hours to reply to."

I stopped brushing my hair. "Can't Johnny do it?"

"He's in court every day this week."

I shook my head and resumed brushing. "Sorry. Meet me for lunch then?"

He nodded. "You take the car. I'll walk over to De Paul Law School and see if I can talk my way into their library."

Picking up the tape was easy. Olivia came right out to the curb and handed me a thick manila accordion file. "The original tape's in there, and a copy of the judge's order. Oh, and there's a psych report, too. He said you'd know about it. You can keep the report, but either get the tape back to me by the end of the day, or return it to the clerk's office by nine in the morning. Or else we'll both be in a lot of trouble." She smiled, a slight pale woman in a too-orange jacket, and waved as I drove away.

When I looked inside I also found a sheet of paper torn off a memo pad. JOHN S. SCARPELLI, ASSISTANT STATE'S ATTORNEY was printed at the top. He'd scrawled only a few words below: *Don't forget our deal.*

Finding a way to copy the tape in a hurry was not as easy. I finally resorted to the telephone book at a battered-looking pay phone, looking under Audiovisual Equipment, Rental. I unfolded the map the concierge had given me, and looked at the two together. It looked like there might be a place not too far away.

"Help you?" said the young man behind the dusty counter of B.I.G. Electronics. At least I think that's what he said, but it was hard to tell in the ambient rhythms that bounced across the small shop from wall to wall and back. I must have grimaced a bit, because he reached for a button in a panel behind him, and the sound level instantly dropped.

"Thanks," I said uncertainly, groping for some appropriate vocabulary. "But that was . . . way def. That's like, rap, isn't it?"

He smiled angelically, showing a gold front tooth with a zigzag design. "Hip-hop. You not from around the way, huh?"

"Sorry?"

He walked out from behind the counter, showing me more of the gold tooth, and a matching design on the side of his head. The black t-shirt tucked into the loose pants sliding down his hips said 2Pac Lives, Biggie Is In Hell. "Around the *way*. The 'hood. I mean, it ain't no haps that white ladies are not comin' in to B.I.G. most days. Can I do for you?"

"I, uh, I wanted to rent some electronic equipment, if possible."

"Word. We got *that*. TV?"

"No, I was interested in a VCR. The kind with two decks, you know? So one could record off a tape."

"Ehh-oh yes." He suddenly sounded Shakespearean. "One cooed, if one wished."

I laughed. "You must think I talk pretty funny."

He shook his head. "I heard everything in here. Indian dude yesterday, you know? *I wohdah if yoah establishment might desire to puhchass some varrah high quality muchandice that has most unfohtunately become available becoss of a mishap befalling the fohmah ownah?*"

"You're pretty good at that. My boyfriend is good at imitations, too."

Zigzag looked dubious. "White dude? They never get it right, they just can't get down with the street. No dis, you know, but that's on the real."

"He's black, actually."

He grinned, then used his eyes and mouth to perform a remarkable imitation of an adding machine doing a recalculation. "Full props, then. Now what you wanna rent? Dual-deck VCR? This a rent-to-purchase?"

I shook my head. "I just need it for one night."

"No can do, Lady Evanston. We rent by the month."

"I'm not from Evanston."

"Where then?"

"Colorado."

"See, this is where I know you tryin' to get over on me. White lady comes in here, talk like Evanston, say she not from Evanston, she from Colorado, she boyfriend a blood, and that's why she be wantin' to rent a dual-deck VCR for one night only. Then she wantin' me to lay this all down to Fly when he come back from bro-dudin' with his homies cross the street."

I looked out through the plate glass window. CAFÉ, said one of the tattered signs above the opposite sidewalk. POOL, said the other.

"Fly is your boss?"

"My brother. I'm not spose to be workin' here until I'm a little older, but sometime he let me look after the place when he need to kick back."

I nodded. "Word."

He giggled, and I realized he was about thirteen years old. "You a-ight, Lady Evanston." He turned suddenly and danced back behind the counter, pulling a dusty silver box of an appliance off the shelf. Then he reached for a pad of forms and a pen. "Come on, we gone write this sucker up so tight not even Fly gone be able to loud."

"Have you watched it yet?" asked Sam as we ate dinner that evening. We were at a place called The Greek Islands, where a message at the hotel had told me to meet him. Waiters were flying around with platters of flaming cheese, calling "Opah!" or something like that. I had been trying to explain about the kid who had rented me the VCR.

"Not yet," I said. "I guess I wanted to wait for you, if you're willing to watch it with me. It's only eighteen minutes, according to the label."

"Does the box say who made it?" asked Sam.

I shook my head. "John Scarpelli told me they found the tape in Leonard Fitzgerald's VCR, but never found a box for it. There's a label stuck on the tape itself, but it's not very useful."

"What does the label say?"

"Just the name of the tape and a copyright tag. Copyright Bodkin Productions, 1994."

"Bodkin?"

I shrugged. "It's a kind of knife. Like a dagger. Hamlet talks about one, when he's thinking of killing himself. A bare bodkin. But it sounds kind of like a child's body, too, doesn't it? So if a child's body were to be cut up with a knife . . ." I pushed at a dolmathe listlessly, no longer hungry.

Sam put down his fork. "Are you sure you want to watch this tape?"

"I have to, sooner or later, I guess. I can't just turn it over to my client without ever looking at it."

"Why not? She just hired you to get it, didn't she? Not to watch it."

"Maybe if I watch it I can find a way to talk her out of watching it herself. Think about it, Sam, it was her child that was murdered in the same way as the girl on the tape."

Sam's face took on a carefully neutral look that I had seen before, and that I suspected meant *These white people are purely crazy.* "Cinda, this lady's obviously obsessed with this crime or she wouldn't have sent you here in the first place. You think that once you have this tape in hand you're going to be able to talk her out of watching it? I don't think so."

I nodded unhappily. "You're probably right. You don't have to watch it with me if you don't want to."

He signaled the waiter. "Let's go get it over with."

How do you prepare to watch a snuff film on a rented VCR in a hotel room? I though about the pleasant rituals associated with my home theater experiences: lowered lights, glasses of wine, snacks, cushions propped against the headboard. The room was already dark, with only the bedside light on, but I discarded the other ideas as obscene. In the end Sam sat in the chair and I leaned against the headboard, clutching a pillow to my middle.

Sam had set up the machine. "Will it be copying while we watch, or do we do that later?" I asked.

"Both at once," said Sam. "Sure you're ready?"

"Let's go," I said.

The sound quality was distorted and thick from the outset, but the visual quality of the first scene was surprising, and pleasing. Someplace green and paradisiacal, a pool in a shaded grotto with a waterfall emptying into its glassy depths, a blonde child in a pink ruffled swimsuit cavorting in the pool with a rubbery floating toy. Reggae music: "One Love," by Jimmy Cliff. Two bronzed, swimsuited adults, apparently the little girl's parents, sitting on a rocky outcropping watching her fondly, sipping at drinks from cups like half-coconuts. Sunlight penetrates the shade trees in spots, and dapples and plays on the water. The girl kicks and splashes; she's singing a tuneless childish song. The parents sip again, then the man puts his hand on the woman's brown thigh. She turns to him, eyes glowing, and slips down the strap of her bikini, revealing a lovely breast. He reaches his head toward the breast, mouth open, but the woman puts a hand on his shoulder and gestures with her eyes toward the child. He nods and rises; the camera locks briefly on a noticeable bulge in his swimming trunks. The two walk behind some nearby bushes, where he slides his hands inside her bikini bottoms and lowers them to the ground, then moves one hand between her thighs; his muscular wrist flexes and pulls as

64

she closes her eyes and moistens her lips. In close-up, the camera watches him draw his hand out, then slowly lick his glistening fingers.

I was horrified to realize that I was excited by this scene. I pinched my arm hard between my fingers, until it distracted me from the screen. I didn't want to look at Sam, and was grateful for the darkness of the room.

The little girl is still in the pool, but she hears a groan coming from behind the bushes, and climbs out to investigate, the rubber dinosaur float still around her middle. She looks around the bush, following the noise, and we see the scene on the ground from her perspective, the brown bodies locked and writhing, the woman's large breasts seeming to be everywhere. The adults are oblivious to the child, who slowly steps out of the rubber float and pulls her own little-girl swimsuit out from her chest. She looks for a moment, then shrugs and pushes the suit to the ground and steps out of it, too. Her childish white body is curiously exotic and delicate after the close-ups of the adults, who seemed so attractive just moments before but now seem hairy and gross in memory. The child runs and jumps back into the pool.

"Tiffany!" calls the woman from behind the bush, smothering giggles. "Are you all right, honey?"

"Fine, Mommy," she calls, splashing again. After a moment, listening, she steps slowly out of the water by the stone steps. She stands with her feet in the water, rippling light reflected off her smooth white belly, and looking down, slowly touches a nipple with her index finger. She puts the finger in her mouth and sucks on it, then rubs the nipple slowly. Her little back arches for a moment, and then she reaches the finger hesitantly toward her child's pudenda. The reggae music is louder, sweet and insistent.

The camera moves. A handsome black man, bare muscled shoulders shining, is watching from the other side of the pond. The girl looks up at him, startled, and he slowly raises a finger to his lips: *shh*. She looks at the still-shivering bush, then back at him. She smiles.

I rose and stumbled into the bathroom. I ran cold water and splashed it onto my face over and over, then filled a glass and drank deeply. My hands trembled in the yellowish light and I willed them to stop. They did, eventually. Mostly.

When I came back out Sam was sitting in the chair. The tape had stopped running, the screen was glowing blue and blank.

"Enough?" said Sam. "That's my opinion, by the way."

"Just give me a minute," I said, and sat down heavily on the bed.

"Would it help to talk about it?" he said.

I shook my head. How could I tell him that what we had seen excited me even as it disgusted and repelled me? Sam knew me better than anyone, but he didn't know this about me. I hadn't even known it about myself.

"You remember the Supreme Court's definition of obscenity?" he said.

"Not exactly." I didn't especially want to have an academic discussion just then, but neither did I want to see more of the tape right away. So I said, "Remind me."

"Patently offensive, that's one part. That means it's revolting, disgusting."

"Okay." I had no idea where this conversation was going.

"Appeals primarily to the prurient interest. That mean's it's exciting, I'm pretty sure."

I nodded tiredly. "Yeah, sounds familiar."

Sam looked at me closely. "Cinda, you're not the only one who has the reaction you're having to this kind of thing. It's in the nature of the material, don't you understand? It turns you on, and at the same time it grosses you out. It makes you ashamed of your own sexuality while it tells you that you can enjoy your shame because everyone else is as dirty as you are."

I rubbed my face with my hands, thinking of John Scarpelli saying he wished he could arrange that he had never seen the tape. "I thought I was prepared for something horrible, violent," I said. "Prepared to be—revolted. But not for the other. I didn't think of that."

"I understand," he said. I wished briefly for the comfort of this wise, kind man's touch, but sat stiffly, unable not to think of the couple behind the bushes, or of the storms of our last two nights in this bed.

Finally we watched the rest of it, while the silver box copied the images and sounds from one tape to the other. What else was there for us to do? Even though I had seen the photographs of Alison Grayling in death, and knew that everyone from Leonard Fitzgerald to John Scarpelli agreed that her death had been modeled on the example of this tape, I still was not prepared for what followed the sunny scene at the grotto, after the man leads the child away. Not for its cruelty, not for its racism, not for the ineradicable terror in the eyes and in the voice of the child when she finally sees that this is not going to end in her lifetime. Not for the everlasting mystery of *why.*

When it was over I sobbed into the pillow that I held against my face. I could hear Sam retching behind the closed bathroom door while a few screens of credits rolled by silently. And then, unbelievably, the movie started again, the buzzy opening music, "One Love," the sunny grotto. I jumped up to stop it, then used the fast forward control to run the tape ahead invisibly to about the midpoint, where I started it again. The little girl was just pulling off her swimsuit. I went back and forth a few more times, until I realized the explanation. The snuff film was recorded onto the tape several times. I fiddled with the controls and figured out how to record the entire contents of the original tape onto my blank without any display or sound, then went to lie on the bed again, watching the digital counter roll forward, as slowly as a clock in hell.

Even after Sam came back out we could not talk, or turn on the television, or raid the minibar for cheap wine. I packed my suitcase mechanically, thinking of my early departure the next morning. Sam finally tuned the radio to a local jazz station and dialed the volume down very low. We lay side by side, and finally I took his hand, but I could not bear to touch him further and I believe he felt the same way. Dawn was breaking pitilessly before I slept a little.

The original videotape was safely returned to the clerk's office, and the copy swathed in my clothes inside my checked suitcase, as my flight back to Denver took off from O'Hare. The lack of sleep had left me groggy, and as the big plane turned away from takeoff and headed west I fell into a fitful and hellish nap. In my disordered imagination the black plastic rectangle in my suitcase stank like death and attracted the attention of a sniffing dog; it melted into a loathsome slime that coated all of my clothes; it exploded and ignited a fire that consumed the plane and everyone in it, even as the vessel continued its voyage across the sky. I called Beverly from DIA and told her that I was sick, and would be going straight home for the rest of the day. She didn't ask me any questions.

When I awakened in my own bed it was dusk. If there had been a bad taste in my mouth I could have tried toothpaste or mouthwash; if it had been a headache, I had plenty of Advil. I even had a reefer tucked away somewhere—I'd forgotten where exactly, probably in my underwear drawer—

against the possibility of nausea. But I didn't know what drug to take against the sickness that had seized me. I was still prowling restlessly around my house at nine o'clock, opening and closing the refrigerator and the medicine cabinet in turn without ever removing anything. I finally went calling on my next-door neighbor Diana, who's one of those dentists you see after your regular dentist has decided your problem is a little too much for him. She took pity on me and gave me a couple of Valium, warning me not to take more than one and definitely not to mix it with alcohol. I went straight home and took both of them with a slug of cabernet sauvignon. I don't recommend this, but I did sleep until six. It was the same world when I woke up, though: sunny, clement, all the glowing green splendor of a Rocky Mountain spring merely illustration on the thin wallpaper covering the chasm of pain and death below.

When I got to the office Beverly looked at me closely but didn't offer any advice or observation, for which I was grateful. She handed me a handful of pink message slips without a word other than "Okay?"

"Okay," I said, and went into my office and closed the door. The top slip told me that John Scarpelli had called yesterday at 4:30, and wanted me to call him back. In the message space Beverly had scrawled *Says remember your deal (?)* I crumpled the slip and threw it behind me. The next few were routine—a book salesman, a reminder call about a bar association committee meeting. Then one from Peggy Grayling. *Call when you get back to town. Wants to know did you get the tape?* I started to crumple it too, but instead tucked it under another piece of paper with only the slightest margin showing. I suppose I thought I could make it disappear that way, without treating it quite as cavalierly as I had John Scarpelli's. I busied myself reading the newest *Colorado Lawyer* and making a tidy list of tasks I had to accomplish on several pending matters, none of them named Grayling. I ordered myself to relax, but that never works and it didn't then. I would notice every few minutes that my muscles were tensed all over and my heart was racing again. A few minutes after ten Beverly rang to say that Peggy was on the line.

"So you're back," she said warmly. "Did you have any luck?"

"Some," I said. "We need to talk, Peggy."

"Sure. I have a yoga class at eleven. Want me to come by afterward?"

I thought of the yoga class I had taken for a while, the serene acquiescence of body and mind after an hour and a half of practice. "Maybe I'll come to the class with you. Do I have to be registered, or can I just show up?"

"It's a walk-in," she said. "But it's Bikram style. Do you like that?"

"I've never tried it. I think what I did for a while was something different. Ash-something."

"Ashtanga," she said. "That's very good, too. But Bikram is—well, why don't you try it? Wear something very small."

"Small?"

"You'll sweat a lot," she said. "Better not to have too much on. A swimsuit is good."

"I always sweat a lot."

"You'll sweat more," she said, and gave me directions to an address in east Boulder, near the airport.


It was a generic industrial building with an entrance in the back. Inside, a petite dark-haired woman in a lime two-piece aerobics outfit sat behind the high counter, sipping from a large plastic bottle of water. A matching lime elastic confined her hair to a fountain on the exact top of her small head; it switched like an animal's tail as she looked up. "For the eleven class?" she asked automatically.

I nodded, and she looked at me more closely.

"You haven't been here before, have you?" She seemed slightly concerned.

"No, but I have studied yoga a bit," I said. "A while ago."

She smiled. "Okay, then. I'm sure you'll do fine. Shaanti's a very good teacher. You brought plenty of water?"

"Um, no, I didn't. But I'm sure you're right. I'll do fine."

"Just a minute. It's sixteen dollars, please." And she vanished into a closet behind the counter while I counted out three fives and a one. She returned with a battered plastic bottle marked *Boulder Peaks Triathlon 1995* in eroding red letters, and put it onto the counter next to my wallet. "Someone left that—you can have it. Just fill it up at the drinking fountain, and next time you might want to bring some that you've kept in your freezer so it will stay colder. You do have a towel?"

Freezer? "Yeah, I brought a towel," I said. "So um, thanks, and not to sound ungrateful since you've been so nice, but isn't sixteen dollars a lot for a yoga class?"

She nodded. "Most are less. But Bikram teachers are specially trained, and that's very expensive, and then there's the heating. It costs a ton."

"The heating."

"Of the studio."

"Oh. I see." I didn't, really. I supposed every yoga studio had to be heated in the winter, just like every other business in this mountain town. But she had turned to greet the next arrival, so I took my gym bag and my new water bottle into the dressing room and changed out of my office clothes into a pair of shorts and a running bra.

Peggy Grayling arrived as I was stowing my clothes and bag in a locker. She gave me a hug and then prepared for the class quickly, merely pulling off her shirt to reveal a black one-piece unitard, kicking off her sandals, and sweeping her hair quickly into a ponytail. "We'll go get something after class," she said, "and you can tell me what you found." I noticed that she had two large bottles of water, both of them frozen.

"How do you drink from those all frozen like that?" I asked her, but just then an acquaintance of hers arrived in the small dressing area, and she turned to greet her.

"Cinda, this is my friend Sierra," she said after the two exchanged a few words. The woman was about Peggy's age, short and round-faced but very fit-looking; she smiled in acknowledgement, and the three of us walked out toward the closed studio door. Many puzzling things were explained when Peggy opened the door and a stunning blast of heat poured out. Peggy and Sierra walked right through it, chatting as though nothing were unusual. I followed reluctantly, immediately dizzy in the furnace, which looked unaccountably like a nice room with a pale carpet and long mirrored wall.

Peggy turned to make sure I was behind them. "The heat is wonderful," she said encouragingly. "It loosens you right up so you can perform the asanas with much more ease. Like in India, you know, where yoga was invented." She walked away a few steps and began to spread her towel on the floor.

I nodded wordlessly. Within seconds my vision blurred as sweat began oozing from my brow and ran swiftly into my eyes in stinging rivulets. Wiping it away with my towel, I blinked and discerned that the dozen or so people in the room were spreading out their towels at intervals, all facing the front where a tall woman in tiny black lycra shorts and a bikini top was conferring with a man in swimming trunks. He nodded and walked over to a thermostat on the wall, which he gave a moderate twist.

"Okay," said the woman, fitting a microphone headset over her sleek brown hair, nearly a crew cut. "I asked Tashi to turn the heat up a bit, it's not nearly hot enough. Sorry, I should have checked it earlier. But we should be over a hundred in twenty minutes or so. Meanwhile, let's start. *Pranayama*, deep breathing. Anyone new today?"

I held my hand up reluctantly, as did one other student, a well-muscled guy standing two towels away, bare-chested in red running shorts.

"Just watch me, and do the best you can," she said. "Breathe. If you have to rest, okay, but keep with the deep breathing. If you get dizzy sit on your towel. I'll come around if I see you need help."

I need help already, I thought, struggling to stay vertical against the shattering waves of heat. I knelt to wipe my eyes on my towel again before standing and attempting to imitate the teacher's posture, her fingers clasped together and then tucked under her chin, her elbows touching below. It was impossible. Shaanti must be double-jointed or something, I thought, but stealing a look around I saw that nearly everyone could accomplish the same.

"Ten cycles," said Shaanti. "Begin. *One.*" The breathing part involved sweeping the elbows in and out slowly in rhythm with one's inhalation and exhalation. There was a plate-glass mirror covering the entire front of the studio, and in it I could see Peggy's reflection, a few towels down from mine. She looked happy, her posture perfect, her face serene as she filled and emptied her chest and swept her arms elegantly. For me, I never had such a hard time breathing in my life. Each inhalation filled me with more of the searing heat, and after five I was already desperately thirsty.

"Excellent," said Shaanti into the mike after *ten* had come and gone, but there was to be no rest period—which would have made sense but for the temperature, as all we had done was breathe and move our arms, but I was faint and dizzy and would have been grateful to stand still for a moment. "Now *Ardha-Chandrasana*, half-moon pose." She raised her arms gracefully over her head into a steeple effect and I followed, thinking this at least I could do. But then it seemed one was supposed to arch sideways as though hinged on the right side of the waist, which I was not. Several of the others seemed to be, however, and they swayed gracefully sideways until their bodies formed ninety-degree angles. This excruciating pose was held for ten, then the hinged ones demonstrated that in defiance of the laws of physics, they could bend just as far to the other side. I and the red-shorts guy, the only newcomers, essayed laughable imitations of this rubber-middle act. I thought my dizziness was abating for a moment, but it returned when I saw the next variation: a backbend with the arms still in the steeple pose. Sure enough, as soon as I tried it my head whirled and I had to step back quickly to keep from falling over. By then my entire body was slick with sweat and I could smell myself and taste salt and fear in my parched mouth. How was I going to get through an hour and a half of this?

Shaanti proceeded without mercy into the next poses, which she called the Awkward asanas, and they certainly were. Then *Garurasana,* Eagle Pose, aptly named, or would be if eagles flapped their wings until they were entangled with one another like pretzels and stood on one foot with other leg wrapped around it as though it were rare bacon wrapped around a hot dog, and tried not to fall over. All while gasping helplessly for breath.

Pointless to recount the rest, the Standing Bow Pulling and Balancing Stick and Locust and Camel and various other unlikely animals. The water in my bottle absorbed heat immediately but I sucked the warm stuff out of the container between every pose; it ran out after the Cobra and I left the studio for a moment to refill it. I stood by the outer door for a moment, the cool air a memory of the heavenly world I had left behind. I should go back, I thought, turning, unhappy with the prospect but way too stubborn to admit defeat.

But I could not resist the opportunity for further procrastination that was offered by a shelf laden with black and white photographs; each one showed the same elfin dark-eyed man performing some of the poses next to a slightly less accomplished companion. I did not know him, but the other faces seemed almost familiar. I wiped my eyes and looked more closely. *Bikram Choudhury with Carol Lynley,* said one, showing the small man and a slender blonde woman in Triangle pose. *Bikram Choudhury with Keir Dullea. Bikram Choudhury with Sarah Miles.* It was like a Sixties film festival. *Bikram Choudhury with Susan Strasberg.* Apparently this Bikram fellow was teacher to a cadre of aging Hollywood stars. I had to admit they looked great in their swimsuits, lithe bodies extended or draped over themselves in imitation of Bikram's effortless posing, although it seemed suspicious that nobody appeared to be sweating.

Sighing, I trudged back into the studio, just in time for the Bow and its associated tortures. I had dried off and steadied up a little outside, but in less than a minute I was slimy with sweat and lightheaded again, even though the Bow is done with belly to the mat. My feet, arched behind me, inched out of my slippery grasp no matter what I tried; I noted to what would have been my amusement in less desperate circumstances that several of the more accomplished students were wearing thin gloves to avoid this effect.

Crazy stuff, a bunch of American yuppies hanging out in a carpeted Hades wearing gloves and getting shouted at in Sanskrit. And although it was true that my joints eventually felt as though they had been buttered by the heat, and by the end of the ninety minutes I could touch things and straighten things that astonished me, I promised myself I would never attend another Bikram yoga class.

Showered and finally finished sweating, I was into my second gallon of ice water, sitting at the Nirvana Juice Bar with Peggy and her friend Sierra. They kept saying things like "Isn't it fantastic?" and "Don't you feel utterly *cleansed?*" It was true I was relaxed, or at least limp, but I was also growing impatient, as I had come there to talk to Peggy about the subject of the videotape. I was waiting to raise the subject until Sierra excused herself but it was Peggy, sensing my purpose but not the reason for my hesitation, who brought it up.

"So Cinda, did you get what you went after in Chicago?"

I looked uneasily at Sierra, who took an innocent sip of wheatgrass juice, her face glowing with contentment, her yellow shirt a flag of cheer.

"It's all right," said Peggy. "Sierra knows a little about it already."

"That's fine, Peggy. But if we talk with each other while Sierra's here, then it endangers the attorney-client privilege. Nothing personal, Sierra, but I can't allow that."

Sierra gave me a no-hard-feelings smile and rose immediately, draining her glass. "I have to go anyway. See you, Peggy. *Namaste.*" She put her palms together briefly and bobbed her head once, a sturdy sunflower of a woman. I hoped that she and Peggy were good friends.

Peggy turned to me eagerly. A light dusting of freckles across her nose made the lines lurking at the edges of her face seem like a mistake or a trick of the light. "Did you get it?" she said again.

"I have it. But listen, Peggy—" And I then embarked on the speech I had planned about why she shouldn't see it. The words were as familiar as

Chicago blues lyrics. *Do no good. Reopen your wounds. Can't bring her back.* Maybe Magic Slim could have put these lines across, but I didn't succeed. Peggy Grayling's stubbornness was less obvious than mine, but as we talked I soon realized that I was overmatched. She was determined to see the tape, and she was the client and entitled to, whether or not it was wise. Before we parted company I had undertaken to be at the office at four so she could come by for the tape.

"And then what?" she said to me.

"That's up to you, Peggy."

"You know what I want."

"There would be so many obstacles to a successful lawsuit. It's important you understand how unlikely it is we'd overcome all of them."

"We'll take them one at a time. What's the first one?"

"Maybe the hardest. We have to find out where the tape was made, and by whom. Unless we can identify the maker or at least trace the path of distribution, we don't even know whom to sue."

She smiled. "I love the way you say *whom.* How many lawyers get that right?"

"It's Tory," I confessed. "She's always ragging on me about my grammar. I guess it has improved a little since she started."

"I didn't realize she was such a grammarian."

"That's not what it's really about," I said. "I don't think."

"What then?"

I shook my head. "I don't know, Peggy. She and I have a really complicated relationship. Practicing law is pretty tense sometimes and we both get edgy every once in a while."

Peggy nodded, as though acknowledging something she knew already. "She doesn't want you to do this case, does she?"

I looked away from the level gray eyes. "Do you want me to talk to an investigator about trying to trace the tape? I have a few ideas, and he'll probably have some more. But it will be expensive, Peggy."

"Do it," she said. "Then what?"

I thought for a second. "I have a friend I could ask to start working on the possibility of proving a link between the tape and the behavior of Leonard Fitzgerald. I got a copy of the psychiatric report that was done on him before trial."

She nodded. "Do you need some money now?"

"I'll let you know. Soon, probably. Maybe we should sign a fee agreement when you come by this afternoon, get the details in writing. I'll do the case on contingency—a third if we win at trial, 40 percent if there's an appeal, which I'm sure there would be. Might not leave too much for you, Peggy, especially after all the expenses. Might not leave anything, in fact." I started to add that the rules for measuring damages in wrongful death cases didn't favor large awards for the deaths of children, but I found I didn't want to say that. I didn't want to explain it.

She nodded. "I know why I'm doing this, Cinda. I never got to look Leonard Fitzgerald in the face, but he's not the only one I blame, anyway. I want to look this guy in the face, whoever's making money supplying ideas to murderous pedophiles. I just want to see him, and I want him to feel shame. I'm a big believer in shame. I'm fifty years old and I have more than enough money to live out my life. I don't have a child, and I'm learning not to be attached to anything. This is what I want to do." She hesitated, then spoke again. "Do you know what a *bodhisattva* is, Cinda?"

I shook my head.

"It's an evolved human being who postpones his own Nirvana so the rest of us can learn from him. I knew that Alison was special while she was alive, but since her death I've come to believe that her life and death had a meaning beyond most, that she may have been a bodhisattva. But it's left to us to teach that meaning, through this lawsuit. It's my karma to bring this person to answer for what he's done. And his karma to be brought. And yours," she smiled, "to bring your skill and heart to the task. If your will is in accord."

I could think of nothing to say, so I touched her arm and told her I would see her at four. As I stood my head reeled and I almost stumbled. Still dizzy from the heat, no doubt.

"Tory's looking for you," Beverly informed me as I walked back into the office at one. "Wow, you look really—relaxed."

"Thanks," I said shortly. "Yes, I'm cleansed of all toxins and shit like that."

"I think if you really were, you wouldn't have to use such ugly language," she said.

"Let me correct myself, then. I am cleansed of most toxins and shit like that, but not quite all of them, and the ones left are the ones that make you use bad words."

She nodded and turned back to her typing. "That at least is not illogical."

"Thank you. Where is Tory?"

"In your office, I believe."

She was sitting in the saggy caned chair I keep in the corner because I can't bear to throw it out, looking straight ahead. I knew something had to be wrong; her usual energy level didn't allow for sitting still. She looked up at me as I came in and nodded distantly, as to a slight acquaintance whose name one can't quite remember, encountered at the bus stop.

"Is that it?" she asked, pointing to the videotape on the desk, still in its plastic ziplock bag.

I nodded. "You won't believe what I went through to get it. First I had to—"

"So are you committed to this case?" she broke in.

"What do you mean?"

"I mean, which do you care more about, Peggy Grayling's case, or this partnership?"

It had been a long time since I had heard that bitter note in her voice. "Do I have to choose?" I asked. "Of course I thought we'd talk about it. She's coming in this afternoon at four. Why don't we all talk together?"

"Carry on a quarrel in front of a prospective client? Doesn't seem very professional." Her eyes smoldered in her pale face and the full lips were pale and set.

I looked at the office door and considered closing it, but decided against. Beverly knew everything about us, and hated being shut out. And I might need her help before long.

I turned back to Tory, and pulled my newly limber legs into a cross in the center of my desk chair. "Talk to me."

"You don't understand about being gay," she said flatly.

"Probably not. But I try, usually. Don't I?"

She made a noncommittal noise, a little puff of air with her lips.

"Come on, Tory. Anyway, this case isn't about that. Is it?"

"That's *precisely* what you don't understand. You know about *don't ask, don't tell?* That nice liberal compromise on gays in the military, according to which they are given the honor of being permitted to die for their country as long as they don't speak the truth about who they are?"

"Yeah," I said. "That sucks. You know I think so. So what?"

"So! So, so—being gay is all about being allowed to say who you are! Hardly anybody minds gay people any more when we hide in the closet or even have nice quiet little lives with guilty discreet sexual encounters that don't require anyone to notice. But that's not freedom, Cinda! Why do you think we have Gay Pride parades and wear lavender triangle pins and get in your face? So you'll *have* to notice. That's why gays hate censorship more than anything. Haven't you noticed that when some gay gets the shit beat out of him, it's always because he wouldn't shut up about who he was? If we let them shut us up, Cinda, we might as well go back to the closet and crawl under the floorboards and stay there forever. Is that what you want?"

"Tory, I can't believe you're asking me. Your best friend!"

"I don't think that's necessarily what you're after. But if you win this case and a lot of other people win others like it, then that's what you'll get. And if you find a way to make censorship okay, who do you think will be the first ones getting censored? It won't be the straight world, I promise you. It will be us."

"Us! Who's *us?* You and I are on the same side, Tory. I'm really getting upset by your willingness to draw a line and put me on the other side of it."

"You put yourself over there! With Brianna Bainbridge, that postmodern feminist princess, and all the other censors."

"What's censorship about what Peggy Grayling wants?" I was shouting now. I heard the phone ring and then Beverly get up and walk to the door to my office, closing it quietly. I tried to lower my voice. "Is it censorship to ask the maker of a very dangerous product to pay when his product injures someone? A lawnmower, a car, a drug?"

"No," she said, "because those things aren't speech." Her face was as hard as I'd ever seen it.

"And this," I said, gesturing toward the black plastic cassette, "is?"

She nodded emphatically.

"You haven't even seen it." I played this glib card with a smugness I regretted in an instant.

"Fine," she said, holding out her hand. "Give it to me. I'll watch in the conference room."

"No," I said. "Someone tried to stop me from seeing it and I wish I had let them. I wish I could prevent Peggy from seeing it. You don't want to see it, Tory."

Her hand remained outstretched. "You think I haven't seen this kind of stuff? The First Amendment is for the speech you hate, Cinda. Nice speech that doesn't offend anyone doesn't need the First Amendment."

I'd tell myself later that it was the self-righteousness in her tone, and her production of that cliché as though it were an original observation, that pushed me to the cruel act I next performed. I took the cassette, still clad in its plastic shroud, and tossed it to her.

"Go ahead," I said. "Have a regular First Amendment film festival in there. I look forward to hearing your review. You know, thumbs up or thumbs down. Let me know what you think of the acting, especially the juvenile lead."

After she left I turned back to my list of tasks. My heart was thumping painfully as I tried to put our quarrel out of my mind and concentrate on reading an expert's report that I'd commissioned for a DUI trial the following week. The expert, a pathologist who seemed to enjoy testifying in court, opined in his report that the margin of error for a blood alcohol test conducted in the field with a Breathalyzer was plus or minus .015%. My client Tad Murphy, a former colleague from the DA's office with a bit of a drinking problem, had blown a .10 after being stopped for weaving in his Lexus. This measure happened to be the precise legal limit for driving under the influence, so the expert's testimony might allow Tad to skate—again, for this was not the first time he'd faced this charge, nor probably the last. Tad had yet to take any one of the twelve steps. I sighed—I really didn't, as we say in Boulder, *resonate* to criminal defense work, but as an ex-prosecutor I got a lot of it and couldn't afford to turn it away.

Rereading his report made me think of the psychiatric report that John Scarpelli's assistant had given me along with the videotape. I rummaged through my briefcase and found it, between a bill for bar dues and an invitation to a fundraiser for a local political candidate, both tattered around the edges. The report didn't look too long. I looked up and listened for the sound of Tory watching the tape, but she must have shut the door to the conference room. I leaned back in my chair and began to read.

NAME: Leonard Campbell Fitzgerald

D.O.B.: January 10, 1973

DATE OF REPORT: April 19, 1997

IDENTIFYING DATA: Mr. Fitzgerald is a 24-year-old who has completed high school and has taken some classes at Des Plaines Community College. Until his arrest, he resided in Oak Park. After being charged with kidnapping and first-degree murder on February 13 of this year, he entered a plea of Not Guilty by Reason of Insanity before the Hon. Vincent Ricci of the Chicago Criminal Courts. The state's attorney, per John Scarpelli, Esq., moved to have Mr. Fitzgerald examined by the undersigned, and Mr. Fitzgerald was transferred to the Elgin Mental Health Center for this evaluation by order of Judge Ricci.

PROCEDURES: The undersigned examined Mr. Fitzgerald in order to form an opinion about his mental state at the time of the alleged offense. I have at all times kept in mind the requirements of Section 6-2 of the Criminal Code, which provides, "A person is not criminally responsible for conduct if at the time of such conduct, as a result of mental disease or mental effect, he lacks substantial capacity either to appreciate the criminality of his conduct or to conform his conduct to the requirements of law. The terms 'mental disease or defect' do not include an abnormality manifested only by repeated criminal or otherwise antisocial conduct."

The examination included several interviews, totaling thirteen hours, between myself and Mr. Fitzgerald. Before these interviews commenced, I informed Mr. Fitzgerald of their nature and purpose, and explained that the results would not be confidential and would be supplied to the court, the prosecution, and his own counsel. He appeared to understand this advice, and agreed to participate in the interviews. I also arranged that he should take a battery of psychological tests, to be administered and interpreted by Bella Larkin, Ph.D., a clinical psychologist employed at the EMHC. In addition, Margery Courtland, LCSW, conducted interviews with various other persons, including Mr. Fitzgerald's mother, Irene Fitzgerald; his landlord, Stanley Kirkendall; one of his instructors at Des Plaines Community College, Paul Wardlaw; his former employer, Jacob Mellis; some schoolmates of the victim Alison Grayling, who will not be named here; and Detective James Fox, who transported Mr. Fitzgerald to Cook County Hospital after his arrest. Dr. Larkin and Ms. Courtland reported their findings to me, and the results of their interviews and tests have been incorporated into this report.

RELEVANT HISTORY: Leonard Fitzgerald was born in Tampa, Florida, to Joseph Fitzgerald, a machinist, and his wife Irene, a homemaker. He was the first and only child born to the couple. When Leonard was five, the family moved to the Chicago area, where Joseph had grown up, because Joseph's mother died and left her home, a small house in Oak Park, Illinois, to Joseph.

Joseph Fitzgerald died in 1982, apparently of cirrhosis of the liver. He was a heavy drinker and according to his wife was verbally and occasionally physically abusive to the boy Leonard. After his death, Mrs. Fitzgerald went to work as a secretary in a doctor's office, and as a result Leonard was often at home in the afternoon with little or no adult supervision. Leonard was an average student in elementary and junior high school, but his grades fell in high school and he barely graduated. He was not athletic and his two serious pursuits were photography and movies. He persuaded his mother to allow him to set up a darkroom in the second bathroom of their home; she reasoned that this project would keep him at home and away from bad influences while she had to be at work in the afternoons. She remembers that he was mostly solitary, and that few of his friends came to their home to visit, although when he was old enough to drive he went out to the movies at least once a week, and she thinks he may have met friends when he did.

Leonard himself remembers that what he went to see after the age of fifteen was mostly pornographic films, but that he soon discovered that those he could see in a theater were disappointing compared to those that could be rented for home viewing. When he was fifteen he persuaded his mother to buy him a VCR as a birthday present, and he would often rent X-rated films and spend the afternoons between the time he got home and her own later return watching these films. He would watch some of them over and over, replaying certain scenes, and eventually bought himself a second, used VCR so he could make copies of the films that excited him most. He often masturbated as he watched. He would listen for the sound of his mother's car in the driveway. The worry that someday he would fail to hear her, and that she would discover his pursuits, added an element of fear but also excitement.

Mr. Fitzgerald denies any substance abuse or use of alcohol, saying that his father's example has deterred him from drinking, and there is no evidence from any source to contradict this claim. After he graduated from high school he told his mother that he wanted to "take a break" from school, but she insisted that he continue his education at least part-time. He enrolled at Des Plaines Community College, and for two semesters took courses in photography and film studies. He made a B in each course, but did not return for a third semester. His mother, having discovered that he was no longer in school, insisted that he get a job, and he went to work in a video rental store in the Bucktown neighborhood. There his willingness to work irregular hours on short notice and to work double shifts made him a favored employee. He displayed a very detailed knowledge of the store's tape stock, especially its X-rated section, and there were many regulars at the store who sought his advice and recommendations.

He soon had enough income to rent a small apartment for himself, and with his mother's encouragement he moved into a one-bedroom apartment on the second floor of an older building directly across the street from the Oak Park Elementary School. His landlord reports that soon after moving in he requested permission to paint black over the windows in one room, explaining that he needed to do so for reasons having to do with photography. The landlord agreed after Fitzgerald made an additional one hundred fifty–dollar damage deposit and promised to restore the windows to their original condition when he moved out of the apartment.

Irene Fitzgerald helped Leonard move into the apartment, in April 1994, and visited him there one time shortly thereafter. At the time of his arrest, she stated that she had not been to his apartment for several years, and that on the occasions they met it was at her house or in a restaurant. During the years between mid-1994 and his arrest in 1996, Fitzgerald did considerable work on his apartment, much of it apparently clandestine. Some time in 1995, the landlord recalls, Fitzgerald changed the lock on his apartment so the landlord could no longer enter with his duplicate key. When the landlord, who also lived in the building, protested, Fitzgerald promised to get him a copy of the new key, but he never did so and the landlord did not pursue the matter.

When he was not working or in his apartment, Leonard Fitzgerald often spent time standing on the front stoop of his apartment building, or leaning on the rail, smoking and watching the children play in the schoolyard across the street. Many of the children reported seeing him there from time to time. Some of the children referred to him as "Wolf" or "The Wolf," although none remembered ever speaking to him and they could not account for how they knew his name.

Fitzgerald claims that he did not keep a diary. He did write poems and short narratives, in which a character named Wolf or Dire Wolf often appears. Some of these were found in a search of his apartment after the crime. In addition, some of the customers at Rainbow Video called him Wolf. The proprietor, Jacob Mellis, says that he doesn't know how the nickname arose.

POLICE ACCOUNT OF THE CRIME: Most of the information in this section was provided by police reports and by Detective James Fox of the Chicago

Police Department, who was lead investigator of the murder of Alison Grayling. Copies of these reports are provided.

At 6:30 p.m. on January 7, 1997, Mrs. Margaret Grayling of Oak Park, Illinois, called the Chicago Police Department to report that her daughter Alison, a fourth-grade student at Oak Park Elementary School, had not come home after school that afternoon. Mrs. Grayling reported that Alison usually walked the six blocks home from her school with a neighbor and classmate; a babysitter would be waiting for her at home. The babysitter had called to report that Alison was not yet home, and Mrs. Grayling had driven home immediately from work and gone looking for her. She had questioned the neighbor child, who said that Alison had not been waiting at their accustomed spot by a tree on the school grounds after school; the neighbor child had grown cold waiting and had finally concluded that Alison had gone ahead, whereupon she came home. Asked whether she had seen anyone or anything unusual around the school that day, she replied "only the Wolf, but he's almost always there." Pressed further, she explained that "the Wolf" was a man who often talked to the children in the schoolyard; the child thought that he lived somewhere "across the street" from the school, but wasn't certain.

Officer Brenda Ashton was dispatched to the Grayling residence, and introduced to the neighbor child, whose mother agreed to allow the child to show the officer the building where she believed "the Wolf" to live. The child identified a three-story apartment building just west of the school, with a stone stoop that offered an excellent view of the school grounds. Officer Ashton then sought out the landlord, Stanley Kirkendall, who also acted as building superintendent. Kirkendall volunteered that he had some doubts about the stability of one of his tenants, Leonard Fitzgerald, who had some time before changed the locks on his apartment so the landlord no longer could enter and painted his windows with black paint. Officer Ashton then called Detective Fox, who instructed her to watch the door to Fitzgerald's apartment while Fox attempted to obtain a search warrant.

Having failed to obtain a warrant, but concerned about the passage of time since the child's disappearance, Detective Fox knocked on the door of the Fitzgerald apartment at about 9:00 p.m. The subject, Leonard Fitzgerald, opened the door, rubbing his eyes. When asked, he agreed that he was known as Wolf. When asked if he knew the whereabouts of Alison Grayling, he said that he did not, but consented to a search of his apartment by Detective Fox and Officer Ashton. Fox searched while Ashton watched the subject, who slumped in a chair and seemed to go to sleep.

In a room off the apartment's central corridor, Fox found the lifeless body of Alison Grayling. It was nude, and had been mutilated severely. It lay on the floor in front of a television connected to a VCR, still turned on although the tape was no longer playing. The floor also contained a child's rubberized swimming pool half-full of water, a spotlight on a metal tower, two potted plants or trees of the palm family, a kit of stage makeup including stage blood and other "special effects" materials, a child's torn swimsuit, and a large knife.

Fox and Ashton took Fitzgerald into custody, advising him of his rights. The officers noted that he was disoriented, his speech was slurred, and he was becoming unresponsive, so they arranged for emergency transportation to Cook County Hospital. Fox accompanied Fitzgerald in the ambulance, and conversed with him to some degree en route. Fitzgerald said that he had made a mistake, and also said, twice, "she was the wrong one." Drug overdose was suspected and in the hospital Fitzgerald underwent gastric lavage, but tests later completed on the blood drawn from him at admission provided no evidence that he had ingested drugs. After this procedure he appeared to recover from his lethargy, although he still appeared disoriented. He was transferred to a locked ward.

Crime scene investigation resulted in the seizure of the items listed above, as well as a videotape that was removed from the subject's VCR, which was turned on but not running, located a few feet from the victim's body. The videotape portrayed an encounter between a person who appeared to be a female child of about ten, and a male of apparently about thirty. The encounter, which takes place in a tropical grotto, depicts the child as a willing participant in sexual acts, some grotesque but none violent, until the last few minutes of the film. In those final minutes, the acts turn violent and the child (if she is one) struggles and pleads. The film depicts the eventual strangulation and mutilation of the child by the man, who then commits an apparent sexual act with the child's mutilated body. The resemblance between the acts there depicted and those apparently committed by Leonard Fitzgerald are, to say the least, marked. An unusual feature of this tape is that it depicts the same eighteen-minute scene seven times, consecutively, until the tape's capacity is exhausted.

Further investigation by Detective Fox failed to determine the origin of the videotape. Jacob Mellis denies ever having seen it, and points out that all of the videotapes available for purchase or rental in his store are marked with a label containing the store's name. Lab analysis found no traces of a store label or any glue on the tape's exterior, although there is a label with the name *Bodkin Productions* and a copyright notice. Investigators apparently found no records of a business organization by that name. It could not be determined whether the acts depicted on the tape were real or simulated, not could it be shown with certainty that the "child" on the tape was a minor, despite her childlike appearance. Detective Fox's researches suggested that producers of pornographic videotapes often employ actors who appear to be many years younger than their true ages, in order to avoid prosecutions for violating the child pornography laws. Nothing more was learned about this particular tape.

An autopsy indicated that Alison Grayling died of strangulation and/or blood loss from massive knife wounds to her abdominal and pelvic area. Either cause would have been independently sufficient to cause death; it could not be determined with certainty which was inflicted first. Her hands bore no defensive wounds, but this was not deemed significant by the examiner, as they were bound when she was discovered. She died between one and three hours prior to the discovery of her body. Ejaculate identifiable as the subject's was found on the exterior abdominal area of the child's body, and also inside two of the wounds in that area.

SUBJECT'S ACCOUNT OF THE CRIME: The subject Leonard Fitzgerald has experienced, for many years, ideas of reference concerning his identity as a wolf, or wolf-man. He remembers coming to believe in his lupine identity when he was in high school. He detected references to himself in, among other works, the novel *Steppenwolf* and the Chicago theater company of the same name, the film *Never Cry Wolf*, and especially a song by the Grateful Dead called "Dire Wolf." When discussing this subject, the subject sings a few lines from the song, in which the phrase "Don't murder me" and "I beg of you, don't murder me," are repeated. He sometimes will say that he is a wolf, but also sometimes talks as though "the Wolf" is another being or entity (e.g., "The Wolf and I work together, but I don't tell him what to do and he doesn't tell me, either.")

The subject also became convinced, at some time in early adolescence, that he was black, although there is nothing in his appearance to suggest this. He believed that his race was a reason that others, including or especially his father, treated him badly.

After leaving college, the subject returned to his obsession with pornographic films. When he was not watching them or working at the Mellis video store, he would spend hours walking the streets of Chicago, looking for women that he could recognize from the films he had seen. He began to prefer films that showed very young women, and on the street he also began to watch children more than adults, expecting to see a girl from a film. He fantasized about approaching such a girl and suggesting that they make a film together, and wrote various scripts and screenplays to have in readiness in case his fantasy should be realized.

Some nights he would wander the streets for hours. Later he would realize that he had lost track of time. Sometimes he would discover scratches or bruises on his body that he could not remember getting. Other times he awakened in a public place, often on a park bench, without memory of falling asleep there or of what had brought him there. Once he was arrested for indecent exposure after urinating in a park, in Cicero he thinks. He remembers that he told the officer he was "marking his territory." When asked what that meant, the subject said, "It was the Wolf. He has his own ways, and follows his own law." (No record of this arrest could be found.)

At some time in the fall of 1996, the subject started watching children playing on the grounds of the elementary school across from his apartment building. He struck up acquaintances among the children, although he spoke only to boys, as the school's crossing guard warned him at one time that the police would be called if he bothered any of the girls (the crossing guard has retired and could not be reached to confirm this episode). Shortly before, he had acquired a copy of the videotape he calls *Sunshade Snuffdown*; he is not sure where, but says he often bought tapes on the street or from persons who would come into the store with "bootleg" that the subject was sure Mr. Mellis would not want to buy, but that he would purchase for his personal collection.

This particular tape became an immediate favorite. Apparently the tape the subject purchased showed the same events repeated numerous times. This facilitated the viewing of the events over and over, consecutively, and that was what the subject did. The subject believed that the film was speaking directly to him and was in some way about him. He thought the protagonist, a black man, had a "wolfish" grin and was "a wolf like me, a black one." He also became convinced that the little girl in the film was one he had been watching on the playground. He asked one of his acquaintances among the schoolboys and was told her name was Alison Grayling. He was also informed that she was "stuck up" and that she talked all the time about her cat, Misty. This knowledge reinforced his belief that she was the girl on the tape, because he knew there was a well-known actress in pornographic films named Misty Climax. He determined to meet her and talk to her about making a film with him. When the examiner asked if he had wanted to kill the girl, as was done in the film, the subject replied, "It's all special effects. If she was the right girl she'd have known how to do it."

On the day of the murder, the subject had prepared a stage and props for a "rehearsal" of the film he wished to make with Alison Grayling. He expected that if he could get her to come to his apartment, once he showed her the tape and told her he knew she was the girl in it, she would acknowledge this and cooperate. He wanted to know how the "special effects" were done, and thought she could show him that as well.

The subject remembers that he waited until the crossing guard was pre-occupied, then called Alison over to the fence. He told her that he was from the vet's office, and that her mother had sent him to get her because Misty was very sick. In this way he persuaded the girl to come with him. He remembers that she was afraid in the apartment, and kept asking for Misty and crying. He denies any other memories of the killing, saying that it was "the Wolf" who did whatever was done. He also says he now thinks she was the wrong girl, but that the Wolf did not realize that.

Other things he will say about the death of Alison Grayling are that it was "a waste" and that he "doesn't mind paying for it." When asked what he thinks is going to happen to him, he says he doesn't know, but "doesn't mind." He says he doesn't think he should be put to death because "it was really the Wolf" but agrees that some people might not see it that way.

PSYCHOLOGICAL TEST RESULTS: Dr. Larkin administered the Wechsler Adult Intelligence Scale (revised) and the Minnesota Multiphasic Personality Inventory. It appears that the subject has a full-scale intelligence quotient of 108, which is slightly above average. The MMPI results were examined chiefly to detect malingering. The lack of elevation in either the L, F, or K scale of this instrument tends to confirm the examiner's clinical impression that the subject was not malingering or misrepresenting his symptoms. The MMPI results also confirm the examiner's impression that the subject is highly suggestible. Copies of Dr. Larkin's report are provided.

DIAGNOSIS (per DSM-IV):
- SCHIZOPHRENIA, PARANOID TYPE, 295.30. Characteristic symptoms include multiple delusions (bizarre) and affective flattening. The disorder had a marked effect on the interpersonal relations of the subject, and influenced his work behavior as well (although not entirely dysfunctional, his employment was subordinated to his obsessions). Continuous signs of the disorder were present for many months or years. There is no apparent connection to substance abuse.
- PEDOPHILIA, 302.2. Characteristic symptoms include recurrent intense sexually arousing fantasies concerning prepubescent children, related to significant impairment in social and occupational function, as well as at least one known episode of violent and destructive acting-out of these urges.
- The undersigned examiner has not diagnosed any form of dissociative disorder, as he believes the criteria are not met. A different examiner

might, however, perceive some features of dissociation in the subject's narrative about the Wolf, and might diagnose Dissociative Disorder Not Otherwise Specified (300.15). This examiner believes that the Wolf is an attribute of the subject, partially disclaimed or denied, but not a separate identity, and for that reason does not believe that a diagnosis of Dissociative Identity Disorder (300.14) would be appropriate.

CONCLUSIONS:

- The subject was unquestionably suffering from schizophrenia, paranoid type, at the time of the offense, and probably for several years preceding it. He also fits the diagnostic criteria for pedophilia, although this diagnosis has fewer implications for his responsibility for the crime. The pedophilia seems to be of more recent genesis, and his attraction to children is entwined in his paranoid belief system to the extent that it is difficult to separate the effects of the two disorders.

- These disorders interfered significantly with the subject's capacity to conform his conduct to the requirements of law. They had less effect on his ability to appreciate the criminality of his conduct. One must also take into account the very powerful influence the videotape had on the subject's fantasies, plans, and behavior. An ultimate conclusion of the issue of sanity is not here included, per the policy decision made by the Elgin Mental Health Center that examiners should not express an opinion on the ultimate issue until asked to do so. The undersigned remains available to counsel for both sides to discuss the ultimate question if desired.

—Lakshman Gupta, M.D.

I had encountered this reluctance to state an opinion in a pretrial report before, a result of some jurisdictions' prohibition of psychiatric testimony that states the examiner's "ultimate opinion" of the subject's sanity. But I thought I could read Dr. Gupta's opinion between the lines of his careful report. In any event, I reflected, the good doctor's opinion of Leonard Fitzgerald's sanity mattered less to Fitzgerald's fate than the jury's opinion. And they had concluded that the Wolf was insane. But what mattered more than his sanity, for what were beginning to look like our purposes, was the role the videotape *Sunshade Snuffdown* had played in his acts. I made a note to try to find a telephone number for Dr. Gupta, and another to call Andy Kahrlsrud.

It was nearly four, and I expected Peggy to come by on the hour to get the tape. I went looking for Tory. Her office door stood open, but the light was off and she wasn't there. There was nobody in the conference room either, and the VCR in the corner was still and empty. I heard the exterior door open and went back out to the reception area to find Beverly coming in, holding a cardboard cup from the Trident close to her nose as though it contained French perfume. Sometimes the sheer awfulness of Beverly's coffee is too much even for her.

"Ah," she breathed. "Hi Cinda. I didn't want to disturb you when I went out. I put the phones on voicemail."

"Fine," I said shortly. "Where's Tory?"

"Went home, she said. She left you that." She gestured toward my inbox, and the flat brown envelope that lay there.

It was the tape, with one of her FROM THE DESK OF TORY MEADOWS post-it notes stuck on. She had written four words on the slip:

## LET'S GET THIS GUY.

I blinked away a spurting ache behind my eyes, then looked up to see Beverly's eyes on my face. "Have you seen Linc lately?" I asked her. Lincoln Tolkien was a musician and occasional private investigator. He and I were good friends, I thought; he'd worked for me not only on the Smiley case but also on Mariah McKay's lawsuit against her father. He had loved Mariah, as had I, but somehow her death had caused an unspoken break in our relationship. I hadn't spoken with him in many months.

"Only yesterday," Beverly said. "You know he opened an office out in that hideous strip mall."

"No," I said. "He has an office for his PI stuff? He must be doing a lot of business."

"Next door to some Indian restaurant. He says he smells curry in his sleep."

"So you've been seeing him then," I said, a little hurt.

"Just ran into him is all. He still plays bluegrass music on the Mall sometimes, down on the corner by the bank. You want me to call him? Ask him to come by?"

"Not yet," I said. "But I may need his help on this case eventually."

Beverly nodded, then turned back to her computer screen. "Maybe Charley could help with something," she suggested, carefully not looking at my face. "He could use something useful to do."

"Out of work again?" I asked.

"I can't actually remember the last time he was *in* work," she said. "Unless you count writing screenplays and looking things up on the Internet. I'm sort of worried because lately he's been talking about day-trading. You know what that is?"

"Yeah," I said, thinking this sounded pretty bad. "I'll think about it, okay? Maybe there's something he can do." I wanted Charley working for me about as much as I wanted a trip to the spa in Nederland where they do colonic therapy.

"Any time you want to tell me what this is all about," she said.

"I know," I said. "I will, soon, I promise."

The last time I visited Andy Kahrlsrud in his office, it had been a discouraged-looking box lined with rust-stained cinder blocks in a dilapidated building in east Boulder County. He worked at the time for an agency that provided mental health services to rural residents, and seemed to thrive on the challenges. I remember thinking on that occasion that his comfortable overstuffed body, sitting behind a scarred desk, was the only cheerful furnishing in the room. But the building is gone now, a casualty of the relentless gentrification of the former agricultural community of Erie. So is Andy's job with the agency, which decided that a trained social worker could handle the needs of the distressed farm community as well as a clinical psychologist. We had talked on the telephone once or twice since then, and I knew Andy had recently opened a private practice in Boulder, but I hadn't been to his new office until today.

It was certainly a change. His name was etched into a shiny brass plate that kept company with several others at the entrance to a townhouse on 11th Street, just off the Pearl Street Mall. The leaves of the vine that clasped the columns on either side glowed with health, as though polished by hand. As I gripped the handle and opened the door, cool air slid out, slightly scented with cedar. Inside the waiting area, a pastel carpet absorbed most of the sound coming from a CD player in the corner—Enya, it sounded like. The room's only occupant, a gaunt man in khakis and running shoes, perused a *Runner's World* magazine. He didn't look up from it as I entered and sat down. I was ten minutes early.

Three interior doors led from the waiting room—into different consulting rooms or whatever they were called, I imagined. My own experience with therapy had been limited to a brief but useful period after my husband Mike left me years before. It seems odd now that it required several dozen hours with a highly trained professional before I realized that nothing I could do would make Mike into someone else, but at the time it was very helpful. I needed something quite different now, and I had no idea whether my old friend Andy could provide it. I gazed at several vivid Georgia O'Keeffe prints on the walls and wondered not for the first time if it was true what everybody said about them, and if so whether that made them an odd choice for a suite of psychologist's offices.

Presently a kind-faced short woman in a linen shift emerged from the leftmost door. The runner guy finally looked up at this, and she smiled and beckoned to him. He stood up as though reluctant, and they disappeared behind her door just as Andy opened another one and came out.

To my immense pleasure he looked almost exactly the same as ever. Perhaps his reddish beard was trimmed with slightly more care, possibly he had lost a few pounds, but he still had his grin and bearish mien, and still covered his unapologetic spare tire with a plaid flannel shirt. I smiled as I rose to greet him.

"Glad you called, Cinda," he said as he led me into his inside room and directed me to a plump wing chair flanked by a small table holding tissues and a water pitcher with matching glasses. "I've thought about you from time to time."

"I've thought of you, too," I responded. "You've come up in the world, Andy."

He looked around impersonally, as though it were someone else's office, and shrugged. "Not up, I think. Over, maybe. It's nice not to have to wonder whether the building's going to fall down or the air-conditioner's going to fail. And I enjoy my clients, don't get me wrong." But he looked away, toward a quilt that hung on the wall, a bit tattered compared to the other decorations.

"You think you might have been doing more good out there?" I suggested.

He jerked his head back and forth once, banishing the subject. "What's up with you? Trouble in mind?"

"Not in mine. At least that's not what brings me here. I'm pretty good, myself." I brushed my hand through my hair, suddenly self-conscious.

He looked unconvinced. "I worry about you sometimes, Cinda. You still think about Mariah?"

"Of course. Every day." Andy had been trying to help Mariah manage an eating disorder, and to remember a childhood event that had become eclipsed in her memory by time and sorrow. In the suit we filed against her father, my success would have had to depend on his in helping Mariah back to her memory. In the end both ventures failed, because an assassin who was looking for me killed Mariah one night while she was driving my car.

"I do too," he confessed. "You ever think if you'd done something different she wouldn't have died?"

"Are you therapizing me, Dr. Kahrlsrud? Because that's not what I came here for."

"Asking you these kinds of questions would be very bad therapy, Cinda."

"What then?"

"Friendship, I suppose. And I ask partly for myself. I know I wonder sometimes whether I failed her. Another thing I'd never say to a client. But I assume you're not here for therapy. Otherwise I would have had to ask you all kinds of questions about your frigging insurance company and you don't hear me doing that, do you?"

I smiled. "No. I'm sorry, Andy. I know you were hurt by her death, as much as I was. I wasn't thinking." But I was. I was thinking, Let's move on.

He nodded, not ready to change the subject. "You know, I've never lost a client before. Had quite a few on suicide watch, some other eating disorder sufferers—they're really at risk. A drunk who wouldn't stay out of his Porsche after he'd had too many. They're all still alive. Struggling, some of them, but still alive."

"Yeah," I said shortly, focusing my suddenly aching eyes on the tissue box. "Yeah, that's good," but I was thinking, resentfully, that it must be nice to have only one dead former client. Jason Smiley, executed more cleanly and lawfully by the state of Colorado but just as dead, joined Mariah in my bad dreams sometimes. It was irrational, I knew, but I wanted someone else to know the feeling of visiting The Gallery of Dead Clients. The Ones You Didn't Save.

"What, Cinda?"

"Nothing. Can I tell you what I wanted to see you about?"

"Sure." He sat back and crossed his large legs, his thighs pushing against the seams of his jeans.

"First, do you ever do forensic work? In-court stuff?"

"Sometimes. Don't like it much. Most of us don't. You want us to tell you how many angels on the pinhead, is there free will, that sort of thing. Who am I to say whether someone's responsible for their acts or not? That's a job for a philosopher."

"Could I pay you to give me an opinion on a matter?"

"One like that? Insanity?"

"Not exactly." And I told him the story of Leonard Fitzgerald, Alison Grayling, *Sunshade Snuffdown,* and the Wolf.

He listened to me without interrupting, fingering his beard thought-fully. When I finished he said, "Why are you doing this case, Cinda?"

"That's not what I'm here to talk about."

"Okay. But maybe you should talk to someone about it. I trust you and Tory are working on this together. Do you and she talk about it?"

"Andy, I don't need your advice about how to do my job, okay?"

"You just need my help to do it."

"If you're willing."

He inclined his head toward the briefcase I had brought with me. "What do you have for me to look at, then?"

"The psych report on Leonard Fitzgerald, done after his arrest. And the videotape."

"You have a copy of the tape?"

I nodded.

"And on what question do you want my opinion?"

"I want to know," I said, "whether Leonard Fitzgerald would have killed that little girl if he had never seen the tape."

"What you lawyers call *cause in fact?*"

"That's right. Or maybe, but I know this is a little harder, whether he would have killed anyone if he'd never seen the tape. If the answer to that was no, that would be even better." I handed him the report and a copy I'd made of the tape. It was at best a second-generation copy, but even so I'd stored it in a ziplock bag because I didn't like to touch it.

"I thought you said he was obsessed with porn and had a shelf full of tapes and worked at a video store. He must have seen thousands of porno-graphic tapes."

"So?"

He looked at the black rectangle inside the plastic bag. "How am I supposed to sort out the contribution this tape made to his acts from the contributions made by all of the others? You realize that there are those who say that only God can have the kind of knowledge you're claiming we can achieve."

"I'd be glad to call God to testify if I can get him served with a subpoena. It would make for a great trial, wouldn't it? *And now, Your Honor, as God is my witness, may the bailiff please summon Him from the witness room?*"

Andy smiled wryly. "He'd have a lot more credibility than I do."

"I just—you know. Hate to ask Him. I think He must be too busy."

Andy touched the side of his waist and I realized his buzzer must have sounded. He peered at it and then looked back at me apologetically. "Sorry, I have to make a call. May be quick. Can you sit here a minute while I use the phone in the conference room?

I nodded, glad to have a minute to sort out the thoughts that seemed to be scribbling over my mental outline of things I wanted to say in this meeting.

God was very big in Texas, but our father did not believe in organized religion, and Dana and I were free to sleep late and read books and work on our suntans on Sunday mornings while our friends went to church, although Dana often attended with a friend at whose house she had slept over, having packed her pearls and cashmere sweater carefully in plastic bags before setting them into her overnight case. This was good practice for her later conversion to Baptism. She had to take classes before Jerry's minister would marry them in his church with the enormous stained glass windows, but she had a good head start.

As I remember, my elementary school briefly experimented with the recitation of a blessing in the lunchroom; it occurs to me now this may have been prompted by the Kennedy assassination. But some of the Jewish parents objected to the invocation of Jesus, and some of the Christian parents objected to any prayer that failed to invoke Jesus, and in any event nobody's God could have been very pleased by the undercurrent of shoving and suppressed giggling during the imperfect silence, and this didn't last too long. I believe the first time I ever experienced reverent prayer was at a football game. I mean in person, not on the television. Even though we didn't pray in my house, of course I remember watching television with my mother that week after President Kennedy died. President Johnson, who was from Texas (but even so, my mother did not seem to like him much), was telling us that we had to have the something, and the something else, and the wisdom to know the difference. This was the Serenity Prayer, my mother explained, and I asked her why not the Wisdom Prayer, and she didn't know. I may have prayed along a little because like most of us I was scared, but this Serenity Prayer was on television, not in person.

I'm pretty sure the first serious in-person prayer I ever participated in was before a junior high football game, a home game, and the first thing I ever prayed for was for the Franklin Falcons to beat the Hayes Hornets. The prayer was offered by our principal, speaking over the crowd noise through a portable loudspeaker on our side of the stadium. *Bless this contest, oh heavenly Father, to the nourishment of our spirits, and our bodies to Thy service. Please grant, if it please you, that no young man be injured seriously in this game tonight, and of course Thy will be done, but we pray it pleases You to grant victory to our fine young men and our excellent student body, which is the best this year that we've had in many years. In His name we pray.*

Amen, murmured everyone, including all of the girlfriends I was there with, and I did too. I don't remember whether the Falcons beat the Hornets or not, but I do remember thinking that the principal of Rutherford B. Hayes Junior High School was probably praying with his smaller group of fans, on the other side of the field, for more or less the same thing, or should I say the opposite thing. I can't claim I really wondered how God decided—like, did He investigate which school had the finer student body that year? Even at thirteen I knew it was idiotic to think about that. I was more puzzled about why nobody seemed very concerned about the position they were putting Him in. And then there was that worrying part of the prayer in which it was asked that no young man be injured *seriously.* Was that because it was thought to be too pushy to ask God that no young man be injured at all? Or just that slight injury is so much part of football that to pray for no injuries would have been asking for an unsatisfying game?

In defense of my intelligence, I want to say I knew there was something wrong with me for asking these questions, even to myself. I couldn't evade the knowledge that there was some mystery to which I had not been admitted. The proceedings that followed the prayer seemed to me to have nothing to do with God, but what did I know? Our family was not very well acquainted with Him, and those who were more so seemed to take it for granted that the football prayer was a proper transaction in their relationship. I tried not to think about the subject too much, but still this experience deepened some essential familiar confusion that I could not explain to anyone.

The inner door opened and Andy was back, carrying a mug of something hot. "I got myself a coffee, too. Would you like one, Cinda?"

"No thanks, Andy."

"So what are you so deep in thought about?"

I shook my head and I blew out a huge sigh as discouragement washed over me in a wave. "My mind was wandering. Listen, I know it's probably impossible to sort out all of the causation questions. But one thing at a time, okay? Will you just read the report and watch the tape, and then talk to me again?"

"I won't deny I'm interested in this, Cinda. There's a lot of research on this pornography question and I've tried to keep up on it. If this goes any further, is there a chance I could interview this Fitzgerald myself?"

"I think so," I said wearily, standing up. "Call me when you're done, okay? And Andy?"

Already scanning the psych report, he looked up impatiently. "Yeah?"

"The tape—it's pretty rough to watch. Actually I wish I'd never seen it myself."

He waved a hand backward in dismissal, then went back to reading the report. "I'll call you."

Mindy Cookson's television set was small, with a built-in VCR, and she kept it in her bedroom. Brianna Bainbridge and Mindy and I sat uncomfortably around the edges of the exuberant quilt covering Mindy's bed; Brianna, in control as always, wielded the remote to start the tape playing. The blinds were drawn against the outdoor sunshine and I could not see Mindy's expression, but Brianna's face was in my line of sight and I could discern it in the light reflected from the screen. It did not tell me anything.

I had approached Brianna first, concerned that what I had in mind would somehow violate Mindy's confidentiality agreement, since I was not certain of its terms. She called me back a day later to say that Mindy would watch the tape so long as Brianna was present, and so long as I understood that Mindy would not say anything during or afterward until the two of them had an opportunity to consult.

I would have given a great deal not to watch that videotape again, but I could not ask Mindy Cookson for something I was unwilling to do myself. As the vignette with the parents and the child unfolded, I found that at least the tormenting sexual heat I had experienced the first time I saw it did not reoccur. There was only sickness, and the desire to turn away. Nobody asked that the film be interrupted; it ran for eighteen minutes before Brianna rose to hit the rewind button and open the blinds. We were silent as the machine whirred and whined. Mindy, who had greeted me on my arrival with a giggle and a glass of lemonade, kept her face turned away and her shoulders hunched. I was grateful when Brianna handed me the tape and said coldly, in unmistakable dismissal, "I'll call you later today or tomorrow." I drove home slowly, the video's images circulating through my body like a toxic substance in the blood. I could have blown a perfect .00 on a breathalyzer, but if I'd had to perform a roadside sobriety test I think I would have performed like an old drunk whose liver refuses to soak up any more booze.

It was almost ten that night when Brianna called me at home. She barely acknowledged my clumsy effort to voice my gratitude to her and her client.

"Forget it," she said. "Here's the deal. We didn't have this conversation, she doesn't know anything, she never saw the tape, got it?"

"Okay," I said uncertainly, wondering if I was promising to perjure myself in some half-imagined future proceeding.

"The actor, the one that played the father. She's pretty sure it's a man she met once, stage name Joel Derringer, real name unknown. Probably early thirties by now. Used to work in fairly upscale porn, the kind that actually has a plot and takes longer than a day to shoot. Like most guys in the business, had wood problems eventually and directors stopped using him because he wasn't reliable. Probably had to start doing the violent stuff because it was that or get out of the business."

"What are wood problems?" I asked.

"Can't keep it up," she said impatiently. "Look, male porn actors aren't hired for their looks, like the women in soft porn, or their availability to be hurt and humiliated like the women in hard core. The director requires one thing from them, the ability to produce an erection on demand. When you're shooting an entire film in one day, you can't have a crew standing around waiting for wood. An actor also has to be able to come on command, for the money shot. These days, usually in a woman's face, since that seems to be a box office favorite." She spoke without apparent emotion.

"Oh," I said faintly.

"I'm not sure you're ready to litigate this case, Cinda."

"I'm trying to get ready. Thanks for the help."

"There was no help. We never talked about this."

"Right," I said wearily. "Anything more that might help me locate this Joel Derringer? Could that have been his real name?"

She snorted. "Not bloody likely. All the male actors in porn have stage names borrowed from weapons. They're Dirk or Magnum or Colt. What does that tell you about the attitude toward women underlying even the most soft-core productions?"

I got it, but I was tired of participating in her professorial dialogues. "Any of them called Woody?" I said instead.

"No," she said shortly. I guess it wasn't very funny at that.

"Can Mindy remember where she last saw the guy? The name of the film, or the studio, anything?"

"San Fernando Valley, but that won't help you that much. That's where most of the pornography in the world is produced. Some studio way out Van Nuys, north of Sherman Oaks, she says. She thinks the film had the word *Vixen* in the title. *Split Vixen* or maybe *Bent Vixen,* something like that. There was an actress in it named Gabriella, very in demand at the time, but who knows now? People have a short shelf life in the business."

"Anything else?" I said, writing on my bedside notepad.

"That's all."

"Thanks again," I said.

"We didn't have—"

"I know," I said, and hung up.

There wasn't a student yearbook at law school—that would have been thought frivolous—but there was a composite photograph made for graduation, and all of us got copies. Miraculously I had kept mine, through

moves and divorce and the other mild cataclysms of middle-class life. That
night I pulled it out of the creaky wooden filing cabinet where I keep tax
returns and love letters and wedding pictures and other unwelcome re-
minders of past mistakes. The individual pictures were in alphabetical order so I found his easily in the array: M. Raphael Russell. Almost all the
portraits were dead-on but he had turned his shoulder to the camera, and
looked over it into the lens with a confidence so breathtaking that once
you caught his eye you had no interest in the pictures on either side. Most
of the guys were wearing that goofy flyaway hair of the period. It made
them look dated and in some cases borderline unhygienic but Rafe, no less
shaggy than the others, carried his cloud of frizz like a crown. He was from
old West Texas cattle money; the M at the front of his name stood for
Marlett, his grandfather's name as well as that of the grandfather's ranch
and the small town it surrounded. I was from new North Dallas lawyer
money, and not nearly as much of it. Still, when we first met in Property
class I believed that our shared histories as Texans transplanted to Colorado
gave us something in common.

Rafe was wild in all the usual ways of the time—motorcycle accidents,
dope smoking, even, it was rumored, getting young women pregnant. His
old man would threaten to cut him off from time to time but Rafe, twenty-
three and an only child, knew that was the least of his worries. Neither his
father nor anyone else, including our cranky Property professor, who ragged
on him endlessly for his careless class preparation, seemed to damage the
confidence that had bred Rafe's smile.

We learned a lot of Latin phrases in the first year of law school: *habeas
corpus, animus furandi, nunc pro tunc, sua sponte.* Rafe thought it was all a
tremendous funny goof, and used to make up his own expressions, like
*habeas caffeinus exigus,* or get me some coffee right now. But his motto was
a phrase invented by someone else: *illegitimati non carborundum.* Don't let
the bastards grind you down.

We dated a few times in law school, but by our second year I was living
with Michael, a graduate student in English whom I later married. I don't
think anything would have come of it, anyway; Rafe was a hit-and-run
artist. I knew he had gone to work right after graduation for a Los Angeles
firm specializing in entertainment law. The periodic law school alumni
reports (which I read addictively even though I never sent in bulletins
about my own uneven progress through the world) had traced his moves

from there to a famous talent agency to Robert de Niro's production company and, for the last five years, Rose Brothers—that creation of immigrant siblings that had grown into one of the four largest film studios in the world.

Once, about ten years ago, he had called me on a Saturday afternoon from Denver. I could hear party sounds in the background. He said he had come to town to close a financing deal for a de Niro film, and that a celebration was afoot now that the ink was drying on the paper. Could I come join him? We could reminisce about old times and catch up with each other. I can't remember what obligation I told him would prevent me from agreeing, but whatever it was I had made it up on the spot. Rafe had too much charm and too little staying power, and I didn't want to start thinking about him again as someone who could be part of my life. But that was then.

Only two operators and a personal assistant mediated my call. The PA sounded weary when she acknowledged my explanation that Rafe and I were old friends, in a way that made me suspect she'd heard the claim many times before. She put me on hold and I began to compose a message to leave for him, but in seconds there was a click and then his lazy voice, unchanged from the first time I had ever heard it reciting in class. "Bet you're sorry now that you didn't come to that party," he said.

"The regret has practically ruined the last decade of my life."

"You know everybody got naked before it was over and they threw Bob into the pool. You'd have some great stories to tell if you'd been there."

"I knew you back in the day, remember? Even without that one I could tell plenty of stories about you. And will if you ever run for public office and they're worth money."

He laughed easily, his rich guffaw so familiar I could feel the years sliding away as though they'd been weeks. "Sorry to disappoint you, but that's not going to happen."

"If I had a chance to see you, you could tell me some more stories."

"When are you going to be here?"

It had always been that way, our conversations like machine-gun fire: no time to think, just *rat-a-tat-tat.* "I was thinking of next week."

"Hold on." He bellowed something over a muffled phone, and was back in seconds. "Tuesday. Lunch. Want to eat at the studio commissary?"

"Sure."

"See you then. One o'clock in my office. I swim at noon." And he hung up, before I could ask how to find his office. Sighing, I rose to look for Beverly and ask her to book a Monday flight to Los Angeles.

There was no room service at the downscale hotel in Sherman Oaks that I had chosen for its proximity to the San Fernando Valley, so I ate dinner out of the vending machine after arriving late on Monday night. Then I fell asleep reading one of those forgettable hotel magazines that you see everywhere, although this one did have some local flavor: at least 50 percent of its ad content was for various forms of cosmetic surgery. There was no concierge either, but even the teenaged desk clerk on duty late the next morning knew how to direct me to Rose Brothers. "Most of the other studios have moved to Burbank or somewhere," she told me, her eyes alight, "but Rosebrose is still in Hollywood."

"Will I be able to drive in?" I asked.

"I think there's a parking lot across the street. Are you going for the tour? I can call to make a reservation for you."

"Actually I'm meeting an old friend who works there."

"That is so cool. Is he in, like, production?" She ran her tongue quickly over her lips; I don't think she was even aware she'd done it.

I didn't want to encourage this girl's fantasies. "Not really. Food service actually."

She drew her breath in audibly. "He must be like a famous chef, then."

"He's in the, uh, postconsumption end of it."

"You mean, like—?"

I nodded seriously. "Dishwashing, laundry, like that, He's very very good at it. Terrific at napkins, irons them and everything."

She nodded brusquely and turned back to her computer terminal, no longer interested in me. "Whatever. Have a nice day."

The uniformed attendant at the imposing and ornate stucco entrance gate listened politely as I explained that I had an appointment with Vice Pres. Rafe Russell, then turned to a telephone and poked efficiently at its buttons. "Just a moment," she said to me kindly, so I stepped aside while she conferred with the next persons in line. After a couple of minutes, a small vehicle like a golf cart drove up and the driver, a young African American woman with a head full of twisting curls and arresting light gray eyes, beckoned to me and said, "Ms. Hayes?"

"Yeah, that's me."

"Hi, I'm Liz. Climb in. I'll drive you to Mr. Russell's bungalow."

She was an intern, she explained, working for a semester at the studio as part of her credits toward a degree in film arts from UCLA. "Usually I drive the tram, for VIP studio tours." She pointed to a vehicle ahead of us pulling an open-air trailer with seating for ten or so.

"I always wonder what people saw on those VIP tours that the rest of us didn't."

Liz smiled as she deftly piloted our little craft around a tight corner, avoiding a rack of costumes being pushed along by a perspiring woman. "We don't like to let this out but the truth is it's exactly the same tour, only you get to ride instead of walk. People are always showing up saying they know this person or that person and demanding special treatment. Sometimes they say they're friends with Cal Rose, and he's been dead for forty years. So the attendant just gets on the phone and says, so the person can hear them, 'We need a guide for a VIP tour, right away.' And then they send me with the tram. And then after the person climbs on I point to the next eight people in line and say, 'I wonder if you would mind if we invite these other people to join you on the VIP tour?' and they always look pleased as punch and go, like, 'No, no, that would be splendid,' and then they act like the host of the whole group for two hours. They'll turn to one of the people who came along and they're like, 'Well, Herb, what did you think of the prop warehouse? Fascinating, wasn't it? I'll bet they didn't see *that* on the regular tour!'"

"So," I said, "what did they say when they called you after I showed up at the window? Another loser for the VIP tour?"

"Not a bit," she said warmly. "I understand you really are an old friend of Vice President Russell. I don't know him, but everyone says he's very good."

"I bet he is. We were in law school together, back in Boulder. He was good at everything."

Liz pulled the cart up in front of a small one-story stucco building with well-tended window boxes stuffed with geraniums and pansies. "Here you are. His assistant Louise will be expecting you."

We were sitting in the commissary, which I had somehow expected to look like a slightly glamorized version of my high school lunchroom; in fact it resembled a very nice restaurant. A fresh-faced waitress who reminded me unsettlingly of Mindy Cookson took my order for Caesar salad with chicken, and Rafe's for gazpacho and a baguette, no butter.

"Have to watch it," he said as he unfolded his napkin, in apparent comment on his abstemious lunch, although I had said nothing. I caught a faint whiff of chlorine emanating from the vicinity of his shirt collar.

"How was your swim?"

"Excellent. Maybe I should have invited you to join me."

I shook my head. "Not my sport, but thanks for the thought. Rafe, you look wonderful. The years have been good to you. And you're a vice president here? That's an amazing accomplishment." He did look terrific, his dark bushy hair trimmed into a modest but impressive sculpture by some talented artist of the scissors, tanned arms muscular and glowing below the sleeves of his polo shirt, waist trim where the shirt tucked into expensive-looking tailored slacks. But something was gone, the mischievous lift of his eyebrows or the tilt of his head that had once conveyed that he didn't take any of it—Law Review, grades, job, money—very seriously.

"There are about seventy-five vice presidents on this lot," he said. "It's not a very exclusive club. 'Scuse me." He turned away to flag down a passing busboy and ask for a Calistoga water with lime. "Would you like one, Cinda? While we wait?"

I shook my head. "So what do you do?"

"This and that. Deals. Financing, licensing, distribution. Foreign rights, a lot of stuff with the Internet now. It's a tougher game every year. For a while video was going to destroy us, then save us. Now I think, I don't know, maybe technology will destroy us after all. The music industry is hitting the problem worst and first, but we'll all have to face it soon. It's practically impossible to eliminate piracy. Who wants to pay to go to a theater when you can log on to a Web site and watch a pirated version over streaming video on a thirty-eight-inch hi-res screen in your own living room?"

I tried to think of an encouraging observation. "So it's pretty challenging, what you do."

"It is. Only maybe not in the way that I used to—well, fuck that. We all had to grow up, didn't we? What about you?"

"I guess I grew up. I have a law practice in Boulder, one partner, plenty of work, a good life. I lost a couple of clients lately and can't quite seem to shake it off, but otherwise life is good."

"Everybody loses clients. They move on, they decide to go with some guy they met at the country club, am I right?"

"Sure, but I lost these two worse than that. They died."

"Oh. I'm sorry. But not your fault, surely." He sounded genuine, but he was looking at something behind me and I saw him smile and wave.

I shrugged. "I don't think so, but I don't know. Maybe that's what bothers me."

He touched my shoulder as he turned to accept his water from the waitress, and when he turned back he said, "Sorry. You gotta press the flesh around here, or at least catch the right eyes. So, you marry again after getting rid of that mope Mike?"

"No. I do have a—a long-distance relationship. He lived in Boulder until about three years ago, then moved to New York. Actually," I said, as the thought struck me, "you might know him. He was in law school with us. Sam Holt?"

"No way! You and Sam are together?"

Were we? I shook my head. "New York's a long way from Boulder," I said. "But we still see each other."

Rafe's eyes looked into the past, and he smiled suddenly. "You know I tried to get him to play with Rasta Bones—that reggae band I played with? He was an awesome sax player in those days. But he was too much into the jazz thing—Charlie Parker and Miles Davis. He thought reggae was simpleminded. I can't tell you how many times I tried to explain that it wasn't the music that was simpleminded, just most of the musicians. He never saw the difference."

Talking to Rafe about Sam made me uncomfortable, so I changed the subject. "Anyway," I said, "you? Are you with anyone?"

"Nah. No woman will put up with me once she really knows me. And dating's too easy in this town. Sometimes I think I could hit the intercom and ask Louise to get me a date for that night the way I ask her to call and get me into the studio barbershop that afternoon. I mean, I really think she'd do it and never even ask any questions. How weird is that? And I used to think it was just great to live in a place where that sort of thing was a possibility."

"Not any more?"

He looked at me then. The marks of time around his eyes were attractive, striking in their contrast between the paleness within and the sun-darkened skin without. I thought he was about to say something in reply, but instead he looked over my shoulder again and observed, "Ah, here's our lunch."

As we ate we talked of old friends and reminisced about law school and Rasta Bones. "I was so blown away that those guys would let a white man play with them," he said, "that I pretended not to notice they were dealing weed out of our van during breaks. I'm lucky I didn't get busted right before we took the bar exam. But still. Damn, we played some great music." He looked away into the middle distance and something about his small secret smile produced a flash of memory: me and Mike holding hands at a table in Tulagi's, the old nightclub on the Hill in Boulder, watching Rafe on the stage through the haze of sweet smoke that had always enveloped the room, his cloudy hair crazed, his eyes red from the smoke and the marijuana as he leaned into the mike and sang. They ended every night with "One Love." We were so young, I thought, and despite the drugs and the alcohol and what I suppose was the promiscuity, so innocent.

"Do you still play your bass?" I asked him.

"Not much. I'm not good enough to make it a worthwhile investment of my time." And so the moment passed and our conversation moved on and turned desultory until, over a dessert of strawberry granita and cappuccino, Rafe finally asked what had brought me to Los Angeles.

"A case I'm working on. I'm trying to find someone, or something, and I thought you might be able to help." I told him about Alison Grayling and *Sunshade Snuffdown* and Joel Derringer and the film called something *Vixen,* and an actress named Gabriella. "Any of those ring a bell?"

He seemed affronted by the question. "No. Not likely to, Cinda. That's a completely different industry, another world. I'm not saying that Rose Brothers produces art like Mozart or Van Gogh. Most of our work is, I'll be honest, commercial, aimed at a large market. But the stuff you're talking about—it's the lowest common denominator. The actors don't act, the directors are guys who would never be trusted with a legitimate project. No production values whatsoever. The producers are scumbags. I mean, I don't really know anyone in that world, or want to."

"I understand. I didn't really think you did, Rafe. I just thought you might have some ideas where I could start. For example, I've been told that sometimes an actress might move from porn into mainstream film, after changing her name. I thought you might know of someone like that, someone who might talk to me."

He shook his head. "That's a myth, frankly, about the actresses. No legitimate studio is going to use an actress who has that kind of a history. And furthermore, from what you say about that tape, it sounds like it was probably produced offshore. Jamaica, Puerto Rico, or even more likely some little island neither of us has ever heard of whose economy depends on porn films and money laundering. Also, I doubt very much it was an actual snuff film. Special effects, probably."

I nodded. "You may be right. Only I was told that this actor was in it who had also been in a film made around here, in the Valley."

"Yeah, I get it, this Joel whoever. Who told you that? Are you sure they knew what they were talking about?"

"Someone I showed the tape to recognized him," I said uneasily, remembering my promise to Brianna.

"Someone in the business?"

"The person doesn't want to be known, Rafe. For good reason." The conversation was beginning to make me very uneasy, so I was relieved when he reached for the beeper on his belt. I had not heard a sound.

"Had it set to vibrate," he explained with a wry smile. "Hold on a second, will you?" He scrutinized the tiny screen, then said, "Will you excuse me a minute?"

"Sure."

He walked to the edge of the room and punched a few numbers into his cell phone. The waitress came by and offered me another cappuccino. I declined with some regret, aware that I was jittery enough without the extra caffeine, wondering whether I could salvage anything from the remainder of the afternoon. Rafe returned to the table in a few minutes.

"Sorry, Cinda. Little fire I have to put out." He put his hand between my shoulder blades as I rose. "Listen, let me think about your problem. Maybe I can come up with someone or something that would be helpful. Did you bring a copy of the tape with you to L.A.?"

I nodded. "Shall I give you the number of my hotel? I don't have a cell phone. Must be the only person in L.A. without one."

He smiled, his eyebrows twitching like back in the day. "I hear Jodie Foster refuses to carry one."

"Well then, me and Jodie." I reached into my bag and found a slender pad of hotel notepaper I had taken from my room. "This is the place. I'm in room 709. Shall I write that down?"

He grimaced slightly as he read the hotel's name. "Maybe you should come stay at my place, Cinda. I've got lots of room."

"Wouldn't be a good idea, Rafe." His eyebrows dropped a degree or two. "I mean that as a compliment, buddy."

"Okay, then. I'll ring you later. Louise is calling the kid with the cart to come back to the front commissary door for you. Let me walk you out."

He kissed me lightly and left me standing in the butter-colored sunshine as he walked away. He did not take the direction toward his bungalow, so I assumed he had been summoned to a meeting. While I waited for the cart, I allowed myself the guilty pleasure of thinking about what would have happened if I had accepted his offer of lodging. I imagined a sparkling swimming pool, a cabana, gin and tonics, maybe some old reggae music, some aching hymn by Bob or Rita Marley on a primo sound system as we watched azure waves curling onto a beach below the enormous picture windows.

It was a rather complete, if preposterous, fantasy. But I couldn't overlook the circumstance that there was no sex in it. Why not? I asked myself. It wasn't out of loyalty to Sam; I had never thought the life of the imagination called for loyalty. Anyway, I had not spoken to Sam since Chicago, unless you count a couple of noncommittal e-mails. It was just, as I was slowly coming to acknowledge, that ever since Sam and I watched *Sunshade Snuffdown*, thinking about sex made me uneasy. Never mind having it. These unwelcome thoughts were interrupted by the arrival of Liz, cheerful in her khakis and blue oxford shirt with the *Rose Bros.* logo over the pocket, jingling keys between her long fingers.

"Hi, you ready? I left the cart around the corner. Listen, you want to see anything else before you leave the lot? I could probably find a soundstage where they're filming, or maybe you'd like to see the back lot."

"I could watch the shooting of a Rose Brothers movie?"

Liz shook her head. "The studio doesn't actually have any of its own films in production on the lot right now. We have several projects shooting on location elsewhere, but nothing here."

"Then what would we be seeing?"

"Television," she said. "Most of the soundstages are shooting television shows. The studio rents its facilities to the networks. And to film-production companies that don't have their own facilities. Most don't, you know. I'd have to check because the director can close the soundstage if he wants, but I bet I could find us at least a television episode to watch."

"I never knew all that," I said. But I wasn't very attracted to the idea of watching a sitcom being made, and I wouldn't have felt right spending Peggy Grayling's money to swan around L.A. like a tourist. "Better not take the time, I guess. I've got some work I need to go do. Thanks for the thought, though."

She lifted her shoulders and let them fall again. "No prob. Shall I take you back to the front gate?"

"Sure."

On the short cruise back in the little cart she asked me about Boulder. "I hear it's beautiful," she said. "Maybe I'll go there someday."

"It is beautiful," I agreed, surprising myself with the warmth of this endorsement.

"Not too many black people, I've heard," said Liz frankly.

"I'm afraid that's right, too," I said, thinking of Sam. And then on impulse, "Liz, you don't by any chance know anything about pornographic films, do you?"

She looked at me in surprise, as though reassessing my character. "It's for this work I'm doing," I added hastily. "A professional project. I was thinking you might have come across something in film school."

"You know," she said, "there *is* a course on sexuality in film at my school. I didn't take it, but one of my friends did. I guess a lot of it's about porn, at least that's what I've heard. The professor's sort of a character or something."

"Could you give me his name?"

"Her," said Liz, pulling the little cart up to the gate. "Sure. Do you have something to write on?"

I had surprisingly little trouble getting hold of Prof. Evelyn Gravehurst. I called the general number at UCLA, mentioned her name, and was connected to her office. As I mentally rehearsed what I would say to an answering machine or secretary, she came on the line.

"Gravehurst," she said brusquely.

I explained how I came to have her name and stammered out some barely coherent version of my mission, which wasn't all that clear even in my mind. "I don't suppose there's any chance you would have any time to speak with me in the next day or so?"

Rather to my astonishment she said, "Why not?" without asking me any further questions. "This paper I'm working on is beginning to bore me to *distraction*. Where are you right now?"

"Ah—at my hotel," I said, naming it. "But it's not a very nice one, I'm afraid. Do you want to name some place we could meet?"

"I know that hotel—it's not too far from here. That will be fine. There's a cocktail lounge, isn't there?"

"There is," I said reluctantly. "I haven't actually been in it, but it looks pretty small and sort of grimy."

"Perfect," she said. "I'm going to leave right now, because the traffic will be *dire* before long. I'll meet you in the lounge in forty-five minutes."

It was more like an hour and ten minutes. Twice I rose to greet women who entered the bar's cavelike darkness alone. The first woman, an attractive blonde in a gray business suit, shook her head slightly when I said "Professor Gravehurst?"; she found a solitary table against the back wall. The second seemed less likely, a crew-cut redhead in shorts, platform sandals, and an ankle-circling tattoo, but even so I gave her a questioning look. She barely glanced at me before heading for the same table. Before long the two women were holding hands and whispering over tall slushy white drinks, the candle on their table flickering with their breath as they shared secrets I would never know.

Two or three couples entered and took tables over the next twenty minutes while I watched CNN on the television behind the bar. Seeing a small commotion at the entrance, I looked up again to see a tall woman with a pale painted face under an explosion of dark hair peering into the room. She was wearing fishnet stockings and a micro skirt, rather obviously a hooker, and when I looked up again she was sashaying away, back out toward the registration desk, the hem of her dress barely clearing her crotch. Looking for her date, I supposed. But a moment later she was back, this time accompanied by the same desk clerk I had spoken with earlier, who was for some reason pointing at me. Even then, my mind resisted the obvious conclusion, but the hooker nodded to the clerk, crossed the room, and sat down unceremoniously across from me.

"Sorry," she said, pulling a cigarette case out of a gaudy leather shoulder bag decorated with grinning suns and mysteriously smiling moons. "Traffic was psychotic."

"Professor Gravehurst?"

"And you were—Cindy Someone?" She reached into the bag again and withdrew a lighter shaped like a fish complete with mother-of-pearl scales, a few of them missing.

"Cinda Hayes. From Boulder, Colorado. You were so kind to make this trip, especially for a stranger."

She shook off my thanks with a piece of the same gesture she employed to light a slender dark-brown cigarette, or cigar, I wasn't sure which. It had a bitter, rank smell to it.

The bartender, a heavy woman in exquisite makeup, was with us instantly. "You know better than that, hon," she said to us cryptically. I frowned in confusion, but it appeared she was not talking to me.

"Well, fuckadoodle, what are you—the fire department?" said my companion.

"No, hon, just a girl trying to make a living who's going to get fired if I can't get you to put that thing out, or take it out. Now, you could sit on the patio out there and you'd be fine. I'll make sure your glasses get refilled and all. What about it?"

"Well," said Evelyn Gravehurst, with evident exasperation. "I guess we don't have any choice." She collected her bag and swayed toward a small door under a sign that said PATIO. I followed her, squinting as my eyes encountered the hazy brightness of the day.

"This is just as bad as where you live," she observed, sliding under one of the four empty wrought-iron tables inside the dusty enclosure.

"Sorry?" Before sitting down I swiped at the gritty-looking chair seat ineffectually with the paper napkin I'd brought along.

"Smoke," she said, blowing out a wide stream of the stuff. "I was at a conference in Boulder last year, and after a day of utterly *drear* lectures and the like some of us went out to a little bar, where we were told it's actually *against the law* to smoke anywhere in your city. Can that *be,* I wondered, but I was *assured* so."

"Not in the whole *city,*" I protested, falling involuntarily into her conversational rhythms, "just not in restaurants, or bars."

"Or in any university building, or in my *hotel* room, or in anyone's *car* since they've all taken out the ashtrays and put in little cup holders. Outdoors, maybe, if you don't bother the *trees,* but it was *January,* it was *arctic.* I'm telling you, it's Prohibition all over again. So," she said abruptly, "you want to know about porno movies?" She crossed her legs, themselves crisscrossed with the black fishnet, with little apparent concern for the brevity of her skirt.

*I see London,* said a child's voice in my memory. *I see France.* But I nodded, trying not to smile. "I'm told you are a world-recognized expert."

She studied me shrewdly, sitting still for the first time. Out here in the bright shade I could see that she was much younger and more attractive than the wild hair and heavy makeup suggested. "So," she said again, puffing on the vile little cigarette, "being a lawyer from Boulder, I bet you went to law school right there in town, didn't you?"

I nodded. "Quite a few years ago."

"And so you must be friends with Prof. Brianna Bainbridge? Such a *brilliant* woman!" Her tone was sarcastic.

"I've met her," I agreed cautiously. "The school is very proud to have hired her," I said, then added "I guess" when I saw scorn gathering in her expression.

"Carrie Nation in Armani," she said decisively. "Confounds the signifier with the signified, has no ear for nuance or irony, essentialist to the core of her being."

"Yeah," I said, nodding. "I've, um, heard others say that too." Was I going to be forced to participate in some weird postmodern academic debate here? I wasn't prepared to defend Brianna Bainbridge against the charge of essentialism. I didn't even know what it was exactly, except I gathered it was bad. I had a small flash of inspiration. "Actually," I said, truthfully if disloyally, "a lot of the time I can't even understand what she's saying."

"Well, *exactly,*" said Gravehurst more amicably. "Anyway, faulty phenomenology aside, she's certainly no friend of the First Amendment. Now, what was your interest exactly?"

"I'm researching the, ah, erotic film industry in the San Fernando Valley. For a project I'm working on. And I was told you were an expert."

Evidently *project* and *researching* were the right buzzwords. She didn't ask for any further details. "Call me Evelyn," she said, stubbing out the half-smoked cylinder just as a waiter joined us. "What are we drinking?"

The answer was a Cosmo for her, an unimaginative glass of white wine for me. The wine arrived sour and lukewarm, but she sipped down her drink with every appearance of relish; she was waving for another inside five minutes. While we drank, she explained her own work to me. "My dissertation was in Latin American cinema, particularly the Mexican films of Luis Buñuel. You know Buñuel?"

"I thought he was French," I said, surprising myself that I even knew that much.

"Yes," she said triumphantly, "and most people don't know that he made quite a few films in Mexico, because every kind of *cost* associated with filmmaking was so much lower in that country. He did some very interesting work there, although the films are hard to find. The UCLA archive has the only prints of some of them. But anyway—can we have another round?" I signaled for the waiter. "Anyway," she continued, "I got the job here, and started work on a book based on the dissertation. Only I got sidetracked somehow. I started thinking about Buñuel's vocabulary of *transgression,* and here I was in L.A., only a few miles from the Valley, where the most transgressive, most in-your-face, cinema in the world is made, where the contest between norm and perversion in the texts is *cosmic,* and the possibility of decentering the entire aesthetic of sexual representation was growing. The Buñuel project stalled out, I just couldn't stay interested in it. So I got some grants and made some contacts and now I have a book contract. *Diverse Desires: The Polymorphous Gaze of the Pornographer's Camera.* At least, that's my working title." Her voice seemed to lose some of its cynical drawl as she recounted this history, and she began to sound more like a graduate student than the world-weary voyeur of my first impression.

"Gosh," I said, at a loss for a more intelligent comment. She swallowed the last of her second drink and waved at the waiter again. Her frantic air was disquieting. *Not waving but drowning,* I thought.

"So," she said, recrossing the formidable legs in their latticed casing, allowing me another visual tour of Western Europe. "What's the nature of your project? Do you have a grant?"

"I'm interested," I said, thinking quickly, "in the actors, actually."

"The actors," she said skeptically, and then more reflectively, "the *actors.* God, you're right, there's so little been done on that." She looked at me with greater interest. "The nexus between desire and professionalism, the commodification question, disgust, *performance* anxiety, exhibition-ism, disguise, simulacra."

There was a silence; clearly I was expected to pursue these suggestions. I thought fast and said, "That, and I've been thinking about the wood problem as a paradigm of class and gender-based issues pertaining to working conditions."

"Oh *God* yes! It's all there, isn't it?" She was tapping her cigarette case on the edge of the table by way of punctuation. "So, what's your research agenda for this trip?"

"Actually, there are a small number of performers whose work I'm really fascinated by. But I don't know how to get in touch with them. You know, they're not in the usual scholarly indices or the like." I couldn't believe I was pulling this off, but Evelyn Gravehurst leaned forward, nodding.

"Of course not. The customary scholarly methods are useless here. You have to look at it as fieldwork. Who are the performers?"

"Joel Derringer," I said. "And an actress who goes by Gabriella."

She frowned. "Hard or soft?"

"Some of both." *Not to mention snuff,* I thought, but something told me to keep quiet about that.

"I don't know them," she said. "Not by those names, anyway. I could ask around for you, but your best source would be Universal Modeling."

"A modeling agency?"

"In theory. In fact it's like central casting for porno films. They have audition calls every other Thursday, the first and third of the month. Practically every actor in the Valley has been through UM at one time or another. Ask for Norm Lagrange, he's the manager, tell him you're a friend of mine. And if Norm doesn't know those names, some of the actors who are waiting to audition will."

"Where is it?" I asked.

"It's on Van Nuys, just north of Ventura. Right across the street from a Humphrey Yogart. You'll see the sign."

"That's a great tip, thanks, Evelyn."

"Oh, fuck," she said, looking at her watch, "I gotta go." She rose, tottering a bit on her spike heels, and again I caught that whiff of vulnerability behind the attitude. I tried to imagine her life, visualize her at a faculty meeting in her baby whore clothes, but could not.

I thought of something else. "Evelyn, did you ever hear of a porn film called something *Vixen?*"

She turned back toward me and narrowed her eyes. "There are only about a thousand of them. Surely you know that?"

"Of course," I said, slightly panicked. "I'm just—I just think the *semiotics* of the word are so, you know. The, ah, *discursive* complexities."

She nodded. "Absolutely. There's at least an essay in that. Ciao." She walked out, her small butt switching like a horse's in its wisp of a skirt. After she was gone I went back in to the bar area, to ask for the check. The two women sitting next to the wall were smiling at me. The redhead raised her right hand, thumb and forefinger joined at the tips in a gesture of approval.

When I got back to my room I found the red light on the phone blinking, A smeary laminated card next to it recommended that I push 6 in such an event, so I did. After a featureless recorded voice informed me that I had a voicemail message left at 5:34 p.m., I heard Rafe's faint Texas twang, more noticeable on the recording than it had been in person.

"Hey *Querida,* where'd you go? You don't have some other boyfriend in this town you're not telling me about, do you? I still think you oughta leave that grunge palace and come stay with me. You should've heard the desk clerk massacre the English language when I asked to be connected to your room. *I'm sorry, sir, but she is like totally not answering her phone at this time.* Anyway, here's the deal: I think we have a guy at the studio who would be willing, as a personal favor, to look at this tape you were talking about and see if he can learn anything from it. I don't know what he could tell, possibly whether things were real or special effects, that sort of thing. This guy analyzes tape for us in copyright infringement situations. He's world class. But he says it's best if he can analyze the original. Is that what you have? Call me. I gave you my mobile number at lunch, didn't I?"

He had, but when I dialed, it rang and rang.

I walked around the hotel's neighborhood, if you could call it that, looking for some place to eat dinner and thinking about how to approach Evelyn Gravehurst's friend at the Universal Modeling Agency. I felt like an alien, walking. Not as in immigrant, as in space. A Martian visitor to the San Fernando Valley would have to conclude that its true denizens are automobiles, and that the rather stupid soft-bodied creatures who variously attend to and scurry out of the way of the powerful indifferent metal monarchs are a slave class. After consuming a small and unmemorable pizza of unlikely ingredients, I walked some more and ended up staring into the window of a place called Provocations, apparently an apparel shop for those unburdened by taste or modesty, and wondered briefly whether I could, appropriately attired, impersonate an actress seeking an audition for a film role. I wouldn't have to be convincing enough to *get* the role, I reasoned, or even get close, just plausible enough not to arouse suspicion.

Did I say briefly? Very briefly. I was at least a decade too old to be even at the upper range of eligibility for that line of work, I decided, thus sparing myself a more searching mental inquiry into other disqualifications that might become apparent if I pursued this unpromising plan. I would have to play this one straight, and see whether Evelyn Gravehurst's friendship with the manager of Universal Modeling would suffice as an introduction.

After a night of fitful sleep broken up by the overpowering hum of my hotel room's air-conditioner and the stabbing sweep of car lights through cracks in its heavy curtains, I woke myself up with metallic-tasting coffee made on the little drip machine in the bathroom. While drinking it on the edge of the king-size bed, I found the address in the telephone book; the place was no secret, anyway. And today happened to be the third Thursday of the month.

About ten in the morning I parked my rental Geo across the street from the Universal Modeling Agency and watched for a while as I sat at a café table on the sidewalk and sipped a cup of coffee obtained from the Humphrey Yogart shop. The agency was a second-floor office at the top of a rusty set of stairs, above a yoga studio. The only identifying marker was a faded circular sign on a rather high pole, displaying a pair of buffed-up bodies; it was curiously quaint, as though left over from a bodybuilding studio of the1950s. I drank coffee and listened to the intermittent buzzing throb of passing cars, their tops down, hip-hop chants broadcasting from their speakers. The day grew warm and I took off the sweatshirt I had worn over my tank top and tied it around my waist. I had decided that dressing informally might get me further than businesslike attire, although I still wasn't sure exactly what I was going to say.

For about half an hour nobody came in or out of the door across the street, but then several cars arrived at once, shiny California rides—Mustangs and Jeeps with high-metallic finishes, and one ferociously clean white Corvette. It was young men who emerged from this sudden convergence of horsepower, five or six of them in jeans and tan shorts and velcro-strap sandals. They all seemed to be friends, greeting one another with high-fives and shoulder punches and other intricate coded gestures of male bonding before clattering up the rickety steps to the second floor and disappearing into the agency. It could have been the ten-year reunion of a fraternity whose selection criteria were clean-cut good looks and being white.

About twenty minutes later a gray Town Car pulled up, and a suited driver emerged and opened the back door, from which stepped a young woman with extremely long dark hair, wearing a clingy aquamarine dress that probably measured fewer inches from shoulder to hem than her hair did from crown to end. As she nodded to the driver and walked away from the car she was joined by a shorter, older man, who had let himself out of the limo's other back door. He was talking to her in an urgent way and tried to take her arm to slow down her progress toward the stairs, but she shook him off and kept on going. He looked back at the driver, still standing by the car, and gave him a what-can-you-do shrug, then hurried after her as she climbed the stairs.

By 11:30, two more men and one more woman had arrived and gone up the stairs. The men had arrived together in a Honda, the least flashy car in the lot; the woman had been dropped off by a black Mercedes whose driver was invisible behind its heavily tinted windows. Nobody had entered or left the yoga studio, which appeared still to be dark. If I had been interested in certain sociological generalizations I would have had plenty of material, but I decided I was going to learn very little that was useful to Peggy Grayling from watching; I was going to have to go in.

I had rehearsed some lines to say to the receptionist, but there wasn't one. The reception area, if that's what it was, reverberated with the sound of rock and roll—Chris Isaak exulting over and over that Baby Did a Bad Bad Thing. The large room was air conditioned to a frigid chill and seemed to contain most, if not all, of the young men I had seen enter, but none of the women. The men had lost their jocular cheer, and lounged in postures of boredom on scruffy formless corduroy-upholstered furniture, reading magazines. Only a couple of them even looked up as I poked my head tentatively into the room.

"Yoga's downstairs," said one of them instantly, taking in my jeans and sweatshirt before turning back to his magazine.

"No," I said, with the friendliest smile I could produce, "this is where I want to be. Mind if I join you?" And I sat down on one of the puffy sofas without waiting for an answer.

The men exchanged uneasy looks but went back to their reading, if that's what it was. I settled my back against the sofa and glanced swiftly at the magazine being perused by the guy next to me, whom I recognized as the slave of the red Jeep in the parking lot. It was porn, all right—naked women in saucy butt-display postures, or holding their unbelievable breasts up in silent invitation. He turned the page, and the two-page layout there was less playful: an Asian woman with beautiful eyes, semireclining, concentrating solemnly on the flesh between her legs, which her fingers spread open to the camera's eye like a tender fruit being offered to an honored guest in a home where certain ceremonious manners are observed.

I looked away, repelled, then tried to get a look at his expression, laboring to keep my head forward and look sideways so I would not be noticed. I needn't have bothered. He didn't have the slightest interest in me, but looked at the picture with ferocious concentration while bouncing his hips slightly to the beat of the music. I expected him to look—I don't know how. Lascivious, or maybe hostile; at least avid in some way. He looked unhappy and determined, like a law student studying for a final exam in his least favorite subject.

Just then the inner door opened and one of the men emerged, talking as fast as he could to a taller, older man who was coming out behind him. "I'm telling you, I was almost *there*. Like another fifteen seconds, I *swear.*" Despite the chill he looked faintly sweaty, his face glistening in the track lights.

"We'll call you," said the older man, who was wearing a Hawaiian shirt over shiny black pants. He surveyed the room from side to side, his wall-eyed gaze falling on a young man with fierce blue eyes and blonde hair to his shoulders. "In," he said to him, jerking his thumb briefly. He continued to propel his protesting predecessor toward the outer door. "I said we'll *call* ya, Christopher, and that's all I can say right now. Don't quit your security guard gig, okay?" As the younger men disappeared through their respectively designated doors, his attention turned to me.

"The fuck're *you?*" he said. "Yoga's downstairs."

"I'm looking for Norm Lagrange," I said, aiming to sound businesslike but unthreatening.

"Yeah? He's not here."

"Oh. Do you know when he might be in?"

"Nah." At this one of the men on the sofa snickered audibly. "Shut the fuck up, Gregory, or whatever you're calling yourself this week," said the older man, cuffing him on the head, "if you want an audition." The blow did not look very hard, though, and might have had some affection in it. The man turned back to me. "What do you want with him?"

"A friend of his suggested he might be able to help me find someone."

"Yeah? What friend?"

"Professor Gravehurst from UCLA."

"He doesn't know anyone by that name." He seemed to realize his mistake, and scowled at me.

"So you're Mr. Lagrange."

He didn't deny it. "I don't know any professors."

The inner door opened and the man who had arrived with the woman in the limousine poked his head out. "Norm," he complained, "what the fuck? This guy's a possible, Natalie hasn't turned her nose up at him yet, he's hung like King Kong and he's got serious wood, and you're out here yakking? C'mon!"

The walleyed man walked away from me toward the door, saying to the other man as he brushed by, "Tony, tell this broad I'm not friends with any professor and get her to fuck off, okay?"

The man named Tony walked over to me and smiled nicely. "I get it. You're a student of that lady professor who wants to be a porn star, right? Graduate student maybe?" he said, looking at me more closely, his smile vanishing. "Listen, lady, get outta here, and tell that meshugge teacher of yours to stick to explaining *Citizen Kane,* okay? She came around here once juiced up, all hot to see what the place was like, throwing her tits around. Norm let her audition, for a goof. She's pathetic. Get her into rehab, and get yourself outta here, before you get in over your head." He jerked his head once by way of emphasis, then stood and watched me until I reluctantly opened the outer door and stepped out onto the pitted metal landing.

"Bye!" called one of the younger men in a high voice. I could hear several of them guffawing as the door closed.

I trudged back across the street to my car, and noticed the man—Christopher, was it?—whom Norm Lagrange had advised not to quit his day job, sitting at the café table outside Humphrey Yogart. He looked toward me blankly and spooned a bite of pink frozen yogurt into his face, which wore a very dejected expression. I walked past the Geo and sat down next to him at the little wrought-iron table.

"Bad day, huh?" I said tentatively.

"Who're you?" he said, but he had a reflexive smile that he couldn't stop.

"Cinda," I said, sticking out my hand. "And you're Chris? I heard that guy say your name inside there," I said hastily, as he looked alarmed.

"Oh yeah." He put the yogurt carton down on the tabletop and rubbed his hands over his close-shorn brown hair. "I wasn't at my best," he confessed. "I fucked up and had sex with some girl I met last night. I *told* her to leave it alone—I told her I had an audition today! Bitch," he added, but without much rancor. "I guess she couldn't keep her hands off me. What're you doing here anyway?" he asked me. "You don't look much like a porn starlet, that's for sure!"

A moment went by, his words hanging in the air, and we both burst into laughter. "I didn't mean anything bad," he said. "I mean it's a compliment! I hate those dykey bitches. They think they're queens of the universe, and they're right. They say who they'll work with, they refuse to fluff a guy up for even five, ten minutes, all they care about is getting on the cover of a video box and retiring and having a house with a swimming pool and being on talk shows or something. And they get away with it! Men are the grunts in this business, that's the truth. A normal guy like me doesn't have a chance. The only guys who make any money in this business are freaks, guys who can throw wood for hours. Dicks of steel!" He laughed bitterly.

"It sounds awful," I said. "Why do you do it? You and your friends?"

He shrugged. "What else am I gonna do? Construction? My old man did that, and now he's forty-nine and so broke down he can't even move without groaning. Busted his knee, his back. I'm a good tennis player, had a job as a pro at a club for a while but then they gave me the boot to hire the son of one of the members. Some guys make a lot doing things with computers but I tried taking a course and we don't get along, me and the computers. There are a lot of guys who try this, after they try to break into movies all the other ways. You gotta admit I have the looks, don't I?" He smiled again, sublimely, flexing his upper arm, and I nodded by way of conceding that I had to admit it.

I was waiting for him to ask me again what I was doing, and considering whether to tell him the truth. But he didn't ask, just started in again on the yogurt. Either Chris had never had much curiosity, or he had lost most of it somewhere along the way.

"Chris," I said. "I'm looking for a couple of people who're in the business. Maybe you've run into them."

"Oh yeah?" he said automatically. "Like what for—you casting a movie? Commercials? I've done commercials! Remember the guy in the backseat in that Burger King commercial about the drive-through? That's me!"

I shook my head. "I'm a lawyer."

"Oh," he said, his eyes retreating back into disinterest. "So who you looking for?"

"A guy named Joel," I said. "Joel Derringer."

"Oh yeah," he said. "I've met him. But haven't seen him for a while now. I think he may have retired."

"How about Gabriella? An actress who calls herself that?"

This arrested his attention. "You're kidding."

"Why," I said. "Do you know her?"

He tossed the yogurt container expertly into a nearby bin. "So you're a cop, really. Why didn't you just say so?"

"I'm not a cop."

"Yeah," he said tiredly. "Just a coincidence you come around asking about some dead porno queen."

"Gabriella is dead?"

"Killed herself, is what I hear, but who knows. Maybe a month ago. Someone said she had AIDS. You're really a lawyer? For her estate or something? I know—someone who wants to inherit her money!"

"Not exactly. Actually, if she's dead, it's probably not of any help to me. I was mostly trying to find Derringer, but someone said she might have worked with him once."

"He worked with a lot of people." He looked at me, a flicker of interest crossing his face. "That's why you were over there at the agency? Trying to find him?"

"Yeah. I didn't get too far with it. They threw me out right after you."

"Assholes. Listen," he said, rotating his shoulders like an athlete warming up for a contest, "I've got an idea." He announced this as though it were an unusual occurrence.

"Go on."

"Why don't you hire me to find this Joel Derringer? I could use a job, you could use the information, right?"

"Don't you have a job? Besides acting, I mean."

"Nah, not really. I do some security work for some of the studios now and again, when they call me. It's not steady."

"I'll think about it, Chris. My client is paying expenses, and I'd have to get her okay to hire on an investigator. But uh, yeah—maybe it would work. Can I call you later in the day?"

"Sure," he said, "do you have a pencil?" I produced one and he wrote a telephone number on a napkin, just below a smear of pink. While he did, I pulled out a business card and wrote the name of my hotel on the back.

"Here's where I'm staying while I'm in town," I said, as we exchanged paper, mine small and crisp, his large and floppy.

"Hey, Carrot-man!" The call came from across the street, in front of the yoga studio. The guy with the shoulder-length blonde hair sat at the wheel of the Corvette, revving its engine.

Chris threw him a friendly finger gesture, and turned to me saying, "I gotta go see how Riley did. I'll kill him if he got the part."

I smiled. "What does Carrot-man mean?"

He looked abashed. "When your wood is, like, puny. Like a week-old carrot. You gonna call me?"

I looked at the napkin to be sure I could read the number. I could, just. "I'll call you."

"They always say that," he said ruefully, then bolted across the street to join his friend.

I found a pay phone and tried Rafe's cell phone number again. This time he answered right away. "Russell," he barked curtly, but after he heard my voice he asked me to hang on. I could hear muffled conversation and then he was back.

"Sorry—I had to get rid of some dickhead screenwriter's agent trying to tell me his client got cheated on points. Cinda, glad you called, I was starting to think you'd gone back home."

"Not at all. I tried you at this number last night but you didn't answer."

"Must have been out of range. So you got my message?"

"Yeah, about the audiotape analysis guy. That's really great, Rafe. Listen, do you have any idea what he charges? I need to clear expenses with my client and she's not rich."

"Didn't I say personal favor? No charge, Cinda. Did I explain about the original?"

"Yeah, and what I have is not an original. It's a copy of a copy that someone bought from a—I guess you could call it a street source. But I don't know what that tells you. Isn't almost every videotape a copy one way or another?"

"Yeah, I know what you mean, I guess so. That technical stuff is not my bailiwick. Don't worry about it. I'll send a messenger over to get the tape from you."

"I'm not at my hotel, Rafe, and I left it there."

"Oh yeah, where are you? Have you found some other leads?"

I became aware of someone waiting to use the phone, a purple-haired teenaged girl in very roomy striped boxer shorts hitched up to form a proud display above the low waistband of a hard-looking pair of black jeans. She had a large bunch of keys hanging from a chain attached to an empty belt loop, and she was starting to finger them with what looked like menace as she glared at me.

"I better tell you later," I said. "Can you come by at the end of the day, and I'll give you the tape? Maybe we could have a drink, or some dinner."

"My day ends when I say it does. How about lunch instead? Swing by your hotel and pick up the tape, then meet me."

"The commissary again?"

He snorted. "Hell no. Meet me at, let's see—the Cache Pinot Bistro on Ventura Boulevard. It's not too far from that place you're staying. Between, like, Coldwater Canyon and Valley Vista."

"Such exotic names."

"Are you kidding? Same kind of names they have in Colorado and Minnesota and Indiana and every other damn place these days."

"Yes, Rafe, I was kidding. How soon do you want to meet there?"

He coughed. "Shit, I really am losing my sense of humor, just like that asshole agent said. I'll be there in an hour. That give you enough time?"

"Plenty," I said.

Over the most exquisitely composed and austerely dressed salad I have ever consumed, I explained to Rafe about the tape: the difficulty of obtaining it from the court in Chicago, the rented machine on which I made a copy at the hotel there. I didn't mention Sam's presence and the effect of watching it on both of us.

Finally I pulled the tape out of my shoulder bag and handed it to him. "So is that all this guy will need to know?" I asked anxiously.

"Are there any other copies?" asked Rafe. "He asked me to ask you that."

"Why does that matter?"

"Hell if I know," said Rafe. "He didn't say."

"There's one other," I said, thinking of the copy I had made for Andy Kahrlsrud.

"Okay," said Rafe. "I'll tell him what you told me and he can sort it out."

"You really think he might be able to help us find whoever shot the original film? I can't tell you how great that would be."

"Let's just wait and see what he says," said Rafe. "So what else have you found out? Were you on stakeout somewhere when you called earlier? V. I. Warshawski on the case?"

"I was trying to find something but it didn't work out." Somehow I didn't want to mention Chris and what I had learned about porn, wood, and the modeling agency. Neither of us had alluded to any residue of our old sexual attraction and I was glad to stay away from the subject of sex altogether. But I would have liked to find something to talk about; Rafe seemed glum somehow.

"Is something the matter?"

"Nah. Bit of a shakeup going on at the studio, it happens from time to time." His expression brightened and he reached into the pocket of his jacket. "Anyway, here's a little present. No," he said, seeing my face, "it's not a big deal. Kind of a joke, really. For old times' sake."

The small red box gave me the worrying idea it was jewelry, but instead it was a tiny cell phone, although small and silvery enough to bear some resemblance to a pendant of some kind.

"I can't take this, Rafe," I protested. "These are very expensive."

"Not in bulk," he said. "Look, the studio bought about a gross of these as Christmas presents last year. There were a few left over and I thought of them when you said you didn't have one and had Louise activate this one for me. C'mon, every makeup girl in Hollywood has one."

"Well, then," I said stiffly.

"I didn't mean it like that," said Rafe. "I've got one just like it myself." He looked forlorn enough that I relented.

"What about monthly charges, long-distance, roaming, all that stuff?"

"I'm telling you, it's a studio deal. It's a flat fee, no roaming charges, no LD, anywhere in the U.S.A. and most of Canada, I think.'

"That's crazy, Rafe, you can't just go giving these things away. You're talking about a fortune."

"This is Hollywood, girl. Fortunes are measured a little differently here and—trust me on this—everything is crazy."

I removed the little instrument from its cushioned case and examined it. Its polished surface winked back the dim lights of the restaurant and I recognized a feeling I had experienced before. I was in trouble: I was in love.

"How do I know my number?" I asked Rafe.

He grinned at me, and showed me how to turn on the power and punch in the code that would tell me my number. "But it's a 213 number," I said. "Where I live is 303."

"It doesn't matter," he said. "No roaming, no LD charges, see. The studio pays the fee. It's a one-year contract, I think. If it will make you feel better, I'll tell them not to renew the contract, and you can pay for service yourself after the year is up. Here," he reached under his seat and handed me a larger box that contained a manual and a couple of cords and plugs, "it's all there."

"Rafe, you're too good."

He knew I had capitulated, and changed the subject quickly, as though to prevent me from reconsidering. "Did I ever tell you about the time Harrison Ford decided he needed to teach me how to fly-fish?"

"No."

And so he entertained me for the rest of the meal with stories about his brushes with the famous and the notorious. These were very amusing, but Rafe appeared in them like one of those sturdy recyclable character actors whose name nobody can ever quite remember, and whose own personality is as much beside the point as his mother's maiden name. They depressed me, and I think I may have more or less stopped listening a few minutes before the check arrived.

"C'mon," he said, after paying the waiter without even letting me see the bill. "You look bummed. Let's go for a ride." During our brief law school affair, it had been his answer to every bad mood, a couple of hours roaring around the hairpin turns of Boulder County's country roads in his ancient and badly maintained Porsche. I'd been ready to part company a few minutes before, but the thought of my dreary hotel room made this idea seemed appealing.

"Don't you have to get back to the studio?" I said. For an answer he took my hand and led me out to the parking lot behind the restaurant, waving off the attentions of a parking valet outside the door with a brief exchange featuring a key and a unit of currency. He opened the passenger door of a teal Jaguar convertible, which sat in the shade of a wooden canopy apparently reserved for cars whose owners preferred to leave down their roofs while lunching. The engine came to life with a throaty roar as he turned the key, and the CD player resumed in the middle of a Sting number.

On principle, and usually in practice as well, I dislike expensive cars, overpriced meals, traffic, and loud music. But my lunch sat lightly in my satisfied belly, and as Rafe steered the Jaguar out onto the street I felt the power of its acceleration pushing me back against the warm leather seat, the heavy sway of its sudden move to the inside lane, and the vibrations of the music carrying through the car's body and into my own. Something in me that had been dead since I first watched *Sunshade Snuffdown*, something that could taste pleasure without guilt or fear, stirred slightly, as though it might be saved from permanent extinction if nourished, and I decided not to resist. I laid my head back against the cushioned headrest and tilted my face up to the sun and closed my eyes, receiving with gratitude the warmth and the wind and the firm clasp of Rafe's hand on my knee.

I kept my eyes closed for quite a while, so I'm not sure how we ended up in Topanga Canyon, the Jaguar's smooth gears and Rafe's skill with them carrying us uninterrupted along the twisting ribbon of pavement that grew more narrow as we climbed. At some point the CD must have come to its end, and Rafe hadn't replaced or restarted it, so the only sounds were the wind and the engine. Shortly after I opened my eyes he turned off to the right onto a dirt track, marked only by a hand-lettered wooden sign: CANON DE CEBOLLA.

"Onion Canyon?" I said.

He nodded, his eyes on the ruts that scored the path, some of them deep enough to swallow the Jaguar's wheels. "They grow wild up here."

"Is this where you live?" I said in surprise, surveying the desiccated landscape. Brown and yellow shrubs sang as the wind blew through them, and the odor of sage drifted into the car.

"Course not. A few years ago I bought a couple of acres up here, thinking I might build a cabin. But I haven't had time to get it done. There's an old shack, water from a well except when it runs dry. I come up here sometimes to get away. Usually I drive my Jeep," he said, grimacing as he jerked the wheel to avoid a crater in the packed brown earth. "I'd better concentrate on driving for a few minutes here."

So I sat in silence and enjoyed the slower pace we were forced to maintain now, as Rafe guided the car between and around the obstacles that littered the broken trail. I saw a few tracks that veered off to one side or the other; they must have led to something, but I saw no other signs of habitation, no man-made structures. Stretching my arms out over the door on my side, I breathed in the warm air, dry and aromatic, nothing like the dense damp atmosphere of oceanside L.A.

"Remind you of Colorado?" said Rafe.

"Yes," I said. "A bit. We certainly seem a long way from the water."

He nodded. "That's why I wanted this place."

It was twenty minutes and one worrying scrape of car undercarriage against rock before Rafe stopped the Jaguar a few yards from a weathered wooden structure, about the size of a large garage. The land rose up above it on three sides, every direction but the one from which we had come.

"Not exactly the Hearst castle," he said, taking my hand.

"No," I agreed, but the duet of breeze and vegetation sang sweeter than ever in this place, and brought with it the faint and delicious hint of onion.

"There's a porch on the other side," he said. "Rickety, but we can sit there and watch the sun go down behind the canyon wall. It's usually gone by 3:30 this time of year." He looked at his Rolex. "Not quite an hour."

I smiled. "Is there a bathroom in there?"

He nodded. "Rustic, but functional." He took my hand as we walked toward the building.

From the inside I could see strips of bright daylight seeping in between the boards, but the rickety shack was surprisingly pleasant inside except for the dust that covered everything. I had to edge sideways up to the toilet wedged in a corner of the tiny bathroom, but it flushed with a satisfying rush, and the warm rusty water that first ran from the faucet soon turned clean and cold. I looked at my face in the small spotted mirror above the sink. The mirror was filmed with dust, like everything else including me, and this circumstance made it a forgiving reflector. By the scattered light I thought I caught a glimpse of my much younger self, the one who had known Rafe before time and necessity had imposed on us. It's so unfair, I found myself thinking, but I could not have told you what I meant by it.

The main room contained a miniature brown refrigerator, as well as a daybed covered with a red Mexican blanket and a pale wooden table flanked by two chairs that matched neither the table nor each other. Rafe was rummaging in the refrigerator, and brought out a couple of tall brown bottles as I rejoined him.

"Beer?"

I don't like beer, usually, but I nodded, the prospect of the cold fizzy liquid irresistible after the dusty ride. He handed me a sweating bottle after twisting off its cap, and showed me to the splintery porch, where two molded-plastic chairs, once white but now pitted and discolored, sat facing the hillside. I settled into one of the chairs and we sat in silence, long enough for me to see that the motion on the hillside was not all from the wind, that it was alive with birds and small animals. A coyote drifted over the ridge toward us and then turned back when it saw me stretch my legs out in front of me.

"Is this like West Texas at all?" I asked him. "Does it remind you of home?"

He turned the brown bottle of beer in his hands and started peeling the label away slowly from a loose corner. "West Texas isn't home any more. I don't know where home is. But yeah, this looks a little like it, except it's too hilly here."

"Your parents must be proud of you," I said.

He smiled and turned toward me, looking me fully in the face for the first time since I'd arrived. "My mom was, I guess, but she died ten years ago. Otherwise folks around Marlett don't have much use for Hollywood. My father tells everyone he knows I'm a big corporate executive in California."

"Well, it's true, isn't it? Vice president at Rose Brothers."

"Oh, yeah," he said. "Mr. Big, that's me." He ripped the rest of the label off with one swift motion.

"You sound a little disillusioned."

He nodded. "Perfect word, actually. Our business is creating illusions, but once you've seen how the tricks are done, the dazzle gets pretty much rubbed off. I'm a little cog in a big machine, Cinda. Just what I never wanted to be."

I tried to think of something to say, but couldn't. He didn't let the silence last long, anyway.

"So," he said, crumpling the stiff shiny paper and dropping it between the boards of the porch, "how come a beautiful woman like you—"

"Please don't do that, Rafe," I said. "I know I'm not beautiful. And I don't need to hear any of your pickup lines."

He looked at me for a long moment then, finally rising to go inside. I drank more of the beer, warmer now, and watched the light edge slightly from yellow toward gold on the side of the hill. When he came back I said, "I thought we were going to watch the sun go down over the canyon wall. But we must be facing east—the sun's behind us."

"This is how I like to watch it," he said, handing me a cigarette, although I had not asked for one. "Reflected on the hillside. Light's interesting by itself, but it's more interesting when it collides with something."

I looked at the cigarette he had given me—ragged, uneven. "A joint?" I said.

"Sure," he said. "I always keep a couple up here. Don't tell your cop friends."

I shook my head. "I haven't done this stuff for years."

He shrugged. "I'm not going to make you, Cinda. But I will say that even the president's drug czar knows some better arguments against the ingestion of marijuana than that one."

I thought for a moment, or perhaps I didn't think, just let the fading rosy sunlight and the life stirring beneath the cover of the sunstruck vegetation work on my hungry senses. "Do you have a match?" I said.

We shared the joint, and, I think, most of another. At one point Rafe went back into the shack, where there must have been a radio. The reception was poor, but behind the static the station offered up Golden Oldies—another thing for which I ordinarily have no use, but on this golden afternoon I briefly understood their appeal.

We danced to the slow ones, at first on the packed dirt in front of the porch, then through the opened door back into the dark of the shack, and onto the Mexican blanket. My feet were no longer on the floor so I could not dance with them but had to use my hips instead, and hands, and to move with Rafe's hands. We were dancing to all of them now, slow and fast. Our clothes were in the way, twisting and pulling beneath us, so we got rid of them. His skin tasted like salt and sunshine and the music was louder in there and at first I didn't hear what he was saying.

"What?" I said sleepily.

"Why do you keep your eyes closed?" he said.

I didn't want to think about this and said, "Shh," returning to the task of getting more and more of my skin against his, more than I had thought was possible. But he put a hand on my belly and stood, his warmth replaced by the cool air that rushed between us. He reached the hand down and pulled one of mine until I had to rise as well, protesting.

"No," I said. "I want to stay here."

"Come on," said Rafe. "I want to show you something." And he led me to the door and then out onto the porch. "Just a little farther."

"Ouch!" I exclaimed, as the sharp dry ground cover assaulted the bottoms of my feet. "Stop it!"

"Just here," he said, and he pulled me to stand beside him on a slight rise, where the sun's last rays stabbed through the air and bathed us in warmth. I could see to the west now, sky and canyon wall in the early stage of a sunset, but Rafe put his hand on my head and turned it back toward the shack. "Look," he said. "There, at the window."

My breath took a small ragged gasp as I saw. Off the dark surface of the shack's rear window our naked selves were reflected, Rafe's torso with its girdle of muscle, my own far more slender than I expected, hips carved like a bowl turned on its side, one of my feet slightly raised to avoid stepping on a thistle. It was true, I thought, light was best when it collided with something. My disordered hair flew about in the wind, across Rafe's face as he leaned his head into mine and pulled our mouths together again.

"You see?" he whispered. "Beautiful."

We must have walked back down to the shack, although I don't remember exactly. I know we slept for a while, entwined on the narrow daybed. But when I awakened Rafe was dressed, standing in the entrance to the little bathroom, the sound of running water behind him.

"Maybe we'd better go," he said, smiling. "If I'm going to drive into a ditch, Triple A prefers that I do it before midnight."

I nodded and sat up, my head throbbing gently with the remembered effects of marijuana, my bladder reminding me of the beer I'd drunk. "Can I come in there?" I said.

"Sure," he said, with a gesture of welcome. When I followed him into the tiny space, he said, "I'll get out of your way. Not much room in here for two." And as I blinked my eyes into focus he sniffed powerfully three or four times, then wiped his nose with the back of his hand, watching himself in the mirror. He rubbed a finger over his gums, catching my eye in the mirror as he did and smiling, his eyes bright. "It's a shame," he said, "but gotta wake up." Then he twisted a cap onto the small glass vial in his hand and held it out to me, his look questioning.

"No," I said. "No, thanks." My own eyes, when they gazed back at me from the still-dusty mirror by the harsh light of the overhead bulb, were red from dust and dope and the knowledge that while I'd slept, things had somehow turned for the worse.

He drove me back to the Pinot Bistro, and handed the valet something. It was nearly ten, and most of the dinner crowd was gone. My Geo appeared inside two minutes.

Rafe got out of the Jaguar and stood at the door of my car. "Do you want to follow me to my place?" he said, but politely rather than urgently. My answer would have been the same in any event.

"I don't think so."

He didn't argue. "Then I'll follow you back to your hotel, make sure you get there safely," he said.

"Please don't," I said. "I know the way perfectly."

"You sure?" he asked, but he sounded relieved. "Then you'll call me before you leave town?"

"Sure," I said firmly, and put the car into gear. I only looked into the side mirror once, as I braked before entering the street. He stood looking after me, but I couldn't see the expression on his face.

The next morning I called the office from my hotel room. Beverly picked up immediately, and I asked her if Tory was around. "Ye-es," she said carefully. "Hold on."

Tory had been in Steamboat Springs when I left for L.A., defending a manslaughter case, and I had not spoken to her since she had watched the tape and left me the note. A conversation about the exact extent of our firm's commitment to Peggy Grayling's case was way overdue. Although I would have preferred not to have it on the telephone, I needed her help right then.

Her first words were, "Did you find the sonsabitches?" Maybe this wouldn't be as difficult as I'd thought.

"Not yet," I said, "but I have a couple of very slender leads. Could you take care of a couple of things at your end?"

"I'm writing," said Tory. She agreed to ask Peggy Grayling to come in and talk about expenses, and also to run down Lincoln Tolkien. "I think Beverly knows where to find him. This is good, we need to get Linc back to work with us again. What else?"

"That's all for now."

"How's the old flame?"

"How did you know about that?" I asked.

"Beverly," she said. "Don't you know by now there are no secrets from Beverly? She knows everything."

"It was never that much of a flame, and the ashes are cold by now," I said. For some reason I didn't want Tory to know what had happened between me and Rafe. Anyway, I wasn't sure what had.

"Um-hmm," she said, ostentatiously unconvinced. "So when will you be back?"

I started to say I wasn't sure, but suddenly the antiseptic smelling, white-noisy confines of the hotel room seemed to close in on me. What was I hanging around L.A. for? I'd done all I could here. "I'll be home today, if I can get on a plane," I said. "See if you can get Linc to come by tomorrow."

I had a bad moment when I thought I had lost the napkin on which Chris had written his number, but it turned up in my jeans pocket. The pocket search reminded me of the little phone, so I used it to try the number. The phone worked fine, but Chris wasn't in. After four rings, his voice came on.

"Don't mean to dis you by not bein' here for your call, but we do have a life, y'know. Leave a message and keep it real."

I reminded him of our meeting and said I would call him from Colorado after talking to my client. I also asked him to call the office in Boulder and leave his full name and address. I should have gotten that before, I thought, looking ruefully at the filthy napkin I was using in lieu of an address book. I copied the number over carefully on a sheet of the hotel's notepad, and tucked the pad into my pocketbook before pulling my suitcase out of the closet and beginning to refill it.

The hotel didn't charge me for that day even though I had reserved the room for one more night, and United Airlines was okay with changing my return ticket to a four o'clock flight that afternoon for a mere $75. I spent the rest of the morning and early afternoon at the county clerk's office in Norwalk, east of the city, searching deeds and utility records fruitlessly for Joel Derringer. Nothing. About two o'clock I gave up, figuring I could just make the flight with enough time to turn in the rental car, and that my decision to go on home would result in a net savings to Peggy Grayling.

I was feeling a little guilty about Rafe; I'd promised to let him know I was leaving town, but my ambivalence had led me to procrastinate and now it appeared there might not be time. Things went more quickly than I expected at the car rental return, however, and once at the gate I found I had a few minutes after all. I used the little phone again and tried his office number, conscious of having become a cliché: only one of a dozen persons making important last-minute calls on their mobile phones before getting onto an airplane. Louise, gracious as always, said Rafe was in a meeting.

"Tell him I decided to catch a four o'clock flight back to Denver," I said, "and that I said thanks for everything."

"Of course," she said. "I hope your trip home is pleasant."

I still had twenty minutes to read magazines before time to board. *U.S. News & World Report,* or *Glamour*? I asked myself as I stood at the newsstand display. Whichever I chose, it wasn't very memorable. I perused it with galloping disinterest until they called for my row to board.

Then the plane sat at the gate, all of us sealed aboard, for nearly an hour and a half. The captain made occasional cryptic announcements. The cabin attendants were solicitous at first, dispensing water and pretzels about half an hour into the ordeal, but toward the end of the ninety minutes they stopped appearing altogether. They must have been hiding out in the little kitchen; I think they feared we would mutiny at the sight of them, and they may have been right. The other man in my row was muttering in Spanish. My Spanish is strictly leftover from high school, and Señora Castellano didn't teach us any dirty words, but I still think I know a curse when I hear one. Most of this fellow's were too intricate for me to follow, but I recognized *chinga* and *pinche*. Finally the captain's voice came over the address system again. We were to deplane, it seemed. Deplane. Ruminating crossly about what a stupid word it was, I gathered up my briefcase and carry-on suitcase and shuffled up the crowded aisle back into the terminal.

There was nothing to do there, either, but wait. We deplanees milled about in the departure lounge or flopped into the bucket seating there. Irritated, I walked up to the desk to ask the agent the reason for the delay. Three uniforms were in worried consultation behind the counter, one of them talking alternately into a telephone and at his colleagues. I heard him say "bomb threat" before one of the others shushed him, pointing to me.

"Please be seated," said a small woman in the slacks version of the navy-blue uniform, waving her plump hand at me with authority. "We will announce as soon as there is any information."

I complied, shrugging at a couple of my fellow passengers who had been watching me hopefully, to indicate that I hadn't learned anything. I didn't want to start a panic by saying anything about a bomb, although I considered leaving the gate. If there were a bomb on the plane just outside, couldn't it injure people back here in the terminal? But if I left I'd miss the promised announcement. I compromised by taking my bags and going to stand against the far wall, next to the entrance to an earring shop, but as soon as I settled in there I started thinking about how guilty I'd feel if the bomb exploded and I survived but the others didn't.

*"Chinganse,"* I thought savagely, now fully in that state of florid impotent rage induced by a bad air-travel experience. I picked up my bags and started back for the departure lounge when a pleasant chiming sound announced that something was about to happen. I stopped and looked expectantly toward the counter, expecting to see one of the uniformed agents about to speak into the microphone, but they were still huddled tensely. Nobody else appeared to have heard the chime, although just then it sounded again. A handsome Asian man standing nearby drinking a coffee

smiled and pointed at my shoulder bag just as the chime sounded again, this time from inside the bag.

"Oh!" I said, setting down the suitcase and burrowing through the bag to pull out the silver phone. It chimed again as I tried to remember how to answer a call. Finally I pushed a button marked SEND (could that be right? what was I sending?). "Hello?" I said uncertainly.

"All right!" said Rafe's voice. "I was afraid you were already on a plane. Louise said you decided to leave town."

How does one talk, when in Los Angeles on a cell phone, to an old lover with whom one has recently had sex and for whom one feels both tenderness and disapproval? I had not the slightest idea. "I was *supposed* to be on a plane," I said petulantly. "*Hours* ago. Some bullshit, maybe a bomb threat."

"Well hey," said Rafe. "Don't be so pissy about it. Every day hundreds of people arrive in LaLa land, having spent their last dime on a bus ticket because they wanted to get here so badly. You don't have to be in such a hurry to leave. Anyway, do you really want to fly on a plane that might have a bomb in it?"

"I guess not."

"You sound awfully far away, Querida."

"Must be the phone. It's awfully little."

There was a long enough silence that I thought the phone's signal might have failed, but then I heard his voice again. "It's the coke, isn't it? You think I'm scum because I used a little after we were together. Look, Cinda, I'm not a saint. I'm fucked up, to tell you the truth. Don't judge me based on just what you've seen so far."

I thought of various cases I'd handled that featured evidence gathered from the interception of cordless and cell phone conversations. "Doesn't seem like a good idea to talk about it here anyway," I said.

"No," he insisted. "Talk to me."

"I haven't—been with anyone like that for a while. Don't get me wrong, Rafe. It was good, but then afterward—it just reminded me of something I'd rather forget," I said.

"Okay," he said resignedly. "But we need to talk about it some time. So what airline are you on?"

"United," I said. "Why?"

"What's the flight number?"

"Eight ninety-four. If it doesn't get canceled. Why?"

"Sorry about the delay. Have good trip then, Querida. I'll call you when you get back home." The connection then seemed to be gone, but just to be sure I examined the keypad of the shiny little instrument, then pushed the button labeled END.

Fifteen or twenty infuriating minutes later, a harried crinkle-haired man with the knot of his red tie pulled away from his open collar and large Adam's apple strode into the lounge area with a wireless microphone. "Ladies and gentlemen," he said plaintively. "United Airlines apologizes in advance for any inconvenience the cancellation of flight 894 may cause you. If you will—" he paused, nearly flinching from the wave of verbal protest that rose from the ranks of those listening—"if you will please line up at the passenger service desk next to Gate 46, our agents are prepared to rebook you onto a later flight, or arrange overnight accommodations if necessary."

I rose wearily, my indignation exhausted, and prepared to perambulate down the corridor to stand in line again. "Cancellation!" expostulated a woman wearing a denim jacket with intricate embroidery work over a t-shirt that said I LOVE JET-SKIS. "They didn't even tell us why!" She headed for the microphone man, who was reading from a note someone had handed him. As she approached, six feet of fury in cowgirl boots, he blanched and held his hand up to stop her so he could speak into the mike again.

"Would passenger Hayes please come to the counter?" he said. "Passenger Lucinda Hayes."

I looked around, then headed toward the counter. The denim lady was giving the poor microphone guy a large piece of her tiny mind, but she paused long enough to give me a hard look as I passed. Several passengers looked at me curiously, and one or two with suspicion, as though I were about to receive some special treatment.

Which it seems I was. "Miss Hayes," said the short woman with the plump hands, "you have been booked on Frontier Airlines flight 4265, which leaves in twenty minutes from Gate 14. You should go straight to the gate."

"Booked? How?"

She tapped at her computer terminal. "That information is not available here. You'll have to ask the Frontier agent at gate fourteen. We were just asked to deliver the message. You'd better hurry—they will close boarding for that flight in five minutes."

They hurried me and my carry-on bags aboard at Gate 14, but I didn't have far to walk once I was inside the airplane. The attendant stopped at the second row, pointing to a wide, cushiony seat and saying it was mine. Mine? First class?

"May I bring you a drink before takeoff?" she asked after ensuring that I had a pillow, a blanket, a set of headphones, and a copy of *Fortune* magazine.

"Maybe after," I said gratefully, still dazzled and confused by this turn of events. Rafe, it had to be. Another little present from the studio. I put away any thoughts about whether I ought to accept his gifts and instead wiggled happily in the roomy seat and tried to remember the last time I had flown anywhere first class. The aisle seat next to mine was empty so I had acres of room. I swished my feet around with abandon. A nicely dressed man seated across the aisle smiled and raised his glass of red wine in my direction, as if to welcome me to this freemasonry of elbow room and comfort.

The attendant walked by again and spoke to me with extreme deference, suggesting almost apologetically that if I was carrying a cell phone I needed to turn it off for the duration of the flight—the first time that advice was ever offered to me so politely, and the first time I ever needed to pay attention to it. I pulled my new toy out of my bag and depressed the power button, then tucked it into my pocket. My neighbor across the aisle watched me and smiled with approval, nodding to indicate his admiration for my equipment.

I was only a little discomfited when the jet-ski lady staggered on just before the door closed, wheeling her oversized black bag down the aisle past me into coach class. She glared at me as she stumbled by, but I looked back at her stonily in the manner of all first-class customers confronted with the class resentment of their fellow travelers. I could hear the commotion of her arrival behind me, past the curtain, where some harried attendant was being required to find space for her suitcase. *Bitch,* I thought idly, my own recent promotion having already caused me to surrender solidarity with other travelers in favor of sympathy for the airline crew.

The plane started to move within five minutes, and as soon as the seatbelt sign went off, the attendant returned and offered me a little bottle of wine. I was given to understand this was no six-dollar, correct-change-is-appreciated deal, but another gift. Red would be lovely, I said. I drank it too fast, and then the alcohol and the airplane's oxygen-depleted air and the residue of the day before combined with the comfort of my padded seat to put me under. I was aware of the distribution of a meal and the collection of trays above me, but only in the shattered way an ocean diver might sense the passage of an occasional cloud over the sun above. I broke the watery surface and struggled back to consciousness as the seatbelt sign was being turned back on; I had a powerful need to pee. I begged the attendant, who was trying to hand me a goblet of ice water garnished with a slice of lemon, to let me use the head. She nodded. "Hurry, though," she urged me, as she placed the goblet on the armrest between the seats. I eased myself out carefully so as not to spill it, and splashed water on my face in the jaundiced light of the cubicle before returning to my spacious throne for the descent. The man across the aisle nodded and smiled at me again, one airborne nomad to another. I smiled back and drank the water, grateful for the real glass of its container and the oily astringent of the lemon, and decided that first-class air travel was an experience not to be scorned.

I didn't feel drunk when I left the plane, only a bit groggy, but as I looked for the Saab in the vastness of DIA's west parking lot I realized I was still tipsy. It took much longer than it should have for me to remember that I had recorded the car's location on the back of the lot's ticket when I parked it two days before. I set down my bags and fumbled through my shoulder purse until I found the chit. Level 2, Row J. Even so, it was an endless and stupefied ten minutes before I was unlocking the car and heaving my bag, which seemed too heavy, into the back. Had I picked up the wrong one at the carousel? No, silly, I hadn't checked my bags. I started to giggle at my own incompetence. Airhead! I said experimentally to myself. This made me laugh even harder. Doofus! I had to hold onto the side of the car to calm down. I heaved a deep breath and told myself sternly to be serious, then got in and started the car.

I remember dropping a hilarious spill of coins and bills onto the floor of the car while trying to pay the parking lot attendant. I laughed so hard my eyes teared. The attendant, a dignified African woman with a spectacular manicure, stared at me expressionlessly. I noticed the car behind me when I turned off Peña Boulevard onto Tower Road, to catch the eastern route back to Boulder. Tinkerbell! I taunted the light in my rearview mirror. Everybody clap and she'll come back to life! I thumped on the steering wheel as the Saab flew down the narrow dark road, but when it swerved sickeningly I realized I was not myself. Nothing serious, I told myself. I needed a nap was all. It was cold. I wished the stewardess would bring me that nice blanket back.

Cold. Where was that blanket? I was in that damn ocean again, that was it. Everything blurred when I looked up, so I closed my eyes again to keep the watery bright light from stinging them.

"Cinda?"

Go away, I thought. "It's cold," I said.

Hands were doing something along my sides and I opened my eyes again. Ouch. It took several rounds before I could keep them open against the brightness, and when I did I saw Tory leaning over me, framed by a very white room. A blanket was tucked around me so securely I felt like a mummy.

"Shit," I said. "Am I in the hospital?"

"University Hospital. For about ten hours now, almost ever since you drove off Tower Road toward some farmer's field. You're lucky a cop came along. What were you chasing, a white rabbit?"

"I guess I fell asleep," I said hoarsely.

"I guess you did. You weren't cut out for the L.A. lifestyle, darlin'."

I struggled to get free of the blanket, no longer cold. "What did I do to myself? Break anything?" I straightened my arms tentatively and looked down: no casts, no tubes. A few tender spots. More inventory: very bad headache. Queasy stomach. "Tory, something isn't right. I wasn't that sleepy."

"Oh, something wasn't right, okay. They know you were roached out, Cinda, you might as well cop to it. You're lucky you didn't hurt anybody."

I was getting confused again. It seemed to me I used to know what that expression meant, but I couldn't remember with my head hurting like it did. Anyway, I thought of something else. "What happened to the Saab?" It had been Sam's, left behind for me to take care of, and I suddenly wished very hard that I had not totaled it.

"Like you. Some scratches, broken headlight, maybe a bent axle. Don't worry, I had it towed to Emmett's. It'll be fine. Who gave you the roofies, the old flame?" I noticed for the first time that Tory's tone was more angry than concerned. "Did they make it nicer to have sex with him? Why'd you take them on the airplane, then?"

*Roofies.* I blinked and remembered. "They found Rohypnol in me?"

"What did you think they were, aspirin? You took two of them didn't you? Of all the fucked-up stupid things to do! You think just because you've been in some producer's bed you have to take every drug he gives you?"

"Stop it! I didn't take anything. He's not a producer and I wasn't in his bed and I didn't take anything!" It wasn't his *bed,* I thought to myself.

Tory just glared, looking angrier than ever. "Is that enough, goddammit, Dombrowski?" she said with unnecessary loudness. Was I still drunk, or was she not making any sense? I closed my eyes again.

When I opened them again a big guy with the largest freckles I've ever seen stepped out from behind the door. He wasn't in uniform but even through the blur I could see he was wearing an Adams County Sheriff's Office windbreaker. "Okay, Tory," he said. "You made your point. Now can I ask your friend a few questions?"

Of course they'd done a drug screen when I came into the ER. A trace of THC, which they attributed to the poppyseed cake United had served its first-class passengers for dessert. I didn't tell them I'd skipped the meal. BAC was .02, but I was full of flunitrazepam. I had first encountered this drug when I was prosecuting sexual assault cases in the Boulder County DA's office. It's a sedative, legal in Europe but prohibited in this country. Still, a lot of the little pills get past the border. They dissolve in liquid and don't have any taste or color. The high school kids who buy them for five bucks and take one of them at a time call them roofies. They would say the drug made them loose and happy—roached out. The predators who drop two or more of the tablets into girls' drinks, and then offer to escort the helpless victims to a safe place to rest, call it the "forget me pill." Prosecutors call it the date rape drug. I'd put a couple of those predators in the slam, and lectured hundreds of high school kids and sorority girls about never accepting a drink from a stranger or leaving a drink unattended in a public place, but I'd never ingested the stuff myself. Until, apparently, now.

A nurse came in and fussed over me while I was talking to Dombrowski, who wanted to know when I could have taken the drug without knowing it. I thought of the delicious lemony water on the plane, and that made me think of the odd way I'd ended up on that flight, in the first-class cabin. And Rafe, with his reefer and his white powder.

"I drank some wine on the plane," I said, "but that was in a sealed bottle and I didn't leave it unattended. Then just before we landed I drank a glass of ice water. I left it alone for about a minute to go to the bathroom."

"Did you notice anyone who might have been following you, might have gotten onto the plane after you did?"

I tried to think, shook my head. "I was one of the last to board." I didn't explain why, didn't want to say anything about Rafe until I had a chance to think things through.

Dombrowski was writing. "Do you remember anybody who was sitting nearby?" he asked.

"Maybe someone you knew?"

"I don't know. I didn't see anyone I knew. I was on the second row, in the first-class cabin. I only noticed one guy, across the aisle from me."

"What was your flight number?" he asked me. "We may have to get the FBI involved."

I shook my head. "I don't remember. It was Frontier. But my boarding pass stub should be in my briefcase." I looked around the sterile little room expectantly. Tory was sitting in the only chair, flopping her foot impatiently up and down. Her gaze slid away from mine.

"So, ah, was your briefcase in the front seat of the car with you, or in the trunk?" said Dombrowski.

"What do you mean?" I said.

"Wasn't that English?"

"I put everything except my pocketbook in the back of the car. It's not a trunk, it's a hatchback."

Dombrowski made a note. "Do you remember whether you locked the back of the car?"

"I was not exactly in a remembering frame of mind. Are you trying to tell me my suitcase and briefcase are gone?"

"And your pocketbook," said Tory. He turned and looked at her; his back looked disapproving. "They did find your new little *telephone,*" said Tory. "In your jacket pocket. It's cute." She looked miffed, as though she'd caught me wearing a Wonderbra or learned that I'd had surgery on my eyelids while out in Babylon.

"Ms. Hayes," said the officer, ignoring her, "did you have anything in your luggage or your briefcase that could have motivated this attack on you?"

"No," I said. "No. I don't own anything that valuable." Tory seemed about to say something but I shot her a look that had the desired effect.

He stayed for another ten minutes, before a resident stuck his head in and announced that he needed to examine me. Dombrowski folded up his notebook and stepped back from the bedside. "We'll be in touch," he said. "I'm going to notify the Bureau there's the possibility of assault committed on an aircraft. They can identify the flight and get the passenger manifest, but frankly I don't think they're going to be able to find the guy. The theft of your luggage is our bailiwick, and we'll work it, but you didn't see anybody, and the officer who called your crash in didn't either. There was a vehicle reported stolen from the DIA garage a few hours ago, but there may be no connection. Unless your stuff shows up somewhere, we don't have much to go on."

"I understand," I said.

"If you think of something, maybe something someone could have wanted to steal from your bags, give me a call, okay? Do you carry a weapon for protection?" He screwed his face up earnestly as he handed me a card.

I shook my head emphatically. "Not interested."

"Because you could certainly get a permit to carry a concealed weapon after this. I'd be glad to send you an application."

I waved him off impatiently.

"Objection on principle, eh?" said Deputy Dombrowski, as he tucked his notepad into a pocket and turned to leave. "Okay, it's your right."

The first real guns I ever saw, except on television, were in Celia's house. Her father's gun case decorated one wall of their living room, across from the several portraits of Peggy and some of Celia and one of their mother hugging their dog Tiller. The case had narrow thick windows and a polished brass lock. The guns, long ones and short ones, glinted with promise behind the glass. I was very attracted to them, to the gleam of the metal and, I suppose, to the combination of display and inaccessibility.

I asked Celia what they were for. Her father must have heard me ask. He came into the room and spoke to me then.

Those are for defending my family, he said. That's the only thing I'd ever use them for, but I would use them for that in a second. Now don't ya'll ever touch them.

It was different at my house. My father was a lawyer, and many of his clients had done things with guns, including shoot them and even kill people with them.

That's entirely different, I heard him say to my mother once.

They didn't know I was listening. You'll defend those scumbags but you won't defend your own family, she was saying.

I defend people with words, he said. We don't need any guns in this house.

I doubt that your fine words will do much good when they come to rape your daughters, said my mother.

What *they* are you referring to? he said.

Don't start with me, she said. You know who I mean, and don't think just because you belong to the NAACP, the only white man I ever heard of who does, I might add, don't think that's going to help the night they come here for Dana and Cinda. You think you can show them your membership card and they'll go away?

I don't have a membership card, Lianna, he said, sounding tired. And didn't I hear you talking last week about how great Chirico Daniels was, what a shame it would be if the Cowboys traded him to Cleveland?

That's completely different. He's a football player. And a Christian. And I'm certain *he* has a gun. To defend himself. Even a big, strong football player, over two hundred fifty pounds, understands he has to defend himself and his family. And he has a right to, it's in the Constitution. I'd think as a lawyer you'd be more interested in our constitutional rights.

I'm sure you're right, said my father, as he always did when he realized he was going to lose the argument.

But we never did have a gun in our house. Nobody ever raped me or Dana, but somebody raped Tory once, in Boulder. He was white, and he had a gun. He was a police officer.

"Cinda!" said Tory. "She's all right, doctor, she's always been a space case. Cinda, the resident is here."

The resident, who looked to be all of nineteen, seemed to have been sent to ascertain that I could be discharged. It's true my mind had been wandering, but there was nothing wrong with me except for a headache. After checking a few vital signs and asking some peculiar questions ("Who is the president of the United States?") that encouraged me to answer perversely ("Willie Wonka"), he told me that I was discharged but with a warning that my sense of humor appeared to be deranged.

"Is there a treatment for that?" asked Tory.

He looked at her and shook his head slowly. "Not when it's this far advanced," he said solemnly. "Now get her out of here."

Tory was driving her newest vehicle, a huge black pickup that looked as though it had been built to pull a train. I was still groggy enough and my perch in the passenger seat high enough above the ground that I was enjoying being driven and looking down on the roofs of the cars beside us on the Denver-Boulder Turnpike, until they made me think of roofies. I turned toward Tory, who looked tired. She must have been up all night, I realized.

"Sorry, Tory," I said. "How did they know to call you, anyway?"

"The insurance card in your glove compartment," she said, shifting down as the traffic thickened near the Boulder city limits. "You'd filled me in under Who To Call in Case of Emergency."

"Whom," I said automatically.

She looked over at me and, for the first time since I waked up, smiled at me. "Actually, the card said *Who*. That guy Dombrowski showed it to me while he was trying to tell me you'd driven off the road after voluntarily ingesting a controlled substance."

"I guess we'd better change to a more grammatical insurance company."

"I guess we better change to one that covers the risk of getting killed because you stubbornly refuse to tell the police all you know about an attempt on your life."

I shook my head. "I just needed to think things through, that's all, before I told him all our client's business. Anyway, nobody was trying to kill me. Rohypnol never killed anyone as far as I know, even with an overdose."

"You could have been killed if you'd run into a pole because you fell asleep while you were driving. Could have happened easily."

"Yeah, but that's so chancy. If someone was going to dose me with a drug to kill me, why wouldn't they choose one that would kill me for sure? There are enough of them. That other party drug, ketamine. Too much of that and you just stop breathing."

"Then what? Why did someone dose you at all?" said Tory.

I pushed away the memory of Rafe's reefers and his vial of white powder. "Had to be because they wanted to get my luggage for some reason. But that makes no sense because there was nothing in it worth anything. I'm going to miss my nice suede jacket, but nobody was going to so much trouble just to get his hands on that."

We were on Broadway now, at a red light at University by the Starbuck's. A man crossed the street in front of us wearing long planks with wheels fastened to his feet, pushing himself along with ski poles. This was Boulder: nobody paid any attention to him, including Tory. She turned her shoulders around in the seat to face me. "What about the videotape?" she said.

"Nobody knew about that," I said. "Anyway, I didn't have one with me. The only one I had I gave to Rafe because some guy at his studio promised to analyze it for us."

"So you had one with you for a while. Maybe somebody knew that you'd had it, and didn't know you'd left it behind."

"Who would that be?" I asked. "The only one who knew I had it to start with was Rafe, and I left it with him."

"Maybe he thought you had another copy with you."

"That also doesn't make sense. Why would I carry two copies? And even if he thought I had another copy with me, why would he want it? He didn't have anything to do with it except that he was trying to help me."

"You really like this guy, don't you?"

"No! I mean, he's an old friend, of course I like him. I'm just trying to be logical."

Tory sighed. "You didn't tell anyone else in L.A. about the tape?"

I thought back over my conversations with Evelyn Gravehurst and Norm Lagrange. And Chris, I reminded myself. But no. "Nobody. My inquiries were very general, just that I was looking for these actors. Don't you want to be in the left lane?" We were about to pass Spruce, and the turn toward our office.

"You're going home," she said. "Until tomorrow. Remember what you used to teach those kids about the aftereffects of roofies?"

I thought back. "You mean nausea?"

She nodded. "You don't want to be talking to Ralph on the big white phone in our office bathroom. Stay home today, come in tomorrow."

I smiled at the expression, certain I knew who had taught it to Tory. "You've been around Linc, haven't you?"

She nodded. "I called him after I talked to you and we had a drink last night before I went home to my very short night's sleep. He'll be in at nine in the morning. I think he's willing to work with us on the Grayling case."

"Sweet!" I said, happy as much for the *us* in her sentence as for the news about Linc. "Now there's one more thing I want to know. Why'd you come?"

"What?"

"I mean, you told me why they called you to come to the hospital in the middle of the night. You didn't tell me why you came." This was shameless fishing, I realized, but I wanted to hear her say something affectionate.

"Don't you know? It's because"—here she assumed a very convincing Sam Spade accent—"when a man's partner is killed, he's supposed to do something about it."

"*The Maltese Falcon.* Very good, except I wasn't killed."

"And except I'm not a man. But I just didn't think *When a girl's partner gets roached, she's supposed to do something about it* had the same ring."

"You're right."

"But the principle is the same."

"Right again." I leaned over and kissed her on the side of the head. "Thanks."

"Yucchh," she said, rubbing her hair with her hand and miming a shudder. "Don't go all femme on me."

I felt stranded, fogged in by the unexpected afternoon at home. The nausea didn't come and I was grateful for that, but my head still hurt. At first sleeping had seemed like a good idea, but it seemed I had been doing enough of that, including while driving, and I didn't like being alone in bed with my thoughts. After a restless hour I climbed out of my rumpled bed, which was now strewn with the newspapers I'd been trying to use as a soporific. I started to sort a little laundry and concluded I'd better go buy some underwear to replace what I'd been carrying in the missing suitcase, since my margin of error in the clean-underwear department was pretty thin. Then I remembered I didn't have a car. *Chinga.* Nothing for it but to continue with the laundry. While turning out the pockets of my jeans before stuffing them into the machine I found the crumpled napkin with Chris's phone number and nearly threw it out before remembering that the neater version I'd recorded on a notepad was gone, vanished with my pocketbook. So I smoothed out the napkin and put it onto my disorderly desktop.

Once I got the washing machine chugging along I paused and sighed, thinking of the need to cancel credit cards, replace my driver's license at the famously inefficient Boulder DMV office, figure out how to get some money without an ATM card or checkbook. My stomach lurched.

That you Ralph? But no, just the body joining for a moment the mind's rebellion against the prospect of the tedious Kafkaesque hassle of it all. I procrastinated for a while by watering my few worthy houseplants, the less loyal having long ago deserted me. One more green soldier had gone AWOL during my absence but I tried not to let it bother me, flinging the traitor's corpse into the garbage bin. Eventually I settled into my desk chair with a sigh and set about trying to find some clues, in my Dickensian filing system, to the numbers to call about my missing credit cards. I found a few, and had a corresponding number of impersonal conversations with persons who seemed to be quite knowledgeable about what to do concerning the missing cards, and stunningly incurious about the circumstances under which we had parted company. I had a couple of woozy moments, but Ralph never came calling. Small favors.

Just before five, done with this task, I swept my desk clear of the bits and scraps and came across the napkin again. I dialed Chris's number, more from curiosity than in pursuit of a coherent purpose, expecting to get the recording again.

"Yeah, wassup?" Music of staggering volume played in the background.

"Chris? Can you turn that music down?"

"Minute." The music stopped in less than that, and he was back, repeating his original greeting verbatim.

"Hi, it's Cinda Hayes. Remember, from outside the modeling studio, yesterday?"

"Yeah." His voice sounded guarded.

"Is there, ah, somebody else there, Chris?"

"Nope."

"I was thinking about your offer to do a little work for me and my client. You remember, to help us find some people?"

"Yeah, well, that's not gonna work out, Cinda." He said it harshly, but it was an actorly harsh and he wasn't a very good actor.

"Oh," I said. "Why not?"

"I got a part, that's why," he said, sounding more like I remembered him. "Big one."

"Well, that's great. I'm glad. But, you know, isn't it possible you could do both?"

"Naah. It's not just one part, actually. It's like, a big contract. This producer, I guess he'd like seen my work and asked for me specially. I'm exclusive with him for one year, and Norm Lagrange is gonna be my agent. But I can't work for anybody else, that was the thing they told me. Not even work security or teach tennis or lifeguard or anything. Which is like fine because who wants any of those crappy jobs?"

"Well, if I'm back out in L.A., or maybe someone who's working with me, could we at least buy you a drink? To celebrate, you know. Cause this contract sounds terrific."

"Yeah, I dunno. I better ask Norm, he's gonna be my acting coach and all, really set me up for the big time, and like he said guard and shape my public image. I think I'm supposed to stop drinking."

"Oh, yeah, I don't drink at all," I lied. "I was thinking just maybe meet for a coffee somewhere. Or juice," I added quickly. "I love juice." Sheesh. But Chris didn't seem to notice anything weird.

"Yeah, maybe," he said unenthusiastically. "Just like, you know. Call me if you get back to town or whatever."

"Okay, I will," I said. I thought he would hang up then, but he told me one more thing before he did.

"It was nice to meet you, anyway," he said, the calculated delivery now gone altogether. "You're a nice lady."

I put the phone down slowly. I hadn't been feeling very nice lately. If Chris thought I was, he must have been hanging with people who were less so. Curiosity is said to lead to death in felines, but Chris was no cat, and I thought he was more in danger of having too little of it than too much.

Maybe this next bit will seem strange, or possibly not; perhaps you've had a similar experience, found your way to an uneasy truce with something you wish you hadn't seen or didn't know. It's not that I stopped thinking about Alison Grayling or the snuff film or the man who made it and the one who loved it—the skull beneath the skin and all that. I carried every filthy scrap of that unwelcome knowledge with me. It cast its shadow on everything, and I was already beginning to realize that it had poured its poison between me and Sam. Nor could I deny being troubled and puzzled about what had happened between me and Rafe. But from time to time these preoccupations lifted enough to allow me to smile and even laugh at the tinny, sunny world as I moved through it.

For example: I had to get to the office the next day on the Skip, the bus that navigates up and down Broadway. The ride costs seventy-five cents and the entertainment is free. This morning the latter consisted of a conversation between the driver and a kid with a tattoo on his forehead depicting a very realistic bullet wound that would surely have been fatal if real. The kid sat just behind the driver, under a sign advising:

NO SMOKING
NO EATING OR DRINKING
NO CHEWING GUM
NO PLAYING RADIOS UNLESS W/ HEADSET
NO PLAYING MUSICAL INSTRUMENTS

The kid also had a accordion. Shortly after I got on, I realized that he and the driver were arguing about whether the accordion fell within the terms of the posted prohibition.

"I say it is," said the driver good-naturedly.

"Isn't," said the kid, fingering the keys a bit for practice.

"Is."

"My dad says it isn't," said the kid.

"Your dad?"

"Yeah." The kid smiled.

"Same dad that let you get that tattoo?"

"He didn't know I was going to. I just did."

"Did he throw you out of the house when he saw it?"

"No."

The driver nodded, but didn't say anything more, as though satisfied this dad's opinion on anything had been sufficiently impeached. The kid shook his head, acknowledging that he'd lost the argument, or so I thought. But then he reached behind him and pulled the cord. Hearing the bell, the driver halted the bus at the next stop, Maxwell Street, and opened the door.

"Bye, Pop," said the kid, stepping off with the accordion still slung around his shoulder.

"Call your mom after your lesson and see if she needs you to bring anything home from the store," admonished the driver. Then he pulled the door lever closed and maneuvered the bus back into the traffic. Noting that I watched him in his mirror, he grimaced. "Kids," he said.

I got off at the Pearl Street stop and strolled down the Mall to the office, enjoying the sight of the Flatirons, crisp and bright in the cool morning. After greeting me coolly, Beverly directed me across the street to the Trident. "Tory and Linc went over there about ten minutes ago," she said in a clipped way. She seemed to be in the grip of barely suppressed indignation.

"Why?" I said, intending to kid her a little. "Don't they think your coffee is good enough?" She didn't reply, but the way she tightened her lips made it clear I had unwittingly hit upon the grievance. "I think your coffee is terrific, Beverly," I said less than truthfully.

She barely nodded in acknowledgement, but I think she was mollified a bit. "They said look for them in the back."

Tory and Linc had not only settled in at one of the big booths in the back half of the Tri, but appropriated nearly the entire floor as well. Linc was occupied by an attempt to instruct Tory in the intricacies of some dance step. From where I stood it looked very sexy, even taking into account my knowledge that their respective sexual orientations precluded any consummation of the attraction suggested by their twined posture. At least I thought so.

"Hi Cinda," Linc called out, looking up at a dangerous moment.

Tory, in a backbend supported only by his careless grip and the purchase of a few of her own toes on the worn wooden floor, didn't seem concerned about his inattention. "Hey," she said, straightening up and raking her fingers through her disordered hair by way of grooming. A few other patrons of the coffee shop were watching with a proper degree of amazement, but not all of them. This was, after all, Boulder. The circus never comes to town here because it can't compete.

Linc greeted me with a hug, a good-looking kid in his mid-twenties whose newest personal style statement involved rather too much hair gel and a very skinny black tie dangling down the front of a white shirt. I felt a surge of fondness for him as we reclaimed the booth where he and Tory had been sitting. "I was showing Tory some salsa moves," he said. "We're going out dancing some night soon. Want to come?" I forebore to answer and surveyed the table instead, noting a copy of Vranesh's *Colorado Water Law* resting on the scarred wooden surface beside their half-filled glasses of milky latte.

"Do we have a case in water court?" I asked Tory, lifting the thick tome.

"No," she said, "that's Lincoln's." I looked at him.

"I'm still thinking of going to paralegal school one of these days," he said. "Just getting a head start."

"How's the private eye business?" I said. "Lively?"

"You wouldn't even believe how boring, Cinda," he said earnestly. "I mean, I read things like that book for the excitement."

"Salsa dancing doesn't supply enough excitement in your life?"

"Oh, playing is mad edgy. It's work that's stupid. I've been climbing and mountain biking, and I rollerbladed down Flagstaff Road last Sunday."

I shuddered. "Linc, that sounds incredibly dangerous."

"Hella," he said, grinning in apparent agreement. He had taken it as a compliment.

I reminded myself that even if nearly old enough for the role, I was not his mom. "We might have some moderately interesting work for you, if you're interested," I said.

"Phh!" Linc's mouth noise suggested that any doubt on this score would be preposterous.

"Okay then." And I told him, Tory interrupting only occasionally, the story of Peggy Grayling and her daughter, Dire Wolf and his obsessions, and my ineffectual efforts to trace the origins of *Sunshade Snuffdown* during my trip to Los Angeles.

"So you need me to sherlock this question of who made the tape, maybe by finding someone who was in it, or whatever."

"That's right. I didn't get very far, but you might try again with this guy Chris. He doesn't want to talk to me now—I'm not sure whether someone warned him off, or whether this new gig of his is for real. But either way, it might be best for you to start fresh with him, not mention me." I handed him a sheet on which I had written Chris's telephone number.

"No address?"

"I never got one. Can't you try a reverse directory or something?"

He nodded. "Sure I can. Do you think he knows something about the snuff film?"

"Probably not, but he knows a lot about the modeling agency. He didn't seem to recognize Joel Derringer, at least not by that name. He told me Gabriella had committed suicide but that's all he knew about her, and anyway we don't have any reason to think she's connected with the snuff tape, except that she was in a different film with Derringer."

"And what's this?" said Linc, looking at the paper I'd given him.

"That address on Van Nuys? It's the agency's."

"I'm on it." He nodded and pocketed the paper. "I gotta write a couple of reports, do some paperwork, and meet with one client tomorrow. But I'll try to be in L.A. by Saturday night and see what's up."

Tory had been listening while playing in the dregs of her drink with a straw, and cutting her eyes at me from time to time. Linc rose as if to leave but turned back when she said, "Hey!"

"Sorry," he said, and took her hand in his. *"Adios, muchacha linda,"* he said, raising the hand to his lips.

She twisted their clasped hands until somehow she was holding him by his wrist, then thrust it toward me with purpose. The meaning of the gesture was perfectly clear: *You're not done with each other.* "Were you think-ing," she asked me, her eyes snapping, "that Linc didn't need to hear about the attempt on your life?"

"It wasn't that," I said quickly, but I knew she was right that Linc needed to know about the roofies. "Sit down," I said to him, and he slid back into the booth beside Tory. I told him about the delayed flight, my fortunate rebooking onto Frontier, first class, my suspicion that Rafe was responsible for it, and the accident. "Tory was the one who had to convince the cop I wouldn't have taken the roofies on purpose," I concluded.

Linc was fond both of Sam and of cars, and he had seen that I was perfectly fine, so probably there was nothing wrong with his first reaction. Which was, "Did you total the Saab?"

I shook my head. "It's gonna be fine. Just be careful, that's all I'm saying. If we can make it happen, this case is going to get us on the wrong side of some bad people. Could be someone was after the tape and thought it was in my luggage."

Linc drummed his long fingers on the table for a moment, his eyes taking him somewhere else. "But nobody knew you were rebooked for Frontier except for whoever did the rebooking, and nobody would have done that but this Rafe character."

"I guess that's true."

Tory snorted. "Of course it's true. For some reason Cinda's old friend arranged for her to be drugged and for her luggage to be stolen. We just don't know why yet."

Linc shrugged. "We'll find out."

"Stay away from that end of it for now, okay, buddy?" I said anxiously. "I need to think about that some more. Don't even call Rafe on this trip."

"Okay, we'll get to that later. Listen, I gotta book."

He ruffled Tory's hair as though she were six and he were her uncle. She smiled back as if smitten and we both watched Linc's narrow backside as he navigated out of the shop between the scattered tables and chairs.

"What's up with *that?*" I said. "Isn't Linc a little young for you? Not to even mention the other."

"What other?" she said innocently. I couldn't exactly tell whether she was teasing me and anyway, I still didn't want to talk about sex. So, leaning across the booth, because I didn't want the fellow at the next table, the one with the lime-colored hair, to overhear us, I turned to the other puzzle that was on my mind. "What made you change your mind about Peggy Grayling's case?" I asked Tory.

"I'll tell you later," she said.

"Later like when?"

"Tonight, six, in the upstairs room at Trio's."

"We're having dinner together?"

"The monthly meeting of the Lesbian and Gay Lawyers Alliance."

"I'm invited? I'm not a member. I'm still pre, you know." One of Tory's more aggressive friends had once informed me that there are only two kinds of intelligent women: lesbian and pre-lesbian. Since then Tory had taken to calling me The Pre, or sometimes The Big Pre.

"Special occasion, and you're a special guest," she said solemnly. "I'm the main speaker."

We left then and crossed the street back toward the office. As we climbed the narrow stairs I could hear Beverly talking animatedly.

"It's not that he doesn't *want* to work," she was saying as Tory opened the door, "it's just that his particular talents—hi Tory! Cinda, Dr. Kahrlsrud is here to see you. He's just giving me some advice."

Andy nodded from the chair he had taken across from Beverly's work station. "Do you have a minute, Cinda?" he said.

"Sure," I said. "You want to finish your conversation with Beverly there first?"

"We're done," he said. "Remember, Beverly, just listen very carefully to your couples therapist."

"Okay," she said glumly. She and Charley had been in couples therapy for years and he was no closer to a job than when they started.

"Holy moly," said Andy after the door to my office closed behind us. "If codependence were contagious, you'd be offering me a large order of french fries right about now." He rubbed his spacious belly.

"She's pretty bad," I agreed, "but what are you gonna do? She loves the guy."

"Couldn't *you* put him to work somehow? Stapling briefs or something?"

"I'd worry about the worker's compensation claims. Charley would staple his fingers together the first day. But that's not what brought you here."

"Leonard Fitzgerald," he said. "Can you get me in to see him?"

"Really? You're interested in working on this?"

"I'd like to see the guy. Never saw a case like this one, and I want to understand him better. It would also help if I could talk to this fellow Gupta, who assessed him and wrote the report."

I leaned back in my chair. "I think I could get you in to see him, or at least I know where to start. And once you see him maybe he'd sign a release for Dr. Gupta if you think you need one, but wasn't Fitzgerald told that his conversations with a court-appointed expert weren't confidential?"

He nodded. "But still, Gupta's a lot likelier to talk to me if I show up with a release than otherwise."

"I'll work on it, Andy, but if my client's going to pay for this I need to be able to tell her you'll be a witness for us if your findings are favorable."

"I'm not even sure what that would mean right now, Cinda. But don't worry about the money—I'll pay my own way if your client won't." His fingernails were white from his grip on the sides of his chair.

"Why? You don't even like forensic work."

"There're just some things I want to understand better, that's all. How someone could do what was done. What effect material like that tape has, and why."

"Did you watch it?"

He looked down at his hands and they relaxed, as if instructed to do so. "I watched it."

"Did it have an effect on you?" I said. I wanted to know, and also didn't.

When he raised his head his eyes were narrow with anger, or something close enough to it. "What do you think?" he said.

"You too," I said, my eyes suddenly wet with the memory unfolding before them. "I did try to tell you. Will we ever be able to forget it?"

"We won't," he said. "We shouldn't."

"I'm not sure I'll ever be able to make love again without thinking about it," I said, choking on the words. I felt just that desolate, even though what I said wasn't strictly true—I had, hadn't I? I suppose I was hoping for reassurance, or at least sympathy, but Andy just nodded and stood to leave.

"You asked me not to try to shrink you, remember? But let me know if you change your mind."

John Scarpelli's secretary told me he was on the phone, but when I gave her my name for a message, she said, "Oh. I think you're the one that Mr. Scarpelli said I should put through right away if you ever called. Just a moment."

It didn't take him long to get rid of his other caller; his voice came onto the line right away. "I was afraid you were going to renege on our deal," he said. "Glad to find out I was wrong."

"What was the deal?"

"You've really forgotten? Then what were you calling about?"

I told him about Andy's desire to interview Leonard Fitzgerald. "And do you think you could find out where that shrink, Gupta, is now?"

"Lakshman's still at Elgin; I talked to him last week on another case. So is Fitzgerald, but I don't talk to him, although I hear he's pretty coherent from the meds they have him on. I could probably get your guy in to see him, but it'd be up to him whether he wanted to talk. And I'd have to run it by his public defender first."

"Would you do that?"

He sighed heavily. "Why should I? You forget your promises, lead me on."

"I don't think there was any leading on, John. And I'm sorry—what was it I promised? I'll be glad to do whatever I promised but I need a reminder."

"You were going to tell me what you thought of the tape."

I did remember, then. "What do you want me to say? It was disgusting, despicable. Grotesque. I try not to think about it."

"Yeah, but do you succeed in not thinking about it?"

"No."

"Say more." He was starting to remind me of Anthony Hopkins in that movie. *Tell me about the lambs, Clarice.*

"No," I said.

The sigh again. "Nice talking to you, Cinda." And he hung up.

"Asshole," I muttered, hoping Beverly wouldn't overhear, and then I dialed again.

"All right," I said. "I have terrible dreams."

"Tell me one," he said.

"I'm at a cabin in the woods somewhere," I said, concentrating on this act of invention. "Alone. I'm sitting by a nice fire, drinking a glass of wine or something, and I hear a wolf howling. Then I realize that the cabin has this room that I've never been in, and the wolf is behind the door of that room. I hear it howling again, and I decide not to go into that room. I curl up in front of the fire and try to sleep but the wolf keeps howling and waking me up. Then I really wake up, and I'm more tired than when I went to bed."

"That's a good one," he said. "Did you just make it up?"

"What difference does it make?" I said. "This is childish, John."

"You're the one who started off talking about dreams. Not that I haven't had some of my own."

I believe he wanted me to ask him about his dreams, but I didn't think I could bear to hear about them. "What do you want from me?" I said.

"How's your love life? How are things with your boyfriend these days? Have you told him about the tape?"

"He's seen it. He watched it with me."

"Oh, that's very interesting. Tell me about that. Did you watch it together more than once?"

"No! No. It was horrible. Why would anyone watch it more than once?"

"The Wolf did. Lakshman told me he figured Fitzgerald watched it several times a day for weeks before he kidnapped Alison Grayling."

"We didn't. I could barely get through once." I decided there was no point to explaining that I had watched it again with Mindy Cookson.

"Are you telling me it didn't turn you on? Or him? Not at all? It's not a moral question, you know, simply a matter of physiological responses."

"I don't believe that, John."

"So it didn't. You're lucky. And you and he went back to fucking every couple of nights just like before?"

"That would not be possible," I said stiffly. "We don't live in the same place. He's in New York." *And when we did it we didn't call it fucking,* I thought.

"Aha," he said. "So tell me more."

"No," I said, thinking of Rafe and my desperate desire to uncouple the pleasures of sex from the burden of guilt and terror. "Hang up on me again if you want to, but no more on that subject."

He must have decided to accept this. "So, the press knows about your case?" he asked.

"No, I don't think so," I said. "You haven't told anyone, have you? We'd prefer to announce it when it's filed, if we ever find the maker of the tape so we have someone to sue."

"I haven't told a soul," he said. "But some reporter was sniffing around here asking after the tape a couple of days ago. Ruth Suarez mentioned it to me."

"A reporter?" I said, seized by a sudden worry. "They didn't let anyone check out the original tape, did they?"

"I guess not. She told me that if there was going to be so much interest in the thing, she'd have a few copies made to sell so she wouldn't have to keep worrying about somebody taking the original out of her office."

"Do you know what paper the reporter worked for?"

"Nah. Why don't you call her?"

"I will if I have a chance. Are you going to help me with the other now?"

"Yeah. But you have to keep talking to me, Cinda. How many people do you think I can talk to about this? I don't know anybody else who's seen that tape but the jurors, who I'm not allowed to talk to. Or Amy Springer, Fitzgerald's lawyer, who I can't very well talk to. Or Lakshman, who talks like a textbook."

"And Fitzgerald," I said.

"Oh yeah. And the Wolf. Yeah, sure, I could talk to him."

Then I called Peggy Grayling, but she reminded me that she didn't care for telephone conversations. "I prefer face-to-face encounters," she said gently. "Would you like to meet me at my Bikram class again? I'm going to one at two this afternoon."

"No," I said quickly. "No, that isn't convenient. How about before?"

"In Eben Fine Park at 12:30?" she suggested. "It's a lovely day."

"That sounds good."

I walked there from our office, along the Boulder Creek Trail, which has worse traffic at noon than Broadway does at five o'clock. It should have been a peaceful walk, but locomotion took less energy than the need to stay alert to the possibility of collision with any of the rollerbladers, bicyclists, scooter riders, and new moms out for power walks with baby strollers as wide and well defended as Humvees. The park was lively with picnickers and energetic kids; at the water fountain several runners lined up for a drink before heading farther up the canyon toward the spot where the city ends and the trail curves uphill.

Peggy Grayling sat on top of one of the weathered picnic tables in the half-lotus position, her face turned toward the sun. She didn't see me approaching. A leaf fell onto her sky blue bike shorts and I watched as she took it between her fingers and scrutinized it before releasing it to flutter to the ground. Her every movement embodied grace; she seemed to have discovered the thread that links body to mind to universe. I wanted to know what that felt like, but didn't think it likely I ever would.

I called out to her, and she turned to greet me with a smile as I sat down next to her on the table. We talked for most of an hour. I gave her an account of my trip to L.A., estimated what I had spent so far in investigating, and explained my plans to send Linc back to California and Andy Kahrlsrud to the mental institution in Elgin, Illinois.

"I'm very pleased with all you've done," she said. "And of course you should pursue your plans. Do whatever you think is necessary, but please remember that the most important thing, to me, is to discover who is responsible for the videotape. Do you really think this fellow from your friend's studio will be able to help?"

"I don't know, Peggy. I don't know enough about videotape technology, but it doesn't seem all that likely to me that he could tell us much just from analyzing the tape, especially since it's a copy."

She nodded, understanding, and I turned sideways on the splintery wooden surface to get a better look at her. "Did you watch it, Peggy?"

She turned her head away briefly, looking toward the creek where a man was pulling a kayak out of the water. When she turned it back, a red stain had spread across her cheeks and her slender neck. "Yes," she said. "I must get to class now. Thank you, Cinda." She rose as soundlessly as a column of smoke and started walking toward the parking lot. Two muscular men running in our general direction on the trail followed her progress across the grass with evident admiration, but she did not seem to notice. Or if she did, to care.

Tory and I walked over to Trios together a little before six. The restaurant was one of the more stylish in Boulder, which is probably not saying much if you happen to live on either coast but still left me worried that my fleece jacket and jeans weren't exactly appropriate.

"Are you *kidding?*" said Tory when I confided this concern. "For a meeting of the LesBiGays? I can't think of anything that would be out of place in this crowd except maybe a pink tutu, and that only if it were on a woman."

"Tory, you sound a little homophobic, dear."

"Not, Cinda. I can say things like that. Just as long as you understand that you can't, you'll be all right."

Near the entrance there was a discreet sign pointing toward the banquet room with the caption *Boulder Lesbian and Gay Lawyers Alliance Monthly Meeting.* The banquet room door bore a larger sign saying *April Meeting of LGLA, Victoria Meadows, Speaker. Subject: Why the First Amendment Does Not Bar Suits for Damages.* Voices swirled around the room, and as soon as we entered, Tory was surrounded by various persons who wanted a word. I knew she would sit at the head table since she was the speaker, so I looked around for an acquaintance to dine with as I sidled toward the cash bar.

"Cinda, don't you look ready for anything!" Karen Spector, a successful litigator with one of Boulder's fanciest law firms, spoke at my elbow; it was

Karen who had once informed me about the two varieties of intelligent women. She wore a gray worsted suit of such fierce propriety and unimpeachable style that I felt as though I had wandered in from a lumberjack's convention, unlikely as it was that such an event would be held at Trios.

"Thank you Karen, so do you." Although in truth I would not like to have to wear clothes like hers all day long; it would be a stiff and clammy experience, I thought, like swanning around in armor. The phrase *suit for damages* seemed quite apposite. Something to wear while inflicting them on others, and protecting yourself against efforts to inflict them on you. Still, the fleece was beginning to seem like a major fashion mistake. I looked around, hoping to see a guy in a pink tutu or something similar that would make me feel more proper, but everyone I could see looked at least businesslike, and many quite spiffy.

"What are you looking so worried about?" said Karen.

"Nothing," I said. "Could I sit with you at dinner?"

"Of course," she said. "Bill Woodruff is sitting with me, too. Do you know each other?" she said, turning to include the young man next to her in our conversation.

"Billy?" I said. I had run into him this morning unlocking his office across the hall from ours, his shorts frayed at the hem, his tattered rubber and Velcro sandals exuding the faint swampy odor of Boulder Creek, where he liked to practice rolling his kayak. But this evening his suit was even grayer and harder than Karen's, the knot of his paisley silk necktie perfect.

"Yes, Cinda," he said, taking in my surprise. "Ah. So you didn't know, did you?"

"Oh, I knew you were *gay*," I said. "Tory told me ages ago."

"Then what?"

"My confusion was exclusively sartorial, Billy."

"What?" he said, but then someone struck a utensil several times against a water glass and bade us all take seats for the program. I settled into a chair between Karen and Billy at the U-shaped table, noticing that Tory was sitting at the base of the U, next to a podium, already eating. She caught me watching her and grimaced horribly, like a bad kid. I didn't know whether it meant the food wasn't good or she was anxious about her talk, but then she pointed at her plate and wrinkled her nose.

There was a business meeting while we nibbled on our choice of salmon mousse or blackened chicken with pasta. I had the salmon, and agreed with Tory about it. While we ate I listened as Mary Schaeffer, an earnest older woman who had worked for legal services for years, detailed the group's campaign to persuade the University of Colorado to offer domestic partner benefits to same-sex couples. Then a young man who moved like a toreador in snug black pants urged us to attend his tango clinic that weekend, as it would be a benefit for the Boulder County AIDS Project. Billy stood and mentioned that the Press Committee was in the process of composing a response to a homophobic letter that had been printed recently in the *Boulder Camera*. Someone else spoke up to suggest that the reply cast a certain aspersion on the original letter-writer's physical and mental endowments. There was laughter and hooting.

Finally Mary Schaeffer returned to the podium and said, "For our program this evening, our friend Tory Meadows is going to share her thoughts about an issue that is of interest to every gay, bisexual, or transgendered person. We know Tory as a former assistant district attorney, currently a partner in the Boulder firm of Hayes and Meadows. She tells me that what she has to say may surprise some of us. Those of us who know Tory would be surprised if she ever stopped surprising us. Tory?"

Tory stepped up to the podium, brushing Mary Schaeffer's shoulders with the hint of an embrace as they traded places in the small area behind the podium. She adjusted the microphone, wincing a bit as it screeched from feedback, and began to speak. As it happens, I still have her written notes, but even without them I'm sure I'd remember almost every word she spoke to that expectant crowd.

*The love that dare not speak its name. That's what they called it—still do, in some places. And for too long, much too long, that's what it was. We were afraid to say who we were, what we needed and wanted. If we tried we were shut up, the hard way with blows and broken bones, or the softer way with a look or a looking away or a pink slip in the pay envelope, or by any of the many methods in between. Our ways of making love were a crime. Our words of love were said to be obscene or pornographic. Some of us could not find love except in places associated with dirt—bathrooms, bathhouses—and then we were told we were dirty because that's where we could be found. We hid.*

*They said to us We won't ask, as though this were a favor. But you, they instructed us, are not to tell. Some of us refused this bargain. I still have a t-shirt I got at a race to raise money for AIDS research. It says SILENCE=DEATH, and although it was meant as a slogan about the cost of failing to educate people about that terrible disease, for many of us it means something more as well: if you can't say who you are, your soul will be injured and die.*

*(take a breath) At some moment, each of us here made a decision to renounce silence and to say, sometimes to shout, who we are. But none of us can say she hasn't felt the cold hands moving to seal her lips, doesn't feel them still from time to time. So it's no wonder that we, as a community, have always taken a strong stand against censorship, which is the polite name for the enforcement of that silence. And because we have always known that labels like* obscene *and* pornographic *have been employed to mark off our speech, we've resisted the idea that some categories of speech can be censored while others must be left free.*

*We have heard that the most important speech to protect is the speech you hate, because nobody would try to censor polite inoffensive speech. And we have agreed, and said it ourselves, and even found ourselves in the familiar First Amendment predicament of defending the speech of neo-Nazis and homophobic radio psychologists and preachers who would not hesitate, if they had the opportunity, to silence us once and for all.*

*In our vigilance to tear down any barriers to speech we have come to the defense of Hollywood, even though sometimes its creations make us cringe. Many of us have decried efforts to regulate the World Wide Web, even as we see the virulence of the hatreds that can grow in that nourishing environment. So we were ready when the* Hit Man *case came along, ready to go to battle again like well-trained First Amendment warriors.*

*Some of you know about this case, because it has a connection to Boulder. But it starts in Maryland, where one night in 1993 Trevor Horn, eight years old and quadriplegic, was strangled to death by a man named James Perry. Perry also murdered Trevor's mother, Mildred, and his nurse, Janice Saunders; he killed the women by shooting them through the eyes, two or three times apiece. He didn't know any of his three victims, and had no grudge against them; he did it for money. He'd been hired by Lawrence Horn, Trevor's father and Mildred's ex-husband, who also acted for money; he stood to receive two million tax-free dollars from a trust fund if Trevor and Mildred were both dead. It didn't work out that way for Lawrence; he was convicted of murder and sentenced to death. James Perry also never got to enjoy his commission for the job; he was convicted and sentenced to life in prison. But Paladin Press, our neighbor here in Boulder County, got to keep its profits from selling James Perry a 130-page book called*

Hit Man: A Technical Manual. *The book contained advice like the following (read slowly):*

- *Using your six-inch, serrated-blade knife, stab deeply into the side of the victim's neck and push the knife forward in a forceful movement. This method will half decapitate the victim, cutting both his main arteries and windpipe, ensuring immediate death.*
- *Although several shots fired in succession offer a quick and relatively humane death to the victim, there are instances when other methods of extermination are called for. The employer may want you to gather certain information from the mark before you do away with him. At other times, the assignment may call for torture or disfigurement as a "lesson" for the survivors.*
- *Use a rifle with a good scope and silencer and aim for the head—preferably the eye sockets if you are a sharpshooter. Many people have been shot repeatedly, even in the head, and survived to tell about it.*

*In later litigation brought against Paladin Press by the survivors of the three victims, the publisher admitted for purposes of the litigation that James Perry had purchased, and followed, the* Hit Man *manual in carrying out his triple assassination. It also admitted that it knew and intended that the manual would be used by criminals and would-be criminals to carry out murders for hire. The publisher made these admissions because it wanted to argue, in a clean fashion without quarrels about factual matters, that even if Perry had been encouraged and instructed by the manual in killing his victims, and even if Paladin Press had known that he or someone like him would use the manual that way, the First Amendment would prohibit any court from entertaining a lawsuit like the one the victims' families filed against Paladin Press. Why would it? Because, to put their arguments in a nutshell, it would be censorship. It would inhibit those who write and create and publish the writings and creations of others, for fear that their creations or publications would inspire one person to do harm to another and they would be required to pay for it. It would have, as we say, a (pause) chilling effect on free expression.*

*I was one of those who said they were right. It might not be as blatant as burning books, it might not be as straightforward as a judge's injunction to prohibit the publication of the* Pentagon Papers, *but the legal theory that would require Paladin Press to pay for the actions of James Perry, just because they had published a book about how to be a hit man, would discourage the publication of such books. And not only books about how to be a hit man, but books about being a hit man. Or a bank robber, or a Mafia boss, or a drug addict. Goodbye to* Bonnie and Clyde, *and* The Man With the Golden Arm, *and* The God-father. *I hated the* Hit Man *book; it's despicable and disgusting. But the First Amendment is for the speech you hate, isn't it?*

*Most of you know all of this. But I'm here to tell you something different tonight. This is it: I was wrong. I was wrong about* Hit Man, *and wrong in general about this kind of lawsuit.*

*I have a friend who makes bicycles; they sell for about four or five hundred dollars. Sometimes bicycle manufacturers get sued; an individual claims he was hurt because a bicycle was badly designed or poorly made. Bicycle manufacturers know this, and they buy insurance to protect them from legal fees and judg-ments; it's a cost of doing business. My friend says that about sixty dollars of the cost of every bicycle goes to these precautions. Have you ever heard anyone com-plain that the possibility of product liability has had a chilling effect on the production of bicycles? Of course not.*

*But Tory, I can hear you saying, bicycles aren't speech. Books and movies and video games are. We have to keep the marketplace of ideas flowing freely or silence will descend on us. I'll forego the glib answer that silence has already descended, hard, on Trevor and Mildred Horn and Janice Saunders. But let's talk about that marketplace. God knows if there's any lesson we've been hit with again and again in the last decade it's that markets are good. But a marketplace is not where products go to be cleansed of liability for the harm they cause. Bicycles and pharmaceuticals and automobile tires and home insulation are all sold in marketplaces. And they're all useful products, more useful than assassina-tion manuals, in my humble opinion. But aside from a few nut cases, nobody says that we should abolish all of the law of product liability in this country because we need to keep goods flowing through the marketplace. In fact, the better thinkers argue that we ought to import a little more of the discipline of the marketplace into the decisions of those whose products spread a harm that they aren't required to pay for or mitigate, in the form of what we call pollution. Economists even have a name for the phenomenon in which the parties to a transaction—for example those who wish to sell or buy polluting vehicles—seek to impose the costs of the transaction on a third party: they call them externali-ties. A market full of externalities is not an efficient market, or a just one. It is a deeply flawed marketplace.*

Yet the so-called *marketplace of ideas* will have just this flaw as long as we say that those who sell ideas, in the form of words or images, have no responsibility for the harms that their words and images contribute to.

But Tory, I hear you shouting. Nobody ever committed a murder, or a rape, or any other crime or atrocity because they read about it or saw it in a movie. But how can that be? I have noticed that some of the same people who make this claim also maintain that freedom of expression is important because books and movies, especially books, can change us, make us see things we never saw and know things we never knew, transform us, in other words, into more than we were before. This proposition I do believe. But if good books can make us better than we were (pause), how can it be that bad ones cannot make us worse?

But here is the thing, my loves, that you have to understand. I'm not claiming that the Hit Man *manual compelled or encouraged* James Perry *to kill those three people, any more than I'm claiming that* Natural Born Killers *encouraged those kids to shoot a convenience store clerk, or the video game* Doom *taught a troubled kid in Paducah, Kentucky, to solve his problems with a deadly weapon. I don't know that. That ought to be for a jury to decide, the same way they decide whether a flaw in a tire or a drug contributed to an injury. What I'm saying is this: if those products did encourage or contribute to some harmful outcome, in a way that those who profited from the product's sale should have foreseen, there's nothing in the First Amendment that says they should be immune from responsibility. That is not censorship; that is the market at work.*

But Tory, you are screaming now, isn't the one responsible for the deaths of those people the shooter, and the one who hired him to do his filthy work? Of course they are responsible; nothing I'm saying suggests they have anything less than full responsibility for their acts. When the Ford Pinto was being built, with the fuel tank that would explode when the car was rear-ended, most of us had no trouble with holding Ford responsible for the deaths of those who died in the flaming wrecks. Of course it was not Ford's fault that the Pintos were rear-ended; almost by definition, hitting the back of another car is negligent. But it was foreseeable to Ford that their cars would sooner or later be struck from the rear, and they had a responsibility to take that possibility into account in designing the car. And of course, the drunks or speeders or inattentive drivers who did the rear-ending were also liable for those deaths. One theory of responsibility does not exclude the other. Rules are available to sort out the relative portion of damages that should be paid by each responsible party.

*We have a decent, not perfect but decent, set of legal rules and doctrines to help us decide when those who put goods into the marketplace should bear responsibility for harm. The harm has to be actually caused by the product, it has to have been foreseeable. Scholars and legislators have tinkered with the details of these rules for a long time, and they have served us well. The First Amendment doesn't have a role in the development of these cases. If a judge ever tries to put someone in jail for what he wrote or said, or issue an injunction against the publication of some book or movie, I'll be the first one you hear screaming. But that's not what we're talking about.*

*If you're not persuaded yet, let me give you one of those hypothetical problems of the sort you probably remember, without affection, from law school. Suppose you are walking through a pleasant plaza, on your way to court or church or the gym or Trios, and happen into a crowd where someone has been preaching hatred of homosexuals. The crowd is all fired up. The speaker sees you and, looking around at the crowd he has gathered, screams "Kill the queer!" And they do.*

*The speaker raised no fist, fired no gun, laid not a hand on you. He has only exercised his power of free speech. And I am not suggesting that the law should stop him from speaking by employing force, or with a writ. But if you should die at the hands of this mob, would you think it unfair to hold the speaker responsible?*

*Of course, if the law holds him responsible, it might have a chilling effect on others who were considering similar speaking engagements.*

*(pause) Don't we hope it does?*

*(pause again) And anyway, however chilled they may be, they will not be as cold as you are, in the ground.*

*Thank you for giving me the chance to say these things to you.*

Later, after everyone had finished hugging her and congratulating her and a persistent few had hung around to explain their own analyses and reactions in some detail until one of the waiters started to vacuum the floor, Tory and I walked together down the Mall back to the office. I hadn't said a word since she had started speaking, and she seemed content with the silence as well. The wind sent clouds scudding across the face of the gibbous moon and I tightened my fleece jacket across my chest and asked Tory whether she had a written version of her talk. She reached into her bag and handed me a sheaf of folded paper.

"I can keep it?" I asked, tucking it carefully under my arm.

She just nodded, her eyes on that amazing moon, and we continued walking toward the silvery silhouette of the Rockies outlined by its light.

There were so many things I wanted to ask her that I got confused and could come up with only a simple one. "What happened," I asked her, "in the *Hit Man* case?"

"Trial judge threw the case out," she said. "Said a suit like that would violate the First Amendment. Court of appeals didn't agree, threw it back in. Now the Supreme Court has a certiorari petition before it, asking them to throw it out again. But the word I hear is that it may settle. Paladin Press's insurance company's got the jim-jams."

"So the First Amendment question still hasn't been decided for sure?" She nodded.

"How," I said, my pent-up questions beginning finally to spill out of me, "how did you figure out all of that stuff you said so fast? It was like, one minute you were against Peggy Grayling's lawsuit, the next you were for it."

"It wasn't that fast. Putting all those thoughts together occupied me for quite a while. I had Brianna Bainbridge out to lunch and she gave me some stuff to read and then I thought about it. I've been spending a lot of time working this out," she said.

"I can tell," I said. "I think that with a little editing for audience, what you said in here can become our brief on the First Amendment motion, when it comes. But it still seems to me you changed your mind in the course of an hour."

"Eighteen minutes."

We walked in silence for a moment or two while I puzzled over her meaning. Finally I said, "The tape? You mean watching the tape persuaded you, and then you started thinking about how to explain why?" If I hadn't been watching her closely I might not have seen the small, slow nod of her head. We had reached the jammed-up little parking lot behind our building.

"Just be sure the jury sees it, Cinda," she said. "At your trial. Night." I wanted to tell her I loved her but I knew she'd think that was femme so I just watched her climb into her Cherokee and held up my hand as she drove away.

I didn't feel ready to go home somehow. I took the back stairs up to the office, turned the lights back on, and sat for a long time with a legal pad, listing all the obstacles to success with this case. Assuming we could persuade a judge on the First Amendment question the way Tory had persuaded the crowd tonight, I thought the list looked like this:

- find the maker (Linc?)
- get jurisdiction in Colorado (find copy for sale here? who? and will that be enough?)
- prove causation btwn tape & Wolf's acts (Andy?)

I thought for a few minutes, then added a fourth item.

- prove Wolf's actions foreseeable to maker (how?)

The real list was probably even longer and more discouraging, but this one seemed daunting enough. I tried to think of anyone I knew who might be available to go around the state to adult bookstores and porn shops, looking for a copy of *Sunshade Snuffdown*. I needed Linc to pursue things in California, and anyway the job didn't require anything like his skill or intelligence. My eyes roamed my desk while I thought, and they fell onto a note from Beverly, explaining that she would be in late tomorrow because she and Charley had rescheduled their couples counseling. I reached for the telephone, thinking for a minute to remember her home number.

"Beverly," I said when she answered. "Sorry to call so late."

"Is there a problem about my coming in late tomorrow?" she said. I could hear the television whooping and thumping in the background. The World Wrestling Federation, it sounded like.

"No," I said. "Not at all. But could I speak to Charley?"

Beverly came into my office the next morning, while I was doing some First Amendment research, to tell me that John Scarpelli had called and asked for my e-mail address. "I gave it to him. That's okay, isn't it?"

"Sure," I said, still absorbed in some footnote written by Mr. Justice Souter.

"And Sam called. We had a nice long talk. I think he's lonely, Cinda."

I looked up at her. "I doubt it, Beverly. Not a guy like Sam in a place like Manhattan."

She held my gaze stubbornly. "I always thought that you and he—"

"I don't think so, Beverly. Too many difficulties, you know?"

She blew out a quick puff of exasperated breath. "Well, whatever. He'd like for you to call him, anyway."

"Okay," I said quickly. "Anything else?"

"Yes. We received a check for $20,000 from Margaret Grayling. For expenses, her note says."

"That's good," I said, still reading from the computer screen. "We'll need to send some expense money to Linc in L.A., and possibly Andy Kahrlsrud. He might be going to Chicago for us to work on the case. He says he'll pay for it himself but we can't let him."

She nodded. "He's nice, I like him better than our counselor. But you did more for me and Charley than any shrink I ever knew."

"What do you mean?" I looked up at her and noticed that her face had a blurred but happy expression, as though she had been up all night, or perhaps not up, but awake. "Have you and Charley rediscovered something?" I said.

She bent down and wrapped an arm fiercely around my neck, giving me quite a good whiff of her perfume. "Oh, Cinda, I'm just so grateful you had faith that he could do this job! It's done wonders for his, his—for both of us, really!" And she was gone, in a flurry of magnolia scent.

It's one of the things I love about Beverly, how little it takes to make her happy. How many women would be ecstatic that their husbands had a new job frequenting adult bookstores?

It was just before noon when the little phone in my briefcase rang, and it still took three rings before I realized what was making the silvery sound. When I did, I rummaged through papers and legal pads and a couple of stray tampons before finding it.

"Hello!" I said expectantly, realizing as I said it who the caller must be; I hadn't given the number out to anyone. "Hello, Rafe."

"Querida, am I the only one who ever calls you?"

"On this phone you are. How are you?"

"Very good. Just closed a big foreign distribution deal. Extremely big, in fact, with a party tonight to match. Wish you were here so we could celebrate."

I said nothing.

"Why don't you fly out? The studio will pay for your ticket. Let me have Louise call and arrange for it." I felt a surprising pull toward the urgency in his voice, but knew that agreeing to his suggestion would be a mistake of some sort, even if I wasn't sure exactly which sort.

"I can't, Rafe, I've got work to do here. Anyway, I couldn't take any more tickets from your studio. I feel bad enough about the phone, and the first-class ticket back to Denver."

"I explained about the phone, didn't I? Look, it's unlimited air time, unlimited long distance. You might as well use it because it doesn't cost any more whether you do or not. Not that I mind having a hot line to you, Querida, but I know you hate waste. I remember how you used to yell at us in law school about how we shouldn't take notes on yellow pads because yellow paper couldn't be recycled."

"I think it can be now," I said irrelevantly. I was waiting for him to deny that he had arranged for my flight back to Denver.

"Lots of things have changed since then," he said. "But some haven't. Come on, I need to talk to you anyway, about your tape."

"Why, did your guy find something out about it?"

"It's very possible. He's working on it some more today, and I think he's making some real progress."

"Can't you tell me about it over the phone?"

"I'd rather see you in person." He said it quietly, and I started to feel like an ingrate despite my suspicions.

"I can't leave now, Rafe. Sorry. This case is heating up, and I need to be paying attention to it."

"Really? What's heating up, if you can tell me?"

"Everything at once, it seems. But it all depends on finding who made the tape, of course. Listen, Rafe, I have an investigator who'll be arriving in L.A. today. Can I have him meet with your tape analyst? Then I'll come back out there myself when I can."

"Cinda," said Rafe, his voice less caressing now. "Do you really understand what you're getting yourself into here? I'll meet with your guy, of course. But have you thought about who's going to be lined up against you when you file this case?"

"Warner Brothers," I said. "Paramount Pictures. Universal Studios, NBC, ABC, CBS, CNN, Fox, the ACLU, *New York Times*, *Washington Post*, *Los Angeles Times,* Reporters Committee for Freedom of the Press, America

Online, the Freedom to Read Foundation, and about a dozen professors of constitutional law. I expect they will all ask to file *amicus curiae* briefs on behalf of the defendant, whoever he, she, or it may be."

"You do have an idea, then."

"Oh yes. I've been looking at who filed briefs in the *Hit Man* case. You do know about that one?"

"I know it," said Rafe. "And you left out one other likely opponent."

"Rose Brothers Studios."

"Probably."

"Will you work on the matter, do you think?"

"Maybe."

"Don't you have a conflict of interest, since you've been, ah, helping me with this?"

"Not on the principle of the thing, Lucinda. Not on the First Amendment issues. I have no conflict whatsoever on those."

"Last time I looked," I said, "the First Amendment said merely that Congress shall make no law abridging the freedom of speech."

"*Merely,* she says. Those founding fathers were really smart, and there's a reason they put that amendment first."

"Just how," I continued, "does a lawsuit of the sort I'm contemplating violate that First Amendment? Has Congress done anything?"

"Come on, Querida, don't insult my intelligence. We both know the Supreme Court has said it's the same rule for the state legislatures. If Congress can't do it, they can't do it."

"And if my client is permitted to sue the maker of a snuff film, for damages, how exactly will that constitute an act of the Colorado legislature?"

"Because the legislature will have abetted your lawsuit by setting up the court system and paying the judges and jurors and supplying the laws that you will invoke, you sneaky, obfuscating merchant of smoke and mirrors." He was laughing toward the end, and so was I.

"So your theory is aiding and abetting," I said.

"*Damn* straight, and an excellent theory it is. Isn't that how they got Al Capone?"

"That was income tax evasion, I believe. Listen, you're full of shit, Russell. Have you forgotten how I kicked your butt in moot court?" I smiled at the memory of the mock arguments we'd done in law school.

"Only because you sucked up to the judge, what was that lecher's name?"

"Did not."

"Did too. Listen, I gotta go. Tell your guy to call me about the tapes."

After he was gone I looked at the silent silver box in my hand for some time, trying to think of a reason to believe that Rafe was not responsible for drugging me and stealing my bags. "I just don't see what he had to gain from it," I said, apparently out loud.

"What?" said Beverly, passing by my office door. "Did you want something?"

I shook my head. "Just talking to myself."

"That's not a good sign, Cinda," she said. "You know what I think you need? I think you need—"

"Shut up, Beverly," I said. "Just because you got it and liked it doesn't mean it's what I need."

"Well," she said, offended, and walked away. I'd have to apologize later; for the moment I turned back to my research. But some trouble or regret seemed to buzz around my head like a persistent insect as I pursued my intention of reading through the entire corpus of Supreme Court decisions on the question of obscenity. It wasn't just that the cases didn't seem to address the questions I thought important, although they didn't. When the static finally got too loud for me to continue reading I sat back for a moment, and knew in that instant what it was: Sam.

It was true that he had left Boulder a long time ago; probably it was not reasonable to believe that our love affair could survive a separation so long, and so unlikely to end. But I knew our recent distance was about more than geography. I could not imagine being with Sam as a lover again. The memory of his presence while my mind and body reacted to *Sunshade Snuffdown* would pollute every caress and corrupt every feeling. I didn't think I could explain this to him, but perhaps he was feeling the same way. Apart from his recent call, he hadn't made any more of an effort to be in touch than I had. Even the circumstance that he'd called me at the office instead of at home suggested a certain aloofness, didn't it? But then I thought I remembered a couple of messages he might have left on my home answering machine since Chicago, calls I hadn't gotten around to returning.

This can't go on, I thought. I signed off WESTLAW and connected to our e-mail server. But before I began composing a message to Sam, I looked in my inbox. One message, it said. From John Scarpelli.

*Dear Cinda: Amy Springer ok'd your shrink talking to Fitzgerald, as long as he checks in with Amy first and shares whatever he finds with Amy and not with me. That's okay by me, I don't need to know any more about the Wolfman than I already do. When your guy gets to town he should call her at the public defender's office and she'll call Elgin to make sure they let him in. Lakshman Gupta will talk to him, too, as long as Fitzgerald signs a release. Gupta can be found at Elgin; your guy should have him paged if he's not in his office.*

*We're not done, Cinda, but that's all for now.*

*John*

When I reached Andy, he suggested we meet at the end of the day at a place called the Terrace, past the north city limits near the Bustop, Boulder's strip club.

"I will if that's what you want," I said. "But you'd have to give me a ride, since my car is still in the shop. And we're both right here in downtown Boulder, within walking distance of at least two dozen drinking establishments of every description. Why don't we just meet in one of them?"

"No," he said. "I'll be glad to drive, and these yuppie bars around here give me the willies. I always think I'm going to walk in and the bouncer will direct me to the special room set aside for people whose cholesterol is over two hundred and who are not wearing a single item made of spandex. Anyway, we'd never be able to hear each other talk with all the trustafarians and dot-commers fresh from their hang-gliding lessons, squawking on their cell phones trying to decide whether to buy or sell."

"Andy, I think those are your clients you're talking about."

"I know. It's bad enough I have to listen to them all day long, isn't it? Let's go to the Terrace."

"Isn't it kind of a biker bar?"

"So what? The bikers are much more polite than the smart set of Boulder. What's more, none of them is going to eye my girth with disfavor if I order a plate of nachos. I'll pick you up in front of your office at 5:30, and I'll drive you home afterward. Look for a Dodge Ram, blue, dusty. I don't mean that's a color. I mean it's blue and it's got dust all over it."

"I think this redneck thing of yours has gone a little over the top, Andy."

"I think if I have to listen to that airhead Enya recording they play in my reception area again I'm going to have to shoot the CD player. See you at 5:30."

Peggy came by in the early afternoon with some photographs of Alison that I had asked her to bring in. Some of them were home snapshots, rather blurry and off-center. In three of them the little girl looked out from the mottled blue rectangular background favored by school photographers, her eyes clear and untroubled. In the last one her face was beginning to narrow and her cheekbones to cast faint shadows. I thought she would have grown into a beautiful woman, with a strong resemblance to her mother. "How old was she in this one?" I asked Peggy.

She looked, then thought for a moment. "Nine. Just a few weeks before," she said, her voice as steady as ever.

"Thank you for bringing these," I said, pulling out a folder to store them. "I need your permission to send one of them with the psychologist who will be interviewing Leonard Fitzgerald."

I thought she might have flinched ever so slightly, but if so she recovered quickly. "Whatever you think necessary. But may I ask why?"

"We don't know what kind of mental state he may be in, or how much he'll remember or be willing to say. Dr. Kahrlsrud is a very good interviewer, and he'll know whether showing the photograph, at some moment, might be useful."

She nodded. "I trust you, Cinda. But will this interview allow us to discover who made the videotape? You must remember that's my main interest."

"I doubt it, Peggy. Even if Fitzgerald will tell Andy where he obtained the tape, that's not likely to lead us to the maker. At most it would allow us to find the store where he rented it."

"Then I'm not sure I understand the purpose of the interview. I want to find the person or people who made that tape. Remember there's another little girl involved, too. Whoever made that tape deserves—I don't know what. To be confronted with what he's done."

"I know, Peggy. We're working on that end of it. I expect a call from our investigator in Los Angeles tonight, and if that trail peters out we'll find another. But we need to be ready if the maker is identified, and one of the things we need to be prepared to prove is that the tape inspired Fitzgerald to kill Alison—that he wouldn't have done it unless he had been exposed to the video."

"I understand then. But even being able to prove that won't get us into court unless we can find out who made it, will it?"

"That's right. But it will help keep us in court, if we do discover whom to sue and they file the sorts of pretrial motions I expect. It will be essential then. But I suppose we could wait for the outcome of our investigation into the maker before spending your money on this interview. It's your decision."

"No," she said, "the money is not an issue. As long as you're pursuing the other as well." She rose and took my hand. "Thank you Cinda."

"Thank you, Peggy. Peggy?" I called her back as she was opening my office door.

"Yes?" She looked over her shoulder at me with eyes as clear as her daughter's. I wanted to ask her whether she was seeing anyone, getting any help dealing with her grief, but she looked so much calmer and more determined than I felt myself that the question stuck in my throat.

"Sorry," I said. "Nothing. Take care."

I went back to my old yoga class at noon, breathed really really deeply and evenly, and tried to think of myself as a link in the great chain of being, as my teacher recommended. I know it sounds as though I'm being sarcastic, but the truth is that no matter what irony I brought into the yoga room, it never survived long in the warm radiance of Mali's voice. I stretched and bent and tried to maintain *ujjayi pranayama* and *moola bandha,* and at the end of the hour, a certain warmth had replaced the chilly clenched grip that lately seemed to have spread from my thoughts to my joints. Still, as I showered and re-dressed, I thought that this respite would not last unless I could find some way to melt the ice in my head the way yoga had warmed my limbs.

By the time I got back to the office, Beverly had a fistful of pink phone messages for me, each a small fire that needed putting out with my telephonic firefighting skills. Some were my clients' conflagrations and some were Tory's, but since she was in federal court in Denver at a bond reduction hearing I was the only smokejumper on duty. I spent the afternoon with the small black club pressed against my ear, arguing and cajoling and reassuring, and lost track of the hour until Beverly looked in to say she was leaving for the day.

"Good then," I said into the receiver to my last cajolee. "I'll send you a memo so we'll have it in writing. Right. Right. Thanks so much. Right." I reminded myself to breath deeply and evenly from my belly, and placed the phone back in the cradle with far more solicitude than I felt for it. "Beverly, what's up? Don't give me any more of those pink slips. Ever."

"No more today. I'm going, but I wanted you to know that the Saab place called and your car is ready for you to pick up any time. Also, Charley called in, and he is really on the case. He's been to two places in Boulder, one in Longmont, and he's on his way to Denver now. Nothing yet, but he says Denver is the most promising. Lots of places to look there."

I leaned back in my chair. "That's great, but isn't he going to be home pretty late if he's just leaving for Denver?"

"I don't mind. Not if he's doing important work like this."

"You're great, B," I said, and meant it. "What time is it anyway?"

"Nearly 5:30."

"Yikes," I said. "Gotta go myself."

Andy was right: the Terrace was much quieter than any of downtown Boulder's oases. He and I sat in a corner booth nibbling on nachos and sipping margaritas, perfectly pleased with the company. If the men were a bit burlier, and the women somewhat more leather-skinned, than the aerobicized and glycogen-peeled hordes thronging the Mall a few miles south, that only made us feel more at home. I even felt kindly toward the fellow at the next table with the braids in his beard and the t-shirt that said SHOW US YOUR TITS.

"Here are the photos," I said, handing Andy an envelope with the school pictures of Alison Grayling, as well as the crime scene photographs. "Maybe one of these will get the Wolf talking."

"Thanks," he said, licking guacamole off his moustache with gusto while he slid the envelope into the unstylish hard-sided briefcase at his feet. "I'll be in Chicago tomorrow evening, and I plan to get to Elgin by mid-morning on Friday. I've been working on an interview protocol, but I want to be sure I understand your goals here."

"Almost anything you can learn about this man's thought processes around the time of the crime would be of interest," I said. "But the main reason he's important to the case is to prove causation. We could prove that he had the tape, and probably that he had been watching it, without his cooperation if we had to. But there's only one way to prove that the tape caused him to do the things he did to Alison Grayling, and that's through him. Gupta's report is helpful, and I suppose I could try to persuade him to be a witness, but I'd be very happy if you were able to come back and report that in your professional opinion, the tape was the proximate cause of Alison's Grayling's suffering and death."

"*Proximate cause* is not a term that means a lot to a psychologist, Cinda."

I thought back to the endless and inconclusive discussions we'd had about this term when I was a student. "It's not one that means a lot to me, either. It's a start if we can establish cause in fact—sometimes it's called *but for* cause. If you're able to say that but for the tape, Fitzgerald wouldn't have done what he did, that's an important part of what we need."

"Okay, that's at least a concept I can understand, but I may not be able to reach that conclusion with any degree of confidence. There are likely to have been many confounding variables in his environment. All the other porn he watched, for one thing."

"I understand. But think about the insanity cases you've worked on. Didn't you ever conclude that *but for* someone's mental illness, he or she wouldn't have done the crime?"

"Sure, but it's not exactly the same thing, Cinda. Serious mental illness is a much more pervasive factor in the conduct of persons who suffer from it than a single environmental stimulus. In fact, I'd guess without having met this fellow yet that I'd rate his craziness as a much more significant factor in his behavior than whatever he was watching on his VCR."

"That's not really a problem," I said. "There can be more than one proximate cause in the law. Like when an automobile collision kills someone, both the conduct of the negligent driver and the faulty design of the car that rolls over too easily can be proximate causes."

Andy shook his head. "This is reminding me of why I never wanted to go to law school. Okay, anything else?"

"This isn't really your problem, but I need your advice about a related question. Another part of the idea of proximate cause is foreseeability. I probably need to show that the wrongdoer should have foreseen that if he did what he did—making and marketing the tape in this case—it was likely to lead to the bad thing that happened, in this case the death of Peggy Grayling's daughter. So I'm hoping to find some research that shows that material of this nature has the likelihood, or the possibility, of inspiring acts like Leonard Fitzgerald's. Do you have any references for me?"

He snorted. "You don't want much, do you? Anyway, your question is all over the place. *Likelihood* and *possibility* are very different things. And what do you mean by likely? How likely?"

"There's no real answer to that in the law."

Andy poured each of us another margarita from the pitcher, leaving it empty. "Let me be sure I understand this. Your profession wants mine to answer a question with precision when you can't even articulate it with any precision?"

"You could put it that way. I didn't invent the law, Andy, I just toil in the vineyards."

He rubbed a napkin across his furry lower lip and nodded sagely as though confirmed in all the skepticism he'd ever had about lawyers. "I will say I like your devotion to hopeless causes, Cinda. I've got a bibliography of work on the relationship between media exposure and violent acts that I put together for you, but I doubt you're going to find anything as clear as you're hoping it is. The best stuff for you is by a guy named Detweiler." He rummaged about in the battered case and came out with a few pages stapled together. I remembered the name from my first conversation with Brianna Bainbridge.

"This is great!" I said, examining the pages without really taking them in. "Did we really drink that entire pitcher of margaritas?"

He nodded, miming an inebriated face, and signaled for the check. But he turned back to look at me with eyes as sober as a child's. "I do have one last question. Why are you doing this case, Cinda? You could be earning a lot of money, or doing a lot of good, or both, if you stuck to goals that were a little more achievable. Don't you ever get tired of losing?"

I thought of reminding him of our agreement that he wouldn't try to be my therapist, but my impulse to defend myself was stronger. "What do you mean? I win a *lot!* I got a deputy DA off on a drunk driving charge earlier this week, and the guy was guilty as Judas!"

He just watched me, saying nothing.

"I'm a good lawyer, Andy." I wasn't sure why my throat felt bumpy on the inside as I said it.

"Everybody who knows you understands that, Cinda. How did you feel when you got the drunk DA acquitted?"

"Don't try to shrink me, Andy. It's been tried; it doesn't take."

He leaned toward me slightly. "All right then, let me put it this way. Why do you think *I'm* doing this?"

"My client is prepared to pay you your usual professional consultation fee and all expenses, of course," I said stiffly.

"I'm sure she is. But I'm also sure you know that's not why I'm doing it."

"I believe you said you were interested in trying to understand Leonard Fitzgerald, and what caused him to do what he did."

He nodded. "I am. And also, you. I'm interested in why a talented lawyer who could be at the top of her profession wanted to take on the representation of a death row inmate, then a confused anorexic kid who was mixed up with some very scary people. And now this."

"You're reading way too much into these things, Andy. I've done lots of other work in the last few years that you don't even know about. Anyway, I was *appointed* to represent Jason Smiley. And Mariah—well, you were as interested in helping her as I was."

"That's true," he said, and when I remembered the help he'd given that troubled girl, a wave of gratitude and affection rolled over me. Some subtle change had affected the lighting in the room: items seemed to have acquired haloes, to have lost their hard edges. Perhaps it was the tequila, but it also had something to do with Andy's voice, concerned, confiding but without the threat of judgment. In a moment, all was changed—the table was his office, I his client. I was not certain why I was talking to him, but unconcerned about that. I knew it would become clear eventually. I was just talking.

"Who knows why we do the things we do?" I said. "Who cares, anyway?"

"Sometimes if we understand that, we can make wiser choices in the future," Andy said mildly.

"I don't have any regrets about my choices in the past," I said.

"Okay."

His easy silence became intolerable. "What is there to say, anyway? Where would you even start?" I said.

"Most people think it's useful to start with their childhood."

"Not me. I've come too far from there."

"Okay. You tell me, then, why you took this case, why you put so much into it."

"I had a client, that's all. I'm a lawyer, I had a client. Now that she's my client, I have to do everything I can for her, no matter what it costs me personally."

"Surely you turn away some clients."

"Not that many. Business isn't that good. Too many lawyers in this town."

"But sometimes you do."

"Sometimes."

"How do you decide?"

"For one thing, Peggy Grayling was someone I'd known years before. We had that in common. And I liked her, a lot."

"How many years before?"

"Well she was—oh, no. I see where you're going. The childhood thing again."

"I wasn't going anywhere, you were. She was what?"

"She was the older sister of a girl I went to school with."

"High school?"

"Elementary."

"And that was where?"

"You just have to make me get into it, don't you?"

"Okay, then, never mind that. Tell me about your family today. Are your parents alive?"

I took another large drink of the margarita and considered clamming up altogether. Andy looked at me thoughtfully, then said, "I'll be back in a minute," and headed toward the door marked DUDES.

My mother is dead but my father is in a nursing home. He still looks like the giant of my childhood, only he's white-haired now and has a beard— easier for the staff—and he's confined to a wheelchair. He's silent. My sister and I still quarrel over whether he recognizes us, cares when we visit, hears us when we talk to him. The doctors say there is no way to be sure. Dana says no. I still think yes, that he hears but just can't respond. Easy for you to believe that, said Dana once when we argued about it. Easy for you, a thousand miles away in Colorado.

Let's not quarrel, I said to her. You're the only family I have left now, you and your kids.

And Jerry, she said.

Of course, I said. Jerry.

It was Jerry who had suggested, during one Thanksgiving dinner at their house a few years ago, that the real shame of the whole sorry mess was that nobody could get over it. All these years passed, he said, and still when I go to an industry convention, and say I'm from Dallas, I can tell that's what they're thinking. *Place they shot Kennedy*. Like I'm responsible, like I *did* it somehow. Man, I was in kindergarten! That's the real shame of it. And this town the best damn place to live in America—I mean, look around you!

His gesture took in the view out their enormous bow-front window: the semicircular driveway curved beneath the Lincoln Town Car from fresh off his lot, the stately brick mansions of his neighbors, the endless sky unmarred by the slightest cloud. My eye was less infatuated than his and also noted the Mexican-American maid in black-and-white uniform standing at the door of the mock Tudor across the street, waiting patiently for an overfed cocker spaniel to finish doing his business so she could readmit him to the house. When I turned my face back Jerry was surveying the inside of their living-dining area with pride as well: the shining breakfront, the polished buffet table softly glowing with reflected firelight, his guns gleaming behind the narrow oblong glass panels of their locked cabinet.

Can we go watch the football game, Dad? said Woody, my youngest nephew. He was the starting halfback on his middle school team.

Sure, said Jerry. Go ahead on, I'll join you soon.

I'd rather stay and talk to Aunt Cinda and you and Mom, said Louis, the older one.

Go ahead on, son, said Jerry. That kid needs to take more of an interest in things the other kids care about, he said when Louis had followed his brother out to the den.

Like football, I said neutrally.

Ya damn betcha, he said.

Please don't curse at my holiday table, said Dana.

I was the usual recipient of this entreaty, a thought that must have occurred to Jerry as soon as it did to me. He winked at me before turning to Dana.

Sorry, sweetheart, he said. Then he turned back to me.

I hate it when that's all they can think about when it comes to Dallas. Son of a bitch wasn't even *from* Dallas. He was from Russia or something, right?

Jerry, said Dana.

Sorry, sweetheart, I'm done. So, Cinda. When are you moving back to Big D, where you belong? It's God's country, you know.

When Andy came back I decided to tell him just a little bit of it. "I grew up in Dallas," I said. "But it always felt to me like an accident, my being from there. I loved my parents and family, but as soon as I learned in school about other places, I started to feel like I was, sort of a changeling or something. That I was meant to be dropped down in Kansas City or Portland, Maine, but accidentally delivered to the wrong place. Then after that day, I felt it more than ever."

"What day?" asked Andy.

"November 22, 1963." And somehow I ended up telling him the story in much more detail than I had intended, including the parts about Celia. "So she looked at me sideways and said *yay. Yay,* they got him." I looked down at my lap.

Andy handed me a ridiculous bulky paper napkin, stained in one corner with red salsa. "Careful," he said. "Use the other end of it. If you get that salsa in your eye you'll be crying for the next two weeks."

"I don't know why I'm crying at all. I haven't thought about that in years."

"And this was Peggy Grayling's little sister?"

I nodded, my nose streaming. "But the thing is, after we reconnected I found out that she'd always felt the same way. Peggy, I mean. Like she didn't belong there. So we sort of bonded over that."

"So this is all part of it?" he said.

"Of what—of why I'm handling this case? Maybe some part. But why do I have to explain it? Every lawyer takes some and says no to others. Why don't you investigate your own head if you're so interested in the hopeless cause syndrome?"

"Maybe that's what I'm trying to do. If you'd talk to me it might help me understand myself, too."

Possibly the alcohol was wearing off, or maybe Andy's questions were too reminiscent of John Scarpelli's inquisitions. Whatever it was that tipped me over into anger, suddenly I had had enough, more than enough, of letting some guy with his own issues take a peek inside my head as the price of his help.

"Fuck off, Andy," I said hotly. I wasn't too drunk to notice that it came out sounding like *oth,* and tried to regain my dignity in the next sentence. "Send me an invoice for your work, but I'd be grateful if you'd keep your diagnoses to yourself,"—*shelf*—"unless they're of the Wolf."

He stood up, nearly toppling the unsteady table as his large torso pushed against it, quickly grabbing the pitcher to prevent it from sliding off the edge. "Sorry," he said. "You're right, it's none of my business. Come on. I was going to drop you off to pick up your car, but I think I'd better just take you home."

Late the next morning, the sun streaming through my window too insistently to be ignored any longer, I rose, made myself a cup of strong coffee, and rode the Skip up Broadway to Scandinavian Motors to get the Saab. What a deal: my insurance company had paid for the damage and the car was even better than before because the radio worked consistently for the first time in ages. I drove back toward home singing along to "Box of Rain," or the parts I could remember the words to, considering a little light gardening or possibly a run around the lake. But the Saab went right by the turn near the house and took me back downtown. It was a University of Colorado football Saturday, and all of the Mall's eateries were jammed with pregame brunch hunters, but I wasn't hungry. I parked the Saab and went upstairs to my office, where I stared at the wall for a while and then at the list I had made the night Tory gave her talk.

It would be a long time before the lawsuit of *Margaret Grayling v. Anonymous For Now* assumed its final pretrial shape, but if I closed my eyes I could sense it growing, like a seed sprouting below the ground. *Find the maker, get jurisdiction, prove causation, show foreseeability.*

I would work on the last item myself, using Andy's bibliography, but for the others I was depending on Linc, Charley, and Andy. I had deployed my troops and now I could only wait for their field reports.

I thought of the evening I had sat in this same chair and had seen in Tory's eyes her attraction to the case, and feared the manic loyalty that seemed to seize her. That fear seemed unnecessary now—since seeing the tape Tory had been steady but detached, supporting the office with unspectacular but remunerative cases while I obsessed over the Wolf and his work. And his accomplice, whomever or whatever it might have been.

The mania was still around, yes, only it pulsed in my veins instead of Tory's. Restlessly, I stood to lean against the wall, looking out the window at the alley behind our office and watching a clump of laughing football fans as they pushed each other jovially along the broken surface of the alley. One of the men stumbled and a young girl with laughing eyes, perhaps his daughter, reached out a hand to help him rise again. Behind this family a couple walked hand in hand, in earnest conversation. She was black, and he white. As he looked up into her face I turned my eyes back into the room, sat down at my desk, and remembered that I had meant to be in touch with Sam. But my hands fell away as I reached for the computer keyboard, and instead I took up the list again, staring at it until my eyes grew tired. I wondered how soon I would hear anything from Linc.

# PART TWO

Lincoln liked Cinda, liked her a lot and liked working for her, but found her very confusing. Half the time she didn't know what she wanted, and then sometimes when it seemed like she *did* know, she'd change her mind. He'd never known anyone to change her mind so often. Most people these days were so opinionated they wouldn't change their minds if you washed their brains with extra-strength Clorox, but even without external influences Cinda would zig and zag like a broken-field runner trying to pull away from a tackle, only Linc didn't think Cinda knew who she was trying to get away from most of the time.

Tory was a lot easier, even if she was a lesbian and all, because she was just as stubborn as everybody else and there was a lot less of the coming and going in her head. Although she did do a 180 about the Grayling case after she saw the tape. Which, if you didn't change your mind after seeing it, you'd be brain dead anyway. Linc was down with violent movies as much as anyone—*Reservoir Dogs* was his favorite (Michael Madsen was epic), but he liked *Pulp Fiction* and *Natural Born Killers* even. He didn't mind if the sex was a little edgy and he didn't believe in censorship, but c'mon! Trying to teach people to get their rocks off about cutting up a little kid? Things like that gave sex a bad name. Not to mention (if Cinda and Tory were right about this one) giving some people who were a few raisins short of a muffin some very bad ideas.

Linc was studying to be a paralegal and had read a lot about product liability. He didn't know why the idea shouldn't apply to stuff like that tape. He knew if he admitted this, his friends would be like, no way, that's censorship dude, what about *Reservoir Dogs?* He didn't know all the answers but all he could say was you gotta draw a line somewhere and that tape is definitely on the other side of any line anybody would draw. Anybody. If someone didn't agree with him, it would just be because they haven't seen it.

He wished he hadn't seen it himself, to tell the truth, as he thought it had messed up his mind a little. After Mariah, he didn't really want to be with any girls for almost a year, and then things got back to normal, some-how. Which meant sometimes you got lucky, sometimes not. But now this thing had really put him off it. Last week this hottie he had met salsa dancing one night had come back to his crib with him. After this and that she put her hand on his zipper and just when he was thinking, Oh man, this could be major, there was something about the way she squeezed her eyes shut and he flashed on the little girl and the knife and that was it.

He didn't want to think about that. Anyway, Cinda as usual couldn't make up her mind; which accounted for what happened after Linc got to El Lay, picked up a rental Prizm (a pretty bogus ride, but it was cheap and the client was paying so he thought he'd better go for it instead of the Mustang he would have liked), checked into this elderly hotel, and tried to call the Chris guy. Which was going nowhere fast because all he got was the guy's goofy message, so he left his own saying he had seen some of Chris's work and thought he had a lot of talent and would like to talk to him about the possibility of some other work, only please no agents yet, as they tended to fuck up a deal when they got into it too soon and there would be plenty of time to bring the agents in if things seemed promising after a preliminary conversation. Linc had already decided this was the only likely way to approach the guy. He said his name and room number and the hotel's phone and hung up; he was still sitting there thinking about how to explain to Chris how he happened to have his name and phone number if he called back, when the phone rang and it was Cinda.

The thing was that before he left Boulder there was some talk about a guy named Rafe, some honcho at one of the studios, and how some other guy there was supposed to be analyzing the tape to see if they could figure where it came from. Cinda told Linc at the time not to call this Rafe, because things were tense somehow between the two of them, which was cool by him. Plus Cinda was drugged on her flight back from here to Denver, and from circumstantial evidence Tory thinks Rafe was behind it although nobody could figure why he would be. So Linc was supposed to stay away from him, but now she'd changed her mind, which is why she'd phoned.

It seemed Rafe had called her and said they were close to some break-through or whatever on the tape analysis, and Cinda said that Linc could call him to get clued about it. So he said he would and as it happened this was one of the best breaks that could have come around on the party dimension, because when he called (after getting past the assistants and whatnot by using Cinda's name) this Rafe said there's a big party that very night in Laurel Canyon and Linc should meet him there and they'd talk. Why not? was his reaction because even if the guy was corroded, he could learn something and fuel up at this party, which was sounding better and better as the food on the airplane was strictly lame. So he wrote down the address and by about six o'clock he was cruising along Mulholland Drive wishing he had sprung for the Mustang after all or at least something with a drop-top.

He'd seen houses like this one before in movies, but he'd never been in one. A valet who was like a guy his own age took the Prizm without making a face even though the car ahead of him was a Mercedes and behind him a Bentley, and a girl in a black and white uniform who looked like Jennifer Lopez offered him a drink before he was even in the living room, which was like a hotel lobby with a waterfall and paintings so abstract and so big that at first he thought they were just very outrageous wallpaper but then he saw that one of them was signed *Leroy Nieman* in the corner. So he edged over to look a little closer and then a big dude wearing a sports jacket that was just a little big under one armpit was standing beside him and asking might he know whom it was Linc wished to see.

Linc thought this was pretty good grammar for a guy who looks like he's strictly muscle. Tory had taught him to be attentive to grammar, the subject versus the object and all, because it was important for lawyers, although Linc had never noticed that lawyers on the whole were all that good at it. But he still paid attention because (although he had not told Cinda or Tory) the real reason he wanted to be a lawyer or at least a paralegal was to get some experiences that would allow him someday to write books about the law like John Grisham, and he knew that proper grammar was essential for a writer. So on the basis of this guy's speech Linc decided that this was a very classy party, and he asked the muscle if he could be taken to Mr. Russell, whose guest Linc said he was.

So the muscle took him through the house out the back, where there was a swimming pool the size of a football field and an epic view of the city down below, not to mention a number of girls whom Linc could not begin to describe although he felt sure Grisham could have. These girls were the bomb, and for the first time he felt just a little like a country cousin. But then the muscle sidled up to this dude in a purple polo shirt that somehow on him didn't look weak and whispered something, and the dude turned around and said to him, "Lincoln, my man," but not phony or anything. This was Rafe, it seemed, and the muscle vanished and Linc was introduced to these insanely beautiful girls and gotten a fresh drink and shown to this buffet that went on for about a mile or so. After that he was free to wander around the pool and through the house and anywhere he wanted, including this monster greenhouse. He never saw the muscle again and even though he used the bathroom twice, he didn't see any drugs at all, unlike in various movies. As the evening went on and he started having a really good time, despite the native suspicion that is the hallmark of a PI, he decided that Tory had to be mistaken about Rafe.

But Linc didn't learn much about the tape that night, because Rafe said that the tape guy was supposed to be there but had come down with a bug or something. So he invited Linc to come to the studio the next day, where the guy and Rafe would tell him what they had found out. Which of course he said he would.

He left the party after midnight. On the drive back to the hotel he concluded that the Chevrolet Prizm, although a fine vehicle in many respects for ordinary uses, does not handle quite as well on curves as might be hoped. He considered himself lucky to arrive back at the hotel unscathed, although it was true that he had mislaid his tie (his only tie, as it happened) somewhere along the way. Still, this was not serious, as he had observed already that a tie was not an important accessory in Los Angeles. Despite the skanky smell of the pillow—like some medicine made out of a mold—he fell asleep right away and woke up just in time to leave for his meeting at the studio with Rafe.

It was pretty edgy driving on the freeways to get to Rose Brothers, and mad cool to be taken to Rafe's office, which was like its own little bungalow, in a little golf cart driven by a pretty black girl. But when Linc and Rafe were settled down in the hum of the air-conditioning with big glasses of o.j., Rafe told him that the guy who had worked on the tape was still out sick. "But never mind," he said. "I can tell you everything he discovered, and frankly it goes a lot further than I expected, because we had some lucky breaks."

"I couldn't exactly see how analyzing the tape would tell you that much. There aren't any secret identifying marks on videotape, are there?" said Linc. He knew this much from another case he'd worked on.

"That's right," said Rafe, "and anyway the tape we had was just a copy Cinda had made of the one they found in the killer's VCR, so analysis of the technical qualities of the tape itself was never a very promising avenue."

"Then how did you learn anything?" asked Linc.

"That was the lucky break part. This tape expert analyzes a lot of material for us, usually because we suspect someone's infringing one of our copyrights, or because someone has accused one of our productions of infringement. He's extremely expert at identifying, for example, who lit a certain production from clues in the style of lighting, or who did the sound because every sound director uses distinctive techniques and choices. It's sort of like the guys who can tell from looking at a poem whether it might be an undiscovered work by, say, Shakespeare, or Carl Sandburg."

"*Why does a hearse horse snicker,*" said Linc, "*hauling a lawyer's bones?*"

"What?" Rafe started to look a little edgy.

"Nothing. Just a poem I came across once. Sorry. So your guy could tell something about the lighting or the sound on this tape?" Probably he sounded dubious. He had seen the tape, and didn't think this very likely. The lighting and sound were totally bogus.

"In this case it was the credits, amazingly enough. Even though the credits were very brief and only identified the performers, exclusively by false names, our analyst was able to recognize them as the work of a particular credit designer. It was a lucky break, and it was only possible because the credit designer has done legitimate work as well as porn. If Stanley were here he could tell you about the particular characteristics that alerted him. Too bad he's under the weather."

This did seem like a useful discovery. "So I should tell Cinda the name of the credit designer, and maybe he'd be willing to tell us more about who made the film? Is it someone in L.A.?"

Rafe leaned back in his chair like a guy who's used to getting things done. "I'm ahead of you, bro. I know a lot of people in this town and I figured maybe I could get somewhere with this guy easier than Cinda could. I didn't know about you then—I mean, didn't know she was working with a professional. This credit designer is pretty hinky when I call him. At first he denies he had anything to do with it. Then we go back and forth a little and he says you can't prove anything and that's when I know Stan was right. He was the one. I figure he's reluctant to say so because he's seen the tape and didn't like the looks of it at all."

"Did he admit it then?"

"Finally, on condition of anonymity. You have to understand, Lincoln, the people in the business of making those movies are not good people. I know Orrin Hatch and Jesse Helms think everyone in Hollywood is a douchebag, but they're wrong. Guys like the ones who made this tape are criminals. They make us all look bad. And they're scary. This credit designer finally agrees that he'll tell me what he knows as long as I keep his name out of it. So I promised, and he told me who the producer was."

"Awesome! But if you can't tell me who the credit designer is, how's Cinda going to prove it? Sounds like I need to look up this producer." Linc was already thinking about how he'd approach the guy, induce his confidence, get him talking.

"Look, Linc, can we talk frankly here?"

"Sure, why not?"

"Cinda—I don't know how to explain about her. I know you and she have worked together some, but I've known her for years. We go way back, and I really don't want her to get hurt."

"Yeah, she told me you knew each other back in the day." Cinda had told Linc she and the guy had been friends in law school, but she'd never said there was any more to it than that. Maybe Cinda just hadn't wanted to cop to having done the dirty with this guy years ago. As if Linc would care. He was thinking about the roofies, too, but even though the guy was coming on a little slick Linc didn't think he was the one who'd busted that move. It didn't seem like his style.

"She's got her hands on this case about the dead little girl," Rafe continued, "and I think she's not completely rational about it. She doesn't understand what she'll be up against if she goes through with investigating it and filing it. She's not going to get anywhere, she's going to waste an enormous amount of her client's money and probably her own, and she's going to piss off some very powerful people."

"One thing I've noticed about Cinda," said Linc. "She's always thinking about the ins and outs of whatever she's doing. Too much so, some people would say. Also, she's always willing to eat her own dog food, if necessary."

"Well, I appreciate that about her. But you and I may be in position to get her and her client what they want from this case without the uncertainties she'd face if she were trying to do it alone. Which I'm glad to see she isn't, by the way."

It was kind of a pleasant novelty to be sucked up to but even so the bro act was pretty transparent. Linc himself had employed it professionally many times. It could work both ways, he thought. "I think the two of us could really help her out if we worked together," he said. "I didn't realize you cared about her that much."

"I do," said Rafe, "but that's not all there is to it. The people you're up against—I can't tell you how much they disgust me. They endanger everything we do in this industry, all the art and craft that go into the movies. I want you to put the craps to them as hard as you can. But it can be done in a way that doesn't endanger the freedom of artists everywhere to do their work and find their audience."

"Right," said Linc. "What do we do next, then?"

It was a funny thing. Charley never thought he'd get tired of thinking about sex but by late afternoon all he wanted was to take a break and sip some coffee in the Starbuck's attached to the Barnes & Noble on South Colorado Boulevard in Denver. It seemed somehow amazing and restful that here was an entire store full of books, and while no doubt quite a few of them, maybe even most, had some sort of sex aspect, probably only a few were about nothing but sex, which was quite a relaxing change from the bookstores where he'd been hanging out for the last couple of days.

Of course, adult bookstores sold a lot of things other than books, too. What he had learned were called lubes, for one thing, tubes of lubes of every flavor and description, lubes out the wazoo. Out the wazoo, that was funny, actually, now that he thought of it. He had to remember that for the screenplay he was writing. Also, every kind of thing you could think of made of leather, and a lot of things you'd never think of. Charley didn't actually get it why someone would want to wear a leather mask over his face to have sex, although he didn't object to it if someone did. He tried to think about what Bev would look like in the red teddy he had given her for their anniversary with a leather mask over her face, but the idea didn't do anything for him. Not that she would have done it even if it did turn him on. Ever since she'd started working for Cinda and Tory she'd gotten very independent in her thinking and sort of sniffy about some of the things she and Charley used to do together, like the doctor and nurse stuff. Still, he had to admit that his being out of work for so long hadn't helped, and that when Cinda called to give him this job it had done more for their sex life than 144 tubes of lube. That was a gross, see, which was also pretty funny and might find itself in the screenplay.

It was a video he was looking for, but he hadn't found it yet. At first he thought it would be helpful that the video areas of most of these stores were organized and classified, sort of like that Dewey Decimal thing only dirtier of course. There were the sections you'd expect, like *Gay*, and *S/M*, and *Tits*, and *Lesbian*. He hadn't seen any lesbians looking at the *Lesbian* section, though. Not that he always knew whether some girl was, but he hadn't seen any women at all in these places except sometimes the cashiers and the girls in the peep booths. The ones looking at the *Lesbian* section were men, just like the ones cruising the *S/M* and *Leather* sections. Then there were the sections you maybe wouldn't expect, at least he hadn't: *Spanking* was big, and then *Discipline*, which to judge from the boxes included spanking only more so, but also truly weird stuff like one tape called *Bathroom Slave*. The box on that one showed a guy licking a raunchy-looking toilet with his tongue while a woman wearing leather pants without any bottom in them stood over him with a riding crop, like to make sure he did a really good job. Charley guessed there was some relationship between the bottomless chaps and the job the guy was supposed to be doing, but to tell the truth he didn't want to think about it that much and it was just about then he decided to drop over to Barnes & Noble to drink a latte and listen to that *Four Seasons* thing that always seemed to be on their sound system.

It was restful, definitely. But after forty-five minutes or so he felt he ought to get back to work. Consulting his list, he got back into his Buick and headed for a shop on Santa Fe.

He had decided on his second or third stop that he didn't really have to cruise every tape, because from watching other customers he saw that he could ask the cashier, who usually seemed to have some inventory list on the computer. But twice when he had asked about *Sunshade Snuffdown*, he was told right away they didn't have any snuff films, that those were illegal. "No kiddie stuff either, Officer," one of the cashiers had said, a tired-looking woman whose face seemed to be falling off her bones in stages.

"Why don't you guys try to solve some murders or something instead of harassing a legal business?"

This was somewhat discouraging, as it had suggested that he might have to rethink his tactics, but as he drove to the store on Santa Fe Charley reflected that it was at least somewhat gratifying to have been mistaken for an undercover officer. It made him think of Johnny Depp in *Donnie Brasco,* not that it was the same situation at all, but that was a great movie. You had to actually, in your own head, become the kind of guy you were supposed to be, that was the trick. Thinking this way gave him an idea, and when he got to the store, after being told they didn't have anything called *Sunshade Snuffdown,* he imagined himself a creepy jerk, sort of a Steve Buscemi character, and asked whether there was a back room. The clerk, a man this time, looked at him appraisingly for several seconds, but then nodded and indicated with a jerk of his head that Charley should go through a grimy door set between two of the shelves. "Close it behind you," the man said.

It was pretty dim on the other side of the door, and noisy with the blast of heavy metal music, but luckily Charley was used to that from having raised Duane and so pulled the door shut behind him and looked around. There weren't any tapes, or books, or lubes, or leather either, just six doors along one side. A metal plate the size of a kid's bicycle license tag hung from a nail on each door. The first one said OCCUPIED, and Charley could hear a droning, repetitive moan coming from behind it. Walking on, he saw that all the others said COME IN, so he chose one and did, turning the sign on the door over to say OCCUPIED and finding inside it a little booth with a narrow shelf against the opposite wall, blank except for an oval fitting about the size and shape of a mask, like maybe for diving (although Charley had never been diving) or maybe a Zorro mask. He sat down in the sticky plastic chair and leaned forward to peer through the goggles, but after blinking and adjusting his gaze he realized that the opening, if it was one, had been blocked by something.

"Do you need change?" said a melodious voice, as though right in the booth with him. It was startling, but he was proud to say he didn't jump at all. Then he noticed a coin slot in the shelf.

"Yeah, I guess I do."

"Garth can give you some at the counter," said the voice. "But be sure you come back to this booth. This is the best one, I promise."

"What's your name?" he said, with excellent presence of mind.

"Sable. Want to know why?"

"Yeah."

"I'll show you when you come back."

When Charley went back out to the counter Garth was talking on the phone, but said "Later" and hung up when he saw Charley.

"I guess I need some change. I didn't realize I was out."

Garth looked bored. "How much?"

Charley examined his wallet and pulled out a five-dollar bill. "A fin," he said, glad he had remembered this term, as he felt it added to his authenticity as a customer of the place.

Garth punched open the cash register and counted out twenty quarters. "Seventy-five cents for two minutes, right? That's, ah, twelve minutes you got there. You sure that's all you need?"

"That should do it," he said cheerfully.

The customer in the first booth was still moaning harshly as Charley passed by and found Sable's booth again. His hand fumbled a bit as he put the quarters down on the little shelf and then fed the first three into the coin slot and settled his face against the peephole. Whatever had been covering the peephole slipped open and Charley was looking into a small room, the twin to his own cubicle, containing only a velveteen-covered stool and, sitting on it, a naked woman with a very dark and very thick growth of pubic hair. He was not dismayed by the involuntary cooperation of his johnson, as impersonation was the name of the game and he thought Sable might notice if he didn't seem interested.

"Hi again. Do you see why they call me Sable?" she said playfully.

"Yeah," he said. "Do you see why they call me Richard the Great?"

"Richard the—oh, I see. Very funny. But I can't see you, of course. House rules. I wish I could, though," she breathed. "Would you like for me to dance?"

"Sure," he said, and so it went. The first two minutes were over quicker than they should have been and Charley was very suspicious of the timer and whether it was altogether fair to the customer, but doubted that complaining would do much good, so he just kept feeding quarters until they were gone. After he was out two and a quarter his professional ethics told him it was time to try to learn something from Sable, so he concentrated on getting her to tell him her real name while she danced. That way, he reasoned, he could track her down later where she lived and get the real scoop on the store and maybe some other stores as well, as there was no reason she might not also work at other peep booths.

"Sable? What's your real name, darlin'? I'll tell you mine if you'll tell me yours. Mine's Charley." As he said it he realized he should have used a pseudonym, but she didn't seem to be paying any attention anyway. She just laughed at him as she spun and caressed herself. She was a fantastic dancer. Amazing muscles. Faster than anything, his money was gone, and the slot snapped shut.

"Sable?" he said.

"Yes," she replied. "Can you see where I'm touching myself?"

"I think you know I can't see shit," he said, proud of this deduction. "I'm out of quarters. Don't go away."

But when he got back to the cashier counter, Garth hosed him. "Get out," he said without particular feeling. "I don't like creeps that try to learn my girls' names."

On a deductive roll, Charley figured that Garth must have speakers that allowed him to listen in on what was going on in the peep booths. "I won't do it again. C'mon, give me ten dollars' worth. I think I'm in love."

Garth shook his head. "G'wan, dickweed, before I lose my famous temper. You're outta here."

Charley thought there was little point to arguing, but he had a plan.

Andy had interviewed individuals in jail before, and in a few prisons and hospitals for the so-called criminally insane, like this one. He was used to the security routine, the searches and cameras and metal detectors, and the bad smells and the indifference of the personnel to his safety. *Goddam yuppie shrink,* he could almost hear them thinking. *Always inventing some new explanation for why the dementos did what they did and it wasn't their fault, then going home to his comfortable bed while we stay here all night. Let him look out for himself.* He'd feel the same way himself, he thought, imagining the men who staffed the night shift in this aging brick compound in this decayed manufacturing town sitting at their posts through the dark hours, missing their kids' bedtimes, turning the pages of motorcycle and truck magazines and wondering when one of the inmates was going to put a shank between someone's ribs and whether it would be theirs.

Andy massaged his neck muscles with one hand, feeling the tightness of his belt with the other and wondering whether there was a way for him to loosen it one notch without being noticed. It had been a long drive from Chicago in his flimsy rented car, and the airless motel room had been so uninviting that he had merely dumped his suitcase in it, splashed water on his face and rubbed his beard, and driven on to the hospital.

"Dr. Karl—Karlsted?" Andy didn't bother to correct the man who was standing before him, clipboard in hand, wooden club hanging from his belt.

"Yes." Andy stood up respectfully.

"You know we don't really have the staff to monitor a meeting between yourself and an inmate at this hour. It says here this was explained to you on the telephone."

"I understand. Do you want me to sign a document releasing you from liability?"

The man nodded, handing him the clipboard, to which a form was attached. "If you would, sir. That's regulation, no matter what time of day you come. Then I'll take you back to see Mr. Fitzgerald. He's in the dayroom of his unit. He's not restrained in any way, do you understand? The courts have limited our ability to use restraints, and Fitzgerald hasn't committed any assaults or given us any reason to use them since he's been here."

Andy nodded, handing back the signed form clipped to the board. "How long can I have with him?"

"As much time as you want, far as that goes and as long as he's willing. That is, until the shift is over. You'll have to get out before we change shifts at five, if you're still here then. Everythin's locked down for shift change." He handed Andy a plastic numbered badge with a metal clip attached, and a small plastic box the size of a tin of aspirin, black with a red button on one side.

"I doubt either of us will last that long," said Andy, fastening the badge to his shirt pocket. "Then I press this button when I'm ready to go?"

The man nodded again but said nothing as he turned and walked away. Andy followed him through three corridors punctuated by airlock vestibules accessed through heavy electronically operated doors. The last door gave onto a large room that seemed to have only a few of its overhead lights in operation. The room's sparse furnishings were all pushed against the walls, and the scattered pools of illumination on the empty polished blue linoleum floor gave it the appearance of a deserted swimming pool, drained for the season. It was a few seconds before Andy's eyes adjusted to the dimness and he could see the figure seated on the right-angled tan couch that braced the far corner of the room.

"When you press the button it'll activate my pager and I'll come for you," said the officer to Andy. "But it may take me several minutes." Then he turned and vanished back into the dimness through the door, which closed behind him with a groan and a clash of metal. Andy watched this departure, fingering the rectangle in his pocket and knowing that there would be no help for him, or none fast enough to matter, if things went badly.

"I've been waiting for you," said the figure on the couch, his voice carrying across the empty room. "There's a lot I want to tell you."

Andy turned and walked toward the voice, his eyes straining to make out the features of the man silhouetted against the light-colored wall. When he reached the nearest corner of the couch, he said, "Shall I sit here?"

"Good as any place," said the man. While Andy was pulling his pen from his pocket, the man spoke again. "I've forgotten your name. Sort of a strange one, as I recall."

"Kahrlsrud," said Andy, extending a hand. "Andy Kahrlsrud." The hand that grasped his was dry and small, he noted, its grip appropriately firm without suggesting a need to impress. He could see the man's face now; a smooth pink expanse connecting unexceptional features. A pleasant face.

"Leonard Fitzgerald," he said. "Were you expecting someone else? Bela Lugosi, perhaps?"

"I didn't have any expectations," said Andy, acknowledging to himself, even as he said it, that this was not quite true. He knew, of course, that someone who had done evil deeds could look ordinary, even benign, but if he was honest he would have to admit to himself that he had experienced the familiar surprise at encountering an instance. "Has Dr. Gupta explained to you who I am and why I'm here?"

"Yes," said Fitzgerald.

"Are you willing to talk to me?"

"Yes."

"Do you mind if I record our conversation?"

"I don't mind."

Andy nodded. "Thank you. Just a moment, please." He extracted his recorder from his case and placed it on the scarred low table that flanked the sofa, carefully positioned the little microphone in its tiny tripod, and plugged it into the device. "This is Andrew Kahrlsrud, Ph.D.," he said. "This recording is being made at the Elgin Mental Health Center, Elgin, Illinois, September 14, 1999. Present are myself and Mr. Leonard Fitzgerald. Mr. Fitzgerald, will you please state for the recording whether you consent to this interview, and to its recording?"

"I do."

They rode in Rafe's blue-green Jaguar; Rafe pressed a button and a motor peeled off the roof and pleated it behind them, adding its faint hum to the Jag's purr as Rafe backed the car out of its spot beside the bungalow.

"This guy we're going to see is actually pretty pathetic," he said to Lincoln, twirling the leather-covered steering wheel with one finger as he maneuvered around a tight corner, waving apologetically to the driver of a small truck marked ROSE BROTHERS LIGHTING SHOP that he had cut off. "He calls himself Dashiell Roman, but I doubt that's his original name. He started as a stage actor in the Sixties, but wanted to break into the movies. He could never get cast in a legitimate film so he turned to acting in skin flicks but never got to the top, then he was too old when the style turned to the pretty boys and the ladies started calling the shots anyway. Apparently he came into some money when his mother died and used it to start producing. It's bottom-feeder stuff, Lincoln. None of the soft-focus, romantic fluff they make for cable television or pay-per-view. No plot, no wit. Just a bunch of no-talent actresses with makeup covering their bruises getting fucked in every orifice by guys whose main qualification is their indifference to what they're putting it into. You know what I mean?"

Linc didn't, exactly, his taste running more to action flicks, so he ignored the question. "So you know this guy, Dashiell Rome?"

"Roman. No, I don't know him. But I guess he turned his little inheritance into beaucoup bucks. Distributes his own films, does millions of dollars of business in a year. Good timing, that's what he had."

Linc looked out at the sidewalk, enjoying the looks that the two of them in the open Jaguar drew from the few pedestrians along the sidewalk.

He reached into his pocket for his shades. "I mean, you seem to know a lot about him. What street is this?"

"This is Sunset Strip, my man. We're going to take Laurel Canyon to the freeway, then on to the Valley."

"That's where he has his studio?"

"Yeah, that's what I'm told. Somewhere on Van Nuys, almost to Pacoima."

After Rafe turned the Jag onto a freeway, they flew over the road, dodging slower vehicles as though threading a moving maze. Linc settled his new Carerras onto his nose and slid down into the leather seat to enjoy the ride and the sound system (Springsteen at the moment, not too shabby). But he was thinking, too, thinking that he needed to take control of the situation once they were in this guy's presence, not let Rafe direct the whole interview.

After about twenty minutes, Rafe nosed off at an exit ramp and turned onto a narrower street lined with decrepit structures. Signs proliferated, not the glossy familiar images of Ford, NBC, Seagram's, or white-mustachioed celebrities asking *Got Milk?* Instead: SE RENTA TELEVISIONES, VCR, NEVERAS, painted on the glass of one storefront. AYUDA CON IMMIGRACION, ABOGADO, CARTA DE TELEFONO, on a rust-streaked metal sign attached to the bricks of a low-slung rectangular building. The sun blasted past Linc's glasses and shattered against his eyeballs, but even so he could see mountains low on the horizon, past the endless blocks of peeling buildings that hugged the ground like bomb shelters.

"I don't know which way it is from here," said Rafe, squinting as he clasped the gleaming rosewood gearshift knob and pushed it back to third. "Do you see a number? Wait, there's one. Shit, we're going the wrong way. Hold on."

There wasn't all that much traffic, but even so Linc thought they were going to chew it when Rafe darted a quick look behind him, put both hands on the steering wheel (that should have clued Linc because it was the first time that had happened), and pulled the car across the center line and around like a skateboarder with a death wish.

"What the *fuck!*" yelled Linc.

Rafe grinned like a maniac, shifting down again and flooring the pedal so the Jag shot forward like a bullet, back in the direction they had come.

Linc almost covered his eyes, but then there they were, no harm done, going the right way, although Linc could see at least of couple of the drivers behind them suffering attacks of major road rage.

The street looked the same in this direction: warehouses, the *Taqueria Mazatlan,* a used-car lot (SE VENDE CADILLAC, CHEVROLET, JEEP), a grocer (LEGUMBRES Y FRUTAS DE BUEN CALIDAD). "Here it is," said Rafe, and pulled over at a two-story yellow brick building with no signage except for the number painted on the curb, and sign attached to the metal front door, which was as smooth and black as the barrel of a cannon: NO ADMITTANCE, THIS MEANS YOU.

Linc grinned. "How do we get in?" he asked. At first Rafe didn't answer, just swung the car around to the back of the building, parked it in the shadow of a giant satellite dish, and pressed the button that would restore the roof.

"He's expecting us," said Rafe as the motor hummed and whirred and the roof unfurled over their heads. "I just have to call up there." He waved a small silver phone as though it were a remote control to the door lock, then punched in a number. Within five minutes the two of them were walking through the door, having been admitted by a skinny guy with bad skin in jogging suit, rubber sandals, and Rolex.

"Up there," he gestured, standing in a small vestibule, holding the heavy door open, and pointing toward an uncarpeted fluorescent-lit staircase behind him. The only other feature of the vestibule was another door, off-white and soiled and smudged by countless hands. A small plastic plaque on it said STUDIO, but the skinny man indicated the staircase again with a jerk of his head. "Top of the stairs to the left. And make it quiet. We're shooting down here."

Linc flashed on a firing squad lined up to execute some poor zeke, but of course it was a movie. He nodded at the skinny guy, who nodded back in a dorky way as if unused to being noticed, and followed Rafe's tidy khaki butt up the stairs. At the top, in a featureless white hall with no furnishings but an ancient metal water cooler, he put a hand on Rafe's arm.

"I'll do the talking, right?"

Rafe looked dubious. "You can ask whatever you want, but why don't you let me get it started? He's expecting me, and he'll be helpful because he knows I'm from Rose Brothers and guys like him are always trying to suck up to us, but he doesn't know you. Once I get it going, you can jump in."

Linc considered. "Okay," he said, not necessarily meaning it.

Rafe looked at him more closely, perhaps hearing the intention in his voice. "Listen, Lincoln. I know you think I'm just an old guy who sits in his bungalow and has his secretary bring him guava juice, but I've got some street cred here. Movies are pretty but Hollywood isn't. I was negotiating deals with guys you wouldn't want to touch with a barge pole while you were learning to play tic-tac-toe."

Linc shrugged and Rafe raised his fist toward the door to the left of the staircase. It was as far from clean as the one downstairs, and whoever had painted the letters DASHIELL K. ROMAN on it needed to go back to art school, or maybe grade school. Rafe knocked twice, *bap-bap* on the cheesy particleboard, and must have heard something that Linc didn't because he grasped the knob and pushed the door in.

The office was paneled with some kind of dark knotty wood, like maybe stuff that had been remaindered by some contractor who worked his way through Peoria, Illinois, remodeling basement rumpus rooms. Dashiell K. Roman sat behind a blocky blonde desk, looking gray. His hair was gray, his face was gray, even the hairless chest framed by the open collar of his silver silk shirt looked colorless, starved of blood.

"Mr. Roman!" said Rafe, striding forward as though eager to make his acquaintance, hand extended. Linc followed along behind, taking in the two small windows, the stench of stale pipe tobacco emanating from the rug, the absence of a computer or any paperwork on the surface of the desk, which held only a copy of a skin magazine. "This is my associate, Lincoln," Rafe was saying, waving toward him.

"Mmph," said Dashiell Roman, nodding but not rising or even leaning forward in his desk chair, "Mr. Russell, Mr. Lincoln." Linc nodded back, not seeing a reason to correct him; Rafe withdrew his hand and covered the awkwardness by running it over his springy hair. Roman gestured toward two gray-upholstered chairs in front of the desk. "Sit," he said.

"You were very good to make time for us," said Rafe, taking the chair on the left. Linc settled into the other, reached into his jacket pocket, and unobtrusively started the tape recorder he was carrying there. He knew from his paralegal studies that Colorado attorneys are not allowed to record conversations without the consent of the other party, but he wasn't an attorney and he wasn't in Colorado either, although he wasn't sure that last part mattered.

"Yeah," agreed Roman. "I could be downstairs watching the fucking, you know?" He made the in-and-out hand gesture. "Would be only about my, say, eight thousandth time. So this better be good." The guy was like a movie character himself, thought Linc.

"We wanted to talk to you about *Sunshade Snuffdown*," said Rafe. "Really interesting piece of work."

"Yeah," said Roman. "It is."

"We've been told that you produced it," said Rafe.

"Yeah," said Roman. "I did."

"Yeah," said Rafe, slowly, "that's what we were told." Nobody said anything for a very long moment. Linc suspected that Rafe's plan for this interview hadn't included the possibility of this unexpected admission, a suspicion that was strengthened when Rafe turned to him and said, "Linc?"

"Um," said Lincoln. "The tape said something else on the label."

"Oh yeah?" said Roman without interest. "Whass that?"

"Bodkin something. Bodkin Productions."

"Yeah," said the old man. "One of my subdivisions." He made a sudden barking laugh that dissolved into a cough. "What else?"

"We were interested in what you could tell us about the film," said Linc.

"Whaddaya want to know? We made it offshore, beautiful little place in the Caribbean. Private island. Shot it in two days. Director was this Czech guy, it's the only film he ever directed for me. I hear he's back in Eastern Europe now. Actors—same old same old, mostly, except for the kid."

"What year was this?" said Rafe.

"Before 1996, that's all I remember. Lost all the records in a fire, unfortunately." He grinned horribly, pulling the corners of his mouth sideways to expose long yellow teeth.

"What happened to her?" Linc said quickly. "The little girl."

The gray man looked back at him with eyes like glaciers, still and deadly. "Dunno. We haven't kept in touch."

"So, she's still alive?"

The man turned to Rafe. "Why don't you tell me what you're after? Stop dicking around, letting this kid do your talking. I understood your studio had some interest."

"It's not the studio exactly," said Rafe. "More of an independent deal."

"Yeah," said the man, reaching toward a grimy chrome ashtray that held a pipe and clamping the cold mouthpiece between his yellow teeth. "Mind if I smoke?"

"It's your office, Mr. Roman," said Linc.

"Probably yours before long," he said cryptically, sucking the flame of a match into the bowl of the grimy pipe. "You the lawyer?"

"I'm a lawyer, Mr. Roman," said Rafe. "Lincoln's not."

"Thought you said you were with the studio," he grunted, eyeing the thin column of smoke as it twisted out of the bowl. Then he drew on the pipe, and immediately started coughing.

It lasted maybe two minutes, the last thirty seconds consisting of a horrible retching wheeze. Just as he seemed to recover, he dropped the pipe onto the smelly carpet, and a clot of burning cinder rolled out. Linc stood quickly, snatched the magazine from the desktop, and brushed the cinder onto its glossy cover, where the fire glowed for a brief moment then went out harmlessly. He replaced the pipe in the ashtray, and looked more closely at Dashiell Roman.

"Can I get you a glass of water?" he asked. Roman was still doubled over his own lap, alternately gasping and trying to clear his throat, but he managed to shake his head, so Linc retreated to his chair. Rafe caught his eye and sketched a shrug.

Roman finally sat up straight, his eyes reddened against his ashen face. "Thanks," he said, gesturing to the pipe.

"No worries," said Linc. "Sure you're okay?"

The gray man looked at Linc, his chest still rising and falling spasmodically. When finally he spoke it was to say, "I'm dying."

Beverly loved the fax machine, even if it was old and cranky. She listened with pleasure to the muted ring and hushed electronic crashing sound that meant a fax was about to arrive, and pulled the first page out with curiosity. It was part of her job, to make sure that faxes were delivered to the right person promptly, and also, how was she ever supposed to know what was going on if nobody would tell her, unless she stayed alert and paid attention?

It wasn't a very professional fax, she could tell that right away, as the first page emerged covered with irregular handwriting slanted across the paper. She grasped it as the machine puffed it out onto the tray, and started to read.

*Cinda: saw the wolf last night, will again tonight. I found a stenographer to transcribe the interview tapes daily—a retired court reporter, so she's good. Hope your client is good for the expenses. I bring them to her in the morning and she gets them done by afternoon. Hope this is the kind of thing that will help. It's slow going—I don't think the transcripts give you a sense of how flattened his affect is. From the drugs, probably—this guy is nearly totally shut down. There are lots of awkward silences, but I told the stenographer only to note a pause if it lasted longer then three seconds, which is a long time in conversation. So far he's pretty cooperative—seems willing to talk, even eager in his numbed-out way. I see him again tonight. You can beep me if you need to talk after seeing this. AK*

Dr. K was a good psychologist, thought Beverly, but he sure needed to improve his handwriting. The fax machine had continued to whir and puff while she had been deciphering the chicken scratching. The pages now arriving were much more legible, she saw, very professional. Beverly looked around, seeing that Cinda had her office door closed. Tory was in court in Longmont. She pulled the next few pages from the tray and started to read.

ANDREW KAHRLSRUD: This is Andrew Kahrlsrud, Ph.D. This recording is being made at the Elgin Mental Health Center, Elgin, Illinois, September 14, 1999. Present are myself and Mr. Leonard Fitzgerald. Mr. Fitzgerald, will you please state for the recording whether you consent to this interview, and to its recording?

LEONARD FITZGERALD: I do.

AK: Can you tell me whether you are taking any medication at this time?

LF: Of course I am.

AK: Do you know what it is, and the dosage?

LF: It's called Zyprexa, I know that. I don't know what the dosage is. The standard one, I think. You'd have to ask Dr. Gupta.

AK: Do you notice that the medication has any effect on your thinking?

LF: Course it does. Now I know I'm not a wolf, for instance.

AK: Was there a time when you believed that you were a wolf?

LF: I thought you already knew a lot about me. That's what Gupta said.

AK: I've read quite a bit, Mr. Fitzgerald, but I'd rather hear it from you.

LF: Yes. For a long time I thought I was a wolf. Or something. I mean, I didn't think that if I went to McDonald's, people were looking at me and thinking oh my God we'd better call the zoo. I was more of a secret kind of wolf.

AK: What did that mean, your being a secret wolf?

LF: Well, you weren't like everyone else. But there were some others like you.

AK: Did you have an idea about how many?

LF (pause): Not too many.

AK: Did you have a way to recognize others who were wolves, I mean, did you know each other as wolves?

LF: Look, Dr.—— (pause)

AK: Why don't you call me Dr. K?

LF: Okay, you call me Lenny if you want to, look Dr. K, this was all part of being nuts, I know that. You don't have to humor me, asking about it like it was real.

AK: I understand, Lenny. I wasn't clear, I guess. I'm interested in what you thought then. It's good that you understand now that it was part of your delusional system, but it's still interesting to me and to the lady I'm working for.

LF: Yeah, I get it. (pause) I only ever saw about five or six people that I thought were wolves too. They were all black people, because I also thought I was somehow secretly black, you know? Like that my father and mother had found me somewhere and brought me up and somehow made it that I looked like a white man, but really I was black, and also a wolf. In school, when I was a kid, a teacher told us about the guys who started Rome—weren't they boys who got brought up by a wolf? I was just the other way round. Wolf who was brought up by people.

AK: What was the relationship between being black and being a wolf? I mean, in your mind?

LF: I'm not sure exactly. I mean, my old man was an old-time racist, and was always bitching about the blacks this and that. Sometimes he said they were animals. But he was an evil person. I used to think animals were better than people, or some people, for sure. Like him. He used to hit my mother, and me, and I know he forced my mother to do things she didn't want to do.

AK: Do you mean sexual things?

LF: I guess so. He'd take her into their room and lock the door to keep me out and I could hear her crying and begging him not to make her.

AK: How old were you then?

LF: I don't know. Maybe eight or nine, who knows how long it went on? I definitely remember one time I was about nine, because it was just a short time before he died. Later when Mom told me he was dead she was crying, and I remember wondering how she could be sad after what he'd been doing to her.

AK: So was this related to the wolf?

LF: I don't really remember thinking that I was a wolf until later, maybe when I was a teenager. But I'd always had this idea that wolves and animals were better than people like my father. And also black people. You know, something like it would be good to be different from him. Different color. Different—I don't know. Not a man at all. Also—I'm not sure about this. But I think one time my father was drunk, I mean he was always drunk, but this one time he was complaining about some black guy at work, the guy got some promotion or something and my old man was pissed about it, and he kept saying this guy had a "wolfish grin." Like it was, I don't know, the mark of evil or something. At least I think I remember that. I got it from somewhere, I know. Also, sometimes he would yell at me and say he wasn't my father.

(pause)

AK: Anything more?

LF: No, that's about it.

AK: Was there more to your reaction when you were listening to your father abusing your mother?

LF: (pause) No.

AK: Are you sure?

LF: What are you getting at?

AK: Just thought maybe there was more. Were you listening to it?

LF: Yeah, didn't I say so?

AK: For how long, do you think?

LF: Which time?

AK: Say the time not long before he died.

LF: Seemed to go on a long time.

AK: Were you listening the whole time?

LF: Yeah, so what?

AK: I just wondered how you were feeling while you listened.

LF: I wanted to kill him.

AK: Understandable.

LF: I thought you were interested in the wolf.

AK: Yeah, I was. What more can you tell me?

LF: It's just that when I was in high school I was kind of small and kids would pick on me some and I don't know. It seemed like suddenly everywhere I turned someone was talking about a wolf or something. I went to the movies a lot, and there was a what do you call it? Movie theater where they show movies that aren't exactly new?

AK: Second-run movie house?

LF: Yeah. I guess there aren't too many of them any more because of VCRs and things, but there was this one close to our house and I'd go there a lot. After school and stuff. There was this movie *Wolfen* I saw there, it was really good. There was this band, you know music group, Steppenwolf, and then someone told me about this book, *Steppenwolf,* which I got from the school library and read, although I didn't exactly get it. But I had this idea that some of us, like people who didn't exactly fit in, were, like, wolves. And that most of the other wolves were, like, black people.

AK: Yeah, I understand.

LF: Look, I know it was, what is it, delusional.

AK: It's okay, Leonard. I'm interested in it.

(pause)

LF: So what else do you want to know?

AK: Anything you feel like telling me. There's no hurry.

LF: Why exactly is it you're interested?

AK: You know I'm trying to help a lawyer who works for the mother of the little girl you killed.

LF: Yeah, I know.

AK: It would help her, the lawyer, if I could come to understand why you killed her.

LF: The little girl.

AK: Right.

LF: Dr. Gupta told me about this, but I'm not sure I get it. Why would it help her?

AK: Well, it's complicated. She'd like to find whoever it was that made the tape.

LF: Can't help with that. I just bought it from some dude who came to the video store.

AK: Yeah, that's okay. Our end of it is more about whether what you did had anything to do with that tape.

LF: Oh.

AK: Do you think it did?

LF: Sure.

AK: Well, we could talk about that.

LF: Okay. But I'm getting, like, really sleepy.

AK: Okay, I understand.

LF: It's the meds, they make you weird.

AK: Sleepy, yeah. I know they do.

LF: But, like, not as weird as you were before, you know what I mean?

AK: Yeah, Lenny, I know.

LF: Can you come back tomorrow?

AK: I'll try to, but I don't know what time. I have to speak to the shift commander again. Maybe same time tomorrow night?

LF: Be good.

AK: Okay. This recording comes to an end at 11:18 p.m., September 14, 1999.

Beverly nodded, impressed, and put the fax in Cinda's inbox. If anyone could get to the bottom of this business, Dr. K was the one. But it was too much for her. She didn't like to think about the Wolf guy, but she liked being part of this case, that poor woman and the terrible way her little girl died. She wondered how Charley was getting on with his part of the investigation.

Sable brushed her fingers lightly over Charley's pectoral region while he lit cigarettes for both of them off the same match.

"Two on a match," she said after inhaling deeply. "Romantic."

Charley grinned, but not too widely, and thought about how he was better than anyone might have guessed at the detective business. Who else would have thought of waiting in the overhanging shade of the Sonic Drive-In across the street until he saw Sable, disguised in jeans and a baseball cap, walk out of the bookstore's back entrance to her spotty silver Escort? He'd followed her home, then given her a few minutes before ringing the bell of the apartment, and she had actually acted glad to see him when she came to the door. She looked as though she'd washed off a lot of makeup in the meantime, and changed the jeans for some kind of silky robe.

"You don't know me," he'd started, but she'd cut him off.

"Charley," she breathed. "I never forget a voice." His heart was hammering painfully and his head felt as though it might slop right out of its container.

"Are you busy?" he said, half hoping she'd say yes.

"As it happens," she said, "I seem not to be, this evening. Come in for a drink?"

She invited him to sit on the sofa in front of the television, which was already on. It was a little set and the small screen reminded him unsettlingly of the peepshow window, weird to be sitting here with her on the same side of it, some news anchor with a necktie up to his chin on the other side. For a while he couldn't think of anything to say and that seemed all right with her, so they just listened to CNN news. Which helped him to calm down quite a bit, it seemed so familiar: trouble in Iran, or was it Iraq? George W. Bush grinning, Bill Clinton weaseling around. The sun had fallen below the horizon by the time Sable got up to fix the second round of vodka tonics and asked him if he had any cigarettes. Thanking the lucky chance that had kept him from trying to quit, a notion he had toyed with the week before, he'd tapped a couple out from the pack. That was when she said the thing about two on a match. The only light in the room came from the flare of its tip and the blue glow of the television.

"So Charley," she said after sucking in several pulls so deeply that he imagined smoke coming out the other end, that fabulous bush on fire. "Why did you want to come to Sable's house?"

"What we had back at the place—it wasn't enough for me. And Garth threw me out for trying to learn your real name."

"He did? Spoilsport." She pouted.

"What are the possibilities here, Sable?" Charley squinted and tried to look as though he did this sort of thing frequently, and actually he had imagined similar conversations quite often as part of his profession of part-time screenwriting. Also, he had watched *Klute* many times.

"What interests you, Charley?" Sable swished her butt along the sofa to get closer and put her hand over his to take a lingering sip from his drink, even though hers wasn't empty.

"I don't want to insult you," said Charley. "You know, by asking for something that isn't your thing."

"Don't worry about that," she breathed. "My thing is whatever yours is. Only some things cost more than other things, of course."

"Of course. Is that a VCR you have there?"

"Sure is. You want to watch a tape with Sable, is that it?"

"I'd really really like to do that."

"We can do that. Do you like to do the things you see on the tapes, Charley?"

Charley took a deep breath. He couldn't read her face in the dark, and hoped she couldn't see his either, because he knew he looked scared. "I like to watch people do things that I'd never have the nerve to do," he said, trying to control the glob of something that had appeared in his throat.

"Oh," she said. "Oh. So do I."

"Do you have any tapes like that?" he asked.

"Not here, but I know where we can get some," she said. "Of course, it will be expensive."

"Of course," said Charley. "Can we go get one now?"

"Why not? I know a place that's always open, if you're the right customer."

"There's just one thing I need to do before we go," said Charley.

"Make a phone call," said Sable, stabbing out her cigarette into an ashtray shaped like a woman's torso. She ground the smoky tip into the navel.

"How did you know?" he said, but he was kidding and he knew she knew it, of course. In her line of work, men were needing to make phone calls all the time.

"In the kitchen," she said, waving toward the yellow instrument attached to the wall by the small sink, and then she rose. "I'll just go slip into some clothes."

"Hey," said Charley in a friendly way, "just not too many."

He was a little anxious about Beverly, but it wasn't necessary once she came onto the line, sounding sleepy, and he explained that he needed to stay in Denver a little longer to work on the new assignment. He figured this was a safe thing to say even if Sable was listening to him somehow, because it was the sort of thing guys would always say to their wives if they were with a prostitute. He was good, all right, thinking of everything, and Beverly seemed to get it too, not asking too many questions.

"Oh," said Beverly, "that's great, Charley. I mean, are you making progress?"

"Well, I can't say much right now," he said, "you know how it is."

"Oh sure," she said, "I understand. Exactly." He could hear sirens in the background and could picture her sitting there on the plaid couch, the afghan wrapped around her feet, watching *ER,* that one doctor she liked because he reminded her of the guy Sam Holt that she had once worked for. He missed her suddenly and wanted to be able to tell her something more.

"But the boss may be very happy about the sales results," he said.

"What?"

"Just think about it. Listen, I gotta go."

"Charley?" she said.

"Yeah?"

"You're my hero."

It had started raining while they were in Sable's apartment, an ugly sullen rain that felt oily on Charley's fingers as he slid the key into the ignition.

"Which way?" he said, turning to face Sable in the seat beside him. She had her legs drawn up against her chest for warmth, or maybe to avoid the cans and paper bags that littered the floor in front of the passenger seat. Her mood seemed to have turned to match the weather. She looked back at him indifferently, her eyes reflecting the orange tint of the streetlight at the curb.

"Back toward Colfax, then turn south when you get to I-25. Can you turn the heat up?"

"It's not on Colfax then?" East Colfax was home to most of Denver's strip clubs and adult bookstores, and its few surviving X-rated movie houses.

She ran her hands briskly up and down her arms, and looked straight ahead. "Just go where I tell you. You'll be surprised, I promise you that."

"Never a dull moment with Sable, eh?" said Charley, but she didn't respond except to tighten her sweater around her. Charley was sweating in the car's humid interior and couldn't understand how she could be cold, but he turned up the heater for her. They drove in silence for a few minutes and then Sable reached forward to turn on his car radio. He kept it tuned to the oldies station; Elton John's mellow baritone swirled out, "Candle in the Wind," and Sable sang softly along. She had a nice voice.

"Just there," she said, pointing, and he steered onto the entrance ramp for I-25 heading south. The tires slid slightly on the wet pavement as he braked at the bottom of the ramp. Again he thought the rain seemed greasy somehow, dirty, but that didn't make any sense. Acid rain he'd heard of, had some laughs about old man Reagan saying it was trees that made it, but oily rain?

He drove tensely on the vehicle-clogged highway, anxious now about slipping, thinking he should've gotten new tires instead of deciding they could last until the spring. Trucks sizzled by, throwing up ragged sheets of water as they passed, and Charley almost forgot that Sable was in the car with him until she said quietly, "The next exit."

Through the windshield he could see the bulk of a large building looming above the highway ahead, its red sign distorted by the rippling rain. "The Western Plaza?" he said, confused.

"The very place. I told you you'd be surprised."

"The Western Plaza has an adult video rental store in it?"

"Sort of," she said. "Remember, though, I said it would be expensive. Do you have a credit card?"

"Of course," said Charley, with a hearty confidence he didn't feel. He moved his arms away from his body a little; his pits were sticky. He wondered whether Beverly had paid the bill since that time his Visa had been declined at the Olive Garden.

The hotel's parking lot was full and they had to park quite a distance from the front door, and walk through the rain. Some kind of high school dance affair was going on: dewy-skinned girls in short black dresses and corsages stood in clusters, whispering to each other as their guys bantered with the bartender in the lobby bar, trying not too hard to get him to slip them a beer. The amplified voice of a deejay poured out from the open door to a nearby ballroom. Charley felt old and filthy, water dripping from his head onto the carpet. Even Sable looked tired and used-up when he turned to her for direction, but her voice was as sweet as ever as she took his arm and said, "Just over here."

She steered him into the registration line. "Don't—don't we need a reservation?" he said.

Sable smiled and sketched a small wave in the direction of one of the desk clerks, who seemed to recognize her and nodded back discreetly. "No problem," she said.

The room was on the twenty-seventh floor, overlooking the highway, and Charley stood at the window watching red taillights reflecting off the shiny dark road while Sable talked on the telephone. She was sitting on the double bed, her leopard sweater limp and sad against the crisp red and gold pattern of the bedspread.

"Is Guy there tonight?" she was saying. "Then who's this? Tell him it's Sable. We want something special up here, pay-per-view. The private collection." A moment's silence, then, "Well, I'll hold on until he's done. Twenty-seven oh nine, right."

She wiggled her fingers toward Charley and, understanding, he reached into his pocket for the cigarettes, but before he could light one for her she spoke into the phone again. "Hi Guy. Yeah, me again. Listen, my new boyfriend wants to ask you about something particular he's interested in. Yeah, very good taste. I don't know, you'd have to ask him that. Yeah, okay. Here he is."

She held the receiver out toward Charley, her sweater falling open to show the tight black and silver affair—Charley didn't even know what it was called—underneath. Her breasts were squashed into it below, spilling out above, and the vertical line between them seemed harsh somehow, a mistake. For some reason he looked away, embarrassed, even as he accepted the telephone.

"Hi," he said, "this is Charley."

"What is it you want exactly, Charley?"

"Something, you know. Edgy. With, um, a little girl in it."

A comradely snort. "Sure. Just one little girl?"

"Yeah, just one. And she has to be blonde."

"You betcha, no problem. Anything else?"

"Yeah, she has to go with a black man."

"Oh yeah? You have very innaresting taste, Charley. Unusual. But I think we can, you know. Find something to innarest you. Hold on."

"Okay." Charley thought that he ought to specify more, but Sable was watching him with renewed interest and it didn't seem like a good idea.

"Charley?" said the man's voice.

"Yeah?"

"I've got something you're really gonna like here."

"Good." Then a flash of inspiration. "What's it called?"

"Called? It's not called anything, Charley-horse. It's not that kind of a movie, you know?"

"Really? I thought some of them had names." He knew the one he was looking for did.

"Some of them do, but not this one. You want it or not?"

Maybe there were versions of the same tape, some with and some without names, what did he know? "Okay, sure. You going to bring it up here, is that the way it works?"

Another snort. "Didn't that Sable tell you anything, Charley? Listen, just turn on your television, in your room. Pay-per-view, like seeing the Holyfield-Moorer match, get it? Sable can show you. But I'm sending one of my associates up to get the money, okay? Or we can put this on your Visa bill, but some guys worry about that. Strictly up to you."

"And how much was that?"

"For what you want, Charley, a man of your exotic tastes, this is going to be fifty. And of course your deal with Sable is strictly between the two of you."

"Okay." But when he put the phone down and turned to look at her, she was huddled under the bedspread, her hair falling in damp tangles across her small face, her eyes closed. "Sable?"

She barely opened her eyes. "Just wake me up when it's time to watch, okay baby? I'm so tired, and I'm cold."

He pulled the cover up over her thin shoulders; at least he wouldn't have to watch it with her. Charley reached for his wallet and found a twenty and three tens just as there was a harsh knock on the door.

It wasn't the one, of course. He had turned the sound all the way off, so as not to disturb Sable. Charley knew after less than a minute that this was not *Sunshade Snuffdown,* but he sat on the end of the bed gazing listlessly at the girl on the screen, maybe thirteen or so, her mouth red, her eyelashes mascara'd to spidery extravagance. She walked into the bathroom where a muscular man was sitting in the bath; she mimed surprise unconvincingly, he leered. He said something and directed her attention to his cock, floating in the water like the wilted bloom of some intriguing plant, or so her reaction suggested. She seemed both interested and clueless, as though she'd never heard of such a thing. Charley watched without much interest as the girl started to take off her plaid schoolgirl skirt and white blouse (preparatory, he was certain, to climbing into the tub). He thought this film had the lamest excuse for a script he had ever heard of, he could tell that even without any sound. Jeez, why was it a guy with a million good ideas like him couldn't even find an agent for his screenplays?

Sable stirred in her sleep, and Charley turned around to look at her. She'd seemed old and worn in the lobby with the high school girls, but under the bedcover, her knees drawn up, she seemed like a sleeping child. While he watched, she snored faintly, then sighed deeply and turned over without opening her eyes.

He didn't have much desire to watch the rest of the film, but thought it might look bad if he turned it off, having accessed it on the hotel's closed-circuit system—would Guy and the bald character who'd taken his fifty dollars know somehow if he didn't watch it to the end? It only lasted about thirty minutes, and by the time it was over Charley found that despite his mind's contempt for the stupid thing, his disgust at the use of the child actress, he had to go into the bathroom to relieve the swelling of his johnson. He didn't think of Beverly, or of Sable under the covers, or of the little girl as he punished his dick with his hand, furious at its indifference to the things he cared about. He did think of Beverly afterward as he washed his hands, looking at them as though they were foreign objects. He wondered if she would worry about him, but decided she was cool, and he went back into the dim room, turned off the television to erase the MENU OF GUEST SERVICES, and lay down beside Sable on top of the bedclothes. Charley Medford, Private Detective (unlicensed), closed his eyes and sleep pushed him down beneath the bed's soft surface, beneath the floor. He fell so far he forgot he was falling, and slept.

In the offices of Hayes and Meadows, P.C., the fax machine groaned and whirred.

*Cinda: Here's the next installment. He's really beginning to trust me, I think. But I feel I'm a long way from understanding him. I'm faxing this from the only Kinko's in Elgin. I'll be seeing him again tonight, so look for more tomorrow.*

AK: This recording begins at 9:38 p.m., September 15, 1999.

LF: Right.

AK: So, did you have a good day?

LF: About average.

AK: What do you do during the day?

LF: Hang out. Play cards. Read. Watch TV, except most of the stuff is stupid during the day. I like the Nature Channel, though. They had a program today about otters.

AK: What do you like to read?

LF: There's some books by this lady who writes about cave people. They're really good. *Clan of the Cave Bear* was one. I asked the librarian to get some more but she hasn't yet.

AK: What is it you like about them?

LF: What does this have to do with your lawyer and that lady's kid?

AK: Just trying to get to know you.

LF: I just like animals, that's all.

AK: More than people?

LF: Usually, yeah.

AK: What would you like to talk about, Lenny?

LF: You wouldn't care about the stuff that's on my mind.

AK: Why don't you try me?

LF: It's got nothing to do with the wolf or the little girl.

AK: That's all right.

LF: You think you'll figure out some way it does after all, don't you?

AK: Not necessarily. I'm not that smart, Lenny. I just think we'll enjoy our time together more if we talk about what's on our minds.

LF: Okay, you first.

AK: You want to know what's on my mind?

LF: Yeah.

AK: Okay, I was thinking I'm glad I get to leave when we're done and I don't have to go through that door that leads back to your cell. And feeling sort of guilty about feeling glad about that.

LF: You mean it doesn't seem fair?

AK: No, I don't mean that. I wasn't thinking about it in terms of fairness. Just that you and I aren't really in the same situation.

LF: That's fuckin'-A right. You got that right, Dr. K.

AK: Seems like you're getting a little more relaxed around me. Less formal.

LF: Yeah, maybe.

AK: So, now how about you? What's on your mind?

LF: Funny, but it's the same thing more or less. I hate this place.

AK: What's the worst part of it?

LF: Knowing someday someone's going to get to me and fuck me up really bad or kill me. It's not exactly popular to be a baby-killer in a place like this. Or a baby-raper. Short-eyes. Some of these guys would like to stick me. In the guts, that's what this one guy says he's gonna do, so it'll hurt worse. Probably will happen some time. It would help if I were meaner-looking but I'm not. Sometimes I wish someone would get me good, cut up my face or break my nose or something so I'd look more like someone you didn't want to mess with. But if someone gets to me, he'll probably kill me.

AK: Are you afraid all the time?

LF: I don't think you can be afraid all the time, it takes too much juice. You run out of it after a while. Listen, no matter what I say to you, I'm still going to be here after, right?

AK: I'm not here to try to get you out, that's right. Even if I thought you ought to be released, and I don't have any opinion on that right now, it's not up to me.

LF: Yeah I know. That's what Amy told me, that it wouldn't hurt or help. Have you met Amy? She's my lawyer.

AK: No.

LF: She's fine.

(pause)

LF: Well let's get on with it.

AK: Tell me about the video.

LF: *Sunshade Snuffdown?*

AK: That's the one. How did you acquire it?

LF: I think it was this one dude, Stringer we used to call him because he was so skinny. He'd come around to the store with a carton full of tapes. Mellis had told him not to come around any more because he wasn't buying any of his stuff because it was too raunchy—the old man was afraid he'd get in trouble with the law. But Stringer kept coming around and I'd buy some of his stuff for myself.

AK: What was it you liked about the tapes he'd bring around?

LF: Just more extreme than the stuff from the store. Stuff that might have been illegal.

AK: What would have been illegal about it?

LF: Kiddie porn, maybe. Except I hear they have some actors who are really eighteen and specialize in kiddie roles. Who knows? But it made Mellis edgy.

AK: Did you have a particular interest in kiddie porn?

LF: Yeah.

AK: Can you say why it was more interesting than porn with adults in it?

LF: No. I don't know. (pause) It's more (inaudible).

AK: What was that?

LF: No, I don't know. I don't know why.

AK: Did you say more touching?

LF: Yeah. Sort of.

AK: In what way?

LF: Because the little kids would, like, trust the adults. Not to hurt them, or anything.

AK: And that was touching.

LF: Well, yeah, because you know that soon the grownups were like doing whatever they wanted. Hurting the kids. And the kids would be crying and stuff. But then in the next one, the kids are trusting all over again.

AK: What do you mean the next one?

LF: The next tape I'd watch, the next night or whatever.

AK: The kids in the next tape you'd watch?

LF: Yeah.

AK: But that would be different kids, of course.

LF: No, that was the thing. Sometimes you'd see the same kids again in another tape. A lot of them you'd see over and over.

AK: I see.

LF: Well, don't you get it?

AK: I'm not sure. Explain it to me.

LF: At the beginning of every tape, the kids would look all happy and okay and everything. So. Either those things that were done to them didn't really hurt the kids, or the kids wouldn't have kept on letting them happen. Or else there were people who could hurt kids over and over and make the kids act like it was okay. Either way. (pause)

AK: Either way what?

LF: I don't know. Either way it made me feel better.

AK: Why?

LF: I don't know.

AK: Better about your own life?

LF: Yeah. I mean, I wasn't such a freak, you know. Here were these other kids who kept coming back for more. Maybe it wasn't so bad.

AK: You felt you and the kids in the tapes had something in common?

LF: Yeah.

AK: Lenny, did your father ever sexually assault you?

LF: I don't remember.

AK: You think it's possible?

LF: Who cares? If he did, it wasn't like the only time in the world it had ever happened to someone. Is it? I mean, we know that.

AK: Can you tell me how all this is related to your beliefs about being a wolf?

LF: Sure. (pause) Well, sure. But it's complicated, I guess.

AK: Okay. Just tell it as well as you can.

LF: The part about believing I was a wolf, that came mostly before I started with the kiddie tapes. I think I stopped thinking about the wolf stuff for a while after I started watching the tapes. Instead of seeing people and thinking they were wolves, I started looking around to see if any of the people, you know, out and around, had been in any of the tapes I'd seen. Especially the kids.

AK: Where would you look?

LF: Just everywhere I'd go, Mickey D's, on the street, in the parks, in record stores, and the supermarket.

AK: Video stores?

LF: Nah, I was working in one of those. I didn't need to hang out in them when I wasn't working.

AK: I see.

LF: You'd be amazed the number of people who perform in porn who are out walking around, looking just like everyone else.

AK: You saw a lot of them?

LF: Yeah, dozens. (pause) I don't know. Now I'm wondering. You think that was part of the (inaudible). (pause) The delusions?

AK: I don't know, Lenny, except it seems unlikely that dozens of actors in porn films would be walking around Chicago, right in your neighborhood. Doesn't it? Like, what if I told you I'd seen Meryl Streep and Tom Cruise and Meg Ryan and, who else? Bruce Willis? All while I was walking around my neighborhood.

LF: Yeah, I see what you're saying. Yeah.

AK: But I don't know for sure.

LF: I might need to think about this for a while.

AK: It's late anyway. Tomorrow?

LF: I'll be here.

AK: I'll try to come at the same time. This recording ends at 10:17 p.m., September 15, 1999.

It blew Cinda away when Linc told her about the producer.

"He just admitted it?" she said on the other end of the line.

"Came right out with it. Even Rafe was spooked. For a minute neither one of us knew what to say. I had my whole Sergeant Friday routine worked out but never got to use it. Rafe says, very stern like, 'We hear you produced this tape,' and the guy says, 'Yeah, I did.'"

"My God. This is the last thing I expected. So what did he tell you about it?"

"The director was some Czech guy, he says, gone back home now. He claims not to know where the little girl actress is now. Doesn't want to talk about her much."

"Where'd they make the film?"

"Offshore, he says, on some island in the Caribbean. They rented out someone's beach place from a travel agency to use. He claims the black guy was a Jamaican, not even a professional actor."

"Do you think they really killed the little girl in the tape?"

"I don't know what to think, Cinda. I didn't ask him that. This guy has lung cancer, he's dying, he says, and I believe that part. So would you if you saw him. He's known about Alison Grayling ever since the Fitzgerald trial, and maybe he feels guilty. Doesn't have any family, his ex-wife hates him, and his son was killed in a motorcycle accident six years ago, so he doesn't have anyone to leave his money to. But he's scared of being arrested, dying in jail or prison."

"This is too easy, Linc, there's something wrong here. I think someone's trying to misdirect us."

"Yeah, I know what you mean. What do you want me to do?"

"Is this guy—what's his name?"

"Roman. Dashiell Roman."

"God, I hope he turns out to be the real guy, just to be able to sue someone with a name like that. You tell a Colorado jury that's the guy's name and nothing will ever convince them he's not a producer of pornography."

"Well, he admits that, Cinda. That's part of what seems too easy, you know? Like this guy came from central casting."

"Here's what I want to know, Linc. Is this guy incorporated? I mean, is there some business entity that made the tape, and has assets? Or does he have personal assets that are really his and not tied up in some trust or offshore account or something? Maybe they're trying to get us to sue some outfit that doesn't have any assets, keep us from finding the real ones."

"Yeah, maybe. Then we have to ask, who's *they?*"

"Rafe led you to this guy, right?"

"I like him, Cinda. And he really seems to care about you. Anyway, you don't really think Rose Brothers produced *Sunshade Snuffdown,* do you?"

"I don't know, but we've got to go where the facts take us, Linc."

He sighed. "I'll find out what I can. Meantime, do you want me to do anything else? I tried that guy Chris, but the number's disconnected."

"Can you find out where he lives, from his telephone number?"

"Sure, city directory should show the address if the number's recently disconnected. I could drop in on him. But what can he tell us now?"

Linc heard Cinda blow into the phone, that little huff of concentration she did sometimes. "Chris told me he knew Joel Derringer, the actor that Mindy Cookson said played the father. See if you can get him to tell you how to find Derringer. I looked at the county records when I was there and didn't find anything in that name, but it's probably not his real one. Be careful, Linc. Do you have my cell phone number? You can call me on it any time."

"Give it to me," said Linc. When she did, he said, "That's the area code here, not there."

"I know," said Cinda. "Just use it if anything comes up, okay? Call me once a day at least."

"Yes, Mom."

"What are you going to do tonight?"

"Rafe and I are going out to some clubs, okay, Mom? He thinks it's for fun but I might learn something. Don't worry, I won't drink out of any unattended glasses."

✧✧✧

AK: This recording begins at 9:22 p.m., September 16, 1999. How are you tonight, Lenny?

LF: Okay.

AK: You sound unhappy.

LF: Yeah. So what?

AK: You want to talk about why?

LF: No.

AK: Okay.

    (pause)

LF: So what, we're gonna sit here for two hours not saying anything?

AK: It's up to you, really.

LF: Yeah well fuck you. What good does it do to talk to you anyway?

AK: I can't say it will do you any good, particularly. Unless there's something you want to get off your chest.

LF: Yeah, like what?

AK: That would be your call, Lenny.

LF: You want me to say I'm sorry for doing that little girl?

AK: To be perfectly honest, that doesn't do much to help the lady that's paying my bills, your being sorry. She's not suing you, you know. But if you are sorry and want to talk about it, I'd be glad to talk with you.

LF: Why?

AK: Why what?

LF: Why would you be glad? I mean, if it doesn't help the lady who's paying your bills.

AK: That's a good question. I guess it's because I'm interested in you, Lenny.

LF: Well, why are you? Aren't there enough freaks in the world for you to study without coming here all the way from—where is it?

AK: Boulder, Colorado.

LF: Yeah, Boulder.

AK: There are a lot of troubled people in the world, Lenny. But you're the one I'm interested in right now.

LF: What you're really interested in is why I did what I did to the girl. Alison.

AK: That's certainly one of the things.

LF: I'm not sure I can tell you.

AK: You said something about being sorry. Are you sorry?

LF: Hell yes.

AK: Can you say more about that?

LF: I was fucked up, Dr. K. I thought I was a wolf, whatever. I lived in some other world. I watched porno tapes all the time—that's most of what I did except for work. I thought the people I saw around me were the same ones I saw on the tapes. I thought this little girl I used to watch in the playground across the street was the same little girl that was on that tape, *Sunshade Snuffdown*. I thought she was teasing me, you know? Looking at me and then looking away like she didn't know me. That was fucked up, wasn't it?

AK: When did you realize that you were mistaken about these beliefs?

LF: Shit, when I got here and started taking the drugs, you know?

AK: Okay, hold on. Ah, I'm going to say something for the tape here, Lenny. Mr. Fitzgerald is crying now. We're going to take a break here for a moment. Lenny, hold on for a minute. Let's get some water from the fountain over there, okay? Is there a cup around here?

(pause)(very long)

AK: You had some very bad chemicals running around in your brain when you did what you did, Lenny.

LF: No shit.

AK: Can you tell me more about that tape? Why it appealed to you, what it made you think about?

LF: You know, I hadn't been thinking too much about the wolf business since I got into the kiddie porn. It was like they were separate things. Like some guys I went to high school with, they'd have like a motorcycle, and that's all they'd think about for a year was the bike, Then one day they sell it and buy a car and it's like, now everything's the car, all the time. It's like this bike that they were so interested in, it's forgotten about.

AK: Yeah, I know what you're talking about.

LF: Okay. Okay. That's the way it was with the wolf, and then the tapes. One day I was like thinking about being the wolf all the time, then the next thing I know it's like with the tapes, all the time, thinking about them, seeing the people from the tapes everywhere.

AK: Okay, Len. Good. Slow down, buddy.

LF: Yeah. Then I got this one tape, that one. And like *bam*. It was all in there, everything. The man, he was black and it came back to me that I was black. And he had this wolfish grin, that's the only word for it. Every time I watched it I thought, man, he's a wolf. He's a wolf. Like I'm a wolf. Everything came together in this tape, you know what I mean? And then the little girl, and she was so trusting, and it was like so (pause)

AK: So what, Lenny?

LF: I don't know.

AK: When we were talking about tapes before you said something about the kids and the way they trusted the adults.

LF: Yeah.

AK: Do you remember?

LF: Yeah. (pause) Touching.

AK: Was this tape touching in that way?

LF: Yeah.

(pause)

AK: So, did you watch this tape often?

LF: Every day. Several times. And watched the girl. Alison. I was sure she was the one on the tape.

AK: What did you want to happen?

LF: I wanted her to be the one. And we would watch it together and I would say to her, Look at you! You're so (pause)

AK: What?

LF: Brave.

AK: You wanted to tell her she was brave?

LF: And see how she was, in person.

AK: Okay.

(pause)

LF: (inaudible). To show me.

AK: You wanted her to show you how to be brave?

(pause)

AK: You want some more water, Lenny? Take a break?

(inaudible, speaker unknown)

(pause)

AK: Okay. You okay to keep talking?

LF: Go on.

AK: You were saying that you wanted to know more about how she was so brave.

LF: Look, I was fucking nuts. It's not like this is going to make any sense.

AK: That's okay. It doesn't have to make sense.

LF: I was going to get her to come to my apartment, somehow. I figured she was a nice girl and all and her parents taught her not to talk to strangers but I was going to think of a way. Then once she was there and saw that I knew, she was going to tell me that I was right, that she was the one on the tape, but nobody else knew it, not her parents, not her bitchy little playmates or her teachers, nobody but me.

AK: This is what you thought would happen.

LF: Right.

AK: But what really happened?

LF: Don't fuck with me, Doc. I know you know what really happened.

AK: I don't know why.

LF: Well, you're the shrink. You figure it out.

AK: I only know what you've told me and I still don't quite understand.

LF: Let's finish this tomorrow.

AK: Lenny. I know this isn't easy, but it's not going to be any easier tomorrow. I think we're almost there, let's keep going.

LF: You expect me to understand perfectly why I did what I did? What's your job then?

AK: Sometimes I'm not sure of that.

(pause)

LF: I thought she was fucking with me, you know?

AK: Alison?

LF: Pretending not to get it, acting like she didn't understand. Acting, you know? Because she was an actress. And I was a wolf, a black one. She liked those things about me, I knew that. She liked doing the things she did on the tape, too. She wasn't as innocent as she made out, that was just a tease. That was okay at first but she took it too far. She wouldn't put on the swimsuit or get in the pool, she wouldn't watch the tape, she just kept crying and crying. She got really quiet after a while. (pause)

AK: Did it occur to you to stop what you were doing?

LF: It was too late. Already she was going to say she had been hurt. The only way was to get to the end of the tape.

AK: That was going to solve the problem?

LF: Yeah.

AK: You wanted Alison to watch the tape to the end with you, and that would make everything okay?

LF: Not watch. Not just watch.

AK: I see.

LF: We had to do the tape, do you see? We had to be it.

AK: Why again?

LF: I don't know. I was fucked up.

AK: I think you know something, though.

LF: Then in the next one, she could be fine again. She would be fine. No bruises or scars.

AK: The next tape?

LF: Yeah. I told you it was fucked up.

(pause)

AK: Lenny, all the time you were watching this tape, *Sunshade Snuffdown*, and the girl, and thinking those thoughts, did you ever talk to anyone about them?

LF: No. Hell no.

AK: You didn't have any friends or anyone that might have understood some of it?

LF: I didn't have any friends.

AK: So there's not anybody who's going to remember knowing about any of these fantasies before the day Alison came to your apartment?

LF: Nope. Can we stop? I need to stop now.

AK: Sure.

LF: Will you be back tomorrow?

AK: Sure. Same time probably, more or less.

LF: Good, there's something I want to ask you.

AK: This recording ends at 10:12 p.m.

The apartment building, a small stucco complex with two stories, was in a part of L.A. called Glendale. Its U-shape didn't completely enclose the swimming pool and patio, so a splintered shoulder-height wooden fence was doing duty as a barrier to kids or dogs who might wander in. Linc opened the gate cautiously, but nobody was in the pool area. The water shimmered in the afternoon sun, a thin film of oil on its surface forming patterns that broke and re-formed when they encountered the leaves that also floated there. Many more leaves lay in the deep crease at the center of the pool's bottom. One of the floaters capsized and began to sink as he watched.

He stood on the pool's concrete apron and looked up. There were no signs of activity along the balcony that ran from door to door on the second story, unless you counted an orange tabby cat pawing a mouse or a spider out of a terra-cotta pot. Linc scanned the apartment numbers, his eyes slowly growing accustomed to the glare thrown off by the white stucco, until he found 212.

The sound of his feet against the stairs spooked the tabby, and Linc wasn't surprised; the metal steps clanged in a way suggesting they were not very well fastened to the building, an impression confirmed by the tremors under his feet. The cat ran toward the far corner, her catch dangling from her mouth, and disappeared.

It wasn't Chris but a small and very pretty young woman who came to the door when he knocked.

"Hi. Chris in?"

"No."

"Oh. You must be his girlfriend. I've heard him talk about you. I forget your name."

"Shelley. Who're you?" She rubbed her large eyes. Her dark hair looked smashed on one side, and there was a red patch on her cheek, same side.

"Did I wake you up? I'm really sorry. I feel like a jerk, but Chris said if I came by here he might be in. Today, I mean. He was going to talk to me about some private tennis lessons."

She peered at him with more interest. "I was taking a nap. Chris told you to come here? I thought he had quit with the tennis."

Linc shrugged. "Well, he told me we could at least talk about it. I've heard he's really a good teacher. Do you think he might be back soon? I mean, I could wait for him. I wouldn't mind."

She turned to look back into the apartment. "It's pretty much a mess in here. Where did you say you met Chris?"

"At the country club. It's been a while, I guess. I was in Europe for six months. My grandfather wanted to go and someone needed to go with him, so I did. But now that I'm back I'd really like to work on my tennis game. Because I'll be starting medical school next year and this could be, you know, my last chance for a while." He smiled like he thought a rich guy might, one without a care in the world except his tennis game. Good job she couldn't see his crappy rental car on the other side of the fence.

His invented respectability worked, sort of. She said, "Okay, you can come on in," but she didn't gesture him toward the door or turn back toward it herself. This girl's a bit disoriented, thought Linc, as she spoke again. "But I don't know where Chris is, or when he'll be home. He's gotten really strange about what he's up to. Do you want a Diet Coke?"

"Do you have a real one?"

"A real—? Oh, no, sorry. Just diet. I might have to stop drinking them, myself. I'm pregnant. Do you think there's some stuff that isn't good for the baby in them?" She turned then and peered back into the darkened room again, as if the answer to her question might be there.

Every interview has one, a moment when the key is in the lock and you can turn it one way, or the other. Choose wrong and you'll never learn what you need to know, but turn it the right way and you'll hear the tumblers fall and see the door swing open.

He waited until she had turned back toward him, then said gently, "Chris doesn't know yet, does he?"

She shook her head, then raised her hand to her mouth, but not before he saw the small crumple there. "He's been so busy lately. A new part, I guess. Legit, not that stuff he was doing for a while. Anyway." Her voiced trailed off.

"It's bad to get dehydrated when you're pregnant," he said. "Let me take you to that juice place back on the corner. We can walk, and I'll buy you a smoothie. That would be really good for the baby."

Shelley drew in her breath, a quick intake like a tiny sob. "What if Chris comes back? Don't you want to see him?"

"Leave him a note," said Linc. "Tell him to come join us."

"If he even comes home." Her voice broke a little on *comes,* but she put a hand to the small of her back as if to straighten it and went inside, coming back with a pad of paper and pencil.

They were in the juice bar for most of the afternoon. It was odd, she was the first girl he'd been attracted to in a while, even though she was pregnant. You couldn't count the girls at that party Rafe had taken him to; they were ill, no question about it, but that was a very superficial thing. He bought Shelley two Very Razzberry smoothies and would happily have kept on buying them until dark, but after a while she said that they should get back, that maybe Chris would be home. When they got to the apartment complex the shadows were beginning to slant across the small courtyard; already the leaf-clogged bottom of the swimming pool was dark. The note she'd left for Chris was still fastened to the apartment door, flapping in the warm wind. Linc thought of a scene in some movie he couldn't remember, a woman waving a white handkerchief to say goodbye. Some western. The woman in the movie was beautiful and when you saw that handkerchief you knew something bad was coming and you wanted to protect her.

He waited until he was back at the hotel to telephone Cinda. "The deal is," he said, "a couple of weeks ago Chris tells Shelley he has this great new part, or maybe a series of parts, it's all a little foggy to her. Something legit, not the porn, but also hush-hush, he says, which she doesn't understand because what's the secret, like when's the last time some actor was secretive about his role? He quits all his other jobs, the security work, he turns down work on commercials. He changes the phone number, so now the phone hardly ever rings at all. And he gets up every day and tells her he has to go to work, and he's gone all day and sometimes into the night, too. But she doesn't think he's really working. Sometimes when he finally gets home his clothes stink of marijuana, and she's found little vials of white powder in his pockets, and also some blue pills that he seems to have an endless supply of."

"Viagra?"

"That's my guess. And see, she's pregnant, she's been sick as a dog. They haven't done the nasty for weeks. You gotta ask, what's he got that stuff for?"

"Yeah. Only maybe professional instead of recreational. I think he's lying to his fiancée about the kind of movies he's making. The guy's a porn actor, and he was having trouble keeping it up, and by his account he wasn't the only one. Now that I think of it, this drug could revolutionize the industry. Maybe they'll call it Blue Wood."

"You have a very weird sense of humor, Cinda."

"Nothing you're telling me makes me think he's stopped working, but I'd still like to talk to him again. We may be getting close to knowing who to sue but I'm still uneasy about Dashiell Roman's confession. I'd like some independent confirmation of who produced that tape. Chris said he knew a guy named Joel Derringer who was in the film."

"Yeah, well Chris doesn't want to talk to me, that's for sure. He told Shelley that if anyone called asking for him to say he'd moved out. Only, she says, nobody ever does."

Cinda was quiet for a minute, then said, "Do you think you could stake out the Universal Modeling place? The guy who runs it, Norm Lagrange, is supposed to be Chris's agent."

"Sure, I can do that."

"Only I don't know how you'll recognize him. I'm the only one who ever saw him."

"No worries, Cinda. When I took Shelley back to the apartment she let me in to use the bathroom. The living room was full of pictures of Chris. Not only will I recognize him if I see him, I'll probably recognize him if I come across him and he has a paper bag over his head, as long as he isn't wearing anything else."

"Their apartment is full of porno shots of him?"

"Not porno, just tasteful beefcake. I got the impression Shelley was embarrassed by it. She said they'd probably redecorate before the baby came."

"Maybe a few shots of the guy washing diapers with his shirt off. Linc, can you also do a check on this guy Roman's business, find out what kind of organization it is and whether it has assets?"

"Yeah, I'm on that already. It's not a publicly held corporation, but I think I may be able to get my hands on a financial statement."

"Audited?"

"You don't want much, do you Cinda?"

She sighed at the other end of the line, and Linc flashed on a picture of her sitting on the edge of her untidy desk, twirling the swivel desk chair clockwise and then counterclockwise with her feet. She often did this when she was on the phone. "I know," she said. "I'm obsessed. Andy Kahrlsrud told me the same thing."

"What are you doing for fun these days, Cinda? You seen Sam Holt?"

"Keep me posted, Linc. And be careful."

"Out there."

"What?"

"I think the line is, 'Be careful out there.'"

"Do it, Lincoln. Because if you get hurt I swear I'll kill you."

It was three nights before Charley went back to the hotel. He thought that would be long enough not to stir up any suspicion. Anyway, what were they gonna suspect him of? If he'd of been a cop, he'd of arrested them that first night, for chrissake. That little girl getting into the bathtub with that guy? She couldn't of been more than ten. That shit was illegal.

Still, he waited the three days. He didn't take Sable back with him either, even though he wouldn't of minded some more of her company. By the time they had both awakened in the morning, groggy and cranky in that soap-smelling room, he felt they'd been through the wars together and become friends. Sable had been underneath the blanket and Charley on top, him waking to find she'd gotten a blanket out of the closet in the middle of the night and spread it over him. Charley was pretty sure she'd figured out he wasn't an ordinary john, but she never said anything, just told him call her some day and tell her how it all came out. Which maybe he would.

Beverly would've come with him this time, if he'd let her. Lately she'd do anything for him. After the night with Sable he was afraid she'd complain about his being out all night, but she was so hot for his body when she finally got home from her office that day, she'd started tickling him around the ears and making jokes of a kind she hadn't since maybe before Duane was born. It seems that employment is a great aphrodisiac. Although he hadn't seen a single paycheck from Cinda, not that it was her fault because he hadn't submitted his invoice yet.

Whatever, Beverly was on him like a bee on a flower, or maybe that wasn't quite right, maybe it was the other way around, but for some reason he couldn't respond. He could've felt guilty about it if he'd of done anything with Sable—and he actually had to think for a minute to be sure he hadn't. It was such an unusual situation for him to be not interested. In his head it had something to do with the little girl in the bathtub, which he felt slimy about every time he thought of. Anyway, tonight he'd told Beverly he better go by himself. She didn't even give him any shit about it, just

French-kissed him when he left and said she'd try to wait up but not to worry if he needed to wake her up when he came in, she wouldn't mind.

It was a long drive down the Boulder-Denver Turnpike, not in distance but in time. Seemed like hardly anyone could afford to live in Boulder these days, and at the end of the day all its teachers, sales clerks, firefighters, plumbers, and, for all Charley knew, private investigators got into their cars and headed south toward the still-affordable towns between it and Denver. Good thing he and Beverly had inherited her mother's house when she died, or they'd never of been able to live there.

It did no good to stress about the traffic, so Charley surveyed the line of cars ahead with a practiced eye, turned on the radio to the oldies station, leaned back in the seat, and used the time to plan his strategy. It was dark by the time he pulled into the parking lot of the hotel. He turned the engine off but left the key turned part way, and sat there listening to the end of "Dancing in the Dark." The Boss, now he was cool. He'd know exactly what to do here. Charley thought about being the Boss, thinking he should of worn a black leather jacket, but he hadn't, so that was that. He twisted the key out of the ignition and opened the door.

This was a weeknight and there were no dressed-up teenagers or glad-handing conventioneers in the lobby. The lobby bartender watched his little television and the lone registration clerk smiled at Charley across the thick carpet as though she remembered him.

"Good evening, sir," she said. "Have you a reservation?" Snooty, like.

"Have you a break you could give me?" he thought, but he smiled back and said, "No, I just dropped by. On impulse, like. Do you have any rooms?"

"Let me see," she said noncommittally. What a load of it. She tapped and squinted and then looked up from her terminal and smiled at him like she was about to tell him he'd won the lottery. "I believe we do. We have a suite on the nineteenth floor, or a nonsmoking double on eight."

"I really only need a single. I'm alone tonight."

"Oh," she said, interested but not curious. "Yes, we have a smaller room on the second floor. Eighty-seven fifty plus tax. Will that be satisfactory?" Charley bet they trained their clerks to use that voice, interested but not curious, no matter what the topic. *I see, so you'll be joined later by your wife, whose name you're not sure of? I should give her a key and direct her to your room? Excellent, sir.*

"Sir? And how will you be paying for the room?"

Charley pulled out his credit card and tapped his fingers on the polished surface of the desk as she swiped and typed. "I, ah, would be interested in some entertainment, too. You know, even though I'm alone."

"Sir?" She handed his card back to him, her face professionally blank.

"Pay-per-view?"

"Of course, sir. You'll find a schedule in your room."

"What about unscheduled?"

"Sir?"

"I was told there were some special movies available for special customers. The private collection," he added, remembering that Sable had used those words.

She looked at him, considering, a girl who couldn't have been more than twenty-two in a navy suit and white blouse, whose feet had to be hurting after standing on them all day. For a moment he was sure she was going to summon security, but then she pulled out a notepad embossed with the hotel's logo and wrote something on the top sheet before tearing it off and handing it to him with a plastic keycard in a small paper folder.

He stole a look at the sheet before tucking it into his pocket. *Guy, ext. 5924.*

"Thanks," said Charley. "Have a nice evening."

"Thank you for choosing the Western Plaza," the girl said.

Linc was on his second cup of frozen yogurt, sitting at the outdoor table on the sidewalk outside Humphrey Yogart and surveying the ratty little shops of the strip mall to see if there was one that might sell sunscreen. He was wearing running shorts and an L.A. Marathon t-shirt he'd bought in the hotel's gift shop and torn the sleeves off; the October sun was starting to turn his arms pink. Nobody had yet come or gone from the Universal Modeling Agency, but as he stood and peered along the shadowed storefronts on his side, a flash of motion across the street caught his eye, and he turned to see a silver Saab pull into the parking lot below the agency's sign. A muscular young man in a leather jacket got out and hurried up the steps, and Linc realized that he was not close enough to discern whether it was Chris.

It was either get out the binoculars, or get closer. Linc tossed the yogurt carton into a stained metal bin and walked across the street. There were no outdoor tables on this side, nor any establishments that provided a pretext for lingering, unless you counted the yoga studio directly underneath the agency. Linc looked at his watch: according to the schedule posted on the door, there was a class beginning in fifteen minutes. The glass front of the studio gave him a good view of the place: a small reception area and a large room, mirrored all across the wall opposite the window. A lithe woman in matching apricot-colored shorts and bra was already spreading a towel on the floor near the center of the room. After smoothing out the towel she pulled her brown hair back and began poking it into a bun of some sort. She turned and saw him watching through the window, and smiled at him.

At one time he'd hung for a while with a girl who did yoga videos. He'd watched her twist and stretch with them a couple of times, enjoying the graceful movements without much curiosity about them. He should have paid more attention, he thought. He pushed open the door and walked in.

"Could I ask you a question about the class coming up?" he asked the guy perched on a stool behind the counter, a liquid-eyed South Asian with an enormous smooth chest. He was wearing nothing but bikini-style swimming trunks.

"Of course," said the man, looking up from the magazine he was reading. "I am Nataraj, the owner. The class is twenty dollars, and worth every penny. It's taught by Ananda, one of our best teachers, trained by Choudhury himself."

"That sounds great," said Linc. "But I—I have this problem. Claustrophobia. I can't stay in a room without windows, and I need to see the light from outside or I get in a panic. In this class, do we face the windows?"

"No," said the man. His speech was very precise. "You always face the mirror, so you can see your form and correct it. But the mirror is across from the windows, so I suppose you would see the light coming in when you looked in the mirror. Do you think you could be okay with that?"

"Yeah," said Linc. "I think I could. Twenty?" He had his wallet in his hand, and pulled out two tens. While the man tucked it into a zippered bag, Linc's eyes fell onto the photographs that covered the walls of the reception area. All these pretty but occasionally baggy people in different poses with a small Indian guy. Their faces looked slightly familiar, but he couldn't place them.

"You can leave your wallet and your shoes in the lockers," said the man, gesturing to a small area behind him. "You'd better get a towel, and some water. Have you practiced Bikram before?"

"I thought it was a yoga class."

"Bikram-style yoga. You will be very pleased."

The view was perfect. Linc could see everyone who came to or left the agency through the plate glass window behind. Or could have if the sweat hadn't started streaming into his eyes after about the third or fourth pose, which had to do with some kind of bird. What the fuck? He didn't remember this girlfriend saying anything about yoga being done in a steam chamber. The poses weren't that hard to imitate and he'd already been identified as a newcomer, so he figured it was good to be doofy, but the heat was unbelievable. At one point the teacher, Ananda, stood by while he tried to make a triangle of his body.

"It's good to look into the mirror occasionally, to monitor your alignment," she said. "But you look there continually. That is not necessary. The proper *drishte* for this pose is to look at your thumb." He looked down, sending a fresh cascade of salty sweat into his eyes. "No, the other one," said Ananda.

"Thank you," he said, looking up at his raised hand, clenching his teeth, and wishing she would move away. Someone was getting out of a white car outside.

"Your facial muscles are very tense," she said. "Try to maintain a composed and serene facial expression. But you are doing very well."

When she finally drifted to the next row of students and called out something in Sanskrit, he pulled up a corner of the towel and wiped his eyes, just in time to see in the mirror a man wearing white slacks starting to climb the stairs outside. Linc blinked, disbelieving, but then the man turned his head slightly as he paused to spray something into his mouth from a small atomizer before continuing his climb. It wasn't Chris, but it was definitely someone Lincoln had seen before; he stepped off the towel and rubbed his face with it vigorously before heading for the door.

Nataraj was still sitting on the stool, and he surveyed Lincoln with alarm as he burst out of the practice-room door. "What is the matter, my friend? The claustrophobia?"

"Yes," said Linc. "Exactly. It just got to be too bad."

"You should take kava root," said the man. "I see this many times in young men. You are fighting an unruly mind that persists in flitting like a butterfly. And I hope you did not leave the lesson without at least performing *shavasana*. It is very unwholesome to end your practice without *shavasana*."

"Right," said Linc. "Right. Listen, I gotta go. Maybe some other time. I'll try that kava."

Nataraj shrugged elegantly, his creamy brown chest glowing softly. "You are in need of calming, my friend. I am sorry you left without taking *shavasana*."

Linc was pretty sure the white Mercedes was the one his guy had gotten out of, and it was still there when he dashed out of the studio. He jogged up and down a few times, still doing extreme sweating, thinking he could pass for a marathoner in training if necessary. After a few minutes passed and the guy didn't reappear, Linc rested under a faded awning in front of a carpet store, making sure he was out of sight of Ananda and the yoga class. Tucked into the shadow near the bottom of the stairs, he swept his eyes along the curb at the edge of the parking lot, in the hollow just where it rose to the sidewalk. Nobody had cleaned the area in a long time; broken glass, discarded plastic eating utensils, and miscellaneous small pieces of discarded metal had collected along it. Linc saw what he needed before long.

He looked up when he heard steps on the stairs, but it was a woman leaving the modeling agency. She had beautiful silvery hair and nice legs, but her blue shorts didn't conceal a pair of ugly bruises on the outside of one thigh. Linc looked away quickly, but not before she saw him watching.

"Yeah, well fuck off, you perv," she said as she gained the sidewalk and headed toward the clustered cars, but not like she really cared. The legs were coltish and long, but she walked as though walking were uncomfortable. Linc watched her drive away in a red BMW that rattled as it turned the corner.

It was ten more minutes before the guy came clattering down the steps. Linc stepped into the shadows underneath the staircase and watched. The man didn't look happy to begin with, but his mood got much worse when he started across the asphalt and saw the flat tire.

"Fucking piece of shit!" He kicked at the side of the Mercedes, then turned to lean against it, patting his pockets, his face still distorted with anger.

He's probably got a phone, thought Lincoln, but he made himself wait another few seconds before jogging out of the shadows, blowing out irregular puffs of breath as though he'd been going for miles. He jogged to the middle of the parking lot and then stopped and bent over, panting, like a runner recovering from a sprint.

"Oh man," he said, looking over to the Mercedes and then at the man, as though seeing him for the first time. "Oh, man, that sucks. Somebody slashed it?"

"Stuck it with a nail, looks more like," the guy grunted. "Buttwipes."

Linc nodded. "Major. Probably jealous because you have such a nice car. Happened to me not long ago, my Jag. Listen, you need a ride to somewhere? No, what am I talking about, you've probably got Triple A." He shook out his hands and heaved a deep sigh, a guy finally getting his breath back.

"I let it expire," said the man, shaking his head. "I'm gonna call my girlfriend, but she'll bitch about having to come over here."

"Well, whatever," said Linc. "I just, you know, just finished my run, and my rental car's over there, piece of shit that it is." He pointed across the street. "I'd be glad to give you a ride somewhere."

"Nah, I'm going all the way over to Silver Beach. It's too far for you to go." But he looked interested.

"No, really. I'm just, you know, a tourist. Came here on business, got it done, but my plane doesn't leave until tomorrow. I just wanted to get some exercise, maybe drive around a little, see some of the city. I don't mind, really."

"You sure? Because you could take me to my brother's garage, bring back one of the wetbacks that works for him to change the tire." He gestured to the white slacks. "I'm just not gonna do it myself, you know? I'm having a fucked-up enough day already."

"Well, come on," said Linc, then stuck out his hand and said, "I'm Linc, by the way."

He nodded and extended his hand, saying only, "Joe." Then the man Linc had seen on the tape, the actor known as Joel Derringer, checked to see that his gleaming white car was locked and followed Linc across the street to the Prizm.

After Salvador had been picked up and then driven back to the Mercedes with instructions to change the tire and drive it back to the garage, Joe turned to Linc and suggested that they find some lunch. "I know a place in Santa Monica, near the pier," he said. "Really old place, like California used to be before the spics and Okies and tourists turned up. No offense." He obviously didn't intend this apology for Salvador, busy removing the lug nuts from the wheel with the flat tire, who looked up with such a flash of stoic comprehension that Lincoln flinched before turning back to Joe with a smile.

"Well, sure," he said, gesturing toward his still-damp shirt. "If I can go in there like this. And if you can stand the smell."

Joe snorted briefly and rubbed his fingers together just beneath his suntanned nose. "Believe me, I'm immune to smells. If you knew what I do for a living, you wouldn't worry about that."

"Oh yeah?" said Linc, unlocking the Prizm. "What's that?"

The lunch crowd was gone by two o'clock, and nine of the ten tables in the dim little shack were empty. It had been decorated, some long time before, in a nautical theme: dusty fishing nets dripped from the roof, the angles of their thick strands repeated in the filaments of spider web that festooned them, and a massive schooner wheel stood on a platform against the back wall. Sunlight slanted through the clouded small windows shaped like portholes; it emphasized the deep scars in the sticky varnished wooden furnishings without doing much to dilute the darkness. The smell of fried fish hung in the humid air, and music from the pier hovered beyond the open door, too distant to be identified.

Joel Derringer was on his fourth gin and tonic and Lincoln Tolkien was drinking along to be companionable, although after the second he had managed, on a trip to the john, to whisper to the bartender that he'd like plain tonic for refills from then on. He'd had no chance to get his recorder out of the Prizm's glove compartment with Derringer in the car, and was working hard at storing the conversation in his head for later retrieval.

"Acting in porn," Linc was saying. "Damn. It just always seemed so much like, you know, a dream job. It's weird to find out it's just a pay-check. And the part you said about always being worried you'll get the boot if you don't perform. Shit, it's just like my job."

"Which is what?" said Joe. "I forget what you said."

"Sales."

"Oh yeah. Sales of what?"

"Medical supplies." Fuck, thought Linc, I should have said musical instruments, I could have talked about that. I don't know anything about medical supplies. He hoped that Joe wouldn't follow up on this subject, but it was too late to take it back.

"Oh yeah? Pacemakers, that kind of thing?"

"Not so much pacemakers," said Linc. "I mean, my company makes them, of course, but I'm in a different department."

"Yeah?" said Joe, sucking the last inch of gin and tonic out of his glass. "Which wunnar you in?"

"Catheters," said Linc firmly. "Unbelievably boring things. Try to talk to a girl about them in a bar, you know? Might as well forget it."

"Yeah." Joe nodded understandingly. "Yeah, well try telling her you act in porn films. Try that some time. See what happens, you know?"

"Yeah."

"Reason I ask," continued Joe, "about the pacemakers, I mean. Once I was on a shoot, a guy has a heart attack right in the middle of his big scene, you know what I'm saying? He's fucking away and I'm thinking this guy, who's not all that good an actor, is like really acting a hell of a sweet orgasm, but then he doesn't pull out in time for the money shot, he just like flops onto the girl. The director yells 'Cut,' he's really pissed the guy ruined the scene, but then the girl starts screaming 'Get him off me! Get him off me!' and what do you know? He's bought the farm. What a way to go, huh? Workplace fatality."

"Wow," said Linc, having discovered earlier that Joe needed very little encouragement to keep talking.

"Turns out the guy's doc had told him he ought to have a pacemaker but he wouldn't do it because of the scar. I mean, he wouldn't have been able to work, you know? Or at least that's what I heard. Does it leave a big scar when they put in a pacemaker?"

"Not that big," said Linc, who had no idea. "At least, not these days. Maybe bigger back then, I don't know, before my time. You know, medicine's like everything else, computers and shit. Everything's getting smaller."

"Yeah, you're a young fella, couldn'ta been in the business long. I've seen a lot of changes come in, you know? Like this Viagra. See, there was a time when a guy like me was really in demand, because I got a fantastic control a my cock. I don't mean to boast too much, but I like got the thing under *control.* I was like the O. J. Simpson of fucking, you know?"

"Wow," said Lincoln.

"Or, okay, bad example, like the Tiger Woods or something. Michael Jordan, what have you. You remember what I said about smells? I was like, nothing put me off my game, smells, sounds, nothing. And I had stamina like you wouldn't believe. I mean that, my young friend. You wouldn't believe it."

"Yeah, I understand. So, you mean that's not important any more?"

"Oh, it's still important. It's just now every Tom, Dick, and Harry, especially the middle one, can do the same, because of the Viagra. Used to be a guy like me, good-looking, you know, handsome, but not some babyface hardbody spends all his nights at the gym, used to be that was plenty good-looking enough, if you had control like mine."

"But not any more?"

"No, that's my *point.* No, because all these wannabes who shoulda stayed in Peoria come out here, they got some long eyelashes like Brad whats-his-name—"

"Pitt?"

"Yeah, him. And they got *no* control. None. But now they got the blue pills, so they don't need it. And a guy like me, worked all his life to hone his skills as an actor, I'm out of the game, almost. Passed over, like. Yeah, well. Who said life is fair?" He gestured the barkeeper over to the table. "You?" he said, pointing to Linc.

"Oh, sure," said Linc, nodding to the bartender to remind him of their understanding. "Listen," he said to Joe, "this is like, so interesting. I've really never met anyone like you. Do you mind if I ask you some more questions about, you know, your work?"

"Sure, I'll tell you what you wanna know. Within reason, of course. I know some trade secrets, of course. Can't talk about those." He made the zipping motion, thumb and forefinger to lips. "But you know, I don't think I could recommend the profession to a young man such as yourself. Too many changes lately, and no loyalty. You'd be better off staying with the medical whatever. Catheters?"

Linc nodded. "Yeah, but actually it's my, ah, medical training that makes me interested. I mean, I keep thinking about your story, you know, about the guy who had the heart attack? This may seem strange, Joe, but even though I work in the medical field, I've never been around a dead body? At funerals maybe, but what I mean, I never saw anyone die. Was it, like, scary?"

Joe's eyes clouded, then he shook his head abruptly. "Not that time. Guy was a jerk, frankly, Linc. Thought he was the best woodsman around, you know what I mean? But he wasn't, cause the ticker is definitely part of the equipment you got to control, behind the scenes, like. So, he croaks, the girl gets upset, I guess that's her right, but they send her home, call the EMTs, they come, he's gone. Disrupted the film a bit, but that's not my problem, that's the producer's, you know? He didn't want to keep filming that day, but if I'da had to step in, I coulda. I coulda maintained control, you know?"

In the brief silence that followed this, the man's head jerked forward briefly before he caught it, and it looked for a moment that Joe might be on the verge of passing out. Linc thought of the lock again, the key. He took a sip from his cold bitter drink and turned the key, hoping it was the right way.

"Joe," he said, "there was something you said there. 'Not that time.'"

"Yeah?"

"Did it—you know. Happen some other time, too?"

"Did what happen?" The words were still slurred a bit, but he looked up sharply from the table.

"You know. Somebody dying while you were making a movie."

"Why do you ask me that?" The glass in his hand wobbled.

Linc shrugged, trying to make it casual even as he could feel the tumblers falling beneath his fingers. "Just, I thought that's what you were saying."

Joe narrowed his eyes, then turned his head toward one of the portholes. When he turned it back toward Linc, the eyes were wet.

"Jesus," he said. "Jesus. The thing was, I had a daughter then myself. That was the thing."

Guy was cranky, but willing.

"I never heard a that one," he said on the other end of the telephone. Charley could hear crashing and gunfire in the background, then the whining voice of Kevin Spacey. *The Usual Suspects,* it sounded like. Great flick.

"That's too bad. It's really out there," said Charley, having rehearsed this description in his mind. "At the end, it's like, I don't know. Like really amazing special effects, or else they really croaked this kid. I only saw it the once, but it would be worth a lot to me to see it again."

"I dunno," said Guy. "I hear what you're saying and I'd like to accommodate you, but I don't think we got it."

"Could you check? Or maybe one of the other hotels around? Do you, like, trade tapes with them?"

"Nah. We don't do that. Too much legal exposure, what that is. We wouldn't even be having this conversation except for you know Sable and I know Sable."

"Yeah," said Charley, discouraged. Maybe it was just as well. If he did turn up the tape and told Cinda about it, he might get Sable into trouble.

"Anyway, lemme check, though. I don't always know what we got. I'll call you in a few minutes."

"I'm in two twelve."

"Yeah."


Charley had the television on HBO, watching Tony Soprano trying to calm down Uncle Junior, when the knock came on his door and he realized he should have had a gun.

"Yeah," he called through the door, standing to one side in case they actually shot through the door.

"It's Guy." And he could tell it was, from the same gruff voice as on the phone, even though it didn't carry too well because the door was thick. This was a pretty nice hotel, quiet. Yeah, great, always best to die in a pretty nice hotel if you can manage it, not some grimy hot-sheet joint.

"What is it?" called out Charley.

"I'm not having this conversation through the door, jerk-off. Open up or we can forget about it."

"Okay, okay, just a minute. Lemme put my pants on." Charley waited for a brief interval he thought sufficient for putting on pants, and while he did he wrote on the notepad next to the phone, "Beverly: I love you. Charley." In case of sudden death. But after that he opened the door, even though his heart was bumping in his chest like an out-of-tune car that won't quit when you turn off the engine. Because what else was he gonna do?

Standing there was a short string bean of a man with a combover Charley could have counted the strands of on both hands, or maybe one. He was armed with nothing more than what looked like a shabby magazine, black and white.

"You owe me big-time, Charley," he said as he stepped into the room. "Close the door fa chrissake."

"You found it?" Charley said, pulling the door shut. He was psyched but also now worrying about the Sable aspect again.

"Better," said Guy. "The catalog. You can order it for yourself, see? Course this is a valuable piece a business property, here, this catalog. I'm sure you appreciate that."

"Oh," said Charley. "I do, Guy. I do. You're the man."

They settled on fifty dollars, and by eight o'clock Charley was back on the road to Boulder, thinking of Beverly in her red teddy, and the way her chubby buns peeked out of the back of it when she turned around. Of course she'd probably want them to call Cinda first, but after that anything could happen, especially if Duane was staying over at his buddy's house for the night.

AK: This recording begins at 9:24 p.m., September 17, 1999. Leonard, how are you doing tonight?

LF: Okay, I guess.

AK: What kind of a day did you have?

LF: I stayed in my house all day.

AK: Your house?

LF: That's what they call our cells. What we call them.

AK: Why did you stay in all day?

LF: Because that's the safest place. Nobody can get to you if you stay in. I mean, maybe someone could if they—I don't know. It would be hard, though. It's pretty safe if you stay in.

AK: Are you more concerned about your personal safety than usual?

LF: Yeah, you could say that.

AK: Why is that?

LF: I figure I might be able to help someone if I can stay alive.

AK: Ah. Anyone in particular?

LF: I figure maybe I could be a witness in this case you're working on. For Alison's mother.

AK: You want to testify?

LF: You know I never did in the other trial. It was just Dr. Gupta and some other doctors, I can't remember their names.

AK: I don't think that's what the lawyer I'm working with has in mind, Lenny.

LF: Alison's mother's lawyer.

AK: Right.

LF: Why not?

AK: For one thing, I'm not sure it's even possible for you to be moved out of this facility to testify. There would be very serious security concerns. Even if it could be done, it would be very expensive.

LF: You said she has to prove, this lawyer, she has to prove that it was the tape caused me to kill the little girl.

AK: Well, yes. More or less.

LF: So who would be a better witness?

AK: I think she expects me to testify.

LF: But you only know what I told you.

AK: Well, that's right in a way. I've studied other reports about you, and talked to Gupta, but it's true that you're the ultimate source. Still, I don't think she's going to try to bring you into court, Lenny.

LF: I feel like maybe I could be helpful.

AK: Maybe you could. It's not up to me, you know.

LF: The lawyer?

AK: And her client, I suppose. This seems very important to you, Lenny.

LF: Yeah. (pause) Yeah.

AK: Is there something else you want to say?

LF: This is the last time you're coming here, isn't it?

AK: I'm going home to Colorado tomorrow morning, Lenny. You've been very helpful, and interesting, and I would like other opportunities to talk with you, but I need to get back to my other clients. I've been away for more than a week.

LF: When is the trial?

AK: The case isn't even filed, Lenny. It may not ever be filed, as far as that goes. The trial may not even happen, because it depends on a lot of other things besides what you and I say to each other. I don't even understand all of them myself. Something about the court's jurisdiction, for one thing.

LF: I (pause). I wish we could talk some more.

AK: I do too, Lenny.

LF: What's (pause)

AK: It's okay, Lenny. Here, use this. (pause)

LF: What's, what's going to happen to me?

AK: I don't know, Lenny.

LF: Yes, you do. Tell me.

AK: Nobody knows everything. But I think it's likely you're going to live the rest of your life in this place, Lenny.

LF: You think I don't know that?

AK: No. I think you know that. You don't need me to tell you.

LF: Yeah, you got that right.

AK: You sound pretty angry.

LF: Yeah. Yeah, well. What do you care, right? You're going home.

AK: That doesn't mean I don't care.

LF: About me?

AK: That's right.

(pause)

AK: It's okay, Lenny.

LF: What does that mean, it's okay?

AK: Right then I meant, it's okay to cry.

LF: You think I need your permission? Fuck you.

AK: No, I know you don't. Listen, Lenny, I'm going to leave now.

LF: Like I care. Used me, is all you did.

AK: I'll think about you, Lenny, and maybe we'll see each other again. This recording ends at 10:18 p.m.

# PART THREE

Constructed in the Seventies after the trial calendar overwhelmed downtown's lovely old art-deco courthouse, the Boulder County Justice Center zigzags like a blocky snake diagonally along Boulder Creek. The creek itself tumbles past in a roughly parallel course a few hundred feet to the south. From the air the building would resemble several dominoes placed almost corner to corner, with a small overlap. And then one more layer of dominoes on top of that, but only one.

The Justice Center is set low to the ground for reasons of economy and, more fundamentally, aesthetics. The latter are also known in Boulder as *politics*. People who complain about political apathy should visit Boulder for a while. Citizens have opinions about everything, especially matters that affect what we like to call our *quality of life*. We are certain, despite evidence to the contrary, that it is deteriorating. Public sentiment about local matters rarely reaches the pleased end of the spectrum; we have more talent for indignation. We are particularly vigilant in the matter of real estate development, tending to believe that all of it in Boulder should have stopped at some point in the past, generally the instant just following the construction or renovation of our own residences.

We dislike any alteration of the remaining natural environment and we emphatically do not tolerate anything that blocks our view of the mountains. We like to look west of a morning and see the sun reflected off Flagstaff and the Flatirons, Dakota Ridge and the Indian Peaks beyond. The Justice Center's creek-side plot near the city's western edge could not have sprouted a tall building without fomenting a revolution. Two stories was the most even considered.

I had come on this day to this ugly building in its spectacular setting to persuade a judge that my client's lawsuit should be permitted to go to trial. The theory of our case had been variously described, depending upon the describer, as solid, original, creative, or outrageous. There was a time when I would myself have chosen the last adjective, but like almost all

lawyers I have a gift for persuading myself that the arguments I once fashioned in desperation now shine with truth and inevitability. The numerous expensive, well-trained, and superbly equipped lawyers on the other
side would be arguing within the hour that if I were allowed to take Peggy
Grayling's case to trial, American law and culture would be forever damaged. I hoped they were wrong, but even more than that, I hoped the
judge would not see it that way. I had come way too far to care more about
such abstractions than I cared about winning.

I had arranged to meet my client in the parking lot at 8:30, but the
traffic had been more clement than usual, and I was ten minutes early. I sat
uneasily behind the scratched wheel of Sam's Saab and reflected on the
events that had transformed me, former card-carrying ACLU member, into
an enemy of the First Amendment to the United States Constitution.

Peggy was right on time, interrupting my reverie by appearing at the
Saab's driver-side window at precisely 8:30. I scrambled out, pulling my
briefcase after me, and locked the car. We started walking together toward
the Justice Center.

"Remind me again, Cinda, what this is about today." She looked both
ways before stepping lightly into the striped pedestrian walkway that crossed
Sixth Street between the public parking lot and the squat building. I carried a briefcase laden with paper, and was having trouble keeping up with
her.

"You remember that the lawyers for DR Films and DR Distribution
Company made the motion to dismiss about a month ago? The really long
one that I sent you in the mail?" Peggy nodded without slowing down,
and I paused to hitch the briefcase higher on my shoulder. Then I had to
take an extra step to keep from falling behind her; somehow she managed
to combine speed with the appearance of sauntering. "Today," I continued, "the judge is going to listen to our arguments, and theirs, about
whether she should grant their motion to dismiss." The September sun
poured down onto the jacket of my black suit, creating something like a
furnace effect. I could feel a sweaty trickle descending between my breasts
under my silk blouse, but I couldn't take off the jacket. Already a news
crew of three men was approaching us, one with a camera, another holding
a mike on a boom. The third was Alex Cho, the pretty young man who
covered Boulder for the Denver CBS affiliate.

"Miss Hayes," he shouted. "Miss Hayes! Could we have a word?"

I waved in what I hoped was a friendly go-away motion, and said to Peggy, "Let's concentrate on getting inside without being waylaid. I'll explain about the hearing once we're inside."

She nodded and kept walking, her narrow feet in their black ballet slippers seeming barely to touch the ground. We gained the entrance just before the news crew caught us, and I turned to give them my nicest smile before disappearing through the door, where they could not follow. "Maybe later, Alex," I said encouragingly to the reporter, but before he could reply a shout went up behind him, and looking in that direction I saw Dan Everett, partner in one of L.A.'s biggest law firms and litigation counsel for several television networks. He was just about to enter the pedestrian crossing, chatting in a relaxed way with a second news crew as he strode confidently along the sidewalk, unencumbered by the need to carry anything. I supposed the younger man struggling along a few feet behind him, a large leather case in each hand, to be his associate. Alex Cho turned quickly, and motioned to his camera and sound men to follow him as he strode rapidly away to the rear.

So useful, I thought, to have someone you can pay a hundred and fifty thousand dollars a year to carry your stuff for you. And then, to myself: *Careful, Cinda.* I had spent the last few weeks in a mostly solitary effort at trying to shovel myself out from under the paper blizzard generated by Mr. Everett and his numerous well-paid associates, not to mention the other lawyers and theirs, and I knew that fatigue predisposed me to bitterness if I didn't watch it.

"Will we have to talk to them, Cinda?" said Peggy as we walked into the building. "I'd rather not."

"We'll decide later, after the hearing. Here, Peggy, we have to go this way." I gestured toward the X-ray machine and metal detector, but it wasn't necessary. She seemed to understand the security arrangements at a glance. She smiled softly at the police officer attending the entryway; he responded to her warmth, just as almost everyone did.

"Here you are, ma'am," he said, obviously enjoying her appearance, the tanned skin against the cream color of her pants suit. "If you'll just put your purse here on the belt, and step through the arch there. There you go." He nodded at me more perfunctorily, as I showed him my attorney ID card. I placed my briefcase on the conveyor belt, and he waved me through the arch. My shoes or earrings or something set off the beep, as always, but I did not stop. Licensed local attorneys are not required to divest themselves of all metal appurtenances before entering the courthouse. Peggy followed me, having instantly taken in the relevant distinction and removed her heavy silver bracelet before passing through. She accepted its return from the attendant with a grave smile.

Because the defendants were out-of-state corporations, we'd had a choice of whether to file our case here in state court, the District Court of Colorado for the Twentieth Judicial District, or in the federal court in Denver. Before drafting the pleadings I'd asked Peggy if she had a preference.

"What do you think?" she'd responded, sitting very straight in my office chair.

"Federal court might be better," I said. "The jury panel there would be drawn from the whole Front Range area, about six counties around Denver. It would be a more diverse group, a little more blue-collar, probably a little less intellectual. Might be less responsive to the industry's free-speech arguments."

"If we chose federal court where would the trial be held?" she said.

"At the federal courthouse in Denver. You probably saw it on television during the Oklahoma City bombing trials. It's a very formal place, very secure. The federal marshals do a good job of handling the press, which could be a good thing."

She sighed. "I like it better here. I feel at home in Boulder."

I shrugged. "It's your choice. I should tell you that if we file in state court, the defendants have a right to move the case to federal court if they want to."

She looked up sharply. "They can do that?"

I nodded. "It's called removal. But I don't think they will. I think they'd prefer a Boulder jury."

She nodded. "Let's see what they do, then."

And I was right. They hadn't removed the case, and now the time for it was past.

The courtroom where the motion was to be heard was on the second floor, so I gestured toward the stairs and followed Peggy's light steps to the top of the staircase. The corridor was still deserted at this early hour, and Judge Meiklejohn's courtroom still locked, so my client and I sat on one of the benches. I set my heavy trial briefcase down onto the tiled floor with relief, and tried to explain to my client what was at stake for her in the morning's proceedings.

"The lawyers for the defendants, that's the production company and the distribution company, are going to argue that this case should not even be tried. They'll say the judge should throw it out without ever picking a jury or allowing any evidence to be presented." This was familiar ground, but it had been a while since we had talked face to face, and Peggy did not like to have any but the briefest telephone conversations.

"Will the man be here today? The Roman person?"

"I don't know, but I doubt it. He's very sick, Peggy, dying of lung cancer. I'll be surprised if he comes for the hearing."

She frowned slightly. "But if we win this hearing, there will be a trial?"

"Yes, unless they make a summary judgment motion later, but I'm not too worried about that. Today's hearing is the big event, legally. That's why all of the news crews are here. Today is when they put forward all of the First Amendment arguments about why cases like ours shouldn't even be possible."

"Yes, what about those news crews? I wasn't expecting them. Why are they here?"

"There's a lot at stake here, Peggy, not only for the defendants in this case. Every studio, every television network, production company, practically every publishing house, newspaper corporation, and author's association has at least one lawyer working on this case. The judge has granted the motion of every one of these organizations to be given the status of amicus curiae. Or amici, that's the plural."

"Yes, I remember. Friends of the court, right?"

"That's what it means. But here, even though they aren't parties to this exact case, they're really friends of the defense, and they're all committed to the same argument because they all have a huge stake in it—that the First Amendment does not allow a lawsuit against someone who creates or distributes a book or movie or magazine just because their product inspired someone to commit a crime. If the judge rules in their favor, there will be no trial. We'd have to appeal in that case. But we're ready for this motion, and I think we have a really good chance to get to trial."

She nodded comprehendingly, and leaned forward to ask a question. "And if there is a trial—"

"Yes?" I was ready to explain any of the technical legal issues that were likely to come up at trial.

"Will he have to come then?"

"Who—Dashiell Roman?"

She nodded.

"He won't *have* to come unless we put him under subpoena, Peggy, and maybe not even then since he's out of state. I haven't really thought that far down the road, but I doubt we'd want to try to bring him here anyway. He's a dying man, and according to Linc he looked like one even a year ago, so he's likely to look even more pitiful now. That's sure to create sympathy in some of the jurors. And we don't have to use him as a witness to prove any part of our case. He's admitted to making the film, producing it and distributing it through his companies. I might want his answers to questions about whether he ever thought about the risk of encouraging someone to act out the things on the tape, but I can get those by going to California and taking his deposition. I'd rather have his words in front of the jury on a transcript than him in person. I want the jurors to think of the defendants as businesses, because that's what this is to him, a business. A way to make a lot of money. I don't want them looking at some sick old man."

"But won't his own lawyers want him to be here?"

The courtroom door was pushed open from the inside, and Judge Meiklejohn's clerk looked out at us. "Courtroom's open whenever you want to come in," she said. "Judge will take the bench at nine on the dot."

"Thanks, Carolyn," I said, then turned back to my client. "They might, Peggy. Or maybe not. I can't exactly tell what's happening with the defense of this case, but you need to realize that DR Films and DR Distribution Company don't have nearly as much interest in the outcome of this case as Paramount and Warner Brothers and Universal and Rose Brothers. And the conglomerates that own them. It's not just the porn industry, it's the entire American entertainment industry. Roman is about to die, and I don't think he really cares about the outcome of this case."

"You said you thought he had a bad conscience about Alison's death."

I nodded. "Linc thought so, and that it was why he acknowledged he made *Sunshade Snuffdown*. He doesn't have any children or relatives; my friend Rafe doesn't even think he's made a will. It looks to me as though the lawyers for the big guys are the ones running this case. And I don't know whether they'll want Dashiell Roman in the courtroom if we get to trial. All I know is, they're pulling out all the stops today to try to ensure that they never have to address that question."

Peggy said that she didn't need to visit the ladies' room so I left her on the corridor bench and went alone, grateful for the small interval of solitude. After washing my hands I scrutinized my face in the mirror, which was overhung with a greenish light of the sort that makes you notice small shadowed specks on your face and faint discolorations on the front of your white blouse that you hadn't seen at home. I'm too young for this, I thought, someone with more experience should be handling this case.

*Over forty, too young?* the countenance in the mirror taunted me. *Wish you were back in traffic court?*

I blinked and for some reason the fickle filing system of memory shuffled forward an image that had nothing to do with anything: the grade school playground, the one boy who spat at my feet and said—what had he said?

*I hate this place. Nothing ever happens here.*

Something was going to happen here, all right. I hoped it was the right thing, the good thing.

Good for whom?

My client, of course. Peggy Grayling.

It was Tory who had first given voice to my own disquiet.

"What is *up* with her, anyway?"

"Who do you mean?"

"*Whom,* Cinda. *Whom* do I mean."

"Yes, all right, whom?" It was after midnight, and both of us had been working frantically on our brief in opposition to the motion to dismiss. Until the motion had arrived Tory had stayed pretty aloof from *Grayling v. DR Films,* but once the paper started to blow in, I'd had to conscript her into service. The two of us and Beverly had been toiling eighteen-hour days to get the damn thing as good as we could make it, as persuasive, as professional, as airtight as we could, not to mention completely free from errors grammatical, formal, or punctuational. Everything that I suppose all good writing consists of, except for original.

You don't want original in a brief. You don't want creative. You don't want to be saying to an overworked judge who desperately wishes not to get overruled by the court above him, *Here you are, Your Honor. An opportu-*

*nity to do something so daring, so original, so completely without precedent that they will be talking about it even fifty years from now, still amazed by your audacity.*

Audacity is for novelists or poets, not lawyers or judges. Lawyers want to be saying *Here you are, Your Honor. If you appreciate the cases and statutes and constitutions and all according to their true meaning, then there is only one thing you can do. Anything else would be original. Unprecedented. In a word, illegal.*

So we had been clickety-clacking away for days, each on her own laptop, feeding our disks to Beverly to be stitched together, renumbered and resectioned, cleaned up, reconciled somehow. Tory's speech to the gay and lesbian lawyer's group, suitably expurgated, made ponderous, and decorated with references to everything from *The Federalist Papers* to a recent decision from the Fourth Circuit, formed the core of our argument. Numb with exhaustion, wired to the gills on coffee and sugary carbs brought in from the Trident, barely coherent, we'd somehow managed to manufacture the eighty-page document. The margins were sharp, spelling checked, every outrageous or desperate argument transformed by such sobriety and wit as we could muster into *only one thing you can do*. Even Brianna Bainbridge had gotten involved, coming by one evening to read our draft and mark it up with suggested revisions—some brilliant and some undecipherable—that left the margins inscribed with an intricate frieze of green ink.

Having received one reluctant enlargement of time from Judge Meiklejohn, we had to file the thing by nine the next morning. Ergo, we declared it done. Beverly had gone home and Tory and I, our breath fouled with coffee and our hair greasy from neglect, were supervising the final printout. Afterward, we would have to make the copies, including one for each of what we had come to refer to as the Fucking Amici, thirteen of them: NBC, ABC, for example. Rose Brothers Studios, for example. Then we could go home and sleep; Beverly had promised to be back in the morning in time to take the thing over to the courthouse and mail the copies.

"Our client. Peggy. Is it just me, or is she strange?" said Tory.

I stopped collating for a moment, pushed away the recognition this question produced. "I don't think so. No. She's—you know."

"I *don't* know. I can't figure her out."

"Well, she's a Buddhist, for one thing," I said.

"Yeah, so what. Billy Woodruff is a Buddhist, but he doesn't walk around looking like he's trying to float off the ground."

"No, he just walks around in rubber sandals so old and disgusting that he smells like a landfill."

"That's what I mean. That's normal, that smelling bad, then smelling good, looking great one day, looking raunchy the next day. That's the way of the world, or whatever they say. She's like, I don't know. Like she's living on some other plane."

"I believe there is a Buddhist belief that desire is the cause of all suffering," I said, resuming my collation duties. "Probably that accounts for it."

"See, you've noticed it too. Anyway, how could that belief, whatever it means, account for the way she is? She hasn't stopped wanting things. She wanted us to bring this case for her, didn't she? If not, I swear I'm going home to bed right this minute." She made a histrionic gesture as though she were about to throw a dozen collated pages into the air, but I knew she wouldn't, and didn't react. She doesn't push my buttons quite the way she used to.

"Why are we talking about this?" I said. "This is dumb. She's a nice woman whose daughter was horribly murdered and who wants someone to be held responsible for it. Maybe her personal style is a little effete for you because unlike some people she doesn't go around crashing into things and breaking them, but so what? Why don't we talk about something else?"

I expected her to react to that *unlike some people* in her usual pugnacious style, and thought the resulting unserious argument would at least keep us awake. But instead she said, "Okay, let's talk about something else."

"Good, okay. You start."

"How's Sam?"

"Oh. Oh, he's fine. He's, you know, Sam."

"When did you talk to him last, then?"

"It's been too long, definitely. A while. You know how it's been around here. And I'm sure he's busy too."

She was silent. I was too, but it got on my nerves first.

"What?"

"You two aren't together any more, are you?"

It was ridiculous to deny it. "No," I agreed. "We're not."

"Well why the hell not?" said Tory. "He's worth about fifty of that Rafe character."

"I'm not seeing Rafe," I said. "I haven't seen him since I went out to L.A. about a year ago. I just talk to him sometimes because Rose Brothers assigned him to this case."

"I'd never accuse you of fucking one of the amici curiae, girl, even if Fucking is their first name, but why do I think things might change when this case is over and you're no longer opponents?"

"He's not my type, Tory, so leave me alone about him. He and I have been over this and it's all settled."

"So, the subject has come up? I knew it!"

"Shut *up, Tory*." I reached for the stapler and applied it savagely to the thick sheaf of paper in my hand. *"Shit!"* I plucked a staple out of the fleshy part of my thumb and sucked hard on the puncture. "Dammit, I'd better go wash this off before I bleed on the brief. Don't we have a first aid kit somewhere?"

She pointed toward Beverly's desk with her elbow. "Don't think this is the end of this conversation. Some day this case is going to end, one way or another, and you need to think about what you're going to do with your-self when it does."

"Just collate the copies, Tory. I'm going to find a bandaid."

I wasn't about to tell Tory, but in fact I had seen Sam once since we watched *Sunshade Snuffdown* together in that Chicago hotel room. He'd shown up at the office late one Friday afternoon about two months before, after Beverly and Tory had left for the day. I was thinking about leaving myself, and wondering what I'd do to make the weekend go quickly. I could always find plenty of reasons to come in and work on both days, but I was starting to worry that my unceasing presence at the office meant I needed to, as the saying goes, get a life. Still, it wasn't clear to me where one was to be found, so I'd probably just come into the office, maybe catch a movie late Satur-day afternoon. I heard a scraping noise and looked up to see Sam standing at the door. These offices used to be his, before he left for New York, and he was looking around in a proprietary way.

"Not too shabby," he said, pointing to the only nice piece of furniture in the room, an antique armoire I'd bought at an auction.

"Sam. How did you get here?"

He reached into his jacket pocket and pulled out an airline ticket, displaying and then pretending to examine it. "This says I have to go back Sunday night. Do you know where I might find some company in the meantime?"

"No, I mean, what are you doing here?" I could hear the way it sounded, cold and unwelcoming, but my brain had gone sluggish and words were coming to me slowly.

"Don't you know?" He walked into the room as I rose from my chair.

At first his mouth tasted the same as ever, its pressure against mine like coming home after a long absence. The chill that had stiffened my face was dispersing and my lips parted to take in more of the heat from his. But as he moved his head slightly away to search my eyes, I thought I saw a glint of avidity, or curiosity, in his. Something feverish, intensified by the darkness of his skin, the whiteness of his teeth. He reminded me of someone, someone to be afraid of.

Like a cunning animal, he picked up on my fear immediately. "What's the matter, Cinda?" He brushed my hair lightly with his left hand, but not so lightly that I could fail to sense the power in his arms and shoulders. It would be easy enough for him to crush me if he chose to. I remembered the fight outside the Bucket o' Blues, the feline ease with which he'd thrown his weight into the other man, and also the excitement that this memory had once aroused in me. My heart was hammering with the memory of that link between violence and desire; I never wanted to feel it again. A hand clenched my stomach in its cold grasp and bile filled my mouth.

"Nothing." But I found that I had taken a step back, and was holding my wrist against my face.

"Don't tell me that. There's something."

I had once cherished his uncanny ability to read my silences, but now it seemed sinister. I swallowed the bitter liquid and said, "I just don't feel like it right now, that's all. You just show up and expect me to fall into bed with you? I didn't even know you were coming."

"You haven't been returning my calls," he said gently.

"I've been busy. You're the one who left Boulder!"

"Then talk to me. Or don't you feel like that either?"

I could only shake my head dumbly.

"Cinda, if you don't want to talk, and you don't want to go to bed with me, there's not very much reason for me to stay until Sunday."

I sank down again into my chair and looked stubbornly at the top of my cluttered desk. "You have lots of other friends in Boulder," I said. "They'll be glad to see you. I have plans."

I kept my eyes focused on a ravaged patch of wooden desktop. I didn't see him leave, and he couldn't have seen my tears. "You can never be with him again," I whispered after I heard the outer door slam, willing myself to accept it.

I hadn't heard from him since, and I was glad. There would have been no point to it.

We finally got the briefs filed. Judge Meiklejohn read them, and she set the matter down for oral argument, half an hour per side. The Fucking Amici had asked for a half hour, too, but she'd told them no. I had been cheered by this small evidence of her failure to be impressed by the star power of the industry lawyers.

I had also admired her handling of an issue that came up after they filed a motion to dismiss for lack of personal jurisdiction over the defendant. Their lengthy and impressively syntaxed argument claimed that no Colorado court could have jurisdiction over a suit based on events that happened in Illinois brought against the makers of a product manufactured in California. In my response I'd submitted an affidavit, signed by Charley, in which I'd described the circumstances surrounding his success in obtaining a catalog from DR Distribution Company from the manager of private video services in a Denver hotel. I'd hoped that this discovery would be sufficient to persuade the judge that DR Distribution and DR Films were "transacting business" in Colorado; that's the test of whether the Colorado long-arm statute would authorize a state court's jurisdiction over them. But it was going to be close. It would have been better if we could have ordered one of the tapes from them, and shown that it had been delivered to us in Colorado, but there was little hope of that: Linc discovered that by the time Charley found the catalog, Dashiell Roman had stopped shipping product. Despite further researches, Charley had never located another copy of the catalog in Colorado, nor had he ever found a copy of *Sunshade Snuffdown* for sale or rental.

On the other hand, the catalog he'd gotten from the hotel had invited customers to order items using an attached envelope addressed to DR Distribution Company of Los Angeles, prepaid as business-reply mail. Linc had been able to learn that during 1998, nearly ten thousand pieces of mail had been charged to this account, maintained by DR Distribution at the postal service. Statistically and demographically, I argued, it was therefore likely that about 120 pieces would have come from Colorado—that is, more than a hundred sales of DR products were made to Coloradans. A few cases I'd read and cited in our brief suggested, at least I thought they did, that a hundred mail-order sales per year in a jurisdiction would constitute "the transaction of business." This argument suffered from the defects of all arguments from statistics, and maybe some others as well. I could have asked Linc to undertake more investigation about DR's mailing list, or could have sought discovery using the court's authority, but either alternative would have been expensive, and Peggy's pockets were growing empty. We'd decided to go with what we had. I was hopeful, but not unworried.

I'd faxed my response to Frank Morales, local counsel for Dashiell Roman, first thing in the morning, a couple of hours before I sent Beverly over to the courthouse to file it. Before noon I got my first phone call from Dan Everett.

"So nice to talk with you, Ms. Hayes," he said, his voice as solicitous as a country doctor's. "Even though we're not on the same side in this matter, I must say I admire your work very much. And your pluck."

I did one of those belly breaths and told myself to ignore the condescension. "What can I do for you, Mr. Everett?" I said.

"I'm authorized to tell you that the defendants are considering withdrawing their motion to dismiss for lack of jurisdiction, having read your very convincing response to it. My compliments on your detective work."

"Thanks for letting me know," I said. "You could have just filed your request to withdraw it with the court, and sent me a copy. But I appreciate the call." This was disingenuous of me, as I was certain he would have done exactly that if he hadn't wanted something in addition. Something else occurred to me, too: the court filings had identified Everett as counsel for Star Cable Network. DR Films and DR Distribution Company had retained Frank Morales at the Boulder firm of Hoffman, Moran, and Steele. "But I thought you represented one of the amici, Mr. Everett. Not Mr. Roman's companies. Was I mistaken?"

"Not at all," he said smoothly. "But we're coordinating, you know. Cooperating. Would you prefer to communicate strictly through local counsel?"

"No," I said. "Just curious. Well, thanks again for your courtesy in calling. I'll look forward to seeing your papers."

"Just one more thing," he said. Pleasantly, like an Ivy League Columbo. "What might that be?"

"We'd be very grateful if, in exchange for our surrender on this important point of jurisdiction, you would join us in a motion I've just filed to seal the documents related to this motion. It should be arriving on your fax machine just about now." I glanced out the door of my office to Beverly's desk, and sure enough the cranky mechanism was beginning its series of wheezes and lurches. "I know the local press is very interested in this case, no reason they shouldn't be. But since our motion will be withdrawn and will have no further importance to the litigation, I don't think it adds anything to the story for them to read about your discoveries at the Western Plaza, do you?"

"I try not to concern myself with what the press might do," I said.

"No? You have to admit you're not exactly the most ardent defender of the First Amendment around," said Everett.

"Gosh no," I said. "That would be you and your cast of a thousand amici. Actually, Mr. Everett, it surprises me that a defender of free speech like you would try to keep public documents away from the press. As I recall, some of the amici are newspapers. Are they down with this move of yours?" I admit I was enjoying myself.

"We are all in agreement," he said stiffly. "What you're trying to do in this case is a far, far more serious threat to freedom of expression than what we're asking, which is simply for the court to prevent the unnecessary embarrassment of a national corporation that was unlucky enough to have one out-of-control employee dispensing unauthorized material to a few guests."

"Words fail me," I said, suddenly tired of the conversation.

"Meaning what, Ms. Hayes?"

"Meaning I cannot find enough of them to tell you how much I disagree with you. But request away. Just don't say I join you in your motion, because I don't."

"Perhaps I didn't make myself clear," said Everett. "What I am proposing is an agreement. Our withdrawal of the motion on jurisdiction, in exchange for your consent to join us in asking the judge to seal the papers."

"You made yourself clear," I said. "See you in court."

I'd always wanted to say that.

I called Lincoln right away, and asked him if he could find out who owned the Denver Western Plaza.

"I don't have to find out," he said. "I know. TriState Accommodations."

"Never heard of them."

"Of course not. They're a subsidiary of TransLandCorp, which in turn is owned by Registry News and Entertainment Corporation."

"Now you're getting around to something I've heard of. What else does Registry own?"

"Name it," said Lincoln. "Newspapers, travel agencies, publishing houses. Movie studios. Why do you ask?"

"Just curious," I said. "What movie studios, for example?"

"Rose Brothers, for example. Your friend's studio."

"You're kidding."

"It's not that much of a coincidence, Cinda. I'm pretty sure that before long three or four corporations are going to own everything on the planet, if they don't already."

"How do you know all this stuff, Linc?"

"Just curious," he said. "My natural state. Cinda, are you going to need me for the next few days? I'm thinking I might take a quick trip out to L.A."

"More business there?" I said.

"Nah," he said. "Just to go see a friend. She's got a small baby and can't travel too well herself, and I think she's kind of lonely."

"She's not in the movie business, is she Linc?" I said. "Because I think it's best for you to stay away from Hollywood and the Valley until this case is over."

"Thanks, Mom," he said, "but no worries. She isn't. She hates the business, actually. She lost her husband to it."

I was ready for a fight on the jurisdiction question, and somewhat apprehensive about it, but to my astonishment the DR companies withdrew their motion, even without my agreement. Maybe they decided that even if they got the action dismissed, we'd just refile the case in California; they had no way of knowing how close to zero our litigation fund had dwindled. But I think it was something else: they cared more about protecting the hotel chain from publicity than they liked their chances of winning the motion, and thought they had a better shot at keeping the Western Plaza episode from public view if they gave up trying to get the case dismissed. With their notice withdrawing the motion they filed an emergency request that Judge Meiklejohn seal all the pleadings and papers related to jurisdiction. When her clerk, Carolyn, called me about it I told her I didn't have a position on it. Meiklejohn denied it anyway.

If I'm right about their strategy, it backfired, big time. The judge's order denying the request to seal the documents caught the attention of a reporter for the *Denver Post* who had thought, until then, that there would be nothing engaging about the case until the trial started. Curious to see what was so interesting that someone wanted it sealed, he read all of the submissions, including Charley's affidavit.

DENVER HOTEL OFFERS CHILD PORN TO PATRONS read the headline. I refused all comments, and instructed Charley to do the same. But the fellow who called himself Guy, whose real name turned out to be Lester Armstrong, was not so discreet. Apparently someone at TriState Accommodations, or TransLandCorp, or Registry, figured out Guy had been the source of the catalog and issued an order to give him the boot. He was both angry and voluble, and full of fascinating anecdotes about the job he'd done at the Western Plaza for nearly four years. The *Post* series ran for three installments. It didn't mention snuff films, but Lester Armstrong insisted that he'd filled many guest requests for kiddie porn. There was talk of a federal criminal investigation. The U.S. attorney's office had no comment.

The series mentioned *Grayling v. DR Films* too, although mostly in passing. I was worried the publicity might make it hard for us to choose a jury, if we got that far, but it had its redeeming aspects. For one thing, Peggy was for some reason very happy about it. And for another, this episode comforted me on some nights when my anxiety about the case kept me from sleep. If the affair of the hotel videos was any measure of my opponents' strategic planning skills, I would tell myself, perhaps I'd been overestimating them. And Judge Meiklejohn was showing excellent resistance to the high-powered importunings of the defense team. Unless (I would argue with myself on other nights) by refusing to seal any papers she was just exhibiting her great and pervasive desire to preserve the First Amendment from any incursions whatsoever. Which, possibly, would not be good. Whether it was optimism or pessimism feeding my insomnia, I was not sleeping very well.

There were other oddly comforting events during the pretrial period—so many that, perversely, I grew uneasy when I contemplated all of them. For example, Linc's amazing discovery of the actor, Joel Derringer, who'd played the father in *Sunshade Snuffdown*.

The way Rafe had led Lincoln straight to Dashiell Roman and Roman Enterprises had been strangely easy—way too easy, I had thought. Even after Roman had signed the affidavits I'd had express-delivered to Linc, acknowledging that his companies had produced and distributed *Sunshade Snuffdown*, I was still suspicious. Even after he'd explained that his age and illness, his loss of interest in his business, and his absence of heirs had weighed in with his remorse to prompt him to "clear his conscience," I was not convinced. Still troubled by the Rophypnol incident and Rafe's possible role in it, I'd thought that maybe Rafe and Rose Brothers, having failed in that scheme (the purpose of which still eluded me) were trying to lure us into suing some designated fall guy, who would prove to have no assets—or something. None of it made any sense.

There were other reasons to be wary. Roman refused to identify any of the actors in the film, or any of the crew. He told me on the phone that this refusal was on principle. Some loony First Amendment hypothesis, I supposed him to mean, but Rafe told me it was because he was afraid the feds would prosecute him for child pornography and he didn't want to die in prison. Still, this meant that he was the only witness we could identify with firsthand knowledge of the film's production. His admissions were plenty of evidence, but it smelled like some kind of setup. And he hadn't offered to settle the case, which you might have thought a logical step for one whose conscience bothered him as much as he said.

But then Linc found Joel Derringer, and broke him down with some combination of sympathy and gin, I guess. Derringer didn't know who Linc was—still didn't now, a year later—and I was glad to leave it that way for a while since we knew where to find him if we had to. But in his drunken revelations, he'd told Linc who produced the film: Dashiell Roman. Derringer claimed to have left the set after his scenes were shot, and not to know what had happened to the little girl. When he saw the film weeks later, he said, he'd been sickened and terrified. Especially since he had a daughter of his own. He'd never work for Roman again, he'd told Linc before passing out on the table. Even if he had to give up acting.

Jesus, Linc had said, telling me this story later. Acting. But Derringer's story was independent confirmation: Dashiell Roman had made the film. And Charley's discovery of the catalog made clear that DR Distribution had sold videotapes of it. Moreover, Linc had been able to obtain financial data on DR Films and DR Distribution, as well as Roman himself. There was money there: a lot of money, and not of recent acquisition. This was no shell company. I finally had to surrender my suspicions that Rafe was jerking us around, at least on the question of whom we needed to sue.

So on the brink of this hearing on the motion to dismiss (it was the *second* motion to dismiss, actually, the first one having been the withdrawn motion to dismiss for lack of personal jurisdiction over the defendant, which is not the sort of thing you enjoy explaining to people who aren't lawyers), we were in better shape than I'd dared hope. The list I'd made all those months before in my office (FIND THE MAKER, GET JURISDICTION IN COLORADO, PROVE CAUSATION, PROVE WOLF'S ACTIONS FORESEEABLE TO MAKER) was down to the last two items now. Provided, of course, we could persuade Judge Meiklejohn that she wouldn't be shredding the First Amendment by letting us proceed.

Which thought brought me back to my wan image in the mirror of the courthouse bathroom. I rubbed my eyes with a little cold water and stared at my mouth. Unaccustomed to the lipstick I'd put on at home, I thought it looked garish in the fluorescent light, so I pressed a paper towel against my lips until they were the pale shade that seemed normal to me. Too pale, it was now clear, but I wasn't going to fish through my purse for the lipstick. To hell with it.

When I was still in the DA's office, we used to admonish whichever lawyer was about to start a trial thus: *Kick ass and take names.* I didn't feel that steady on my feet, and decided to settle for taking names. Given the number of Fucking Amici and their lawyers, it would be a long list. I pushed open the door and started the walk back to my client and the courtroom where something was going to happen.

Peggy Grayling was standing beside the bench, rising up and down on her toes, watching my approach with an intensity I could feel before I could see her face.

"What's wrong?" I said.

"They've all gone in already," she answered. "We're going to be the last ones."

"It's all right, Peggy. We've got a whole table set aside for us in there, just you and me. There have to be about twenty of them. It's going to take them a while to figure out who sits where. Don't worry, they won't start without us."

"Isn't your partner going to be here? Tory?"

"She'll come later if she can. She had to appear in another matter, on a trailing docket. Impossible to say if she'll make it. Come on." I had never seen Peggy look anxious before. But if she was going to get nervous, this was as good a time as any.

The scene inside the well of the courtroom was comical, in a way I might have enjoyed if I had been less jumpy myself: two dozen very expensive suits jockeying for the best seats. Carolyn, the judge's clerk, was attempting to herd some of them into the jury box, but there was considerable resistance, and a little discreet elbowing going on. It was clear that the most desirable seats, only four in number, were at the defense counsel table; the next best consisted of spots along the front of the pew that forms a barrier between the well of the courtroom and the spectator section. Then there was the jury box, empty of jurors on this occasion. This enclosure afforded a great view of the proceedings, but it was across the room from the defense table, since by tradition the counsel table nearest the box belongs to the plaintiffs. Accepting a seat in the jury box would mean conceding that it was unlikely the lead lawyers, at the counsel table, would experience an urgent need to consult with you in the course of the proceedings. This concession, I could see immediately, was one that few of the assembled personages were prepared to make.

"Oh, Cinda," said Carolyn, hurrying in my direction. Her face was pinched with worry and little spots of red had bloomed on her neck and chest. "Would you do me a *huge* favor? Would you mind if we traded the plaintiff's and defense tables for this hearing only? I mean, put you away from the jury box and them near it? Otherwise I don't think I'm ever going to get these guys to sit down."

I smiled at her. It never hurt to be especially courteous to the courthouse's working staff, and anyway I liked Carolyn. "No problem. We don't need that much room. In fact, two of their guys can sit with me and Peggy if they want to."

She looked back at me with a sudden grin. "I'll tell them. But I don't think you'll find any takers."

She was right. I waited briefly for Dan Everett and three other splendidly barbered specimens to move their expensive leather goods off the defense table before setting my own much-abused briefcase on it and claiming it for us. "Sit down, Peggy," I said, gesturing to the seat beside us.

"Very kind of you Ms. Hayes," said Dan Everett, as he moved a yellow legal pad and silver fountain pen over to the table nearer the jury box. One of the younger lawyers had already transferred Everett's briefcase, causing me to wonder if the great man ever touched it at all.

I nodded at him, catching a whiff of his cologne, and turned to the lawyer settling into one of the middle chairs of their table, Frank Morales, the Boulder lawyer who signed papers as counsel for DR Films and DR Distribution. "Hola, Paco," I said, and he grinned back. He was smart and successful, a partner in one of Boulder's best law firms, but I didn't think he was anything but the guy who signed the papers in this gang.

"Is that your friend from law school?" Peggy whispered to me.

"No," I said. "His name is Raphael Russell. Let's see." I scanned the room for Rafe and finally caught sight of him behind the bar, chatting with a journalist. The back of the room was full of them, I noticed, with a little good-natured competition for seats going on back there, too. The broadcast journalists were distinguished from the lawyers by better looks, brighter clothes, and more makeup. I noted the Denver correspondents for two of the television networks, mixed with local television reporters. There were print journalists, too, on the whole not as photogenic nor as well groomed. Marcus Maynes, the reporter who'd broken the *Denver Post* story about the Western Plaza, smiled at me and waved. I smiled back, partly because I liked him but also because he had a smudge of ink across his crooked nose. I saw Brianna Bainbridge, resplendent in coral silk, seated in the first spectator row chatting with the legal affairs correspondent for CBS, the one who'd covered the Clinton impeachment. Rafe was also absorbed in a conversation and did not look my way.

"That's him in the gray suit," I said to Peggy. "With the great haircut."

She strained to look, and then turned to me with an exasperated expression. "That doesn't help a lot. There are at least four guys back there who fit that description."

"Light gray."

"Three, then."

"I'll introduce you later," I said, having noticed that Carolyn had taken a position just to the right of the judge's entrance and seemed to be clearing her throat. "Here comes the judge."

The invocation was intoned with suitable gravity by Carolyn *(Hear ye, hear ye, hear ye . . . ),* and then the judge requested that counsel identify themselves and their client; this ritual, called entering an appearance, was of course very brief on our side but on the defendants' slightly clumsy, once again inflected by a subtle uncertainty over the pecking order. Then the judge got down to business.

"I have before me," she said, peering over her half-crescent reading glasses, "the motion to dismiss of the defendant. Will you be arguing today on behalf of your client, Mr. Morales?"

Paco rose, looking a bit embarrassed. "May it please the court, Mr. Everett will be arguing the motion." He motioned toward the man sitting beside him.

"Mr. Everett," she said, nodding at the older man curtly. "You have entered an appearance on behalf of the defendants here?"

Dan Everett rose to his feet in a sweeping motion, exuding confidence like an acrobat before leaping up to the balance beam. "No, Your Honor," he said. "I am counsel for Star Cable Network, an organization Your Honor was kind enough to grant friend of the court status by your order of several months ago. After extensive consultation, Mr. Morales and I have determined that the position of his client, and the position of mine, on the very principled questions embodied by this motion, are identical. Under the circumstances, we have agreed that I will present the arguments directed to these principles, if it please the court."

"This is irregular," said Judge Meiklejohn. "Ms. Hayes, how do you and your client feel about the propriety of Mr. Everett arguing on behalf of DR Films and DR Distribution?"

I looked briefly at Peggy, who shrugged. "We have no objection, Your Honor, if Mr. Morales represents to the court that his clients have consented to this arrangement."

Paco was on his feet. "Mr. Roman knows of this arrangement and consents to it," he said quickly.

"Is he in court today?" said the judge.

"No, Your Honor. He is not well, and his physician has advised against travel at this time."

Peggy leaned toward me. "What if Roman dies before the case is finished?" she whispered.

I turned a cautionary palm toward her and spoke toward the bench. "May I have a moment, Your Honor?"

"Surely," said Meiklejohn, and busied herself with the papers in her case jacket.

"Peggy," I said to her, "don't worry. If Roman dies the case can go on, and if we win, any judgment can be collected against the companies. We didn't sue him personally, and even if we had his death wouldn't stop the case. I don't see any reason to object to letting Everett make this argument, but the judge seems unhappy about it. Do you want me to say we object after all?"

"No," she said, looking across me toward the jury box full of lawyers. "Sorry, I guess I got ahead of myself. No, I don't care."

"We have no objection to Mr. Everett's making argument, Your Honor."

"Proceed, then. Mr. Everett."

Everett was good, very good. But not original. Which is, as I've said before, a good way for a lawyer to be—conventional. Still, I was expecting to hear some new twist on things, something I'd not thought of in exactly that way before. Instead it was the familiar, still somewhat stirring, refrain. *Founding Fathers . . . came to understand importance of a Bill of Rights . . . first and foremost among the freedoms they treasured . . . freedom of expression. A complex constellation of concepts . . . not always universal agreement . . . one principle, however, commands the allegiance of all . . . there shall be no censorship except for the most compelling and extraordinary of reasons. What Ms. Grayling and her able counsel Ms. Hayes would have the court do . . . insidious . . . in the guise of an action for damages . . . seek to treat an instance of expression as though it were nothing more than a lawn mower. This the court must not allow.*

Then there was more along the lines of *preposterous in any event to assume that exposure to a single speech product, however distasteful, would function as the proximate cause of a criminal act. Free will is the touchstone of . . .*

You get the drift.

Then it was my turn.

There comes a moment when all of the belly-breathing, serenity-invoking, mantra-saying practices in the repertoire are insufficient to ward off the edge of terror, and this is one of them. I think that's a good thing, too. My favorite law professor, encountered many years after my graduation, once asked me how I liked oral argument and laughed when I said that even after dozens of them, it was always like making love with someone for the first time. But it's true. If you're calm, something's very wrong, and probably matters are not going to come to a satisfying conclusion. Of course, if you're properly terrified, there's also an excellent chance they are not going to come to a satisfying conclusion. Auden said that law was like love: in both we often weep, and seldom keep. Thinking of him, I stood and took a useless belly full of air.

"Your Honor," I said, "I have listened with care to the arguments of Mr. Everett, and studied with care the arguments in his written brief. They are excellent arguments, but they are addressed to a different case than this one. Mrs. Grayling, my client, and I do not seek to prohibit the defendant from distributing the film known as *Sunshade Snuffdown.* We are told that it is no longer being distributed in any event, but we would not try to suppress it. That is not our prayer. We are also not asking this court or any court to permit the prosecution of DR Films or DR Distribution, or their majority shareholder Mr. Dashiell Roman for the distribution of obscene material, or any crime at all. Whether such a prosecution would be wise or possible is a matter for the criminal authorities, but we have not sought it or encouraged it. If we were seeking one of those outcomes, perhaps the accusation that Mr. Everett makes—*censorship*—would be justified. Or perhaps not. But in any event that is a decision for another court on another day, for what we seek is neither of those outcomes but exactly what millions of others seek when they ask the civil courts for justice—compensation for a loss.

"Margaret Grayling is a mother, but she has lost the most important thing a mother can ever have—her child. Many causes contributed to this loss, to be sure—the circumstance that her child was a girl, the choice of a public school for the child to attend, the availability of a vacant apartment across the street from that school at a particular moment in the life of a very disturbed young man, and, of course, the acts of that young man on the day of Alison Grayling's death. As with almost all tragedies, it is possible to identify a hundred or more circumstances, any one of which might have headed off the tragedy had it been different. But this observation does not mean that some of the circumstances that contributed to the death of Alison Grayling cannot be identified as the most important, the most blameworthy, and the most predictably destructive. When these circumstances are the freely chosen acts of a person or institution, we describe them as a *proximate cause* of the harm, and ordinarily we require that those who did the acts must pay for the damage. This is not new, not extraordinary, not in any way shocking.

"What is shocking is the suggestion, by Mr. Everett and the many other eloquent lawyers who signed the brief amicus curiae in this court, that under no circumstances can this ordinary and accepted and proper assignment of responsibility occur if the act that caused the harm—even if it was the death of an innocent child—was the act of creating a text. By a *text* I suppose they mean among other things a book, a magazine, a film, a play or theatrical performance, or a videotape.

"Of course, they agree that there are some exceptions, as they have to. A newspaper ad soliciting the commission of a murder for hire—they agree the author of the ad can be liable for a crime or for damages. They don't talk about this, but what about the set of instructions for how to operate a piece of machinery, a car perhaps, that recommends a procedure that has fatal results? I think they would agree, would have to agree, that the First Amendment wouldn't prevent the survivors of a dead driver from recovering, provided it was shown that the instructions were foreseeably likely to result in such a death. And yet an instruction manual is a text, too, Your Honor, just like *Ulysses* and *Sunshade Snuffdown*. They are texts of widely varying genres and certainly different artistic merit, but they are all texts. What about a text that is defamatory, libelous—a text that tells a damaging lie about someone? We *know* the First Amendment doesn't prevent the recovery of damages by a victim of libel. Sure, there are things that must be proved—that whoever published the libelous material was negligent or reckless about the possibility that it was false. But the First Amendment is not a complete bar to a suit for libel, and it should not be a complete bar to Mrs. Grayling's suit, either."

I looked up at the judge and nodded, indicating I was done. It felt all right. Nothing eloquent—eloquent is not in my toolbox. But I thought I'd said what I needed to say.

"Ms. Hayes," said Judge Meiklejohn, "I am so glad you finally paused for a breath. I was afraid I wasn't going to have a chance to ask you any questions until perhaps tomorrow."

"Oh," I said. "Sorry, Your Honor."

"My court reporter is grateful for the respite as well, I see." And it was true that Sonia, her reporter, looked relieved. She looked up, smiled at the judge, and shook her hands gently for a moment. I must have been talking faster than I realized.

"Ms. Hayes, how on earth do you think you will be able to prove that Mrs. Grayling's daughter's death was caused by the killer's viewing of this videotape?" said the judge, leaning earnestly over the bench as though she really wanted to know the answer. The courtroom's overhead track lights were reflected in her glasses and I couldn't see her eyes. The room was so quiet I could hear the scratching of some journalist's pen behind me, recording her question verbatim.

"That's a very good question, Your Honor," I said, "and one that has occupied us from the very earliest days that we considered filing this action. I will be happy to answer in a general way, but first I would like simply to observe that although yours is a very *good* question, it is not a *First Amendment* question. It's not related to this motion to dismiss. In any action for personal injuries, or for death, the plaintiff is required to prove that the acts of the defendant were a proximate cause of the harm to the plaintiff. This case is no different. At trial (*if we ever get there,* I was thinking, my heart hammering like an entire percussion section inside my chest) we understand the need to persuade the jury of the strong causal connection, and we expect that we will succeed. Our evidence will include the circumstances in which the child's body was found, expert testimony from a mental health professional who has had extensive interviews with the killer, and transcripts of the words of the killer, who has described the effect of viewing the tape repeatedly on his own mental processes. We also have the killer's diary, describing his thoughts and mental processes. In effect, Your Honor, the videotape recommended that he kill the little girl, and he responded to this recommendation. That is what we expect to be able to prove. But we do not think we are required to prove it to Your Honor, here today. That is for trial."

Judge Meiklejohn turned to the newly created defense table, looking around as though unsure which of the dark-suited, close-shaven men she was seeking. Dan Everett rose swiftly. "Your Honor?"

"Ah, Mr. Everett, there you are," she said. There were nervous titters from the observers behind the bar and it seemed that of the dozen attorneys seated in the jury box, about ten (which is to say, all of the men) shot their cuffs at once. It looked like a set piece from the Gilbert and Sullivan operetta *Trial by Jury,* and that thought and the adrenaline coursing around my body brought me dangerously close to giggling myself. "What say you to Ms. Hayes's argument?" continued the judge. "Is the question of causation one for trial, rather than a reason that the First Amendment compels me to dismiss this case?"

"Not at all, Your Honor," said Everett, a dozen well-barbered heads nodding in unison behind him. "Your Honor, this country is filled with cultural productions of every sort, millions of them, with thousands more published or released every day. It would not be too much to say that the freedom that allows this stunning flow of ideas and their expression is the essence of our society, of America under its brilliant Constitution. But I'm sorry to say that we live in a society where some persons do not subscribe to the premise of personal responsibility. They always want somebody else to blame, for their own misfortunes or for the acts of others. Preferably, someone with very deep pockets. If this suit is allowed to go forward to trial, no movie studio, no book publishing house, no magazine publisher, no television production studio—none of the great engines of our culture—will be free from the constant threat and reality of litigation by someone claiming that a movie, a play, a book, an article, caused someone to hurt or to kill. Their wealth will make them easy targets but soon all of their resources will have to be committed to defending themselves against lawsuits. The funds necessary to publish a novel by Gabriel Garcia Marquez, or to make a film by Stanley Kubrick, or publish the essays of our great historians and political scientists will dwindle and America will become a place where nothing can be read or watched or broadcast except the most innocuous, uncontroversial, and frankly boring—"

"All right, Mr. Everett, thank you," said the judge. "I believe I understand what you're saying. Your argument is at bottom about how much this is all costing your client. Or, rather, Mr. Morales's client." She surveyed the phalanx of lawyers in the jury box with what I hoped, but could not be sure, was an ironic expression.

"Not just in dollars," said Everett in a hurry. "It's a matter of the freedom, the privacy if you will, to engage in the work of artistic expression without having to open one's files and disclose one's secrets to any comer who makes a claim of damage. Your Honor very properly postponed any discovery in this case until this motion to dismiss was disposed of, and we appreciate your recognition that the obligation to respond to invasive questions about proprietary matters can itself make inroads on the protection of free expression. Moreover . . ."

There was more of this colloquy between the judge and Everett, but his last statement snagged my attention like a log arresting the progress of a leaf in a rushing stream. *Invasive questions about proprietary matters.* It was true that the judge had not allowed us to undertake very much discovery—the formal process of requiring our opponents to produce documents and answer questions before trial. Once DR Films and Distribution had conceded the jurisdiction motion, the lack of access to discovery had not been much of an impediment, because of Roman's admission that he had produced and distributed the film and Andy's access to Leonard Fitzgerald. But Everett's comments suggested that there was still something they didn't want us to learn about *Sunshade Snuffdown* and its making or distribution. What could that be? I put the thought aside and forced my attention back to the judge's voice, which was saying my name.

"Ms. Hayes, do you have any precedent for a trial court allowing such a suit to go to trial?"

"Not exactly, Your Honor," I confessed. "But I do have a precedent suggesting that a trial court should have—the *Hit Man* case."

A collective noise of derision arose from the jury box, but didn't persist for long after the judge turned her fierce gaze toward it. It resolved itself into some mild synchronized head-shaking.

"Your Honor is familiar with that case? We cited it in our brief," I said.

"I remember it," she said. "As I recall, the trial judge in that case dismissed the case before trial, exactly what Mr. Everett and his numerous colleagues are asking me to do today."

"That's correct, Your Honor, but on appeal the appeals court said that had been a mistake, and ordered the case back for trial."

"Ah, yes," she said. "And please remind me what happened after that? Did the bereaved families convince the jury to hold the publishers of the *Hit Man* manual liable for the deaths of their loved ones?"

Dan Everett was on his feet, but the judge frowned at him. "Sit down, Mr. Everett, I'm asking Ms. Hayes. You'll get your chance again."

"The publishers of the manual asked the United States Supreme Court to hear the case before letting it go back for trial, and while the Court was considering their petition, the parties settled," I explained.

"Settled," she said.

"That's right."

"Mr. Everett?" Judge Meiklejohn's helmet of steely curls flashed in the track lights as she turned her head toward him. He was still on his feet.

"That's correct, Your Honor. It was right after the Columbine High School shooting incident and I guess they got cold feet. I can guarantee Your Honor I would not have recommended that a client of mine pay a cent on such a claim."

"Thank you, Mr. Everett. Your guarantee is not of much interest to me, but I thank you both for this enlightenment. So the law of the *Hit Man* case, up until the moment it was settled, was that the case could be tried without offending the First Amendment."

"Yes," I said quickly.

"Yes, but . . ." said Dan Everett, but he was too slow for Meiklejohn, who banged down her gavel as though dispatching a errant spider that had climbed onto her bench by mistake.

"Thank you, counsel. The motion is under advisement."

After the judge had disappeared through her private door behind the bench, Peggy turned to me, her eyes as transparent and untroubled as glass. "You did very well," she said simply.

"We had some luck," I said. "I'm optimistic, but it's not certain we won. You can't always tell from the way the judge acts."

"I think she didn't care for all the lawyers they brought in here," said Peggy, sliding her gaze to the right, where the jury-box lawyers were now mostly standing and talking, evidently exchanging impressions of the hearing. "Which one is your friend?" she asked me.

I turned around to see that the back of the courtroom, behind the bar, was emptying of spectators. No doubt the broadcast journalists were hurrying to join their crews outside the courthouse, in hopes of cajoling comments out of some of the departing lawyers—and of Peggy, if they could. "He must have stepped out of the courtroom already. I think he was sitting in back, with some of the journalists. Listen, Peggy, do you want to say anything to the press? They're going to be after you for a statement. It's fine if you just want to say no comment, but if you have something you want to say we should discuss it."

"I don't want to say anything today. Maybe some time, but not now."

"Then we need to figure out some way to spirit you out of here without getting caught in that crush out front. The print journalists can buttonhole you in the corridors inside here, but they're not the worst. It's the cameras I'd like to spare you."

"I could go to Sierra's office. I'm sure she'd let me stay with her for a while. Maybe even go out to lunch. I think she has a parking space underneath the courthouse somewhere."

"Sierra?" I knew I'd heard this name before but couldn't remember where.

"You remember, my friend that I take yoga lessons with. You met her in the juice bar that day. Sierra?"

I had it, a visual memory of a round-faced woman in a yellow shirt. "That's a great idea. She works in the courthouse?"

Peggy nodded. "In the Traffic Division, processing traffic citations."

"Perfect, then. I'll walk you there, and tell the reporters you'll have no comment."

"For now," she said.

Sierra was as quiet and kind as I remembered her. Hers was a regulation steel desk jammed into a badly lit corner, but she had covered odd patches of its surface with small objects—Zuni fetishes with tiny feathers tied to them, a silver paper knife, a brass sculpture of a carp or koi in mid-turn. It looked like a comforting small museum. An African violet bloomed in defiance of the poor light, and the poster behind Sierra's chair said PRACTICE RANDOM ACTS OF KINDNESS AND SENSELESS BEAUTY.

Sierra asked how the hearing had gone, and told Peggy that if she'd wait in the chair next to her desk for about twenty minutes, until Sierra's weekly report was finished, they could go out to lunch. "Don't worry," she told me. "I have a parking space in the basement. We can get to it from the security door here. We won't even have to go back into the corridor, and they'll be so busy watching the front door they'll never see us going out."

"I believe you're right," I said, admiring her generosity. "Peggy, are you okay?"

She looked up at me from the chair, her face shadowed suddenly with sorrow. "Sometimes, when things go well like this," she said, "I forget what this is really about."

"I know. Alison," I said. "Look, Peggy, from time to time we're both going to forget it, and so will the judge and the jurors and the court reporter and everyone else. That's okay. You don't have to be thinking of it every minute, Peggy, and it's not wrong to take pleasure in a small victory. If we get one here."

"When will we know?" she asked.

"I'm not sure," I said. "But I'm thinking maybe soon. In any event, I'll call you as soon as I get the judge's order."

"You say a small victory, but if they win, it would be a big one, wouldn't it? For them?"

"If they win," I said, "then there's no trial."

She looked back at her hands, twined in her lap. "That's right. I knew that."

Someone must have told a reporter where I'd gone, because when I emerged from the Traffic Division office into the main courthouse corridor again, there was an untidy gaggle of them waiting for me.

"No comment, sorry," I said automatically.

"Is your client in there?" one of them said.

"Why would she be in there?" I said.

They looked at each other, smirking. "Traffic ticket?" one of them ventured.

"I'm afraid I couldn't comment on that." After a quick round of whispering, it appeared they were going to stay there and stake out the door, figuring Peggy would have to come out eventually. Good, I thought, and started walking toward the exit, trying to prepare myself for the pushing and shouting, the metal tripods and other objects littering the sidewalk for my uncomfortable shoes to trip on, the idiotic questions to which I could think of only idiotic answers. *(How do you think it went, Ms. Hayes? Oh, very well. Do you think you won? We'll have to wait and see, won't we?)* I felt tired, the usual letdown after a high-stakes court appearance but something more, too, an unease I couldn't name. I was almost to the door, already smiling at the officer at the X-ray machine, when I heard my name called from behind. Or, not my name exactly.

"Querida!"

I turned. "Rafe," I said, and saw that he was not alone. He smiled the remembered crooked smile and gestured toward the beautiful tall woman beside him.

"I understand that you and Professor Bainbridge are already friends," he said, grinning like a maniac. "I was just telling her how much I admire her work." To her great credit, Brianna was having none of this.

"I just met this guy this morning," she said to me. "He tells me he's known you forever. Was he always this annoying?"

"I suspect only since the day he started talking," I said.

"Cinda," she said more urgently, "I really need to sit down with you. You did an outstanding job in there, by the way."

"Right now?" I said, looking back toward the Traffic Division at the knot of hungry reporters impermanently arrested just outside the door. "This isn't a very good time."

"Anyway," said Rafe, "I'm taking her to lunch. Yes, I am," he added when he saw my face. "I have an official proposal from the amici curiae to put before you, which you are compelled as a matter of professional responsibility to consider and put before your client."

"Then perhaps Brianna could join us," I said. "What an interesting lunch *that* would be."

She shook her cloudy head and strands of shining red filament flew around it like visible electricity. "I need to go make a phone call. But Cinda, please, don't make any agreements with him or anyone until we've talked. I have some very important information for you."

"There aren't any deals on the table, Brianna. Anyway, I wouldn't agree to anything without consulting my client. You know that."

"Of course," she said. Her narrow nose rose a degree as she turned toward the door. "But call me as well." She stalked back through the security door. The officer watched her all the way out, waiting until she was on the sidewalk to suck in a deep appreciative lungful of her perfume. Through the smoked glass I could see her turning aside reporters and waving off an effort to invite her in front of a camera.

I felt Rafe's hand on my elbow. "Remember that time you beat my brains out in moot court?" he said.

"Sure I do. You said it was just because the judge was a lecher."

"Yeah," he said. "What's my excuse gonna be this time?"

I concentrated on smiling at the freckled young man who had come to take our order at Dolan's. We both ordered the scampi linguini and I listened carefully to the choices of salad dressing and forbade my face to betray any reaction to the sum of money that Rafe had just invoked.

"We have parmesan Italian, southwestern ranch, and balsamic vinaigrette," said the waiter.

"God, they all sound great," I said desperately. "How about, ah, parmesan ranch?"

"I'm so sorry," said the waiter with every evidence of sincerity. "But that was parmesan Italian, or southwestern ranch."

"Of course. I meant the Italian, of course. Italian. Yes."

"Sir?"

"The vinaigrette," said Rafe, not bothering to conceal much of his grin. He put his hand under my chin after the waiter left and turned it toward him. "You seem a little flustered."

"Not at all," I said. "I was up a little late last night, is all. I'm slightly fatigued. I'm sorry, what were we talking about?"

"You used to be better at not letting your surprise show," he said. "We were talking about two and one half million dollars."

"Oh, yes. Well, of course I'd have to talk to my client."

"Of course you would. And then I'd have to talk to mine, and it's possible mine might go a little higher but I doubt it, really, and—"

"What do you mean *yours?*" I broke in. "Rose Brothers? Or do you represent DR Films and DR Distribution now, too, along with Dan Everett?"

"Cinda, don't be so difficult. It must be clear to you that the industry is pulling together on this. DR and Paco Morales will have to agree, but everyone is going to chip in a little. I was asked to talk to you on behalf of the entire team. And of course we want a stipulation that there is no admission of liability whatsoever."

"Small change to you, isn't it?" I was feeling pretty hostile for some reason, even though this was far more money than I ever expected to recover for my client.

"Not to your client it won't be small. But you need to be very clear with her—this is a window, and it only stays open until the judge rules. If Meiklejohn issues a ruling this afternoon, it's off. Our courthouse sources think she'll take a day or two, to think things over and write a good opinion, but that it won't be long. I'm not going to shine you on about the

odds because you know as much about them as we do. You've got a sympa-
thetic judge and you did a hell of a job for your client on that motion. The
industry is interested in avoiding a ruling that will encourage a series of
cases like this one. But once the ruling is out, it's on the books no matter
what settlement we arrive at afterward; at that point our motivation is to
whip your butt at trial."

Despite my irritation I had to smile; even in a negotiation he talked
like a scriptwriter. "And if the judge should rule against you," he continued, "the settlement value of your case goes in the same direction as a guy
who's gotten pushed out of a plane. At about the same velocity."

Our salads arrived and this gave me a moment to collect my thoughts.

"Of course I'll communicate this offer to Ms. Grayling right away," I
said. "It's her decision, as you know. I'll advise her about this very carefully."

"Yeah, and we both know the advice you give her will have a large
effect on that decision," he said. "So think about it this way: three million
dollars for the death of a nine-year-old girl in a case of highly dubious
liability, with an obvious perp that you *haven't* sued sitting in a padded cell
in Illinois—and don't think we won't have a lot to say about that—tried to
a blue-ribbon jury from a college town where more people probably worship the First Amendment than worship at church. You gotta be kidding
me. What's to think about?"

"For one thing," I said, taking a sip of water, "the way you said three
million in that last sentence, after you started at two and a half."

He didn't lose his deadpan expression, I'll give him that, but even
though his shirt collar was buttoned high under his striped yellow tie I
thought I could see the fingers of a blush creeping above it. "Shit, Cinda,
I did that on purpose. See if you were paying attention. Three is what it is.
I have authority to offer three, always did. Why don't you call her right
now, on your cell phone?"

"No way, Rafe, you know better than that."

"But you still have it? The one I gave you?" He sounded so plaintive I
rummaged through my briefcase and showed it to him. "It follows me
everywhere," I said. "Now, let's eat. And while we do, you can tell me what
it is that you and your friends and their clients don't want me to learn if
this case goes into discovery."

He insisted there wasn't anything I didn't know already.

"What could be secret? We've already admitted almost everything.

There's nothing left except causation and foreseeability. Not that you'd be able to prove those things," he added hastily. "Now let's enjoy our lunch and talk about something else."

So we talked about other things, old friends and being back in Boulder and the nightclubs where he used to play when he was in law school. He told me Boulder had changed, didn't feel like it used to. I told him that was true of every place, or at least every place he'd want to live.

"Place is full of rich people," he complained.

I laughed. "How much did you make last year?"

"But L.A. has all kinds of people," he said. "It's not fun being rich in a place where everybody's rich."

I made the tiny violin gesture with my thumb and forefinger, and he laughed too.

"Anyway," I said. "Not everyone in Boulder's rich. How much do you think that busboy makes? Being in glamorous Boulder just means he has to live in a trailer, probably."

Rafe shook his head slowly. "That's one thing that hasn't changed—you, busting my chops over something."

We parted company about 1:30 in the sunny back parking lot of Dolan's. Rafe kissed me on the cheek and drove off in a bronze rental Infiniti. I'd discarded my suit jacket in the restaurant, and sat in the Saab for a long time after he left, letting my bare arms enjoy the feel of the breeze that had kicked up and thinking about the things that were and were not available for three million dollars. Finally I started the engine and drove slowly back to the office to telephone my client.

Beverly handed me a pink message slip as I arrived. "She made me promise I wouldn't let you make any other calls until you called her back," she said meekly.

"She did?" I said, amazed and impressed at this evidence of Brianna Bainbridge's persuasive powers. Ordinarily, Beverly would find a way to discourage those who tried to tell her how to do her job, most commonly by losing their message.

"She has a way about her," said Beverly, as I took the slip toward my office. It must have been Brianna's home number; it didn't have the university's prefix. "You can't settle this case," she said without preliminaries when she heard my voice. She must have known there was little point to exercising on me whatever graces had charmed Beverly.

"Not that I'm planning to," I said, "but just out of curiosity, why not?"

"There has never been an opportunity like this one," she said urgently. "I was there, I saw and heard Meiklejohn. She's going to rule for you. This is going to be the case that breaks this whole field open. But I know those industry whores, Cinda. They've already made you an offer, haven't they?"

"If they had, Brianna, it would have to be between me and my client."

"I thought I was on your legal team," she said stiffly. "God knows you could use someone on yours. You're badly outnumbered."

"I am very grateful for your advice and help," I said. "But I'm Peggy Grayling's lawyer. My only loyalty can be to her and to what she wants. You're free to have other loyalties, and I imagine you do. Nothing wrong with that. But this decision, if and when there is one, is for Peggy to make."

"Just let me talk to her, give me a chance to make her understand what's at stake," she said. "That's all I ask. Listen, Cinda, I'm on the governing board of the Center for Women's Constitutional Interests. I called a telephone meeting of the other board members during the noon hour. The Center is willing to get involved in this case at this point. Help pay expenses, provide more lawyers. I know you haven't been able to do any discovery yet, and that will be incredibly expensive. We can help. Please let us."

"When the time comes," I said, feeling like a broken record, and a lying one at that, "I'll talk to my client."

"You know," said Brianna, "there are some angles you may not have thought of that could be very productive."

"Like what?" I said, annoyed.

"Like what happened to the little girl in the film? Have you made any effort to find her parents? Imagine making them co-plaintiffs with Peggy."

"We thought about that a lot," I said wearily. "That's one subject Dashiell Roman absolutely refuses to talk about. Look, if she was a minor, which she almost certainly was, then identifying her in a way that made it possible to prove her age could get him prosecuted for violating the child pornography laws. And if she was really killed—if it was a genuine snuff film—he could be prosecuted for murder. The man is dying; he's not going to tell us anything that sends him to prison. I even talked to the U.S. attorney's office out there about offering him immunity, but they won't do it."

"But in discovery, you could force him to answer."

"That's right, and he'd refuse, and then we'd ask the judge for sanctions and then it would drag the whole thing out longer and he'd probably die before the case ever got to trial."

"But Cinda, don't you see—the longer, the better. This story is huge! The longer it goes on, the more people hear about it, follow its every twist and turn. You're talking about a cross between O. J. and JonBenet. In education we call this the teachable moment. Millions of people will finally come to understand what the First Amendment does and does not allow."

"I understand you, Brianna, and I don't disagree. But Peggy's interest may not be in public education. She may care more about something else."

"The money, you mean."

"I'm not sure I understand what motivates her," I confessed. "I doubt it's the money. Closure, maybe."

She snorted in a ladylike way. "That overused concept! You want people to remember this outrage, not forget it."

"It's not a question of what I want. She seems concerned about some kind of public assignment of responsibility."

"Exactly, Cinda! Exactly! That's just what we're talking about. Anyway, quite apart from the other little girl, what about going after whoever provided the place where the film was made? That's definitely worth trying to find out in discovery, and including them as a new defendant."

"It was made somewhere in the Caribbean, Brianna. We'd never get jurisdiction to sue whoever owned the place. It sounds like it was some vacation villa or something that the film crew rented out, anyway."

"That's bullshit, Cinda. Just because Roman told you that doesn't mean it's true. You know where most porn films are made?"

"I guess not," I said, sighing inwardly as I surrendered myself to what I'm sure she saw as a teachable moment.

"Mindy's told me all about this. The parts that can't be filmed in an indoor studio are shot in the backyards of tract homes in the San Fernando Valley. The people who own these houses are dentists and airline pilots and day traders, and they rent their houses out for a day or two to a porn director, for thousands of dollars."

"You think that's what happened here?"

"I saw that tape, remember. I'm no botanist, but that vegetation didn't look Caribbean to me. It looked like Southern California."

"Surely they could have brought potted plants onto the set, or artificial ones," I protested.

"Sure they could have. By why would they? If you were shooting a scene around a pool in the Caribbean, why would you bring in potted plants from California?"

"Okay, you're right," I admitted. "But why would Dashiell Roman lie about that after admitting that he was responsible for the film?"

"I don't know, Cinda. Protecting someone, maybe. Imagine if you could discover where it was made, though. Some corporate executive's house, or maybe even a politician's! People don't know about this aspect of the pornography industry. They'd really be interested! We're talking about *Sixty Minutes* here."

I could hear the excitement in her voice and knew that yielding to her wishes would be like jumping into a carriage harnessed to a team of tigers: you were far less likely to get where you wanted to go than to be eaten up. "You were talking about dentists and pilots before," I pointed out. "And anyway I don't think I'd like to argue that responsibility for Alison Grayling's death could be laid at the feet of some homeowner who let a film crew use his premises for the day."

"A porn film crew? Why the hell not?"

"I'll pass all of this on to Peggy," I said, too weary to continue the argument. "And I'll let you know what she decides."

"Let me talk to her," she said insistently. "I tried to call her earlier but she has an unlisted number. I just want to make sure she understands the kind of help we could make available."

"No," I said, and hung up.


Before calling my client, I needed to consult my partner. The fee agreement we had with Peggy Grayling gave us a third of any recovery—if Peggy accepted this settlement offer, that would be a half million each for Tory and me. After taxes, and after sharing it with Beverly and Linc and paying Andy if he'd take any, maybe two hundred fifty thousand apiece. I could not for a moment suspect Tory of coloring her advice to advance her financial interest, and anyway she was, unlike me, a gambler at heart. But I knew that she and her lover Linda would find uses for the money. They'd build a cabin on their steep timbered mountain lot, the one that would take a lot of engineering. Spend six months in Bali, climb to Everest base camp, buy the llama ranch they'd been talking about.

I couldn't think of a single thing I wanted. My loans were all paid off, I owned my house in Boulder, small but perfect for one person. I didn't want a new car. I had nobody to sail or climb or lie in the sun with, nobody with whom I could pore over architect's drawings or prize-stud books. My eyes welled as I considered this circumstance, and I remembered being told that Alexander the Great had wept when he believed that he had conquered the last scrap of the known world. Tears ran down my face as I sat at my desk and considered how desperately I wished for something to want.

As for Peggy, I knew she wanted something, but I was no nearer to understanding what it was than I had been the day she faxed us the photographs of Alison's body. I shook my head in an unsuccessful attempt to clear it, and went to find Tory.

She was busy drafting a motion in a burglary case she was handling, to be filed by the end of the afternoon, so our discussion was brief. We kicked around a few strategic considerations, but her final comment—"Whatever the Dharma Ditz wants"—summed up her position.

Then I talked to Peggy—it meant arranging to meet her at the Trident since she had her well-known dislike of telephone conversations. When I walked in I scanned the front room for her but there was nobody there except a dreadlocked blonde sipping green tea and reading Sartre's *Nausea* with an intensity that suggested a medical interest. I ordered a straight espresso and asked Jackson, the *barista,* if he had seen Peggy Grayling.

"I don't think I know her," he said, pulling a piston to force the dark fragrant stream out of his big machine.

"Fiftyish, beautiful, she belongs to the sangha?" I said. I knew Jackson was a practicing Buddhist. But he shook his head without recognition. Then I looked into the back room and there she was, alone in one of the booths, leafing through an old *New Yorker.*

"Peggy," I said, and she looked up and smiled. "I have something to discuss with you."

It was late afternoon by the time I telephoned Brianna, whom Peggy had authorized me to call. We didn't talk for long. Finally I punched in the number that Rafe had given me.

"Boulderado," said the well-trained voice that picked up after the first ring. "How may I direct your call?" I should have known he'd be staying at the stately dowager, Boulder's oldest hotel and landmark.

"Rafael Russell, please." I listened to part of a Bach cello solo—Yo-Yo Ma, I think—while waiting. The sublime music put me in an even more somber mood and when Rafe finally came on, I didn't kid around.

"She says no," I told him.

"Well," he said, "it was just an opening offer. Where are you?"

"Still at the office," I said. "But I'm going home now. See you in—"

"Come on over here," said Rafe. "I'm right down the street. We need to talk."

"There's no point, Rafe," I said. "It's not about the amount. She won't settle. She wants a trial."

"Okay," he said. "But that's not what I wanted to talk to you about. Come on, Querida. You've busted my chops enough for one day. Meet me in the Mezzanine Bar, just for a drink."

"Okay," I said, not sure why, and I did and we drank a bottle of Merlot and listened to a smoky-voiced alto rasp her way through a series of jazz standards. I waited for him to make another offer, for despite his claims I was sure his settlement authority went higher than the three million. But he didn't, didn't bring up the case at all, only told me he'd be flying back to L.A. in the morning. Then he sat back in his brocaded chair and hummed along and twitched his eyes in a friendly way when they met mine and eventually reached across the dark little table, past the guttering candle, for my hand. When the alto took a break, he said, "Come upstairs with me. I've got one of the old original rooms, it has a claw-footed bathtub. You've gotta see it."

"No," I said. It had been a long day, and *no* seemed to be its theme.

"You think it would be like sleeping with the enemy," he suggested drowsily, massaging my knuckles.

"That's not it," I said. He took it well, but I left shortly before the singer came back, tired and not trusting myself not to change my mind if I stayed much longer.

Judge Meiklejohn's order came three days later, its twelve pages of text thickly punctuated with cases, authorities, citations. Of course, I thought it was brilliant. "The First Amendment to the United States Constitution," she wrote in a sentence that became oft-quoted in the media, "does not promise the speaker that what he says will have no consequences, for such a guarantee would contradict the justification for protecting the freedom to speak. Speech is protected because it is powerful, not because it is pointless. Nor does the Constitution promise that the speaker must be freed from responsibility for those consequences."

Brianna Bainbridge was ecstatic when I faxed a copy to her. I've always suspected she sent it to someone she knew at the *New York Times*. In any event, it made page 13A of that publication the next day, and was mentioned in the *Washington Post, Los Angeles Times, San Francisco Chronicle*, and a number of other publications, many of which were numbered among the Fucking Amici. It was on the front page of the Boulder and Denver papers. My telephone began to ring at all hours, until I finally stopped answering it, relying on the machine to pick up determined callers.

The judge's order set a trial date six months hence, much sooner than I expected. We couldn't have gotten ready in time if it hadn't been for Brianna.

Our little office became the command center of an almost military campaign. Two weeks after the trial date was set, three young Women's Studies majors from a college in rural Massachusetts showed up, their travel and living expenses paid by the Center for Women's Constitutional Interests. Their school was, incredibly, giving them credit for an internship under the auspices of the famous Professor Bainbridge, but as far as I could tell they were at our disposal. For weeks I didn't have to make a copy, carry a paper to the courthouse, or make a run for office supplies. It was with difficulty that I managed to dart across the street to get myself a coffee from the Tri: Caitlin, Tamara, or Jeffrey was always willing to go get it for me. Beverly was in heaven with so many assistants to boss around. I will always enjoy the memory of the lecture she gave Jeffrey about why his nose ring was not appropriate office attire. She also cajoled our landlord into renting us the vacant office down the hall for six months; he had been looking for a three-year lease, and I still don't know what persuasions she offered him. The triplets, as I came to think of them, worked like demons off an enormous folding table, slinging files like mad in and out of blue plastic milk carton crates.

Tory handled every other piece of legal work that came into the office during that time, and often enough she'd stay late with me to work on *Grayling v. DR Films:* the documents we had to file listing all of our witnesses and evidence, or a motion *in limine* or, toward the end, the all-important jury instructions. Linda, coming by late to pick her up or calling from their big house up in Nederland, grew shorter in her greetings and encouragements as the weeks passed, and I realized she was suffering from the serious unacknowledged affliction Litigator's Partner Syndrome, characterized by feelings of abandonment, irritation, and hostility to the legal profession. I don't know how I would have coped if I'd had a partner, or even a pet. By the time the trial began, all of my houseplants had died.

It was Brianna who introduced me to Dr. Bradley Detweiler. Beverly later took to calling him Dr. Dolittle, and he did somewhat resemble Rex Harrison in that ancient cinematic clinker, but there was nothing cute about his research. A professor at Johns Hopkins, he had spent fifteen years investigating the relationship between violent pornography and violent behavior. I met him in Brianna's office one afternoon shortly after the trial date was set; he would be giving a lecture at the university that evening, but he made time for me.

He was intelligent and distinguished, but what made me want him for a witness was his conversation. Two- and three-syllable words predominated, and he had a way of looking straight at you and conveying that he actually wished things weren't the way they were, but there was no use trying to get around it. We talked for two hours, and at the end I went back to my office and endorsed him on our pretrial disclosures as an expert witness.

Above my desk, tacked onto the corkboard, was a ragged, edge-curled sheet of yellow paper, with the list I had made many months before:

- find the maker (Linc?)
- get jurisdiction in Colorado (find copy for sale here? who? and will that be enough?)
- prove causation btwn tape & Wolf's acts (Andy?)
- prove Wolf's actions foreseeable to maker (how?)

I had lined through the first two items, one in ink, one in pencil, thanks to Linc and Charley. The heart of the trial would be my efforts to accomplish the third and fourth tasks. Andy and now Detweiler were my chief hopes for the third. But even under our theory of what we would need to prevail at trial—that is, mine and Tory's and Brianna Bainbridge's—I needed proof that the defendants, DR Films and DR Distribution, had some reason to know or suspect that the production and distribution of *Sunshade Snuffdown* could cause someone's death. Since Dashiell Roman mostly owned and individually managed those companies, that meant showing that he knew that his products were creating this risk. Or at a minimum should have known, but it would be much better if I could argue that he knew there was a link between the kind of stuff he produced and the possibility of harm. Detweiler could testify about the research concerning the connection between pornography and violent acts, but I wasn't sure how I was going to prove, or even suggest with a straight face, that Dashiell Roman was aware of it.

I'd seen Detweiler's résumé, and noted the publications in which his work had appeared. I certainly wasn't going to be able to rest my case for Roman's negligence on the argument that Detweiler's work was so famous that Roman had to have known it. If I tried, I could imagine how the examination of Dashiell Roman by his lawyers would go:

> *Lawyer: Mr. Roman, are you a subscriber to Journal of Personality and Social Psychology?*
>
> *Mr. Roman: No sir.*
>
> *Lawyer: How about The Annals of the New York Academy of Sciences?*
>
> *Mr. Roman: Nope.*
>
> *Lawyer: Perhaps The Journal of Sex Research?*
>
> *Mr. Roman: Never heard of it. (coughs violently, prompting sympathetic grimaces from jurors)*

What I needed was to take Dashiell Roman's deposition. I reached for the telephone to call Paco Morales and set it up.

Then I called Andy, and arranged to meet him at the North Boulder Coffee Shop for lunch. It was another of Andy's favorites, an unapologetic greasy spoon next door to a laundromat, its clientele a mix of slumming professionals and residents of the homeless shelter up the street. He was waiting for me at a table in the back, already forking home fries into his mouth from a golden mound on the plate in front of him.

"Sorry," he said, his baritone a bit muffled by the potatoes. "I was starving, thought you wouldn't mind."

"Of course not," I said, and gestured to the waitress, thinking I'd just have some coffee. I swear the waitstaff at the NBCS is clairvoyant. In less than half a minute, and without having spoken a word, I had a thick mug of the lovely stuff, throwing off clouds of steam.

"Andy," I said, "we're going to have to try this case. I read your report, I went through all of the transcripts, I admire your technique and your perception, but give me something close to the bottom line here. Are you prepared to testify that in your professional opinion, Leonard Fitzgerald would not have killed Alison Grayling, but for his exposure to *Sunshade Snuffdown?*

"Sure," he said, still chewing. I let out a huge sigh, realizing how uncertain I had been of his answer. "But I wouldn't be your best witness for that," he added.

"What do you mean?"

"Why not put Fitzgerald on the stand?"

"You're kidding." In all of my scheming, I had never considered this possibility. "I'm sure there's no way I could get him here. The Illinois authorities would have to give us permission to move him, and we'd have to get the Boulder sheriff to agree to transport him and keep him in custody. It would cost a mint, and even so I don't think we'd ever get everyone to sign off on it. But, just out of curiosity, what do you think he'd say?"

Andy shook his head. "He'd say all kinds of things, but I think they'd point to the unmistakable conclusion that the tape influenced him, hugely, to do what he did. I'd testify too, of course, but it would be a lot more convincing with both of us."

I reflected on this for a moment while the waitress refilled my coffee cup and dropped an enormous omelet, various vegetables poking through the yellow layer, in front of Andy. "You want anything besides that coffee, Hon?" she asked me.

"No thanks," I said, and she nodded and left, as though she'd known that would be my answer. "What kind of omelet is that, anyway?" I said to him.

"Omaha, I think it's called," he said through a mouthful.

"Because it's roughly the size of?" I asked, and he nodded. I watched him and thought about things while he worked his way through the platter like a man in love. I couldn't decide whether watching him eat made me want to eat, or want never to eat again. Finally he wiped his mouth on his paper napkin and sat back.

"Did it make your toes tingle?" I said.

"Yes, Cinda, it did. Listen, who would you go to for permission to do this thing, if you were going to do it?"

"Well, the sheriff at this end. If my client could come up with the money to send a couple of his guys for the Wolf and pay for his stay at the jail, I think he'd be willing. He's a good guy—I've known him since I was in the DA's office."

"And at the other end?"

"I wouldn't know where to start. I guess that guy John Scarpelli from the state attorney's office might know how to get it done, but I don't really want to talk to him."

"Why not?" asked Andy.

"I just don't," I said.

"Then leave him to me," he said, making the smallest possible hand gesture, which prompted the appearance of the check. "He and I got along okay. And you work on this end, and let's see what happens."

"Okay," I said, still skeptical. "And I'll need to talk to my client, see if she'll pay. She's already had to shell out a lot."

"Money well spent," was his only comment, and he may have been talking about the restaurant check.

We took Dashiell Roman's deposition in the offices of Dan Everett's firm, which had a conference room with panorama windows offering a view of the smoggy Los Angeles basin and, barely discernible through the haze, the ocean beyond. The conference table was a huge polished slab of some endangered species of hardwood. Not only the lawyers, but also the secretaries and even the caterers who slipped in and out maintaining our supplies of iced Perrier and fresh fruit, were exquisitely dressed. I counted twelve lawyers around the table, and only one of us was there for the plaintiff. Rafe was not among them, although I was certain he was the one who'd had a vase of freesia and gladiolus delivered to my hotel room the night before. The card said only *Illegitimati non carborundum*.

We had a little skirmish before we got started about how the deposition would be recorded. In my notice of deposition, I'd designated stenographic recording, but when I arrived and was directed to the conference room, I found a young man with a glossy bald head, dressed in pleated linen pants and black silk shirt, setting up a video camera on a tripod.

"Wait!" I said to him, and he looked up with eyes as blue and guileless as the distant water. "This is not supposed to be a videotape deposition."

He shrugged without emphasis, as if used to this sort of thing. "You better take it up with Mr. Everett, then. He's the one told me to get set up."

I went back out to look for Everett, fuming. The receptionist told me that his personal office was on an entirely different floor of this law firm's suite, and offered to get him on the phone for me. When he came on I erupted, not sure why it mattered so much how the deposition was recorded, but determined not to be intimidated by the distance I'd traveled from my home turf.

"Mr. Everett, I'm sure it was an oversight that led you to set up for a videotape deposition," I said tightly.

"And what would I have overlooked?" he said, still charming.

"The circumstance that my notice designated stenographic recording. I've engaged a stenographer, who will be arriving any minute."

"No problem," he said, with the air of one who has just applied his excellent skills to achieve that condition. "We'll have both. You can order a transcript from your reporter, and we'll even let you have a free copy of the video."

"That's not satisfactory," I said. "The Colorado Rules of Civil Procedure, under which we are operating here, provide that you must give me reasonable notice if you want to use a different method of recording from the one I designated."

"Very well, then," he replied. "Consider yourself hereby notified that we intend to videotape the deposition of Mr. Dashiell Roman, concurrent with your stenographic recording."

"Eight minutes notice?" I said, glancing at the clock on the wall. "I hardly think that's reasonable."

"Oh come *on*, Ms. Hayes," he said, some asperity finally creeping into his voice. "What difference does it make?"

I wasn't certain I had a sound legal reason, but I knew a practical one: I was damned if I wanted a jury to see Dashiell Roman wheezing and gasping like each breath might be his last. I much preferred that they see his answers in cold letters on paper. "I would have prepared differently if I had received timely notice of your intention to videotape," I said stiffly.

"Oh yeah?" he said. "Bad hair day?"

"I will," I said, "register my objection on the record."

"Do that," he said.

The receptionist gave me an eye-wrinkling little smile as I handed the telephone back to her. "All set?" she inquired perkily.

"Oh yeah," I assured her.

Paco Morales ushered Dashiell Roman into the conference room at twelve minutes after ten. I had never met our adversary before, and despite Lincoln's descriptions I was shocked by the fragility of his appearance. Oxygen tubes ran from his nostrils to the tank that he pulled behind him on a small wheeled cart. His hands were clawed and ropy, spotted profusely on the backs. He seemed barely able to navigate, his feet shambling and floppy in their oxfords as though they were no longer receiving the commands of his will.

He scowled at all of the assembled lawyers impersonally, and seemed no more ill-disposed toward me than toward anyone else. I thought perhaps he didn't realize who I was, so I arose from the chair I had taken and walked over toward the seat into which he was being settled. Once he had waved off further assistance I lowered my face to the level of his and extended my hand tentatively.

"Mr. Roman," I said, "I'm Lucinda Hayes. I'm Margaret Grayling's lawyer."

"Figured as much," he said hoarsely. "So let's get on with it." Paco, seated next to him, leaned over as if to explain something, but Roman turned his head toward him and spoke first. "Shut the fuck up," he said. "Let's get this over with." A bitter smell arose from the uncovered flesh of his head and hands.

He hated all of us, it seemed, in equal measure. I surmised that he had refused to undergo much preparation for this deposition. Good. I returned to my chair, smiled at the stenographer, and began. I named the time and place, identified myself and the lawsuit, and for the stenographer's benefit I asked everyone present to give his or her name and spell it. The bald video operator was filming away, but I just smiled in his direction and stated for the record that I objected to any method of recording the deposition other than stenographic, but that in the interest of economy I would allow the deposition to go forward and bring my objection to the attention of the court later.

"I will represent for the record," I said, looking into the camera, "that I was given no notice by any attorney for the defendant or amici of any intention to videotape this proceeding until eight minutes before its scheduled beginning. If any person present wishes to claim otherwise, now is the time to do so."

Silence. Dan Everett looked very pissed off, affronted that I'd call attention to his neglect with all the other lawyers around. But contained, like he would be waiting for the right moment to get his own back. Good.

"I assume," I said sweetly, "that Mr. Morales will be making objections, if any, on behalf of Mr. Roman?"

"What do you mean?" said one of the younger lawyers. Perkins Rostow, I think his name was, appearing for one of the publishing houses; he was wearing one of those suits for damages.

"I mean," I said, "that I've been double-teamed and triple-teamed before, and I don't mind the crowded conditions in here, but depositions are meant to be *mano a mano*. I don't propose to duel with all eleven of you at once. I believe you are required to designate one gladiator for purposes of making objections to my questions. None of which objections will have any merit," I added.

"Mr. Morales will make objections, if any," said Everett, looking less charming and less charmed by the moment.

"Good," I said.

I asked the stenographer to swear the witness, and then got to work. I had, in truth, only one objective in this deposition, but didn't want to get straight to it, so I started with something simple. I smiled at Dashiell Roman, and he glared back at me.

*MS. HAYES: Sir, is Dashiell Roman the name given you at birth?*

*THE WITNESS: I don't remember. It was a long time ago.*

*MS. HAYES: Have you ever gone by a different name?*

*THE WITNESS: Long time ago.*

*MS. HAYES: And what was it?*

*THE WITNESS: Same first name, Dashiell.*

*MS. HAYES: But a different last name?*

*THE WITNESS: Yeah.*

*MS. HAYES: What might it have been, this different last name?*

*THE WITNESS: Rodinsky.*

*MS. HAYES: Dashiell Rodinsky.*

*THE WITNESS: Yeah, I guess so.*

So it went. He stopped fighting with me not long after that, seeming to run out of energy even for hostilities. I was waiting for objections, but none came, as we went through his birth in Idaho, his family's move to Los Angeles in 1947, when he was eleven. Then his first job, after high school, as a grip on a movie set at Warner Brothers, his union card, his training as a sound tech, lighting tech, and assistant director, his occasional acting jobs in blue movies. He was subject to fits of violent coughing, and once he reached behind him to adjust a knob on his oxygen setup. I tried to watch him with a juror's eye, weighing the sympathy that his sickness and frailty would generate against their likely distaste for his crudeness and hostility. But there wasn't too much of the latter: after his initial resistance he didn't seem to mind telling me anything I was interested in knowing.

I needed to make him angry at me for what I had in mind, and was looking for an opening.

*MS. HAYES: What was the highest grade you finished in school?*

*THE WITNESS: Twelve.*

*MS. HAYES: You graduated from high school, then?*

*THE WITNESS: Yeah.*

*MS. HAYES: You're sure about that.*

*THE WITNESS: Yeah, I'm sure. You got someone says otherwise, bring him in here.*

*MS. HAYES: But no college.*

*THE WITNESS: I didn't need no college, I had a good job, union card, everything I needed.*

*MS. HAYES: But you do read?*

*THE WITNESS: Read?*

*MS. HAYES: Yes.*

*THE WITNESS: Course I read.*

*MS. HAYES: What sorts of things?*

*THE WITNESS: Every sort.*

*MS. HAYES: Do you know who win the Pulitzer Prize for literature last year, 1999?*

*THE WITNESS: Jesus Christ on a stick, I—*

*MR. EVERETT: Ms. Hayes, we've given you a lot of latitude, but I have to step in here. There is nothing of relevance to this lawsuit in your inquiry. You are just trying to embarrass the witness.*

*MS. HAYES: I thought we agreed that Mr. Morales would be handling objections.*

*MR. MORALES: I adopt Mr. Everett's objection on behalf of my client.*

*MS. HAYES: Your objection is registered, Mr. Everett. Now, Mr. Roman, will you answer my question?*

*MR. EVERETT: You don't have to answer, Mr. Roman.*

*MS. HAYES: Are you instructing the witness not to answer?*

*MR. EVERETT: I just did, Ms. Hayes. Let's move on.*

You'd have to be around courtrooms for a while to understand the calculated insult in Everett's words. *Let's move on* is what an impatient judge says to a lawyer who's wasting the court's time. For one lawyer to say it to another carries an unmistakable message, in this case reinforced by the posh surroundings and Dan Everett's comfortable place in them: *I'm in charge here.*

Good, I thought, and tried to look flustered.

*MS. HAYES: Let's turn to the production of the film Sunshade Snuffdown. I believe you have acknowledged that you produced that film, Mr. Roman?*

*THE WITNESS: I was the executive producer, yeah. It was produced by my company.*

*MS. HAYES: That would be DR Films?*

*THE WITNESS: Yeah.*

MS. HAYES: *And it was another company that you controlled, DR Distribution Company, that distributed it?*

THE WITNESS: *Yeah.*

MS. HAYES: *What year was Sunshade Snuffdown filmed?*

THE WITNESS: *Not sure. Before 1996, I know that much.*

MS. HAYES: *What makes you so certain of that?*

THE WITNESS: *My lawyer at the time told me I had to stop using minors in my movies because of some change in the law, and—*

MS. HAYES: *So you had used a minor as an actor in Sunshade Snuffdown?*

MR. EVERETT: *Ask that you let the deponent finish his answer, Ms. Hayes.*

THE WITNESS: *Yeah, if you don't mind. Even adults that looked like kids, he told me. So the one I used in Sunshade Snuffdown sure looked like a kid didn't she? I stopped that kind of thing in 1996, that's all I know.*

MS. HAYES: *Is it your testimony that the actor who played the child in Sunshade Snuffdown was not a minor?*

THE WITNESS: *No.*

MS. HAYES: *She was a minor?*

THE WITNESS: *I don't know what she was. I didn't care. My casting director found her, that's all I know.*

MS. HAYES: *Who was that?*

THE WITNESS: *My casting director?*

MS. HAYES: *Yes.*

THE WITNESS: *Artie Sanborn.*

MS. HAYES: *Where is Mr. Sanborn now?*

THE WITNESS: *I have no idea. Haven't seen him in years. Doesn't work for me any more.*

MS. HAYES: *When was the last time you saw him?*

THE WITNESS: *No idea.*

MS. HAYES: *Your memory isn't very good, is it, Mr. Roman?*

THE WITNESS: *I'm getting tired of your insults, lady. My memory is fine, I can read as good as you, I watch the History Channel, I know what's going on in the world.*

*MS. HAYES: Where was Sunshade Snuffdown filmed, Mr. Roman?*

*THE WITNESS: We filmed a lot of places in those days. I can't remember for sure.*

*MS. HAYES: Didn't you tell my investigator that it was filmed in the Caribbean somewhere?*

*THE WITNESS: I don't remember what I told him.*

*MS. HAYES: Well, was it filmed offshore?*

*THE WITNESS: I don't remember.*

Here he looked murderously at Paco Morales, who tried to smile at him encouragingly. It seemed this piece of testimony pained him more than the rest, and I wondered why. For my client's purposes his answer didn't matter that much, but I knew Brianna would expect me to pursue this question further.

*MS. HAYES: Did you ever, for this film or some other, rent someone's house in or near Los Angeles to use as a film set?*

*THE WITNESS: Sure. It's a common practice.*

*MS. HAYES: Is it possible that you filmed Sunshade Snuffdown, or part of it, in such a place?*

The merest cut of his eyes toward Paco, who was looking intent and unhappy. All of the lawyers seemed extremely still, wearing expressions of practiced disinterest.

*THE WITNESS: Is it possible? Yeah, I suppose so.*

*MS. HAYES: Well, did you?*

*THE WITNESS: I don't remember.*

*MS. HAYES: But it's possible.*

*THE WITNESS: I guess anything is possible.*

*MS. HAYES: Do you remember any of the locations of people's homes where you filmed any of your productions over the years?*

*THE WITNESS: You mean their addresses, like?*

*MS. HAYES: Sure, if you remember.*

*THE WITNESS: I don't.*

*MS. HAYES: Do you have any records that would help us locate them?*

*THE WITNESS: Nah. We had a fire a couple years ago.*

As bogus as this sounded, I knew it was true. We'd encountered the same answer when we asked, earlier in discovery, for various records of the two companies. They had been kept in a warehouse near the studio, which had been destroyed by a blaze in 1997. Lincoln had found a copy of the fire department's report. Arson was not suspected.

*MS. HAYES: Well, perhaps you'd just tell me anything you do remember about the house where you say it's possible Sunshade Snuffdown was filmed.*

*THE WITNESS: Nothing, I'm telling you.*

I gave up on this. At least Brianna couldn't say I hadn't tried. And it seemed as though the time might be right for my true purpose. I tried to look flustered and disorganized, shuffling a few papers and peering at them randomly.

*MS. HAYES: Whose idea was it, Mr. Roman, for the eighteen minutes of filmed material in Sunshade Snuffdown to be repeated several times on the videotaped version?*

*THE WITNESS: That was mine. We started to do that with some of our productions. They were short, you know, some of them, and it didn't cost hardly any more to put them on the cassette several times than just once. Gives the customer more value, so to speak.*

*MS. HAYES: So a customer could watch the film over and over without having to rewind the tape?*

*THE WITNESS: Yeah, that was the idea. I was the first to have it, but now lots of the distributors are doing it.*

*MS. HAYES: Good. Now, Mr. Roman, as we've established that your memory is imperfect, and your reading habits less than conscientious, let me—*

*MR. MORALES: Ms. Hayes, I object. It's not proper for you to insult my client gratuitously, and you have not established anything of the kind.*

I tried to look confused and sheepish. Three of the lawyers on the other side of the table were whispering together; one of them moved his hand away from his mouth and I saw his smile. I knew what they were saying to each other: some version of *She's getting nowhere.* Dan Everett was leaning back in his chair, making or reviewing some entry on his Palm Pilot. Probably checking to see what time he had reserved the handball court. The atmosphere in the room had changed since I had abandoned the subject of where the film was made. But Dashiell Roman was not feeling relaxed. His jaw was rigid and his hands trembled with what I hoped was anger.

MS. HAYES: *Sorry. Let me put it this way. You have no awareness, do you, of the current state of research about your industry?*

THE WITNESS: *The hell I don't. I read everything I can get my hands on. I know as much as anybody.*

MS. HAYES: *You mean about the film industry, don't you?*

THE WITNESS: *Yeah.*

MS. HAYES: *But what about the place of your own particular work in the industry? I mean pornography. Isn't that a fair description of your work?*

THE WITNESS: *Porn, yeah, some call it that. I don't mind that.*

MS. HAYES: *But you don't read the stuff, the current research, what have you, about porn, do you? Or don't you remember?*

THE WITNESS: *I read it all. I remember it just fine. I know what's going on in my industry.*

MS. HAYES: *You're not claiming to be familiar with the work of, say, Dr. Bradley Detweiler, are you?*

Everett finally looked up, recognizing the name.

MR. EVERETT: *I object, this—*

MS. HAYES: *Mr. Everett, there was an agreement that all objections would be stated by Mr. Morales.*

MR. MORALES: *I adopt Mr. Everett's objection.*

MS. HAYES: *Mr. Everett has not stated the grounds for an objection, but I will accept for the record that you have objected to the question, Mr. Morales, but may I say that it is improper to object merely to protect your client from revealing his ignorance.*

THE WITNESS: *Shut up, all of you. I'm not the hick you think I am, Miss. I read it, and I remember it.*

*MS. HAYES: Recently, I imagine, after your lawyers suggested you read Dr. Detweiler's work?*

*THE WITNESS: Long before that. I read all of that stuff.*

*MR. EVERETT: This witness is exhausted and it's time for a break.*

*MS. HAYES: Certainly.*

There was more, but I had gotten what I came for. By nightfall I was on a plane back home. A couple of weeks later, after I got the stenographer's transcript and was gratified to confirm that he really had said what I remembered him saying, I was explaining to Peggy what a fortunate set of occurrences these were.

Peggy's spirits had been holding up well, I thought. She'd been happy when the Center for Women's Constitutional Interests had agreed during the preceding week to pay the cost of bringing Leonard Fitzgerald to Colorado for the trial. And whatever combination of sweaty yoga and herbal remedies maintained her external serenity appeared still to be working. So I was unprepared for her obvious unhappiness when she understood what I was saying about Roman's deposition. Although she sat quietly in the saggy guest chair in my office, the low-angle sunlight playing on her slight figure, I could see that her body had grown rigid, her face set.

"I'm not certain I quite understand," she was saying. "You mean he won't be a witness?"

"I'm hoping not," I said. "Here he is on paper, admitting the only things I need for him to admit for us to win this case. But he looks terrible, Peggy, sick and exhausted. I know they were thinking the same thing. That's why they wanted the deposition videotaped, so if it was used it would stir up the same sympathy as his personal appearance. But I'm pretty sure I can persuade the judge that the videotape is inadmissible, because they didn't give proper notice of it. Then we're left with the transcript, which I can read to the jury, emphasizing all the important parts. That's much better for us."

"But he'll be here, won't he?" she asked me. "For the trial?"

"I don't need him to be," I repeated. "And I don't think he will be. His doctors said he was too sick to travel a couple of weeks ago, and he doesn't look like a man who's getting better."

She stood up from the chair and placed her hands on the edge of my desk, leaning her weight into them. "I don't understand, Cinda. I told you

I want him to take responsibility for what he did."

"I know you do, Peggy. So do I. If we win—and I'm feeling incredibly optimistic, although I probably shouldn't say it out loud—the verdict will make that happen. It will say he's responsible."

"But he won't even be here when the jury says it?" She pressed harder on the desk; I could see the blood leaving her hands.

"No, he may not be. But that doesn't mean he won't be responsible."

"Can't you make him be there for the trial?"

"No," I said. "I can't. He's not a named defendant, and he's outside the subpoena power of the court. He won't be here unless his lawyers want him to be."

She paced around, as much as was possible in the small room, the tails of her long sweater swirling as she turned. "Then try to make them want him to be here!" she said. "Don't you understand? I need to look him in the eye, and make him look in mine and know what he did. And understand that I am going to make him pay for the death of my child. That was the entire point!" She collapsed back into the chair and rubbed her small face so violently with her hands that I stood and moved toward her, alarmed. But she looked up from the hands and waved me away. "I'm fine!" she hissed.

Her outburst would not have been surprising from any other client in Peggy's situation. I'd been waiting since the day I met her for some loss of composure, some reassuring evidence she was human like the rest of us, but its appearance so late was inconvenient. My head was full of trial preparations and strategies, in a cold realm of pure calculation where sympathy and compassion could find little purchase. It was a moment of maximum unavailability for counseling a distraught client.

"Here's what I'll do," I told her. "I'll ask the judge to rule before trial that the videotaped deposition is inadmissible. If she does, then they'll be likelier to try to get him here, because that would be the only way for the jury to see how old and sick he is."

"Okay," she said, and it really seemed to be. She looked as though she, too, was engaged in some calculation, some reorganization of her expectations. Good, I thought.

Despite Rafe's suggestion that the amici's interest in settlement would end with the issuance of the judge's order on their motion, the settlement offers continued to come. They were no longer conveyed by Rafe, however, but came from Dan Everett. I had dutifully passed each one to Peggy, who repeated each time that she wasn't interested in settlement at any price. The last one, ten days before trial, was for twelve million, which was at least seven million more than the combined assets of DR Films and DR Distribution.

"Peggy, I feel I have to mention that it's not entirely rational to turn down this offer," I said to her on the phone. "It's more than we could possibly recover after a trial, even if the jury pulls out all of the stops. He just doesn't have that much money."

"Then how can he be offering it in settlement?" she said.

"Apparently all or most of the amici are throwing in money toward a settlement," I said. "But we didn't sue them, so they couldn't be compelled to contribute to a verdict. It's a very unusual situation."

"They must be afraid we're going to win," she said.

"They must be," I agreed.

Then she said what I expected her to say, the same thing she had said to all the other offers: only a trial would force someone to stand up and take responsibility for her daughter's death, and a trial was what she wanted.

When I called him back, Everett refused to believe that it wasn't a matter of the amount. "I'm not kidding this time, Cinda," he said. "There is no more in the kitty, this is a final offer."

"I know," I said. "She does too."

"She's deranged and you're a fool," he told me before hanging up. I decided not to tell him how often I had that thought myself.

Jury selection started on a brilliant February morning, three days after a storm. The streets were clear, only their edges crusted with the gray banished remains of the snowfall, but the temperature had not risen above freezing in days. Early that morning as I pulled on the hated pantyhose and stretched my arms to button a silk blouse behind me, looked for my gloves, and tried a little deep belly breathing to dampen the fluttering of my stomach, I thought of the jury panel, those two hundred or so citizens of Boulder County who had received summonses to appear in the courthouse this morning for jury duty. Thirty or forty of them would get sent to our courtroom. I tried to imagine them doing what I was doing, dressing, eating breakfast, wondering what the day would bring for them. They might be eager or apprehensive, curious about what trouble or dispute might require their attention. And always, I thought, prospective jurors wondered whether they would be chosen, often torn between hope and fear.

I had offered to pick Peggy up at her townhouse, but I was relieved when she said she would get a ride with Sierra, who lived close by. The crowd of journalists and cameras outside the Justice Center seemed slightly less crushing than it had on the day of the motion to dismiss hearing, but perhaps I was just getting used to it. In any event I was glad that Peggy's friend would be able to get her into the building without the need to brave the cameras. When we met outside the courtroom Peggy looked once more composed and rested, although I thought her smile might be a bit tight. She sat on one side of me, and one of the triplets, Caitlin, on the other, to take notes during the jury selection.

Since the jurors would be filling the jury box, the presence of the legion of lawyers that had attended the argument on the motion to dismiss would have posed a problem, but on this day the defense was represented by only three: Paco Morales, Dan Everett, and one of the younger associates from Everett's firm. This was intelligent on their part, as jurors drawn from the population of what some liked to call the People's Republic of Boulder would likely have been put off by the presence of too many thousand-dollar suits.

Dashiell Roman was not there, but I still hoped he might turn up once the jury was chosen. Four days earlier Judge Meiklejohn had granted my motion to exclude use of the videotape of Roman's deposition, and without that I was guessing that Everett and Morales would want him there, fiddling with his oxygen tank and coughing into his copious handkerchiefs, when the jury started thinking about how to assign blame for Alison Grayling's torture and death.

Carolyn opened the court with her *oyes,* the judge entered and seated herself behind the bench. The bailiff brought the jury panel, wide-eyed and disoriented, into the room. They settled into the jury box and overflowed into the front seats of the spectator section, to the displeasure of several displaced media representatives who were sent next door to listen to the proceedings over a sound hookup. I shuffled through the juror questionnaires we had been given, on which they had filled in a few particulars like name, age, occupation, and family, trying to match faces to the data, surprised as always by how little some people's appearance resembled their statistics.

Judge Meiklejohn said a few soothing things to the panel, as though calming a herd of nervous cattle, and then turned to us and we were off. The judge made an exception to her usual practice and allowed me and Everett to question the prospective jurors ourselves, instead of submitting questions to her, but she made us move it along.

She sustained only one challenge for cause made by each side. I succeeded in getting rid of the co-owner of a comic book store who, when I asked him his understanding of the First Amendment, told me earnestly that he was sure it promised that nobody could ever be held responsible for saying the wrong thing.

"What do you think of this?" I asked him. The others were listening intently. "The First Amendment to the United States Constitution does not promise the speaker that what he says will have no consequences, for such a guarantee would contradict the justification for protecting the freedom to speak. Speech is protected because it is powerful, not because it is pointless. Nor does the Constitution promise that the speaker must be freed from responsibility for those consequences." It was from Meiklejohn's order denying the motion to dismiss, but of course there was no way the poor guy could know that.

"I can't agree with it," the honest fellow said.

"Suppose I told you that was the law and you had to follow it in this case?" I asked him.

"I couldn't do that, ma'am," he said. His fingers twitched minutely.

"Suppose Her Honor here told you the same thing?"

He squirmed unhappily. "I just don't hold with it," was all he could come up with.

I asked to approach the bench. Everett was looking unhappy but didn't put up much of a fight, and juror number eight was excused. Not a bad piece of work, I thought as I walked back to our table. Not so much getting rid of him as impressing on the others that some questions had already been settled.

Everett got one too, a University of Colorado student who, when asked if she had any strong opinions about pornography, said she thought it might be the only crime that deserved the death penalty. Goodbye, juror number fifteen. But nobody else was excluded for cause. We asked questions all morning; at noon Peggy and the triplets and I huddled over the questionnaires and Caitlin's notes while we ate sandwiches in the courthouse coffee shop, arguing in hushed tones about this one and that one. After lunch we went back for more questions, and then huddled again about how to use our peremptory challenges. We got rid of the ones we liked least, and watched the ones we liked best walk out as well, peremptoried by Morales and Everett. By the end of the day we had a jury, newly re-numbered one to eight: an atmospheric scientist, a massage therapist, and a retired geography teacher, all men; and a motorcycle mechanic, a nurse specializing in cardiac care, and a mother and part-time writer of some software whose exact nature I did not understand, all women. Two alter-nates, both men: a musician and a postal carrier. I liked them pretty well. I had my doubts about number five, the motorcycle mechanic, because of her occupation. In the motorcycle shop of my imagination there is a lot of porn hanging around, but she was a pretty woman and I thought maybe she just loved the machines and was tired of looking at wall calendars featuring other women's asses bent over Harleys, and of getting hit on by the men. Anyway, I was out of strikes, so she stayed.

"Do you like them?" I asked Peggy softly, as the judge was swearing them in. She was watching this procedure attentively, but when the oath was done she turned to look at me and nodded.

The judge told them, and us, to be back at nine o'clock the next morn-ing. For the first time since I'd walked into the courtroom, my chest felt fizzy and my head untethered. Jury selection was just an exercise in social skills, but tomorrow we would begin in earnest. I told Peggy I'd see her in the morning, and went home to contemplate the order of my witnesses.

I sat in my comfortable desk chair, looking at the blank legal pad, wishing the witness order list would write itself. You want to start with a bang, of course. And you'd like to end with a bang, and it would be nice if your case didn't sag in the middle and you had a few lively bits there, too, but in fact very few trials go bang-bang-bang. One of the most shocking things to most people about attending a trial from beginning to end is the utter tedium of so much of it. Even trials where literally life or death is at stake—maybe especially those, because they tend to be long—fairly ooze ennui. The Nuremberg war trials after World War Two were staggeringly boring, I've read. I remember that Rebecca West, reporting on the proceedings, said that the judges were "dragging the proceedings over the threshold of their consciousness by sheer force of will."

I didn't think our case was going to take that long, but some of it was tedious, no getting away from it. Things were this way in part because Roman's lawyers had admitted so much in discovery: that DR Films had made *Sunshade Snuffdown,* that DR Distribution had shipped nineteen hundred copies of the tape, that it was an unaltered copy of the tape that the police had found in Leonard Fitzgerald's VCR at the same time they found Alison Grayling's lifeless body. At some point all of these stipulations had to be read into the record. Since I wasn't sure our jurors would have the force of will of those Nuremberg judges, I decided to get this routine stuff out of the way fairly early, while they were still fresh. But I still wanted a start that would bring them around to seeing the case the way I saw it: not a case about whether we would continue to enjoy free speech in this great country, but a case about a little girl who would have been twelve now, had the defendants not decided to produce and distribute *Sunshade Snuffdown.*

I wore a different suit the next morning, and braided my hair into a plait. As I did I thought about our jurors, especially the motorcycle mechanic, wondering whether she would wear the leather jacket again, whether she'd wear it every day. I tried to think for a bit about each one, getting ready in his house. It was a ritual that had become a habit while I was a prosecutor, thinking of the jurors every morning of a trial. I don't know whether it did any good, but I did it.

I was running a little late and pushed my way through the shivering news crews with more brusqueness than I liked to use. I met Peggy coming out of the Traffic Division, removing her leather gloves. "Hi," she said. "We just got here. Sierra's car wouldn't start, so I drove."

"They let you park your car in the garage?" I said.

She shook her head. "She said that wouldn't work, so I parked in the lot. But she still had a card that let us in the side door, so the news guys didn't see us."

"Good," I said. "Let's go in."

There were a few more of the defense lawyers in court this morning, but they sat discreetly behind the bar, singly or in pairs. I don't think the jurors knew who they were, probably took them for journalists. Rafe was sitting alone in the next to last row. He smiled at us as we entered the room.

"Who is he here for again?" said Peggy. She found the changing cast of amicus lawyers bewildering, and I couldn't blame her.

"He represents Rose Brothers, the movie studio." I said.

"And they just care about this case because of its—what did you call it?"

"Precedential value. Yes. But they care a lot, and so do all of the others. Enough to send these expensive lawyers to our trial."

She looked at Rafe again and then at me, dissatisfied. "I'll never understand how they live with themselves, defending that murderer."

"To them, it's a principle. Free speech, unconstrained by the fear of consequences. At least, to some of them. I know it is for Rafe. Let's sit down," I said. "They'll be bringing our jury in soon."

Then they did, and the eight of them were seated and looking expectantly toward the bench, where Judge Meiklejohn settled herself at twenty seconds past nine. She wore the same robe as the day before, as far as I could tell. The motorcycle mechanic was wearing a celery-colored turtleneck sweater and black pants. Either she didn't wear the leather jacket today, or she'd left it in the jury room. The massage therapist, number three, wore a nice camel-colored blazer. He smiled at me nicely as I rose to give my opening statement, and I decided to take that as a good omen.

I tried to get that good air way down in my belly, and then I spoke. "Ladies and gentlemen of the jury," I said, "this case is about a little girl who should have been preparing to celebrate her thirteenth birthday but instead is now dead, cold, and underground. The most we can hope for her is that wherever she is, she doesn't remember how she died. This case is also about her mother, who is determined that those who are responsible for causing the little girl's death should acknowledge that responsibility, and bear its consequences." Once I had gotten that far, I forgot to think about whether I was nervous and just talked; it always happened that way. Meiklejohn had given me an hour, and I took forty-five minutes. It flew; time always does when you're litigating. The trick is to make it go as fast for the jurors as it does for you. I hope I succeeded, but I don't know. They all looked attentive and maybe half of them kind, and that's about the best you can hope for.

Paco Morales gave the opening for the defendants, and he came down pretty hard on the freedom-of-speech thing, which I thought was a mistake on his part, but maybe not. I watched the jurors pretty closely while he spoke, and I thought it possible they were wondering where his client was. I wondered myself if we'd ever see Dashiell Roman, nee Rodinsky, and I turned my head back toward my client. She was listening gravely to Morales, but I suspected she was thinking about the same thing and I realized that if she never set eyes on him she'd never be satisfied with this case, even if we won big.

The judge called a recess at the end of the openings, fifteen minutes. I cautioned Peggy not to say anything to anybody, then left for the ladies' room. When I got back, I saw that she was standing behind the bar, talking to Rafe. I started to join them, concerned about what she might be saying, but Carolyn announced the judge's return and we had to hurry back to our table. Peggy didn't respond to my questioning look.

"Plaintiff," said Judge Meiklejohn, "may call her first witness."

"Your Honor," I said, "the plaintiff calls James Fox."

The police detective was a terrific witness. He was about forty-five, an experienced cop, and I started by leading him through his twenty-year career with the Chicago Police Department: patrolman, sergeant, detective bureau, vice, narcotics, homicide.

"Would it be fair," I asked him, "to say you've seen some pretty terrible things in your career?" It was objectionable, leading my own witness that way, but I figured Paco wouldn't object, and he didn't.

Detective James Fox looked at his shoes before answering, softly, "Yes."

Then I took him through the day of Alison's Grayling's death, letting him do almost all of the talking. We had rehearsed this once when he arrived in town Sunday afternoon, and I knew he'd do fine without prompting. He'd probably testified a hundred times.

His voice got softer and softer as the morning passed, and the jurors leaned forward farther and farther in their padded chairs. The nurse began to cry quietly at one point, searching in her pocket for a tissue.

Toward the end of his testimony I showed him the videotape, bagged and labeled PLAINTIFF'S EXHIBIT 1. I had made sure it would have that number.

"Have you seen Plaintiff's Exhibit One before?" I asked him.

"Yes. That's a videotape I found in the videocassette recorder in Mr. Leonard Fitzgerald's apartment."

"Did you remove the tape from the VCR yourself?" I asked.

"Yes."

"Did you note whether it was at the beginning, or the end?"

"Yes," he said. "It was at the end. It had been played through, and not rewound."

"Detective Fox," I said. "In all your years in law enforcement, what is the worst thing you have ever seen?"

He knew I was going to ask this question, but even so he thought for a moment, or if not he was a hell of a good actor. His eyes lingered for a beat on the spot where the ceiling met the far wall of the courtroom and then he spoke, softly. "This crime scene would have to be the worst," he said.

After he described taking Leonard Fitzgerald into custody, I asked him whether his prisoner had said anything to him on the way to the hospital.

"Yes," he said promptly, but no more, well-trained witness that he was.

"What did he say, Detective Fox?"

"He said he had made a mistake. He said, 'Maybe she was the wrong one.'"

"What did you understand him to mean by that?"

Paco and Dan Everett were both on their feet at once, objecting that the question called for speculation by the witness, and the judge was right to sustain them. But at least I had the jury thinking about it, a little.

Paco's cross was brief, but good, more or less what I would have done myself.

"Detective Fox," he said. "Why did you arrest Leonard Fitzgerald?" As if he didn't know.

"It appeared he was the perpetrator in the death of the girl," the cop replied.

Paco's next question was leading, but you're allowed to lead on cross-examination, and anyway I could hardly object, having used the same phrasing myself not too long before. "Would it be fair to say that you believed he was responsible for the death of the little girl?"

"Yes," said James Fox. "Yes, I did."

The jury followed him with their eyes as he was excused, but afterward many of them looked toward Peggy. She had her hands on our table, studying them. She had not shed a tear during Detective Fox's testimony. I put my hand over hers and pressed gently, but she did not respond.

During a hurried lunch in the Canyon Café, the grimy little coffee shop inside the Justice Center, I asked Peggy what Rafe had said to her. "You shouldn't talk to him," I said. "And it's unethical for him to try to talk to you, unless you start the conversation."

"I just wish I could understand what would make someone defend someone like his client," she said. "That's all I asked him."

"You understand that DR is not his client, Peggy? His client didn't have anything to do with *Sunshade Snuffdown*. To him it's the principle of the thing."

"To me they're all in this the same way, to defend their clients' right to do whatever they want."

I couldn't altogether disagree with her. "Just don't talk to him, okay?"

She sipped her soup and said nothing.

"Peggy?"

"All right."

I called the coroner's assistant right after lunch. He did a good job describing the condition of Alison's body and the autopsy findings, and his testimony flowed smoothly without interruptions until I had him identify the autopsy photographs and offered them into evidence.

Dan Everett objected, as I knew he would. They were gruesome, he said, offensive, inflammatory, and unnecessary. They didn't prove any point in dispute.

"They are necessary, Your Honor," I said, making sure the jurors could hear every word, "because they demonstrate that the wounds inflicted on Alison Grayling are nearly identical with those inflicted on the child portrayed in the film that these jurors are to see later."

This time it was Paco on his feet. "Object to the characterization of the actor as a child," he said. "There's no proof of that."

"I withdraw the characterization," I said. "The jurors can decide that for themselves, if it's important. But the pictures are relevant, Your Honor, for the reason I stated."

Meiklejohn looked at the defense table in a way I recognized: if you don't say something to change my mind here, I'm about to rule in your opponent's favor. Everett got the message, and he and Paco put their heads together for a moment.

Everett stood. "We'd be glad to stipulate, Your Honor, that the wounds are similar."

Now the judge gave me the look. "They are *strikingly* similar, Your Honor," I said. "I'll withdraw the exhibits if they so stipulate."

"Agreed," said Everett quickly, and the judge smiled and explained to the jurors what a stipulation was and how the attorneys had just agreed on something and they were to accept the agreed-upon matter and not think any further about the exhibits, which had not been received in evidence. Some of them looked a bit confused but I think they got it on the whole. It had all worked out well for me; I didn't really want them to see the pictures anyway. They were shocking and horrible, and sometimes jurors hold it against you that you're the one that made them look. Before long I was going to make them look at *Sunshade Snuffdown,* and that would be enough.

There was no cross-examination of the coroner's assistant.

I looked at the clock on the courtroom wall: four o'clock. I wanted the videotape to be the last piece of evidence before court was adjourned for the day, so I filled in with some of the boring stuff, reading some other stipulations and admissions into the record. The jurors looked interested despite the inherent boredom of being read to aloud. I tried to observe them as I looked up from time to time, and thought that our case might be coming together in their minds. There was no dispute that the little girl had died, that *Sunshade Snuffdown* was found in her killer's VCR, that her wounds resembled those of a little girl portrayed in the film, that DR Films had made the tape and that DR Distribution had shipped it. *What's next?* their alert faces seemed to be asking me.

"At this time, Your Honor," I said, "I ask that the contents of Plaintiff's Exhibit One be shown to the jury."

While Carolyn was asking one of the bailiffs to turn out the lights in the well of the courtroom, I turned to Peggy and suggested she might want to leave for the day. She seemed subdued or perhaps exhausted. It can't have been easy for her to listen to the day's testimony, and not for the first time I wondered how much energy was required to maintain that serene exterior. I didn't want her to be there while the tape was screened. She nodded, and said she would go by the Traffic Division for Sierra and ask whether she might be able to go home early. I silently blessed Sierra and squeezed Peggy's hand in farewell. The eyes of several of the jurors followed her as she departed.

Paco had already made a motion to prohibit me from showing the tape all the way to the end, its evil rituals re-enacted seven times without variation. He'd offered a stipulation that the tape consisted of seven repetitions of the first eighteen minutes, and Meiklejohn had agreed that in light of the stipulation, I'd be confined to showing only that much of it. I was just as glad, and in addition I thought their victory on this point had distracted them from a much more important objection they ought to have made, but did not.

I nodded at Caitlin, and she pressed the button to begin the VCR projector running. The sound was shockingly loud in the small courtroom, and the image on the five-by-seven-foot screen was enormous. It was odd that a consortium of Hollywood lawyers had not thought to object to exhibiting the tape on a large screen—after all, the Wolf had only watched it on his television, as far as anyone knew. As sickening as the tape had been on a small screen, its impact was unspeakable when it was magnified to the size of one's visual field—I knew, because I had tried it. I looked toward the defense table and could see Dan Everett conferring urgently with Paco Morales as the grainy juddering light from the screen played on their faces, but it was too late to object.

Probably I could have seen something of the jurors' faces in the same partial illumination, but I didn't look toward them. Remembering my own reactions the first time I'd seen *Sunshade Snuffdown,* I thought it would be indecent to watch them. Nor could I bear to watch the screen again myself, so for the next eighteen minutes I stared at my hands, knotted on the table in front of me. There was no escaping the sound, however, the child's lisp, her terror and pleas, toward the end the amplified sounds—surely added in postproduction—of the knife doing its work. I fought back tears and breathed as deeply as I could manage, grateful that it would soon be over.

Thanks to Meiklejohn, I didn't have to say anything when it was done. The judge rapped her gavel on the bench, more gently than usual, and said that court would be in recess until nine o'clock tomorrow morning. As was customary at the end of the day, the lawyers stood as the jury was led out. Not one of them looked at me, or at anyone else—not even at each other. I felt dirty and complicit again, responsible for one last showing of

*Sunshade Snuffdown,* for having forced it on eight people who hadn't asked for the experience, while at the same time I hoped perversely that it would haunt their sleep and destroy their peace of mind, that they would wish they had never seen it.

I went to the Canyon Café and sipped on a styrofoam cup of burnt caffeine for half an hour, hoping the press gang outside would be gone by the time I left. The poisonous-tasting stuff somehow made me feel a little better, and eventually I shrugged on my heavy black coat and gathered up my books and briefcase. The crews were sparser than they had been the day before, and Brianna Bainbridge, who hadn't been in court but had come over after her class to do a few stand-ups, was talking away like mad in the harsh glare of a tower light.

"—*very* important," she was saying. "Because it will establish once and for all that the First Amendment cannot any longer be employed as a tool for the oppression of women and children. This case has forced the legal system to come to grips with one of its—"

I looked at the ground and walked right on by. I made it to the parking lot across the street unhindered and was about to unlock my car, thinking I'd stop by the office to see Beverly and Tory and find out what was happening outside the confines of *Grayling v. DR Films,* when I heard a sound behind me, the scrape of a shoe sole against pavement. Goddamn media jackals, I thought, but when I turned around it was Rafe.

"Cinda," he said. No *Querida* this time, and to my surprise I felt dismay at this.

"Hi buddy," I said, turning back to the Saab's balky lock. "So what did you have to say to my client? I saw you two talking."

He shook his head ruefully. "She doesn't like me," he said. "No surprise. That's all, Cinda. I hardly said a word to her, and she started it."

I nodded, certain what he said was true. "Well don't talk to her, all right? I've told her the same."

He nodded absently, started to say something, stopped.

"You've made yourself pretty inconspicuous in there," I said. "How's the view from the back row?"

"Pretty good," he said, sticking his hands into the pockets of his suit jacket. It was plenty cold, but he had no topcoat. "I have a good sight line for watching you."

"Oh?" I said, as the cylinder finally turned. "How'm I doing?"

"Cinda," he said, "when this is all over, we need to talk, all right?"

It was the urgency in his voice as much as what he said that arrested my attention. "Talk to me now," I said, opening the car's back door and shoving in my briefcase and cartons and books. "Come on, get in. We'll go someplace."

He shook his head and took a step backward, then looked around. He waved at someone two rows over and I saw it was another one of the Fucking Amici's lawyers, a tall young woman who was getting into a silver luxury vehicle.

"Gosh," I said. "I didn't know you could rent a Lexus around here."

"Listen," he said. "Please, just wait until it's over. I hope you win, I really do, and I think you just might. But don't judge me until we have a chance to talk, okay? There were things I didn't know at the beginning, didn't know until just a few days ago. They don't change the merits of your legal claims, but I just—I just didn't know, that's all. Talk to me after, please?"

"Rafe," I began, but he turned and walked rapidly away. I saw him again as I pulled out of the parking lot; he was striding west on the Boulder Creek path, although there was nothing in that direction but snow-crusted trail and the freezing, rushing water of the creek.

My quick trip off Tower Road under the influence of roofies seemed like a long time ago; I hadn't given it much thought in the last year, more concerned with getting ready for the trial, but Rafe's strange apology, if that's what it was, made me wonder again: who had done it, and why? It made me think, too, of the cell phone that he had given me. I reached behind me at the stop light at Canyon and Broadway, pulled it out of my briefcase, and turned it on. It beeped and glowed the same as always, but its silver surface seemed different from what I remembered, somehow sinister. Had the defense team been listening to my telephone calls, or tracking my location? I tried to think whether I had ever discussed anything on the phone that the defense would have wanted to know, or taken it any place I didn't want them to know I'd been. I didn't think so. Still, I turned the little instrument over in my hand until the light changed, and vowed I would have someone take it apart to see what was inside.

Beverly had gone home by the time I got to the office, but Tory was at her desk, marking up a printout of some document with slashing strokes. "Hey!"

she said, looking up. "How's it going?" She came out into the darkened reception area and gave me a hug, and I tried to remember the last time she'd been that affectionate.

"I think good," I said ungrammatically, nearly faint suddenly with gratitude for her loyalty, and her steadiness. I started unbuttoning my heavy black coat, wearily. "Tory, I thought you were supposed to be the wild woman of the law, and I was going to be the workaday little mouse holding things together while you pursued your eccentric schemes. What happened?"

Tory laughed, in great chiming peals that carried so much joy I almost flinched from it. "We switched places for a while, that's all," she said. "That's the way it happens sometime."

"Some*times,*" I said automatically. "Is there something up?"

"Actually," she said, grinning like a lunatic, "yes."

"Well," I said impatiently, "what?"

She shook her head. "Can't tell you yet. But soon, I promise. Now come in here and sit down and tell me about your day in court."

"Let me ask you, first. Do you know anyone who knows about cell phones? The technology, I mean."

"No, but Linc would. He's got some friend he calls BioTech that Linc claims can make any electronic device do anything."

"Can we call him?"

"Linc? He's out in California," she said. "I think he's seeing some woman out there. But I'll ask Beverly to track down this BioTech guy. I think he did some work for us before, cleaned up some virus in our computers. Why?"

She rubbed the pencil back and forth between her hands while I told her about Rafe's odd behavior, then put it down and reached for my cell phone. She turned it over twice on her hands and ran her fingernails along its seams, but finally shook her head. "I don't know, we'd better ask Linc's friend. But even if the phone is hinky, that still doesn't explain the roofies, does it? I mean, what did anyone have to gain from that?"

"Nope," I said. "It doesn't explain that. Now I gotta go home and figure out what to ask the distinguished Dr. Detweiler tomorrow."

"Your Honor," I said after court had convened the next morning and our jurors were settled in their chairs, "I would like to begin the day by reading to the jurors some excerpts from the deposition of Mr. Dashiell Roman."

Judge Meiklejohn looked at Morales and Everett and the third lawyer who had joined them at the counsel table today, a colorless young man in a gray suit. There were plenty of other amici lawyers in court today, seated behind the bar, although I hadn't seen Rafe. I wondered how they decided who got to sit at counsel table on a given day.

The judge had the air of expecting an objection, but none came. "Is Mr. Roman an unavailable witness, then?" she said to all of us. If he were, his deposition would be admissible under the hearsay exception for former testimony, and I suppose that's what she was thinking. I was relying on a different hearsay exception—the one for admissions by the agent of a party— and I think the defense lawyers must have realized this, and that's why they didn't object. It was beyond argument that Dashiell Roman, president and CEO, was an agent of the two defendants, his companies. But even as I started to rise and explain this, it occurred to me that I would be interested to know how his lawyers would answer the judge's question, so I sat down again.

They exchanged looks, and then Paco Morales stood up. "We do not expect Mr. Roman to be attending any of this trial," he said slowly. "He is suffering from end-stage cancer, and his doctor has forbidden him to travel." The nurse, juror number four, looked up sharply at this. "We do not object to the use of his deposition," Paco continued, "although we renew our request that the available videotape version, instead of the transcript, be used."

"I have ruled on that already, have I not?" said the judge, paging through the case file.

"Yes, Your Honor," I said, and pulled my copy of her order out to give to Carolyn.

"Ah, yes, here it is," she said. "Very well, then, Mr. Morales, your request is denied. In the absence of other objection, Ms. Hayes may read to the jury from the deposition transcript."

I didn't want to read the whole thing, of course. That would have been stupefying, and unnecessary. I read them the part I was interested in, leaving out the objections and arguments of the lawyers. It was short, so I thought it bore reading slowly, with particular emphasis.

*MS. HAYES: Sorry. Let me put it this way. You have no awareness, do you, of the current state of research about your industry?*

*THE WITNESS: The hell I don't. I read everything I can get my hands on. I know as much as anybody.*

*MS. HAYES: You mean about the film industry, don't you?*

*THE WITNESS: Yeah.*

*MS. HAYES: But what about the place of your own particular work in the industry? I mean pornography. Isn't that a fair description of your work?*

*THE WITNESS: Porn, yeah, some call it that. I don't mind that.*

*MS. HAYES: But you don't read the stuff, the current research, what have you, about porn, do you? Or don't you remember?*

*THE WITNESS: I read it all. I remember it just fine. I know what's going on in my industry.*

*MS. HAYES: You're not claiming to be familiar with the work of, say, Dr. Bradley Detweiler, are you?*

"Here," I said sweetly, "were some comments back and forth by the lawyers, which I will spare the jurors." And then I continued.

*THE WITNESS: Shut up, all of you. I'm not the hick you think I am, Miss. I read it, and I remember it.*

*MS. HAYES: Recently, I imagine, after your lawyers suggested you read Dr. Detweiler's work?*

*THE WITNESS: Long before that. I read all of that stuff.*

I smiled at the jurors, trying to take them all in. "Thank you," I said, "for your attention."

"Next witness."

"Call Dr. Bradley Detweiler, Your Honor."

He was short and round and had a midwestern accent so flat it made your teeth ache, but he was good. I had not been able to prepare him in person, as he had just arrived back in the country from Austria, but we had rehearsed by telephone. I could tell after the first few minutes that he was a professional every bit as confident as Detective James Fox. It took nearly ten minutes just to work through his degrees and honorary degrees and faculty appointments and research prizes, but I didn't notice the jurors becoming tired of it. After all, this was the man whose work the mysterious and absent Dashiell Roman had read all of.

He then described the careful, ingenious experiments he had conducted over more than a decade to try to tease out the effects of violence and explicit sexuality on those exposed to materials with those ingredients. By lunchtime we had established that his research suggested a link between exposure to violent pornography and various bad consequences: desensitization to violence; aggression, especially toward women; indifference to the suffering of others, especially victims of sexual assault; a tendency to think that women invent complaints about sexual aggression; and the admission that one would, oneself, commit rape if there was no possibility of detection or punishment. During the lunch break I sent Peggy off to eat with Sierra, and spent the hour with Detweiler in the attorneys' lounge, trying to prepare him for cross-examination. I knew Everett would be doing it, and I thought it might be rough, but Detweiler didn't seem concerned.

After lunch, the jury back in their chairs, I asked him if he had seen a videotape called *Sunshade Snuffdown.* Yes, he said, he had watched it at my request. Did it contain any elements that he, based on his work, thought likely to have any of the effects he had described? Yes, it did.

"What were the elements of the film that seemed dangerous in this way, Doctor?" I asked him.

"The circumstance that the child is depicted in a way that blurs childish curiosity with adult sexuality," he replied, as though counting. "The use of an explicit but nonviolent sexual encounter to arouse the viewer, followed by the immediate transition to a sexual situation involving the child. The portrayal of the child as a willing participant in the earlier minutes of the encounter, and the very evident sexual release afforded the male perpetrator by the most violent and grotesque acts. And, I would say, most of all the circumstance that the eighteen minutes of tape is repeated seven times on a single cassette, as though designed to encourage repetitive viewing."

"What is the particular significance of that last feature, Dr. Detweiler?"

"I think it likely to encourage the belief, at the subliminal level, that the child actually survived this murderous violence and mutilation, as though it were simply a game she participated in, as though the protests and screams and whimpers that were so exciting a few minutes before could now be understood as a mere pretense, a charade or a deception on the child's part. As though she were not a victim at all, but a tease." He hesitated for a breath, then added, "I think it quite the most diabolical thing I have ever seen." We had not rehearsed that last comment, and I tried not to wince at it. I knew what Everett would do with it.

"Thank you, Dr. Detweiler," I said. "Your witness."

Everett went to work just as I had expected. *"Diabolical,"* he said. "That's quite a word, Doctor. Is that a word that has some technical meaning in your profession?"

"No," Detweiler said shortly. I think he had come to realize his mistake.

"It means of or pertaining to the devil, if I am not mistaken," said Everett smoothly. "Is that right?"

"I believe so," Detweiler muttered.

"So, does the devil figure in your ideas about pornography and evil, Doctor?"

In my desperation I remembered a provision of the evidence rules, and rose to object. "Your Honor," I said. "Rule six-ten provides that evidence of the religious beliefs or opinions of a witness may not be employed to impair the credibility of the witness."

Meiklejohn gave a me a look over her reading glasses. "The witness mentioned this notion of the devil first," she said. "I believe this is proper cross-examination. Please answer the question, Doctor."

"I was using the term colloquially, Mr. Everett," he said stiffly. "The devil does not figure in my work."

"By colloquially, you meant merely that you found this particular work of art to be evil, did you not, Doctor?"

"Leaving aside whether I would characterize it as art, Mr. Everett, I do not in my work think in terms of good or evil. Only likely consequences."

"But you used the word, Doctor, didn't you? Isn't it true that this particular work that we are discussing offends you in some very profound moral way?"

The little man was silent for a brief moment. "In truth I think I would have to agree that it does. But that has had no effect on my conclusions."

"Come, Doctor," said Everett. "Isn't observer bias one of the most elementary premises of psychology?"

"I suppose so."

"But you think you're immune to it?"

"I only believe that I can do my best to guard against it."

"Your best."

"Yes."

"But many other researchers have disagreed with your conclusions, have they not?"

"Some have."

"Some have criticized your methods as well, haven't they?"

"Yes. This is a controversial field, and there is not a great deal of agreement."

Everett let that hang in the air for a moment before moving on.

"None of your research focuses on the effect of violent sexually oriented material on the mentally ill, does it?"

"No. The subjects in most of my experiments have been college students. There is a screening process as well, and any subject who showed signs of psychosis would be eliminated from the experiment."

"So you can't really tell us anything at all about how a mentally ill person, not a college student, might react to the film *Sunshade Snuffdown*."

Silence. I took advantage of it to rise. "Your Honor, Mr. Everett is making speeches, not conducting a cross-examination. I didn't hear a question there."

"Can you, Doctor?" said Everett, before Meiklejohn could say anything.

"One can only extrapolate," said Dr. Detweiler. I stole a quick look at the jury. I don't think many of them were impressed by the verb. I don't think some of them knew what it meant.

"Doctor, your research has not investigated the effect of a repetitive presentation of material, isn't that true?"

"It is true, although after this case I hope to get funding to investigate this question. I have designed an experiment—"

"Thank you, Doctor. But until you have investigated this question, your comments about the repetitive presentation merely represent your hunch or guess about the effect of such a presentation, isn't that so?"

"An educated guess, Mr. Everett," replied Detweiler.

It was pretty weak, but what else could he say? Then Everett took one last tack.

"Isn't it true, Doctor, that in your book *Pornography and Its Effect on the Viewer*, you say that you don't believe that the legal regulation of pornography is likely to do any good?"

"Yes, it is true."

"You argue that the best remedy for the harm of violent pornography is to educate those who may come into contact with it, don't you?"

"Yes."

"No further questions."

I did what I could on redirect, and on the whole I think Detweiler did us some good, but it wasn't as clean as you'd hope for. Apart from the devil business, the most damaging aspect of Everett's cross had been his point about the lack of data on mentally ill subjects. Andy Kahrlsrud was going to have his work cut out for him.

The thought of Andy sent my thoughts on a brief worried detour. He should be on his way back right now, I calculated. He'd gone to Illinois yesterday, to Elgin. He thought it important to talk with the Wolf about this trip to Colorado, to try to calm him down and reassure him that he would be there at the other end, when the Wolf was unloaded from the sheriff's caravan at the Boulder County Jail, where he was scheduled to arrive tomorrow evening. My plan was to put Andy on the stand first thing tomorrow, then Peggy, and then, if Andy still thought it advisable, to call the Wolf himself. Apart from a few remaining stipulations and transcripts, that was our case.

I wrenched my attention back to the present, noted the jurors watching me expectantly. "Now, Your Honor," I said, " I would like to read the jurors another portion of the deposition of Mr. Dashiell Roman."

"Your Honor," said Paco Morales, looking theatrically aggrieved. "Ms. Hayes has already had a chance to read from this deposition. It's not right for her to chop it up into little bits, out of context, and feed it to the court one spoonful at a time."

"I've tried to place these portions so they make a coherent case alongside the remainder of our evidence," I said. "I think that's proper. If there are some parts I left out that Mr. Morales wants to read, he can do that."

"Go ahead, Ms. Hayes." The judge was starting to look tired, or maybe she was thinking of the TRO hearing in another case that she'd had to schedule for three o'clock. The clock said two-forty. We'd get a break soon, but she might be here for hours still.

"Thank you, Your Honor," I said, and then read the jurors one more piece of Dashiell Roman's deposition, hoping they would see the importance of it now.

MS. HAYES: *Whose idea was it, Mr. Roman, for the eighteen minutes of filmed material in* Sunshade Snuffdown *to be repeated several times on the videotaped version?*

THE WITNESS: *That was mine. We started to do that with some of our productions. They were short, you know, some of them, and it didn't cost hardly any more to put them on the cassette several times than just once. Gives the customer more value, so to speak.*

MS. HAYES: *So a customer could watch the film over and over without having to rewind the tape?*

THE WITNESS: *Yeah, that was the idea. I was the first to have it, but now lots of the distributors are doing it.*

I looked at the jury quickly as I walked back to the counsel table from the podium. Juror number six, the retired teacher, was nodding his head sagely. He got it. I hoped he'd have a chance to emphasize its importance to the other jurors, when the time came.

Meiklejohn admonished the jurors about not watching television or reading about the case in the newspapers or talking to anyone, and then let us go for the day. I walked Peggy to Sierra's office and then left the building myself. The news crews were sparser than ever, their attention having been diluted by a capital murder trial in Denver, and I was able to wave them off without much difficulty. I walked to my car thinking about the remainder of the trial: Andy, then Peggy, then Leonard Fitzgerald. Then the defense case. Then closing statements. I knew the defendants had lined up a couple of experimental psychologists, rivals of Detweiler's, who would discount his results and attack his methods. Probably they would claim there was no scientific evidence that exposure to violent sexual material has any effect on behavior. Apart from their First Amendment defense, this was the part of their case in which they had the most invested. I had some reading to do before I was ready to take on their experts. Still, I felt calm, thought things were going as well as we could have hoped. I should have recognized this particular calm for what it was, or rather for what it preceded.

Beverly and Tory were both in the office when I arrived there a little after three. Tory danced out of her office and hugged me, again. Twice in two days. "How's it going?" she asked, but before I could answer, Beverly handed me a couple of pink telephone message slips.

"Don't forget it's an hour earlier out there," said Beverly. The top slip contained only the word "Linc" and an area code 818 telephone number.

"Linc called?" I said to her.

"He's in California," she said.

"And Andy? Where's he, for Christ's sake?"

"Still in Chicago," she said. "Maybe you better call him first. It's an hour later there, of course. And Bob Tucker, that friend of Linc's who calls himself BioTech? He said I should get your phone from you and he'll take a look at it." She held out her hand.

I shuffled pens and coins and keys aside to pull the silver phone out of my purse and pass it to her. "Get me Andy," I said. I guess it came off a little like Jason Robards in *All the President's Men*.

"Sheesh," said Beverly, and it was true I didn't ordinarily use that peremptory tone, but a lawyer in trial is entitled to be cut a little slack in the deportment department, I figured. I went into my office and slammed the door. Fuck! I hated being a trial lawyer! Why couldn't things just happen like they were supposed to!

The phone buzzed and I grabbed it irritably, just like I hadn't asked Beverly to connect me to Andy. "Okay, put him on," I said.

"It's not him, exactly," she said. "It's that lawyer in Chicago, John Scarface or whatever his name is. He says Andy's there, but not there right this minute, or something."

"Beverly, what the fuck are you saying?" It was out of my mouth before I could stop it. I'd forgotten for a second how it offended Beverly when I took the name of sexual intercourse in vain.

"*You* talk to him then," she said, and she was gone, another item for my list of eventual apologies. And then there was another voice.

"Cinda? It's John Scarpelli. Listen, Dr. Kahrlsrud is here, he's just gone down the hall for a moment. He'll be right back."

"What's he doing in your office?" I said. If I had made a list of people I didn't want to talk with that day, John Scarpelli would have been very

high on it. I hadn't spoken to Scarpelli since the day he'd done his Hannibal
Lecter number on me. Andy had accomplished all of the negotiations with
him about transporting Leonard Fitzgerald, and John had secured the necessary court orders and administrative permissions. All I'd had to do was
send a few faxes, which was as close as I wanted to get to any intimate
communication with the guy.

"I'm going to let him tell you," he said. "He'll be here in a minute or
two, I'm sure."

"Fine." But the silence grew uncomfortable very rapidly. "So how are
you?" I said grudgingly.

"Good," he said. "Much better. Andy Kahrlsrud is a very amazing guy,
Cinda. I've—listen, I'm sorry for that last conversation we had. I was strung
out, you know? It's been really good for me to talk to him. How are you?
How's your trial going?"

"I don't know," I said. "I need Andy to be here, and Leonard Fitzgerald."

"Well, here's your guy," said Scarpelli, sounding relieved. "Good luck,
Cinda."

Andy's voice was as reassuring as ever, but his news wasn't. Leonard
Fitzgerald was in Chicago General Hospital recovering from three serious
stab wounds. Andy had just returned from visiting him.

"Who did it?" I said.

"Don't be paranoid. It doesn't have anything to do with your case,
Cinda. Another inmate who's had a hard-on for Fitzgerald for a long time
got to him in the shower. Thought he'd be a hero, taking out a short eyes."

"What's that?"

"It's what they call a child molester. Listen, Fitzgerald's going to live,
but he can't be moved now. Maybe in a month or so. You'd better ask that
judge to continue your trial."

"No, Andy, I can't do that. She'd either turn me down or declare a
mistrial, and we'd have to start all over. We're doing too well for that, not
perfect, but as well as we ever could, and I like this jury. We'll have to go
on, and you'll have to make the jurors understand the Wolf. Get on the
next plane back here, okay? I need you."

"I'll do what I can. I already missed the flight I was supposed to be
on."

"No shit, Sherlock," I said. Meaner and ruder by the minute, that was
me. I can only plead in mitigation that I felt the ground loosening beneath

my feet, an avalanche of bad luck beginning to stir and shift. "Get here, and call me when you do, even if it's the middle of the night."

I started to open the door and yell out to Beverly, demanding that she get Linc on the phone, but I thought better of it and dialed the 818 number myself. A soft voice, young and female, answered.

"May I speak to Lincoln Tolkien?" I asked the voice.

"Just a minute," it answered, and then I heard her calling Linc, still softly.

"Wassup, Cinda?" said Linc.

"I'm asking you," I said testily. "I understand you called. As you know, I'm in trial. Is there something important we need to talk about?"

"Stressing, aren't you?" he said sympathetically. "I don't know if this is going to make things easier or harder, but it's something you need to know. I'm going to let Chris tell you."

"Chris? Who's that?"

"You've met him before, Cinda," And of course I had. Linc was gone but I recognized the other voice as soon as I heard it.

"You remember me?" he said, and I did. Chris of the Universal Modeling Agency and Humphrey Yogart. I remembered that I had once asked Linc to try to find him, but that had been months ago. I was tired and my thinking wouldn't stay on track, kept curling off into useless spirals.

"Of course I do, Chris, but I'm very busy just now. Was there something you wanted to tell me?"

"Yeah," he said. "Linc tells me I should. And he's been looking after my wife and baby while I was off getting fucked up and fucked over, so I owe him."

"Was that your wife, then?" I said. I didn't remember that he was married.

"She's going to be soon. My son needs a father, you know?"

"Well, what is it, Chris?"

After we talked, I asked him to put Lincoln back on the line. "Are you sure this is right?" I asked him.

"Hold on," he said, and I could hear him explaining something, then the muffled percussion of a door closing. "Didn't want them to hear. Yeah, it's true. I've held onto Joel Derringer's number, talk to him every once in a while, you know. Just in case. After Chris told me about this today, I called him. He was just sober enough to remember, and just drunk enough to tell me. It's true, all right. True enough for them to put Chris on their payroll for the last year and a half. He showed me his pay slips."

"Rose Brothers paid him all this time?"

"Yeah, but he never went to their studio, in fact he was instructed never to go near it. He just did what Norm Lagrange told him to do, mainly act in a lot of phony porn movies that were never released. I'd guess Lagrange was getting paid off, too, to keep him busy. I'm not even sure they had film in the camera. His main job was not being in touch with you."

"You mean, they did all this to keep him from telling me about what happened?"

"Sure. He found out that after he talked to you, they followed you to the airport and drugged you to make sure you didn't have his telephone number."

"But I did have his telephone number! I called him after I got back to Boulder." Even as I said it, I remembered that I'd called him at the number he'd written on a crumpled napkin I'd found in my pocket. The paper on which I'd recorded it more carefully had been in my missing briefcase.

"I can't explain that," said Linc. "That's just what he heard, from some woman he met at that modeling agency place. She was the one who followed you, and put the stuff in your drink. That's how serious they were. Except it wasn't supposed to make you crash your car; you were supposed to nod off before you got to it. Guess you were tougher than they figured."

I remembered the woman, tall with a t-shirt that said something about jet skis. "Why did Chris decide to tell you these things?" I said to Linc. "I mean, why now?"

"He got pissed when he realized the movies he was acting in were never going to be released so he took off and came looking for his girl-friend, Shelley. He found her right away because she was still living in their old apartment. He didn't even know he had a son. And when he showed up, here I was."

I thought I heard a note of resignation in his voice. "Are you in love with this girl, Lincoln?"

"Doesn't matter, Cinda. She's in love with him. So that's what I thought you ought to know. I'm going to help Chris and Shelley move to another place—I'm not sure they're safe here, if someone comes looking. I'll be back in Boulder by the end of the week. See you then."

It certainly explained some things, and complicated others. I didn't think it changed any of the issues in the lawsuit, but I didn't trust my weary mental equipment to make this judgment, so I went looking for Tory. Linda was in her office with her, and the two of them were looking at something that lay on Tory's desk, a watery-looking black and white photograph of some sort. Tory's hand held Linda's loosely, and their expressions suggested that they had together discovered a long-lost Leonardo da Vinci masterpiece, but they looked up simultaneously, guiltily, as I rapped on the frame of the open door.

"Cinda!" said Tory, and the two of them burst into giggles. Tory flipped the photograph face-down and looked up at me with an expression of contrived innocence. Loneliness washed over me. I had not after all traveled very far from that third-grade classroom, and saw in Tory's the face of Celia as she clapped her hands and watched for my reaction. Willing to leave me out.

"Good night," I said, and closed the door to her office behind me.

Sam, I thought. Sam would know what this meant, what the right thing to do was. But even as I turned toward the phone I knew that I couldn't call him now, in frantic need, after neglecting our relationship for so long. Beverly had left, too, and I wondered what it was that had left me so friendless. It's the work, I told myself, it's your commitment to doing everything for your client. And I realized that, of course, I'd have to tell her what I had learned.

Peggy Grayling's address was on our client intake sheet, but I'd never been there. It was in a featureless neighborhood of identical townhouses in the Devil's Thumb area of southwest Boulder, and the numbers and lanes were confusing. For a moment, after the door opened in response to my knock, I thought I had made a mistake, but then I realized the woman looking out with a worried expression was Peggy's friend Sierra.

"Where is she?" I said, looking beyond Sierra into the dim living room.

"In the shower," she said, and stepped back to let me in. "I'm glad you're here, Ms. Hayes. I'm worried about her. She seems, I don't know. Agitated. Maybe it wouldn't be surprising in anyone else, but she's, like, the most together person I've ever known."

"It's a hard thing she's going through," I said. "But I appreciate your concern about her."

"I was going to make her some dinner, but I ought to get home to my kids," she confessed. "My daughter doesn't do her homework unless I stay on her. Anyway, you probably need to have some confidential talk with her."

I nodded. "Can she ride to the Justice Center with you again in the morning?"

"Oh, sure," the round-faced woman said. "Tell her I'll pick her up at the usual time." She gathered a few belongings and left, a nice woman trying to help a troubled friend, but one with a few worries of her own.

The hiss of the shower was audible, coming from somewhere in the back of the townhouse. I sat down in the living room–kitchen area on an austere sofa covered with beige fabric, no extra cushions, and thought about how little we know about each other. I had expected—what? Crimson wall-hangings, a Tibetan *thanka*, some evocative line drawings, something. Some evidence of a taste that I expected to be both bohemian and cultivated, or of her spiritual pursuits. This room might have been a furnished suite at a mid-priced short-term residential hotel. It contained almost nothing personal, except for a silver-framed photograph of Alison, an enlargement of one of the pictures I had seen before. No television, even. I thought of the enormous checks she'd been writing to cover the expenses of this trial, and wondered if she'd had to sell things to underwrite them. Did she spend her evenings sitting here, looking at her daughter's photograph? I couldn't believe that, decided she must have a television, as well as some books, back in her sleeping area, but I didn't investigate, inhibited by both fatigue and propriety.

She didn't seem surprised to see me when she emerged from the back of the house, wrapped in a blue terry cloth bathrobe. "Sierra gone?" she asked, not too interested.

I nodded. "I came by because I've just learned something we need to discuss," I said. "Two things, really."

She nodded as she dried her hair on a towel and drifted toward the kitchen area on the other side. "Tea? I have black and herb."

"No thanks." But I waited while she brewed a cup for herself then settled into the chair across from me.

"First," I told her, "Leonard Fitzgerald is not going to be appearing as a witness after all." I told her about the attack on him, his injuries, his inability to travel. "I was always uncertain whether using him was a good idea," I said. "Andy Kahrlsrud was more interested in it than I was. So I am not too concerned about this. Andy can testify, and tell the jurors exactly what Fitzgerald told him. I'm pretty sure we can even get the transcripts of his interviews with Fitzgerald into evidence, since they're part of the data Andy used to form his opinion."

I could see her growing restive during this lecture. "That's not the same!" she said emphatically. "Can't you ask the judge to postpone the trial for a few days until he's well enough to travel?"

"No. Andy says it will be at least a month, and by then the jurors will have forgotten what's come before. There's a logic to this case, and we need the momentum of that logic. Anyway, I doubt the judge would continue a trial for that long; she'd more likely declare a mistrial, and we'd have to start over again with a new jury. This is a good jury, Peggy. And this trial has been going pretty well for us, I think. We need to keep going."

"So we say that Roman is to blame for Alison's death, but he's not going to be here. Detective Fox says that the Wolf is the one to blame, but he's not going to be here either!" She was as close to weeping as I've ever seen her.

"I thought you believed the Wolf wasn't really responsible. Because of his illness," I said, reaching out to touch her on the knee.

"Somebody's responsible!" she burst out. "Somebody needs to *take responsibility!*" Her hands plucked clumsily at the loose fabric of her robe. "If we need to start all over with a new jury, then that's what I want to do!"

"We didn't sue Leonard Fitzgerald, Peggy, and Dashiell Roman doesn't have to be here for the jury to find against his companies," I said. "You know that, Peggy." She didn't respond, only began to twist the sash of her robe in her lap, her eyes downcast. Her fixation on forcing a live person to stand up in court and take blame, or have it ascribed to him, was not new and not surprising. Hadn't Tory told me long ago that this was what our clients wanted? But now I saw it threatening to unravel all that we had accomplished so far. "Let me tell you the other news," I offered. "It's very interesting."

"What are you telling me?" she asked after I finished recounting my conversation with Chris. "That we sued the wrong one?"

"No, not at all," I replied hastily. "DR Films really did make the film, and DR Distribution really did distribute it. That part's certain. But they lied to us about where it was made. It wasn't a Caribbean island, and it wasn't some rented house in the Valley. It was filmed at Rose Brothers Studios. Keeping that secret must have been the deal that Rose Brothers and the other studios made with Roman—they'd provide him with a defense as long as he lied about where the film was made, and admitted the rest so we wouldn't investigate any further. It doesn't change our case, I'm sure," I added. "I'm not sure it's even relevant to the trial. But I thought you should know."

"If it doesn't change the case, how come they took so much trouble to hide it?" she said.

"Think of the publicity," I said. "Remember how hard they tried to hide the stuff about the hotel in Denver that was showing pay-per-view hard-core pornography to its guests? It's the same thing. The big movie studios and the conglomerates that own them prefer for the public to think they have nothing to do with the sleazy world of hard-core pornography. It's worth a lot to them to conceal the truth."

"And how did this Chris know about it?"

"He was an unsuccessful actor who worked part-time as security for various porn film production companies. He was there the night *Sunshade Snuffdown* was filmed."

"At Rose Brothers Studios. The one your friend works for."

"That's right," I said. "They'd rented DR Films their back lot. They do that—rent their shooting space to other production companies. I doubt they knew what the film was about. They didn't care. It was purely a business deal to them. Even if we had known about this from the beginning, I don't think we could have made a case to include Rose Brothers as a defendant. Anyway, it's too late now. We need to go ahead and finish our case. And I may need to put you on the stand first thing tomorrow if Andy Kahrlsrud doesn't get here before nine. We haven't really had much opportunity to prepare for your testimony. Do you think you're ready?"

She sat for a moment, her hands finally still in her lap, as though once again enveloped by the peace in which she seemed to be wrapped during our first meetings. Then she nodded. "I'm ready," she said, and then, "How are we going to get the news out about where the film was made?"

"After the trial," I said promptly. "That's the best time. I'll call a press conference, I promise. But if we bring it up in front of the jury it's just going to muddy up the case. Remember, we didn't sue Rose Brothers. If some of the jurors start thinking that someone we didn't sue is really partly to blame, it could affect their willingness to bring in a big verdict against the DR defendants."

"And they would be right, wouldn't they? You can't put all of the blame on the ones we sued. Others played a role as well." But there was no hint of protest or quarrel in her question.

"Of course," I agreed, relieved that she seemed to have regained her calm. "I can't absolve Fitzgerald altogether, even though the other jury found him insane. His father, who mistreated him so terribly. The video stores that sell and rent violent pornography, because they keep the industry going. The people who buy it and watch it—the whole culture, really, Peggy. The law can't really deal with that kind of complexity in cause and effect, but sometimes blame needs to be assigned. We're oversimplifying it a little, that's all. Out of necessity."

"All right," she said, rising. "I'm ready to go on the stand tomorrow. Now I'd better get some sleep."

It was after ten when I got home, relieved but exhausted. The message light on my telephone was blinking, and the synthesized voice told me I had three messages. I dropped into my desk chair and pressed the playback code wearily, then turned on the monitor so I could listen without holding the receiver. My eyes were barely able to focus on the objects in the elliptical pool of light cast by my desk lamp.

"Hi, Ms. Hayes, this is Bob Tucker, BioTech, they call me. I'm a friend of Lincoln Tolkien's, and I have a cell phone of yours that your secretary brought me this afternoon to examine. There's—it's a perfectly ordinary cell phone, Ms. Hayes. Nothing unusual about it, no hidden transmitter or anything. I'll drop it back by your office tomorrow, but I thought you might want to have this news tonight."

"Cinda, this is Andy. Listen, the first flight I could get on leaves O'Hare at 6:30 in the morning, arrives DIA 7:20. United Flight 276. I'll catch a cab back to Boulder and go straight to the courthouse, but if my flight is delayed I may not be there by nine—you know how the traffic is coming into Boulder in the mornings. Sorry, but I thought you should know. If you have any other witnesses or evidence, I guess you better slide them in if I'm not there."

"Querida, I'm at the Boulderado, room 247. I know you're angry, and so am I. Please call me, no matter what time it is."

I have *nothing* to say to you, I said out loud to the indifferent telephone.

A chinook wind started blowing in the night, its warm breath melting the remaining snowdrifts even as it lashed at every structure in its path and tore thousands out of their sleep, including me. Despite my fatigue I lay awake from five o'clock until I arose at six, my eyes inflamed and grainy, my nerves sandpapered. I couldn't seem to get the water in my shower to the right temperature, and I shivered and flinched alternately through a hasty ablution. The only pantyhose I could find had a small run beginning at the heel; I could only hope it would not crawl up my calf in the course of the day. The milk in my fridge had gone sour, separating into small bitter spherical particles as I poured it into my coffee. And United Airlines, or the synthesized voice that answered their telephone, informed me that Andy's flight would be a half hour late arriving at Denver International Airport.

Court was to convene at nine, but it was only 8:30 when I went to the Traffic Division to see if Peggy had arrived with Sierra. I found Sierra at her desk, tapping efficiently at a computer.

"Oh, Ms. Hayes," she said. 'Peggy just went to the restroom."

"You're a good friend, Sierra. Peggy's lucky to have you."

She smiled, her small eyes closing even further as she did. "She might be looking for you in the courtroom," she said.

"Thanks, Sierra."

I walked up the stairs to the second floor, noting as I had outside that the news presence seemed to be up again today. I slipped inside the door, to encounter a small knot of people standing and chatting there, making entrance difficult. Looking around, I noticed Brianna Bainbridge standing in the back next to Mindy Cookson. They waved, and I started to move in their direction but then saw, on the far side of the spectator section, Rafe talking with Peggy. Furious, I crossed the courtroom toward them.

"What the hell do you think you're doing, Mr. Russell?" I said. "I warned you about this. You think I won't file a grievance against you for talking to a party you know to be represented by counsel?"

He looked back at me steadily. "She initiated the conversation, *Ms.* Hayes," he said. His face looked as worn as mine felt, and he had a small abrasion on his chin that suggested his morning shave hadn't gone well. I looked at Peggy for confirmation but she ignored me, intent on her own purpose.

"If your studio isn't ashamed of its work, why are you lurking back here like some kind of voyeur?" she said. "I haven't seen you sitting up there with the other lawyers, not once."

"Come on, Peggy," I said, but then Rafe was speaking.

"I'm ashamed of some things," he said quietly, looking to be sure I had heard him. "There are some things I only learned of recently."

"But others in your company knew about them all along. They had to!" said Peggy, her eyes flashing.

"That's true," said Rafe softly.

"And you're still their lawyer."

"Also true."

"Then why don't you take responsibility for what they did, instead of acting like you're too high and mighty to acknowledge that you have anything to do with the poison that killed my daughter?"

He looked at me again. "That's a fair criticism," he said.

She stood there for a full half minute in silence, looking at him, while other lawyers and journalists and onlookers flowed by, jostling all three of us in their haste to get to their seats. He broke their gaze first, turning to walk toward the defense table, where Paco Morales and Dan Everett were already arranging pens and books and legal pads. Rafe put a hand on Everett's shoulder and spoke into his ear. Everett seemed surprised, but after looking around the room, he turned back to Rafe and nodded, and Rafe pulled out the third chair at the table and sat in it. He stared resolutely forward.

"Peggy," I said. "You're going to have to take the stand as soon as we begin. Andy's plane was delayed."

She took a step and turned toward me, a lovely small woman in a tailored blue pantsuit, light on her feet and serene in her expression.

"I'm ready," she said, and then Carolyn appeared and said her *oyes* and another day of court had begun.

"Margaret Quinn Grayling" were the first words she said, after assenting to the oath, and from then forward the jurors could not take their eyes off

335

her. We had not prepared this as well as I would have liked, but she was extraordinary, her recent distraught state replaced by the tranquil composure I remembered. Guided only by my hasty and ill-composed questions, she told them about Alison, identified one of her photographs without hesitation, described their home in Oak Park, the school they'd chosen for its safety, Alison's failure to come home that day, the frantic telephone calls, the terrible discoveries, the funeral. Then the trial of Leonard Fitzgerald, the verdict, her inability to see the tape that so many said had influenced Fitzgerald in his grotesque acts. There was more than a little hearsay and other objectionable material mixed into her testimony, since I had not had time to prepare her or my own questions to avoid it. But Everett and Morales and, to one side of them, Rafe watched her from the defense table without moving or speaking, seemingly as spellbound as the jury.

We were almost done when I heard the courtroom door open. I turned around quickly, to see Andy slip into the courtroom, his khaki pants rumpled like an accordion, his blue blazer straining across his broad back.

"Your Honor," I said. "I see one of my witnesses has entered the courtroom. Since The Rule has been invoked—"

Everett was on his feet. "We will waive The Rule as it pertains to Dr. Kahrlsrud, Your Honor." I nodded my thanks and turned back to Peggy. She was rummaging in her oversized purse, as though for a tissue, but she looked up as I spoke her name.

"Mrs. Grayling," I said, "will you tell the court and jury why you decided to bring a lawsuit against the defendants in this case?"

"Yes," she said firmly. "Because I was raised to believe in responsibility, and in my own right and responsibility to protect my family. Because someone has to stand up before the law and acknowledge that he bears some of the blame for what happened to my daughter." At this she reached down into the bag again, and I thought in amazement: how strange. How curious that it would be here, and not at any earlier point, that she would begin to cry. But it was not a tissue that she brought out in her hand.

When I saw the gun I started to move toward her, slowly, thinking absurdly of the rule drilled into me in law school: never approach a witness without the permission of the court. She's finally broken, I thought—it's finally become real to her that no matter how it ends, this trial is not going to bring her daughter back. And without anything to look forward to, she's yielded to despair. But I felt sure I could talk her out of taking her life in this place.

"Oh, Peggy," I started. "Please don't give up now. What we're doing here means a lot, to a lot of people." I held my hand out toward her. "Give it to me, okay?"

I had no idea what the judge was doing, or thinking, nor did I know how the jurors were reacting to this surreal scene. It seemed important for me to keep my gaze locked on Peggy's. But as I drew closer I saw that she was not looking at me, but beyond. Toward the defense table.

As I watched, she rose from her chair behind the witness stand and stood. She aimed the gun with both hands, her legs braced in a stance that suggested practice, hours at the firing range. I looked behind quickly, but even before my eyes confirmed it, I knew. She did not plan to turn the gun on herself. It was aimed at Rafe.

Did the judge have a panic button or alarm that she could activate in these situations? I had no idea. There was no sound, but perhaps it was a silent alarm. Perhaps sheriff's deputies were on their way, would arrive in moments, would know how to disarm a small determined distraught woman.

Keep her talking, I thought to myself, and then: Andy would know what to do. But he was behind the bar, it might as well have been miles away. I dared not even look away from her to see whether he was sitting or standing.

"Mrs. Grayling," I said, trying to think of what Andy might say, "how do you feel about your daughter's death?"

"That," she said levelly, "is a very stupid question."

"Of course," I said, my head so light and my feet so leaden that I was not sure I could move again, but I did, a little to the side. "But the jurors here need to hear your answer. In words, Mrs. Grayling. In words, for the record. For everyone to read and hear, for as long as words mean anything." I was edging out from behind the podium, between her and Rafe. My notes were in my hand, and they did not flutter. Tremors thrilled through my knees, but my hands were mysteriously steady, although not as steady as hers.

"For the record," I said. "Please explain to everyone here—there are a lot of people here, Mrs. Grayling, from television and newspapers and even from other countries. They need to understand what you're thinking, why you feel so strongly you would bring a gun to this room with you. Why you think someone here would deserve to die. Don't make them wonder, Peggy. Don't leave *me* in the dark. Tell us."

"Move, Cinda," she said. "Don't you think I know what you're up to? Why do you protect him? If you stand between me and him I'll shoot you, too, I swear."

"Mr. Russell," I said. "You're angry at him." I could hear scraping and stirring behind me, imagined the spectators easing themselves to the floor, or sidling toward the door. *Keep talking*, I thought, but now she was speaking.

"You think," she said scornfully, "that it's some kind of excuse that it's a matter of *principle* to him. That's *worse!* He's not the only one, but he's a perfect example of them."

"Example of what?" I started to say, but then I heard his voice behind me. Behind me and far to the side—he'd moved.

"Mrs. Grayling," he said. "Take it out on me. Ms. Hayes never did anything but try to help you."

My memories of the next moments are jangled and unreliable, as I suppose is common in such cases. There was the sharp report of the gun, and the odd way she held it at her side after, stiff-armed, pointing toward the floor. After that, the film jerks and flips when it rolls again in my mind. Looking at the bench, seeing that Judge Meiklejohn is gone, and that uniformed persons are pouring into the courtroom through the entrance behind her empty chair. A deputy taking the firearm away from Peggy, her unresisting surrender of it. The terrified faces of the jurors I can see, about four of them. The backs of several others, who are crouched on the floor of the jury box.

Do I see Rafe before or after those things? Wouldn't I turn to him first? I replay it endlessly, but I can't be sure. I know he was still on his feet when I first looked, propped against the courtroom wall between the jury box and the bar. Between the last time I'd seen him and the gunshot, he'd left the defense table and moved farther into the room, away from the door. His handsome face bore a look of mild surprise while the bloody flower blossomed across the front of his gray suit. He folded slowly, his back sliding down the wall, his body tilting to the side only at the last moment.

I pushed someone out of the way and reached toward him, I don't know why. Perhaps I believed that I could pull him back from the place he had gone, but of course I could not. Nobody, not even the paramedics who arrived minutes later, could do that.

Did I say anything? "Rafe," was probably all. Nothing eloquent. I put my hand lightly on his chest before I was pulled away.

"Don't touch him," someone said.

Later, I put my bloody hand to my mouth and tasted him for the last time.

There's always a denouement, isn't there? Although sometimes it isn't easy to get to it, to pass through the barrier, transparent but ever so strong, that endeavors to imprison you in that last frozen moment. Andy assures me that it is always a struggle over time, not an instant's shattering, no matter how much you might wish for one.

It wasn't the first death I'd ever witnessed. I had seen killing before and surrendered pieces of my heart to be burned or buried with the dead, but Judge Meiklejohn's courtroom, that chilly well-lit cabin of disrupted order, is the place that I cannot seem to leave behind me. It's cloudy in waking memory but when it comes to me in sleep it's too clear, everything sharp and unmistakable in the bright radiance of the courtroom's overhead lights. It's the scene from which I awaken in the middle of the night shivering with the sobs I did not allow then.

We won the case, eventually—I suppose *won* is the right word. I suppose *we* is the right word. Of course there was a continuance, of ten days, during which Peggy was kept in the Boulder County Jail and the jury admonished not to speak with anyone about the case or what had happened until the court had made a decision about how to proceed. What that must have been like for the atmospheric scientist, the massage therapist, the retired geography teacher, the motorcycle mechanic, the nurse, the mother and part-time software writer, the musician, and the postal carrier, I cannot imagine. I barely remember what it was like for me.

The media, of course, went berserk. The press encampment in the parking lot of the Justice Center erupted to the size it had been during the last days of the JonBenet Ramsey grand jury. I think none of my friends or acquaintances escaped the phone calls and cameras, the microphone thrust into the face for comment. Three days after the shooting, a correspondent for Fox Network walked right into our office one evening about nine, seeing a light under the door and thinking he might find me in. I was nowhere near—Tory and Linda had taken me to stay at their house for a few days—but he scared the shit out of Tamara, who thought him a burglar or worse and threw a stapler at him, inflicting a black eye that gave him an unusually rakish appearance on camera for a few days.

The media attention made everything more difficult, I suppose. Linc, back from California, drove me everywhere for a time and did a little blocking and shoving when necessary. I was grateful, but relatively indifferent to the media entourage—at least to the best of my memory, which is not all that good for that period. I was more afraid of my own thoughts, and the pictures that would start to flicker behind my eyes whenever I closed them. Post-traumatic stress reaction was Andy's diagnosis. I wasn't the only one suffering; I heard that several of the jurors had accepted counseling from the police department's victim and witness advocacy program.

"How long had you been planning this?" Those were my first words, after I was seated across from her in the jail's visiting area. I couldn't think of any others.

"Forever," she said, smiling.

"How do you reconcile what you did with your Buddhist beliefs?"

"I'm not a Buddhist," she said. "I told you what I was once, but you weren't paying attention."

"What's that?"

"A gifted impersonator." She smiled and I remembered her telling me, the day we'd walked on the Mesa Trail together.

"Then—what brought you to Boulder? You told me it was the Buddhist community here."

She laughed, a tinkling silvery sound that managed to be ugly. "For you, Cinda. Didn't you figure that out? I needed a lawyer who was willing to take on a hopeless case so I could find the one who killed my daughter. Celia told me that even when you were little, you liked hopeless causes. She told me how you wanted to take on the world after the Kennedy assassination, and I knew you and I could bond around that."

She then lifted her springy hair and released it to cascade over the collar of the blue jail jumpsuit, before leaning forward confidingly. "I hope you know I would never have shot you. I'm very grateful to you. It was you who gave me the idea, actually."

"*I* did? What are you talking about?"

"You know, actually shooting someone in a courthouse."

"You really are nuts, Peggy," I said. "I never had any such idea, and never would."

"Oh, we talked about it," she said airily. "You know, Oswald. Jack Ruby. The courthouse." She raised her hand, cocked her thumb, and made the gesture. "At first I just wanted to know who'd made that tape, and to sue him. But after you mentioned the Oswald shooting I couldn't stop thinking about it. Before long I knew that was what I wanted. Remember when you told me we could file the case in federal court if we wanted?" She laughed softly. "Like I'd want the trial in a place with that kind of security. Here in Boulder I knew that all I needed was a friend who could get me into the courthouse without having to go through the front door. So I found one."

"Oh my God. Sierra didn't know about this?"

"Of course not." She paused, twirling a ringlet around the same finger that had pulled the trigger. "Roman was the one I wanted, but you just wouldn't do what I asked, make him be there. And then it looked like the Wolf would be there, and I thought, all right, he's another one. Time he took responsibility. But then he didn't come either."

I tried to think about this, but my thoughts kept slinking away like whipped dogs.

"Why Rafe? Why not one of the other lawyers, Roman's lawyer, even? Surely Rose Brothers' responsibility, whatever it was, couldn't—"

"That Morales," she said with scorn. "He was just a hired gun, brought in for the occasion. You told me so yourself. But your friend—he believed in what he was doing. A matter of principle, you said it was." She tilted her head one way, then the other, radiant and quietly victorious, like one who's climbed a difficult peak and returned satisfied. "Now, what about the rest of our trial?"

"You're not serious, of course."

"Quite serious. I'm going to need the money to pay a criminal lawyer. Brianna Bainbridge was here yesterday. She thinks I'll have some excellent arguments in my criminal case."

"Excellent arguments," I repeated stupidly. God, I was tired of those.

"She also tells me there's no reason our trial can't go on, if the other side agrees," said Peggy. "Why don't you ask them?"

"You're kidding. Are you kidding?"

She shook her head. "I believe it's my decision, isn't it? As your client?"

Rafe was to be buried on his parents' ranch outside of Lubbock, but there was a memorial service in Los Angeles. It was a Saturday, before the trial was to resume on Monday, and I had every reason not to go, but I was there. I needed to visit L.A. for another reason, anyway.

I found Chris and Shelley that morning at the address Linc had given me, a small place in Venice a few blocks from the beach. The label on their mailbox said *Jacob and Nancy Boldt.* I sat in their tiny living room and sipped a Coke, watching the filmy curtains flutter in the damp salty breeze and their baby, Mac, stagger around the room chortling at some baby joke that he had not told us.

"It wasn't Rafe at all," said Chris. "It was Lagrange. After Norm found out I'd been talking to you outside the agency that day, he had some guy and Sally tail you to the airport. Then they got Sally—I don't know her last name—on the same flight as you, only it was canceled or something, wasn't it? So she had to follow you onto the next plane, all huffing and puffing, the way she told it. She almost didn't make it. Man, she bitched about it for months."

"What was the point, though? Did they think there was a copy of the videotape in my bag?"

He shook his head. "I guess they were thinking for a short time of trying to round up all the tapes and destroy them. They even sent someone to Chicago at some point, but they figured out pretty fast there were too many copies around to hope to get rid of all of them. Nah, it wasn't about that; it was because you had my phone number. I'd told them that. I guess they didn't trust me not to talk if you called. Then when I told them you'd called me anyway they made me change my number."

"All that to keep me from talking to you again?"

"Well, I guess it was supposed to be a lot easier than it was. It was just meant to be a bag-snatch at the airport, you get woozy, she helps you to a seat, leaves her bag and takes off with yours, that sort of thing. But you get into your car, like the roofies didn't even affect you, and off you go! She had to hot-wire a car out of the airport garage just to follow you, and scarf your luggage after you drove off the road." He made a truck noise for the amusement of Mac, who tried to imitate it.

"So whose idea was it, someone at Rose Brothers, or Norm LaGrange?"

"It's the same deal, Cinda. Norm is connected to the chief of security at Rose, you know? He does them a lot of favors, and they used to let his friends use their soundstages and shit. He's the one who got me the job doing security on Rose's back lot during guest shoots."

"When they were shooting *Sunshade Snuffdown*," I said.

"I didn't know what it was called," he said. "Anyway, even if I had, you never told me that's what you were looking for. I didn't realize I knew anything about your case—you never told me enough about what you were up to. But they knew. It was the first time they ever treated me like I was important, you know?" His face was full of rue, but pleasure replaced it as Mac tugged on his knee.

"Chris," I said, "did they really kill that little girl?"

He looked up reluctantly. "I don't know," he said. "It was only the outdoor scenes they filmed at Rose. I remember watching her leave—they were taking her to a car. They must have filmed the second half back at their own studios." He started to say something else but then fell silent, his eyes again on his son. It was a minute before he spoke. "I didn't know what was going to happen in that film, Cinda. You have to believe that." I did, and forgave him for his lack of curiosity. I remembered that it had never been one of his strong points.

I thanked him and rose to leave, detouring on the way out to place my empty glass into the sink of the miniature kitchen. Shelley had gone to the grocery store, but she'd be back soon, with diapers and peanut butter and maybe a bottle of wine—you could buy that in grocery stores in California, couldn't you?

Loneliness squeezed my throat closed, and I couldn't reply when Chris called out goodbye, just closed the screen door quietly behind me. I fumbled for my sunglasses before crossing the street to the taxi. The driver was leaning against his fender, smoking a cigarette. He cast it aside and opened the door for me, pretending he hadn't seen my face.

The memorial service was at a big church; I can't even remember what kind. There were lots of faces I recognized—you'd know the names if I said them—but it wasn't the Academy Awards. The studio must have supplied the security; the press was kept well away. It was quiet and sad, and sometimes funny, when people who'd worked with Rafe told their stories about him. I knew things that nobody spoke of: Rasta Bones and habeas caffeinus exigus and illegitimati non carborundum, and his ramshackle cabin in Onion Canyon and the way he'd told me he didn't know where home was any more. But I didn't say anything. A few people smiled vaguely or kindly, but I kept on my sunglasses and was grateful that as far as I could tell nobody seemed to know who I was.

The service had been going on for more than an hour when I thought I recognized someone else, not from the movies. He was right in front of me, about six rows ahead, so I could only see the back of his head and my vision was blurred by tears, but even so I was pretty sure it was him. I believe I didn't hear much of what was said after that. When it was over I stood and waited, listening to the church organ sending out the notes of *One Love.* He didn't speak to anyone, but stood for a few moments looking straight ahead; perhaps he was listening to the music, too. I watched through the sunglasses until he turned his head and I could see him in profile.

"Sam?" I said in wonder. I may have spoken aloud but if so he couldn't have heard me over the organ music. Still, he turned then and looked straight at me, as if he had known I was there all along. He didn't smile, but inclined his head gravely and I understood exactly. I turned and started pressing gently against the lingering remnants of the crowd, heading for the door.

He joined me under a pair of yew trees, and took my hand without speaking.

"I wasn't expecting you," I said idiotically, as though I were the hostess.

"He was my friend too, you know," he said, a hint of reproach in his deep voice. "A long time ago. We played music together a few times, but jazz wasn't his thing. I was trying to remember that thing he used to say—some kind of pig Latin—about the coffee. What was it?"

I shook my head, speech momentarily beyond me.

"Anyway, where's your car?" said Sam.

"Is that why you came here?" I asked him. "After all this time, to say goodbye to Rafe?"

He stopped and turned toward me as people flowed by us toward the exit. "Beverly told me you were here. I figured if I followed you all the way to the ocean so you couldn't run away, maybe you'd talk to me."

My eyes filled. "I don't have a car," I said. "I've been using taxis."

"Come on then," he said. "I'll give you a ride. You must be tired. And I hear you have a trial to finish next week."

Everett and Morales and the others agreed to go on with the trial, of course—they'd have been idiots not to, or so it seemed to everyone, including me, at the time. What defendant wouldn't want to finish a case in front of a jury that's watched in horror as the plaintiff committed a murder in front of their eyes? Judge Meiklejohn was disbelieving; she even ordered a psych exam of Peggy, who scored quite high on the competency scale. But once the judge satisfied herself that this was the choice made by all of the parties, she acquiesced. She had the jury called back, debriefed them carefully, instructed them sternly, and allowed the trial to go on.

Peggy wasn't in court—she was being held without bail. To Meiklejohn's great relief, and mine, Everett waived the opportunity to cross-examine her, saying only that he thought the recent conduct of the plaintiff spoke for itself and reflected upon the positions she and her counsel had taken in the litigation. It wasn't really proper for him to be speaking that way in front of the jury before summation, but I was beyond caring.

I called Andy as a witness the first day back. He was brilliant, made me feel that the Wolf was there in the courtroom with us, perhaps sitting alongside Peggy, another virtual presence—the two of them antagonists no more, each the victim of a terrible hunger that could never be satisfied. Then it was time for the defense case. I did what I could with their experts; I don't remember that much, to tell you the truth. Much of the time, after we went back into the courtroom, my thoughts were somewhere else. Brianna told me my summation was brilliant, but I couldn't repeat a single sentence from it now.

It wasn't the biggest civil verdict in the history of the Boulder courts, but it was in the top five. It was the bizarre circumstances as much as the size of the award that made the case a seven-day wonder in the national and international press. I referred all callers to Brianna Bainbridge, who had sat at counsel table with me during the second half of the trial and probably kept the proceeding from disintegrating altogether at the moments my mind went walkabout. Brianna was an excellent spokeswoman, somehow able to suggest that Peggy Grayling's acts were only more evidence of the correctness of Brianna's theories.

The defendants are appealing the case, of course, although I hear Dashiell Roman is in a coma; soon he will soon join Rafe and Alison and Jason Smiley and Mariah McKay and Pres. John F. Kennedy and Lee Harvey Oswald and Jack Ruby in perfect indifference to the outcome. I don't know what the lawyers will do then, but meantime Brianna is handling the appeal for Peggy Grayling. If the award is upheld, Peggy will have plenty of money to pay the fellow from Los Angeles—you've seen him on the evening news—who's representing her on the murder charges. I hear she doesn't mind jail that much; she's teaching a yoga class for the other inmates.

Brianna's very busy, of course, so she's taken a temporary leave from her teaching job, and the associate dean at the law school called me last week to ask if I wanted to teach her course in Pornography, Feminism, and the First Amendment in the fall semester.

I didn't think long before telling him no.

I'm still only half here. I wish I could smash the glassy box that keeps me confined in that chilly too-bright courtroom, instead of exhausting myself with this Sisyphean daily climb up its slippery sides. But sometimes, at infrequent and unpredictable moments, its transparent walls seem to dissolve without notice, leaving me in the world that everyone else seems to inhabit effortlessly. It happened last night, at Tory's. She and I were sitting at opposite ends of the sofa, drinking red wine. Sam sat across the room, looking at my godchild Maia over the edge of his Black and Tan.

Maia finally pushed herself up onto her knees, giggling at the giddy height of it before collapsing again, and for a moment I was really there, nothing between me and my friends. Linda was on the carpet doing situps, to try to get her stomach flat again, she said, but she stopped long enough to remark, "Oh my God, for a minute there she looked just like her father. What if she grows up and notices that the guy in the office across the hall from yours has the same nose she does?"

"Billy promised not to let on," said Tory lazily. "He's afraid every lesbian in town will ask him for a sperm donation if he does. Anyway, she'll change again, and again."

"Already she doesn't look anything like those ultrasound photos," I said. But then at the sound of my voice saying the innocent word *photos*, the memory of Alison Grayling, whom I had only seen in pictures—her school portraits and the terrible crime-scene photograph that her mother had faxed me so many months before and the videotaped images that were never far from me—made my heart lurch, and the box descended again. Its presence seems so unmistakable I sometimes think that others must be able to see it, too.

They can't, of course, although sometimes I wonder about Sam. "Hey," he said, and he crossed the room to sit down next to me, taking my hand. "Are you okay?"

"Just cold," I said. "A chill." I smiled at him, but despite the warmth that flowed from his hand into mine I knew he was really on the other side. Still, he didn't let go, and as I told Andy, that's something. That's a start.